Day of Reckoning

DAY
OF
RECKONING

John Katzenbach

G. P. PUTNAM'S SONS
New York

G. P. Putnam's Sons
Publishers Since 1838
200 Madison Avenue
New York, NY 10016

Library of Congress Cataloging-in-Publication Data

Katzenbach, John.
Day of reckoning.

I. Title.
PS3561.A7778D3 1989   813'.54   88-26473
ISBN 0-399-13449-2

Printed in the United States of America
3   4   5   6   7   8   9   10

For the Two Nicks

Day of Reckoning

1

TUESDAY
AFTERNOON

ONE: *Megan*

She felt incredibly fortunate.

Earlier that month she had been sure she wouldn't be able to help the Wrights, and that they would take all their new Boston stockbroker's money over to Hamden or Dutchess County and start looking for their little farmhouse retreat with some other realtor. Then, as she had racked her memory, she had remembered the old Halliday place on North Road. No one had been in it for years, probably not since right after the ancient Mrs. Halliday had died and her estate—nieces and nephews who lived in Los Angeles and Tucson—had listed it with the company. All the realtors at Country Estates Realty had made the obligatory caravan trip down the back roads to inspect the listing, remark upon the leaky roof, the barely adequate plumbing, the mustiness of age, and to figure it would never move, especially in a community that was experiencing a construction boom. It had slid, then, forgotten, like a fallow field slowly being taken over by the advancing forest.

She had driven the Wrights through the woods, bouncing down the half-mile of loosely packed dirt to the front door. The last autumn light had seemed to slice through the darkness of the forest with a special clarity, as if searching out each withered leaf, probing, inspecting, illuminating every ridge and curl. The great mass of rain-black trees stood out, catching the sunlight as it bounded through the brush. "Now, you realize you'll have to do major reconstruction work . . ." she had said, but to her delight, they had ignored her, seeing only the last weak hues of fall foliage instead of the steady gray approach of winter. Almost instantly they had started in: "We'll put a greenhouse there, and add a deck to the back side. Don't worry about the living room, I'm sure we can bring that side wall down . . ." They had still been talking design as they signed the offer sheet in her office. She had joined in, suggesting architects, contractors, decorators, as she collected their check. She had been sure the offer would be accepted, and that the Wrights would turn the house into a showpiece. They had the money and the inclination: no children (just an Irish wolfhound) and two large incomes with the time to spend.

This morning that certainty had been rewarded with a signed contract from the sellers delivered to her desk.

"Well," she said out loud, as she pulled her car into the driveway of her own home, "you're not doing so bad yourself."

Megan Richards spotted the twins' red sports car, parked, as usual, so that it would partially block the front walkway. They would be home from high school, probably on the telephone already, Lauren on one extension, Karen in the next room, but seated in the doorway, so they could maintain eye contact, jabbering away in the language of youth. They had their own phone line now, a concession to teen age, and a small price for peace and quiet and not having to get up and answer the phone every five minutes.

She smiled and glanced at her watch. Duncan wouldn't be home from the bank for another hour. Assuming he didn't have to work late. She made a mental note to talk to him about working extra hours, stealing the time from Tommy, especially. The girls were off in their own world, and as long as it didn't include booze, bad boys and drugs, they were fine. They knew how to find him if they needed to talk: they always had. She marveled for a moment about the special rapport between fathers and daughters. She had seen it in Duncan when the twins were toddlers, the three of them rolling about on the floor in tickle-and-poke play; realized it too, from her own father. It was different with fathers and sons. There, it was a lifetime of struggles and competition, territory gained and lost, the ordinary and essential battle of life. At least, that was how it should be.

Her eyes caught the shape of Tommy's red bicycle, thrown haphazardly into the bushes.

But not my son. The thought made her flush. She could feel her throat grow uncomfortably tight. Nothing was quite ordinary about him.

As always, she felt her eyes start to redden, then spoke to herself in a familiar mock-stern tone: Megan, you've cried all you're going to cry. And anyway, he's getting better. Much better. Almost normal.

She had a sudden image of her son at her breast. She had known right in the delivery room that he would not be like the twins, with their regular mealtimes, naptimes, schooltimes, adolescent times, fitting into every schedule easily and perfectly, as if drawn up by some thoughtful and sensible master plan. She had stared down at his tiny, struggling shape, all instinct and surprise, trying to find her nipple, and understood that he would break her heart a hundred times, then start in and break it all over again.

She got out of the car and trudged over to the bushes. She pulled the bicycle out of the damp hedge, cutting an expletive off in midburst as she splattered rainwater on her skirt, and, holding the handlebars gingerly and trying not to scuff the toe of her shoe, thrust the kickstand down. She left the bicycle righted on the pathway.

And so, she thought, I just loved him all the more.

She smiled. I always knew it was the best therapy. Just love him harder.

She stared at the bicycle. And I was right.

The doctors had revised their diagnoses two dozen times, from retardation to autism to childhood schizophrenia to learning disability, to let's just wait and see. In a way she was proud of the way he'd defied all their categorizations, taken every expert's opinion and shown it to be wrong, skewed or simply inaccurate. It was as if he'd said to hell with all of them, and simply set out on his own course through life, dragging the rest of them along, accelerating sometimes, braking others, but always devoted to his own inner pace.

If it was a hard course, well, she was still proud of it.

She turned and looked back up at their house. It was a colonial design, but new, set back forty yards from the street in Greenfield's best subsection. It was not the largest house on the street, but neither was it the smallest. There was a large oak tree in the center of the lawn and she remembered how the twins had hung a tire from it a half-dozen years before, not really that anxious to swing themselves, but knowing that it would attract the neighborhood children, and bring their playmates to them. They were always a step ahead. The tire was still there, hanging straight down in the gathering darkness. She thought of Tommy again, and how he would rock there endlessly, back and forth, hour after hour, oblivious to other children, the wind, rain, snow—whatever—kicking his feet into the air and leaning back, his wild eyes open, staring up and absorbing the sky.

Those things don't scare me anymore, she thought. And she no longer cried over his eccentricities. The time he brushed his teeth for two hours. The three-day fast. When he wouldn't speak for a week, and when he wouldn't sleep because he had too much to say and not enough vocabulary to say it. She glanced down at her watch. He would be home soon, and she would make him beef barley soup and homemade pizza, which was his favorite dinner. They could celebrate the sale of the Halliday house with some peach ice cream, as well. As she planned her menu, she mentally figured her commission. Enough for a week at Disney World this winter. Tommy would like that, the twins would complain that it was immature, for little kids, then they would have a wonderful time. Duncan would secretly adore the rides and she could sit by the pool and get some sun. She nodded to herself. Why the hell not?

Megan glanced back up the street to see if she could spot her father's car, saying a small prayer of thanks. Three times a week her retired father picked Tommy up at the new school. She was glad he rode the bus only twice a week, and she appreciated how her father, all gray-haired and wrinkled, brought out the excitement in his namesake. They would assault the house, filled with wild schemes and descriptions of what went on at school, all mile-a-minute talk. The two Tommys, she thought. They are more alike than they know.

She opened the front door and called out: "Girls! I'm home!"

There were the unmistakable sounds of teenage voices murmuring on the telephone.

For a moment she was filled with a familiar disquiet. I wish Tommy was here, she thought. I hate it when he's in transit somewhere, and I don't have him in my arms, ignoring his halfhearted complaint that I am squeezing him too tightly. She exhaled slowly and heard a car come down the street. That's probably them, she thought, relieved, then slightly irritated with herself for feeling relief.

She hung up her raincoat and slipped off her shoes. She said to herself: No, I wouldn't change anything. Not one bit. Not even all Tommy's troubles. I have been lucky.

TWO: *The Two Tommys*

Judge Thomas Pearson strode down the corridor as the bell for the end of school rang. Doors popped open on either side, and the hallway filled with children. The flood of young voices washed over him, a joyous bedlam of children gathering book bags and raincoats, opening to let him pass, then closing in behind him. He danced out of the way as a trio of boys raced headlong past him, their coats trailing behind like some squad of swashbucklers' capes. He bumped into a small red-haired girl, with her hair in bows and pigtails. "Excuse me," she said, all childish well-drilled manners. He stepped past, bowing slightly in exaggerated politesse, and the little girl laughed at him. It was like standing in the froth at the beach, feeling the spent wave bubble and boil around him.

He waved at some of the faces he recognized and smiled at the others, hoping that some of his height and age and austerity would seem diminished, that he would blend better with the bright colors and lights of the school corridor. He spotted Tommy's classroom and maneuvered through the press of small bodies toward the door. It had a large multicolored balloon painted on the exterior, next to a placard which read: Special Section A.

He reached down to open the door, thinking how much he enjoyed picking up his grandson, how young it made him feel, but it swung open suddenly. He waited a moment, as first a shock of brown hair, a forehead and finally a pair of blue eyes peered around the edge.

For a second he stared at the eyes, and saw his late wife instead, then his daughter, then finally, his grandson.

"Hi, Grandfather. I knew it would be you."

"Hi, Tommy, I knew it would be you, too."

"I'm almost ready to go. Can I just finish my drawing?"

"If you like."

"Will you come watch me?"

"Of course."

The judge felt his hand seized by his grandson's and he thought of the tenacity of a child's grip. How they hold on to life, he thought. It is adults who cheapen it. He allowed himself to be pulled into the classroom. He nodded to Tommy's teacher, who smiled back.

"He wants to finish his drawing," Judge Pearson said.

"Good. And you don't mind waiting?"

"Not at all."

He felt his hand released, and waited as his grandson slipped into a chair at a long table. A few other children were drawing as well. All seemed preoccupied with their work. He stood and watched as Tommy seized a red crayon and scratched away.

"What are you drawing?"

"Leaves burning. And the fire is spreading to the forest."

"Oh." He didn't know what to say.

"Sometimes it's disconcerting."

He turned and saw Tommy's teacher standing next to him. "I beg your pardon?"

"It's disconcerting. We'll set the children down for drawing or art, and the next thing we know they've come up with a battle scene, or a home burning down or an earthquake toppling an entire city. One of the others drew that last week. Very elaborate. Very detailed. Right down to the people falling into a crevasse."

"A little . . ." He hesitated.

"Macabre? Sure. But most of the kids in this section have so much trouble with their feelings, we encourage any fantasy if it brings them closer to what they're really afraid of. It's really a pretty simple technique."

Judge Pearson nodded. "Still," he said, "I bet you'd prefer pictures of flowers."

The teacher grinned. "It would be a change." Then she added, "Would you please tell Mr. and Mrs. Richards to call me, so that I can set up an appointment with them?"

The judge glanced down at Tommy, who was busy with his paper. "Something wrong?"

The teacher smiled. "I suppose it's human nature to assume the worst. On the contrary, he's been making great progress all fall, just as he did in the summer. I want him to join the regular third graders for a couple of classes after the Christmas holidays."

She paused. "Oh, this will still be his main room, and he'll probably have a setback or two, but we were thinking that we might challenge him more. He's really very bright, it's just when he gets frustrated—"

"—He gets out of control." The judge finished her sentence.

"Yeah. That hasn't changed. He can still get pretty wild. But, on the other hand, it's been weeks since he had one of his vacant spells."

"I know," the judge said. He thought how frightened he'd been the first time he'd seen his grandson, as a toddler, simply stare off into space, oblivious to the entire world. The child would remain like that for hours on end, not sleeping, not speaking, not crying, barely breathing, as if away in some other place, only to return abruptly a few hours later, acting as if nothing had happened.

He looked down at Tommy, who was finishing the drawing with great, bold streaks of bright orange across the sky. *How you terrified all of us. Where do you go on those trips?*

John Katzenbach

Probably a better place than here, he thought.

"I'll tell them. They'll call right away. It sounds like good news."

"Let's keep our fingers crossed."

They walked out the front door of the school, and for a moment the judge was struck by how swiftly the end-of-the-schoolday excitement dissipated. There were only a few cars left in the parking lot. He felt a cold breeze that seemed to reach through the front of his overcoat, penetrate his sweater and shirt and chill his skin. He shivered, and buttoned his jacket.

"Button up, Tommy. These old bones feel winter in the air."

"Grandfather, what are old bones?"

"Well, you have young bones. Your bones are still growing and getting bigger and stronger. My bones, well, they're old and tired because they've been around so long."

"Not so long."

"Sure, almost seventy-one years."

Tommy thought for a moment.

"That *is* long. Will mine grow that long?"

"Probably longer."

"And how come you can feel things with your bones? I can feel the wind on my face and hands, but not with my bones. How do you do that?"

The judge laughed. "You'll know when you get older."

"I hate that."

"What?"

"When people tell you to wait. I want to know now."

The judge reached down and took his grandson's hand.

"You're absolutely right. When you want to learn something, don't ever let anyone tell you to wait. You just go ahead and learn it."

"Bones?"

"Well, really it is just a figure of speech. You know what that means?"

Tommy nodded.

"But really it means that when you get old, your bones are brittle, and they don't have as much life in them anymore. So when a cold wind comes along, I can feel the chill, right inside of me. It doesn't hurt, it just means I'm more aware of it. Understand?"

"I think so."

The child walked along in silence for a few paces. Then he said, more to himself, "There's a lot to learn," and he sighed. His grandfather wanted to laugh out loud, thinking what an extraordinary observation that was. But instead, he gripped his grandson's hand tighter and they proceeded through the grayness of the afternoon to his car. He noticed a late-model sedan parked next to his, and as they approached, a woman got out from the rear seat. She seemed middle-aged, was tall and very sturdy, and wore a large, floppy black hat. Striking red hair flowed down in unruly sheets from beneath the brim, and she wore a large pair of dark sunglasses. They made the judge momentarily uncomfortable: How could she see out? He slowed and watched as the woman approached them briskly, with a businesslike solidity.

"Can I help you?" the judge asked.

The woman unbuttoned her tan raincoat and slowly reached inside. She smiled.

"Judge Pearson," she said. "Hello." She looked down at his grandson. "This must be Tommy. Well, aren't you the spitting image of both your mother and father? A regular little chip off the old blocks. I can see them in your face."

"I'm sorry," the judge started. "Do I know you?"

"You were on the criminal court bench, weren't you?" the woman asked, ignoring his question. She continued to smile.

"Why yes, but—"

"For many years."

"Yes, but I beg your—"

"Well, then I'm sure you came to be familiar with devices like this."

She slowly removed a hand from inside her coat. She gripped a large revolver. It was leveled at his stomach.

The judge stared at the gun, confusion filling him.

"This is actually a .357 Magnum," the woman continued. The judge noticed that her voice had a steadiness that spoke only of rage.

"It would make a large hole in you. An immense hole in little Tommy there. And I'd do him first, so your last seconds would be filled up knowing you'd cost him his life. Don't make everything end here, before it's begun. Just quietly get into the back of my car."

"You can take me, but don't—" the judge started. His mind automatically began to search through the volumes of cases he'd had, decisions rendered, sentences passed, wondering where was the one in which the standard threat had cascaded past reason, where was the one who had sought him out for revenge. He saw the faces of a hundred angry men, eyes scarred with age and crime. But he couldn't remember a woman. And certainly not the woman who gently prodded his ribs with the barrel of the handgun.

"Oh no, no, no," the woman continued. "He's essential. He's the key to all this."

She gestured with the gun.

"Nice and slowly. Remain as calm as I am. Don't move suddenly, judge. Think how silly it would be for the two of you to die here. Think of what you would be stealing from your grandson. His life, judge. All those years. Of course, you're familiar with that. You're the type that stole years easily. Pig! Just don't do it."

He realized that the car door had been pushed open, and there were people inside. A hundred ideas flooded his head. Run! Scream! Call for help! Fight back!

But he did none of them.

"Do what she says, Tommy," he said. "Don't worry, I'm with you."

A pair of strong hands seized him and he was flung abruptly to the floor of the car. For a moment he smelled shoe leather and dirt mingling with the acrid smell of nervous sweat. He saw blue jeans and boots, then a black, suffocating cloth bag was thrust over his head. He suddenly imagined it was like the bag an executioner used on his subjects, and he started to struggle, only to feel a pair of powerful hands grip him and push him down. He felt Tommy's light body land on his, and he grunted. He tried to speak to him, his mind forming the reassuring words: Don't be scared, I'm here—

but only groans came out. He heard a male voice calmly, but bitterly, say, "Welcome to the revolution. Now, go to sleep, old man."

A weight crashed against the side of his head, then darkness exploded about him and he passed out.

THREE: *Duncan*

His secretary knocked lightly on the glass door panel, then stuck her head around the corner, into his office: "Mr. Richards, are you expecting to work late again today? I mean, I can stay, but I need to call my roommate to pick up the groceries . . ."

Duncan Richards looked up from the spreadsheet in front of him and smiled. "A little bit, Doris, but you don't have to stay. I just want to finish the paperwork on the Harris Company's application."

"You sure, Mr. Richards? I mean, it's no trouble . . ."

He shook his head. "I've been working late too often," he said. "We're bankers. We ought to work bankers' hours."

She smiled. "Well, I'll be here until five, anyway."

"That's fine."

But instead of returning to his paperwork, Duncan Richards leaned back in his chair and placed his hands behind his head. He pivoted so he could see out his window. It was almost dark, and the cars leaving the parking lot had turned on their lights, carving small white spaces from the blackness. He could just make out the line of trees on Main Street that rose up against the last gray light of day. He wished for a moment that he was still in the old bank building, up the street. It had been cramped, and the office space was inadequate, but it had been set back from the road, up a small rise, and he'd been able to see much farther. The new building was all architecturally sound and soulless. No view, save of traffic. Modern furniture, state-of-the-art security. Things had changed since he had started. Greenfield wasn't a little college town anymore. Businessmen, developers, money people from New York and Boston, all moving in.

The town is losing its anonymity, he thought. Maybe it means we all are.

He considered the application in front of him. It was one he'd seen a half-dozen times in the past six months; a small construction firm wanting to buy a tract of farmland that had a view of the Green Mountains—twenty-four acres would become six spec houses. Fill the houses at nearly three hundred grand each and the small construction firm would instantly be a medium-sized firm. The numbers seemed fine, he thought; we will write the purchase loan, then the construction loan and probably end up holding the mortgages on the houses when they sold. He didn't have to use a calculator to see the substantial bank profit. He was more concerned with the builders themselves. He sighed, thinking how strapped they would be. Take a chance, mortgage everything, become a success. The American way. It has never changed.

But a banker must be old-world cautious. Never hurried, never pressed.

That's changing, too. Little banks like First State Bank of Greenfield were being pressed by the megabanks. Baybanks of Boston had just opened an office down Prospect Street and Citicorp had purchased Springfield National, which used to be the major competition.

Maybe we'll be bought, too. We're an attractive target for takeover. The next-quarter figures will show a real jump. He made a mental note to exercise a stock option, just in case. But there haven't been any rumors, and there usually are. He wondered whether he should ask old Phillips, the bank president, then thought against it. He's always looked out for me, since the first day. He won't stop now.

He remembered walking through the bank door for the first time eighteen years earlier. Megan's father had held the door open for him, as he'd hesitated. His new haircut had bothered him, and he'd kept running his hand through his hair, feeling like an amputee must in the days after an operation.

His stomach tightened as he remembered his fear and how hard he'd struggled to hide it that long day.

Why am I thinking this?

He looked back out the window, and despite trying to refuse the memory, it still intruded on his imagination. It had been morning, and bright. The bank had been busy. Filled with sunlight and people and activity so that my nervousness hadn't been noticed. I had thought that I would never have the strength to walk into a bank again. Phillips said I could start out as a teller because Judge Pearson vouched for me. They were golfing buddies. My hands shook when I first handled the money and every time the front door swung open, I thought it was over. I expected sullen men in nondescript suits. That they had finally come to get me.

He wondered when he'd lost that anxiety. After a week? A month? A year?

Why am I thinking this?

It's gone. It was eighteen years ago and it's gone.

He could not recall the last time he'd thought of his start in the banking world. Certainly not for years. He wondered why it should come back to him now, and he rolled his tongue around inside his mouth, as if trying to erase a bitter taste. And I will not remember it again, he promised himself. Everything is different now. He picked up the spreadsheet, staring at the numbers. Conditional approval, he thought. Run it past the board and see what they think. No builders going belly-up now, not like the early eighties. But the Fed had raised the prime a half-point that morning, and maybe they ought to have a real discussion at the next staff meeting. Get the forecasting boys to do their job. He made a note on his calendar.

The phone on his desk buzzed and the intercom switched on. It was his secretary.

"Mr. Richards, Mrs. Richards is on the phone."

"Thanks."

He picked up the receiver.

"Now listen, Meg, I'm not going to be home late. I'm just finishing up now—"

"Duncan, did Dad say he was going to take Tommy out? They're not back yet, and I wondered whether he said anything to you."

"Not back?"

Duncan Richards glanced at his watch. Almost an hour late. He assessed the concern in his wife's voice. Minimal. Not scared, just bothered.

"No."

"Well, did you call the school?"

"Yes. They said Dad was there right on time, as usual. He stayed a bit while Tommy finished up some project, then they left."

"Well, I don't think I'd get too bent out of shape. He probably took him over to the mall to play video games. Actually, they haven't done that in a couple of weeks, so I suspect that's where they are."

"I asked him not to do that. It gets Tommy too stimulated."

"Oh, c'mon. They have such a good time. And anyway, I think it's your old man who likes playing the games."

A touch of release slipped into her voice. "But I made a special dinner, and he's probably feeding him greasy cheeseburgers."

"Well, you can talk to your dad, but I doubt it'll do any good. He likes fast food. You'd think after seventy-one years he'd know better."

She laughed. "You're probably right."

He hung up the telephone, pulled out a legal pad, and started to rough out a few thoughts for presenting the loan to the committee. He heard a rap on his glass partition and saw his secretary waving. She wore her coat. He waved back, and thought, finish this tomorrow.

The phone on his desk buzzed again, and he picked up the receiver, expecting his wife's voice.

"Hi. Look—I'm pretty much on my way now," he said, without introduction.

"Really?" said the person on the other end. "I think not. I don't think you're on your way anywhere. Not anymore."

It was as if in those few words, those sounds and tones that tore with horrible familiarity into his memory, that everything around him shattered and was suddenly, abruptly, blown away by a great wind. He seized the edge of the desk to steady himself, but felt his head spinning nonetheless and knew instantly: It's all lost.

Everything.

FOUR: *Megan*

Megan Richards hung up the telephone, more irritated than concerned. Duncan always has so many damn reasonable explanations. He's so levelheaded, sometimes I could scream. She walked through the house to the living room, pulling back the curtain so she could see down the street. It remained black and empty. She stood still, watching, until frustration forced her aside. After a moment, she thrust the curtain closed and paced back into the kitchen.

She thought to herself: Fix the dinner anyway. Maybe they won't have eaten. She glanced at her watch and shook her head. Tommy is always famished after school.

For a few minutes she busied herself with pots and pans, checking the temperature on the oven. She went into the eating alcove and checked the five place settings. An idea struck her, and she briskly marched back into the kitchen and opened a drawer, quickly seizing an extra knife, fork, and spoon. She grabbed a plate and glass from a shelf, a place mat from behind another cabinet door. There, she thought, and arranged the setting. When Dad gets here he will see that I've set a place for him, as well. Maybe then he'll feel guilty about stuffing Tommy with cheeseburgers.

She surveyed her work, then heard a car. Relief filled her, and she marched back into the living room, this time gingerly pulling the curtain aside, not wanting to be spotted spying on them, but thinking: For the hundredth time I'll have to tell Dad that if he wants to take Tommy somewhere, it's fine—he just has to let me know.

But he's done this before, and I wasn't so nervous. She shook her head as if she could shake loose from her feelings by force.

She stared out again, and cursed as she saw the headlights cruise past on the street and pull into a driveway up the block.

Damn!

She looked at her watch again.

Laughter came from upstairs, and she decided to see if perhaps the twins had taken some message and forgotten to pass it on. That made such sense that she was surprised she hadn't thought of it in the first place. She glanced out again at the empty street, then pounded up the stairwell.

"Hey, Lauren, Karen?"

"In here, Mom."

She opened the door to their room and found them spread out amidst sheets of notepaper and textbooks.

"Mom, did you have to do homework in high school?"

She smiled. "Of course. Why?"

"I mean when you were a senior, like us."

"Of course again."

"It doesn't seem right. I mean, we're going to college next year and I don't see why we should have to fool around with all this rinky-dink assignment stuff. Ten math problems. I feel like I've been doing ten math problems every night since I was a baby."

Karen started giggling and cut her mother off before she could answer.

"Well, Lauren, if you tried getting the answers right, maybe you'd do better than a B-minus."

"They're just numbers. They're not as important as words. And what did you get on your last English test, anyway?"

"That's not fair. It was on *Bleak House*, and you know I hadn't finished it, because you took my copy!"

Lauren took a small pillow and threw it at her sister, who laughed and tossed it back. Both shots missed.

Megan held up her hand. "Peace!" she announced.

The twins turned toward her, and she was pierced again by the sameness of their eyes, their hair, the way they looked in unison up at her. What magic they are, she thought. They can feel each other's feelings, think each other's ideas, salve each other's hurts so easily. They are never alone.

"Look," Megan said. "Did either of you talk to Grandfather today? He picked up Tommy at school and they're not back yet. I was just wondering whether he gave you guys a message about being late."

She tried to keep anxiety from her voice.

Both Karen and Lauren shook their heads.

"No," said Karen. She had been the first by ninety seconds, and now always seemed to be the first to speak. "Are you worried?"

"No, no, no, it's just not like your grandfather not to let somebody know if they were going to the mall."

"Well," said Lauren, "it's not exactly like he would call, either. Grandfather just does things, you know. It's like he still thinks the entire world is his courtroom, and he just does what he wants because he's in charge."

It was said without bitterness, pure reportage.

Megan smiled. "It does seem like he thinks that sometimes, doesn't it?"

"He treats Tommy special," Karen added.

"Tommy is special."

"I know, but—"

"No buts. He is."

"Well, sometimes it seems as if we get taken for granted and he gets all the special treatment."

This was an old, but legitimate, complaint.

"Karen, you know that it's not the same thing. The reason that everyone is treated differently is because everyone has different needs. Tommy's just got more needs than you guys. We've talked about this before."

"I know."

"Are you worried something might have happened?" Lauren asked.

"No, just worried the same way I'd be worried if you guys didn't come home from school on schedule. See, that's the same."

But she recognized that for a lie. She wondered why she felt more vulnerable with her son than with her daughters. It should be the other way around. Everything's backward.

"Would you like us to go over to the mall and try to find them? I bet I know where they are."

"Sure," said Karen. "At the arcade, playing that space invaders game. We'll go, Mom, come right back?"

She shook her head. "No, no, they'll be along. And anyway, finish that homework. No television unless it's done."

The twins grumbled and she closed the door.

Megan walked into her bedroom and stripped off her skirt and stockings, tossing on a faded pair of jeans. She hung her blouse in the closet and slipped into a sweater, then pulled on an old pair of jogging shoes and went over to the window. Even in the darkness, she could still see farther from upstairs. The street remained frustratingly quiet. From her vantage point she could see into the Wakefields' living room across the street. Shapes were moving inside. She turned and saw that the Mayers' two cars were parked in their driveway next door. She peered down the street again and checked her watch. Late, she thought. Very late.

Something within her seemed to boil up and she felt hot. Late, late, late was all she could think. She sat down hard on the edge of the bed.

Where?

She felt a need to do something, reached out for the telephone, and dialed 911.

"Greenfield police and fire."

"Hello, this is Mrs. Richards on Queensbury Road. This isn't an emergency or anything, I don't think, but I wonder . . . you see, my son and father are late coming back from school. He picked him up today and they usually come straight home, right along South Street and then Route 116 and I was worrying and thought—"

The voice interrupted with an experienced quickness. "We have no reported accidents this evening. No traffic tieups in those locations, either. No ambulances dispatched. No patrol cars dispatched to anything. I haven't monitored any state police activity, either, except for a three-car out on the interstate near Deerfield."

"No, no, that wouldn't be them. That's the wrong direction. Thank you."

"No problem."

The line went dead and she hung up the phone feeling slightly foolish, but slightly relieved as well. Worry was replaced with irritation again, a much improved sensation.

"This time I'll skin his hide," she said out loud. "I don't care if he is seventy-one years old and a judge."

She stood up and smoothed out the bedspread where she'd been sitting. She went back to the window.

Where? she thought again. By forming the word it was as if in her mind, she opened the box of worry again.

She returned to the bedside phone and dialed her husband's number. There was no answer. At least he's on his way, she thought, and that was reassuring.

She moved about the room, thinking about where she should go next. Downstairs, check on the dinner.

But as she moved out from her bedroom, a flash of color from behind the door in Tommy's room caught the corner of her eye. She went over and saw a pile of red sweaters and blue jeans, dirty socks and underwear, all rolled up into a bundle and thrust out of the way. He'll never learn to use a laundry hamper. It's simply beyond him. For an instant she hesitated and remembered: We thought everything was beyond him once. She refused to let all the nights of defeat and despair fill her. Now we're winning, she thought. We're finally winning. Now it seems that nothing may be beyond him. She realized she had allowed herself to indulge for the first time in the most common of parental fantasies, imagining what their child would become when he grew up. He will grow up, she thought. He will become something. She let her eyes wander about the room, over to the barely made bed, the toys and books and oddities that slowly fill any boy's room, so much junk that masquerades as so many small treasures. She tried to find some evidence of Tommy's problems, but there was none. She thought: Don't let that fool you. They're there. But they're leaving. She remembered one doctor suggesting years before that they pad his room, in case he turned violent. Thank God we always listened to ourselves.

She sat down on his bed and idly picked up a toy soldier. He was always brave as a soldier. All the tests, the pokings and proddings, EEGs and sensory stimulation tests. He suffered through them all. It was easy for Duncan and me. All we had to do was worry. He was the one who showed us bravery.

She put the toy down.

Where is he?

Damn!

She stood up sharply, marched downstairs, and went to the front door. She flung it open and stepped out into the cold night air, standing there until the cold scoured her arms and legs.

Where?

She walked back inside and grabbed the hall table.

Cut out the histrionics, she thought. You're just going to be embarrassed in a couple of minutes when they come running through the front door, shouting for dinner.

The admonition steadied her, momentarily. Then the misshapen fear floated about inside her again.

She walked to the stairwell and called up, "Girls!"

She heard Karen and Lauren answer.

"It's okay," she said. "I just wanted to let you know dinner is pretty soon."

It was a halfhearted lie. She had just wanted to hear their voices for a moment, to be persuaded that they were safe.

This is foolish, she thought.

No, it's not. They're very, very late.

She went to the kitchen telephone, dialed 91, and stopped. Her finger hesitated over the last digit. She sat down, the phone still in hand. And then, like a flash of light in a dark room, she heard a car pull to a stop in the driveway.

Relief filled her. She slapped the phone back down on the hook and quick-marched to the front door, opened it to the night and saw her husband—not her child, trailed by her father—striding toward her.

"Duncan!" she called out.

He covered the ground between them in three leaps.

Even in the weak light thrown through the open door, she could see his eyes were red.

"Duncan! Oh, my God! Something's wrong! Tommy! What's happened? Is he okay? Where's Dad?"

"I think they're okay," Duncan said. "I think. Oh, God, Megan— they're gone. They took them. It's all over. Everything."

"Who took them? What do you mean?" She fought for control.

"I've been so stupid," Duncan said. He wasn't talking to his wife, but to the night and the flow of years. "All these years, and I thought it was over—just a bad memory, or maybe a bad dream. *It never happened*, that's what I thought. What a goddamn fool."

Megan used what she thought was every bit of strength to prevent herself from screaming.

"Tell me!" she said, her voice rising. "Where's Tommy? Where's my father? *Where are they?*"

Duncan looked at her. "The past," he said quietly. He dropped his arms and pushed past her into the house, turning in the doorway.

"Nineteen sixty-eight."

He turned and pounded once on the wall.

"You remember that year? You remember what happened then?"

She nodded and felt as if her entire life stopped in that moment. A hundred awful images flooded into her head and she closed her eyes to try to block them away. Dizzy, she blinked her eyes open and stared at her husband.

They stood then, slightly apart, unable to touch, in the weak doorway light that battled the darkness outside. They did not really understand anything, except that the disaster they had thought was lost and would never find them had overtaken them by the heels and wrapped its great tentacles about them.

2

LODI, CALIFORNIA.
SEPTEMBER 1968

Shortly after dawn, the brigade awoke.

Early-morning light insinuated itself through the heavy curtains hung over the windows, piercing into the corners of the small, one-story wooden frame house as the occupants moved about with the stiffness of the hour. A teakettle started to whistle in the kitchen. There was some grunting as mattresses were taken from the center of the living room floor and shoved against a wall. Sleeping bags were rolled. The toilet flushed repeatedly. Someone kicked over a half-empty bottle of beer, and its contents splashed across the floor, accompanied by a curse. A raucous laugh came from the rear of the house. The heavy leftover smell of cigarettes and angry speech from the night before remained in the stuffy, still air.

Olivia Barrow, who had taken the *nom de guerre* Tanya, went to one of the front windows and pulled back the curtain from the edge just slightly. Her eyes traveled up and down the dusty street outside, searching for signs of surveillance. Each person that entered her view was inspected; each vehicle that passed, examined. She looked first for anything out of the ordinary—the newspaper delivery truck that paused, the derelict in the doorway who seemed more alert than stuporous. Then she searched for anything in the street that seemed too ordinary—the street-sweeping truck, the line at the bus stop. She let her eyes rest on each element, waiting, looking for some telltale sign. Finally, satisfied that they were not being watched, she shut the curtain and walked to the center of the living room.

She pushed aside a stack of old newspapers and trash. For a moment she surveyed the living quarters. Political tracts and military handbooks on weapons and explosives were piled in a corner, which she called the library; the walls were an odd pastiche of handwritten revolutionary slogans and rock and roll posters. She eyed The Jefferson Airplane idly.

Olivia was oblivious to half the clutter and filth, the inevitable result of too many people living together in a small, cheap, and anonymous place. Actually, she liked the limited confines of the house. There are no little places to hide secrets, she thought. Secrets are weakness. We should all be naked together. It makes the army more disciplined, and discipline is strength. Taking the .45-caliber semiautomatic pistol she held in her hand, she quickly slapped back on the gun's action, chambering a round with a distinctive clicking sound that penetrated all the morning fuzzy bad tastes and exhaustions and gained the instant attention of the six other people in the apartment. She loved the snapping-to that followed the sound of a gun being readied to fire. The classic attention-getter. "It's time for the morning prayer," she said in a loud voice.

There were shuffling sounds and the metallic noise of weapons being checked, as each of the other members of the group searched and found their designated arms, then moved into a circle in the center of the room. There were two other women and four men. Two of the men wore beards and hair that hung to their shoulders; two were black and wore bushy afro haircuts. They were dressed in a motley collection of blue jeans and army fatigues. One of the black men wore a bright headband and sported a gold tooth when he smiled. One of the white men had a red scar on his throat. Both women were dark-haired and pale. They all placed their weapons—

John Katzenbach

several handguns, two shotguns, a Browning semiautomatic rifle— on the floor in the center of the circle. Then they joined hands and Olivia began to intone:

"We are the new Amerika," she said, coming down hard on the last syllable, delighting in the flow of rhetoric off her tongue. "Black, brown, red, white, yellow, women, men, children, we are all equal. We have risen from the ashes of the old. We are the Phoenix Brigade, the light-bearers of the new society. We stand against the pig fascist racist sexist antique war money-loving values of our fathers and signal the new horizon. Today is Day One of the new world. The world we forge with guns and bullets out of the corrupt carcass of this rancid society. The future belongs to us, the believers in true justice. We are the new Amerika!"

The entire group repeated it together: "We are the new Amerika!"

"The future is?"

"Ours!"

"Today is?"

"Day One!"

"We are?"

"The Phoenix Brigade!"

"What do we bring?"

"Guns and bullets!"

"The future belongs?"

"To us!"

"Death to the Pigs!"

"Death to the Pigs!"

Olivia held her pistol high and shook it in the air above her head. "All right!" she exclaimed. "All right!"

There was a moment's silence while the group remained still, eyes cast up toward where Olivia waved the gun. Then one of the women dropped her hands to her sides and whispered a muffled, "Excuse me!" The woman stepped abruptly over the pile of weapons, and, starting to rush, broke through the circle on the opposite side. Her sneakers slapped on the linoleum as she dashed down a hallway and into the bathroom, slamming the door behind her.

The others remained in the living room, staring after her.

Olivia spoke first: "Hey, math-man, better check on your squeeze."
Her tone was edged with derision.

One of the bearded men stepped out of the circle and hurried
down the hallway, hesitating at the bathroom door. He whispered:
"Meg? Can you hear me? Are you okay?"

Behind him, the group broke up. Weapons were retrieved and put
into safekeeping. There was laughter from the kitchen as some breakfast was started.

The bearded man could hear the sounds of nausea.

"Meg! C'mon! Are you okay?" he continued to whisper.

He was not aware of the presence behind him, and started when
he heard the voice.

"Maybe your squeeze isn't ready, huh, math-man?"

The bearded man turned abruptly, his voice high-pitched with
tension. "I told you she'd be okay! You asked, and I told you! She's
as committed as any of us. She understands why we're here! So give
it a rest, Tanya!"

"You have to purge yourself," Olivia continued, steadily, her voice
filled with disdain. "You have to lose all your old bourgeois thoughts
and replace them with pure revolutionary fire."

"I told you, we're ready!"

"I think you're the weak link, math-man. Still filled with all that
old learning you got at that school. Still a little bit of the college boy
in you, playing at revolution."

"Listen, Tanya, I'm not playing at anything, and I wish you'd get
off my back. We're here, aren't we? I'm not your precious fucking
mathematician anymore. I put all that behind me. You're the one
that keeps reminding me of it. You know, we've been over this a
couple of times now, and it's starting to piss me off. College was the
past. I've finished it. The Phoenix is as real for me as for you. You
weren't a revolutionary all your fucking life, you know."

"No," Olivia replied, voice even, smooth and bitter. "I was a pig
once. But no longer. I have given everything to the movement. That's
why I took this name, that's why I could die today and I would die
happy. Could you die happy, math-man? What have you given up?
The pigs still know Sundiata and Kwanzi by their old prison names,

but we know them by their revolutionary names. And they're willing
to die. They've lived through the battle of the ghetto, and they're
willing to die in the war today. The others, too, Emily and Bill
Lewis—nice, normal, American names, right?—but now they're
Emma and Ché. They are real soldiers. Nobody's play-acting. But
you two, you're the ones I'm worried about."

"I wish you'd cut out the rhetoric."

"You're one to talk. Because that's all we've heard from you is
talk. About all the times you've been gassed and arrested and beaten.
Where are the scars, math-man? We'll see. Now you have the chance
to fight back, I just wonder whether you can really do it. No more
pacifist bullshit, no more nice Sunday civil disobedience. War! They've
asked for it, now they're going to get it."

"Do I have to die to prove myself?"

"Others have."

He hesitated.

"I told you. We're ready. We'll do what we have to."

"We'll see, won't we? We'll see real soon."

Olivia glared at the bearded man. She was almost as tall as he and
able to look him directly in the eyes. Then she laughed derisively.
Before the bearded man could say anything else, she turned on her
heel and disappeared toward the rear bedroom. The bearded man
watched after her for a moment, filled with anger himself. "She
thinks she's the whole fucking show," he said under his voice. Inwardly, however, he added: And she is.

He turned back toward the bathroom door. "Meg, c'mon, are you
okay?"

He heard the toilet flush, and after another second the door swung
slowly open.

She looked pale and shaky.

"I'm sorry, Duncan, I just got sick. Nerves, I guess. Don't worry,
I'll be okay. You just tell me what you want me to do." She stared
down the hallway toward the room where Olivia had just disappeared. "You know what I think. But I'll do what you say."

"Look, we're all nervous. This is an important day."

"I'll be okay."

"It's going to work out fine. Look, really this is more of a gesture than anything else. And anyway, nobody's going to get hurt. So don't be nervous."

But she knew it wasn't nerves. She knew it was life quickening within her, and for an instant she considered whether this was the time to tell him. No, she thought, not here, not now. But when? Time was short.

Megan reached up and stroked his cheek. "Is everything okay with you?"

"Sure. Why not?"

"I was just wondering."

"Why? I mean, what could be wrong?"

She simply looked at him.

"Goddammit," he whispered angrily, "now don't you start in as well. We're going through with it. We've talked about it, and that's it. I'm tired of marching. I'm tired of protests. They've never done a damn bit of good. We've been over this, and over this and over this. The only thing that the people in power in this society under-stand is violence on their own terms. So strike at their heart. Maybe that'll change things. It's the only way."

He hesitated, then added: "It's the only kind of symbolism that they'll understand. It'll get attention. It's necessary."

At first she didn't say anything. Then she said quietly, "Well, fine. Believing in change is one thing. But don't start sounding like Tanya, because that's not you."

He sighed in frustration.

"We've been through this."

She nodded.

"Dammit, not now. Just not now!"

He grabbed her by the shoulders, but not angrily, merely to hold her at arm's length. She slid her arms around him. "Not now," he whispered. "Oh, Christ," he said. "I should never have brought you here. This wasn't your scene. I knew it."

"My scene is your scene," she said. She laughed. "Boy, that really sounds corny." She knew the joke would help to relax him. She could see the tension in his eyes. She hoped it was tension caused by doubt. I've got to find a way out of here, she thought. I've got to get us out of here.

After a moment he released her. "Let's eat," he said in a normal voice. He cupped her chin in his hand.

She shook her head. "I don't know if I've any appetite." She hesitated, as if thinking. "Funny," she said. "Actually, upon reflection, I think I could eat a horse. With whipped cream."

"For breakfast?" He laughed.

"C'mon," she said, taking him by the hand. But her smile masked an anxiety that cried within her: Tell him! Everything has changed now. It's not just us anymore.

She despaired of finding the right words and the right time.

Olivia Barrow stood at a small dresser in the rear bedroom and looked at herself in the mirror. She had cut her hair short; it gave her whole face an edge. She examined her features, the straight nose, high cheekbones, and wide forehead that had driven her mother to stroke her head so often, standing behind her as they both looked into the mirror, and tell her that she would always be the prettiest girl at whatever party she was heading to. She laughed at the thought: Her mother probably didn't have today's kind of party in mind. She remembered the modeling agency that had tried to sign her to a contract when she was a freshman in college, and she snorted. I need a scar, she thought. Some horrifying bright red-purple badge that runs through the middle of these good looks like a crease across a painter's final canvas. It would be better if I looked more dumpy, more nondescript. I should have become some baggy-bodied, stringy-haired hippie girl, with sagging breasts and buttocks, chanting mantras about peace, love, and flowers, looking like my only concern in the entire world is where to find another hit of acid. I would be harder to recognize.

But she was equally aware of the strength her beauty gave her. She bent down swiftly, touching her toes, then, still jackknifed at the waist, putting her palms flat on the floor. It was important to be physically fit.

Her mother had been a dancer. She remembered watching her

leap, twist, and fly in her studio. She was always strong. Olivia felt a sudden rush of anger. Why hadn't she fought? Why had she just let the disease rob her of life? She remembered how shocked she'd been at how swiftly the cancer had sliced strength from her mother, diminishing her in moments, it seemed, rendering her small and pathetic. Olivia hated the memory. She hated the defeat, the murmurings and ineptitude of the doctors. She hated her father's impotent acquiescence.

She wondered what he was doing that minute. Probably stuck in that musty den in the apartment overlooking Washington Square, reading law books, getting ready for another legal assault on behalf of some hopeless cause, inevitably destined for failure. My father, she thought, with a small measure of kindness, always tilts at windmills. If one won't come to him, then he'll go find one.

In an odd way, she both hated and loved him. She was aware how much he'd taught her, how his commitment to causes had affected her. He had instructed her that going through life without passion and beliefs was a cold, vapid existence. He had shown her that action, social duty, protest were the foundations of intelligence. Their Village apartment had always been filled with songs from one movement or another. It seemed as if she was forever awakening in her father's arms in the middle of the night, as she was transported from her own tiny bedroom to a daybed in the corner of her parents' bedroom, to make room for some important visitor, usually bearded, usually carrying a guitar, who would spend the night in her bed. My first sacrifices for the struggle.

In third grade, when the others were doing book reports on *Charlotte's Web* and *The Wind in the Willows*, she was talking about Joe Hill and the Wobblies. Her mind flashed back to a hundred demonstrations he'd taken her to. She remembered at age seven or eight being led by the hand into a cavernous hall in Greenwich Village filled with hundreds of people, all crying, "Free Them! Free Them! Free Them!" She had learned later that it had been a meeting on behalf of Julius and Ethel Rosenberg. She remembered how impressed she'd been at the volume of voices, at the strength of unity in the hot, stuffy space of that hall. She'd been certain that this cause that her father was such a part of would be successful, and had cried when she'd seen the headline in the paper a few months later. Now she laughed out loud at the memory. That was my father, she thought. He was there to show support. He was there to lend his body, his prestige, his money to the cause he perceived as right. And to what effect? The state murdered the Rosenbergs. The state always thumbed its nose and laughed at men like my father.

But they won't laugh at me.

She pictured her father again. He would wear either a blue, brown, or gray pin-striped suit every day. He called it corporate camouflage. Look like the enemy, he would laugh. He always lost with humor. I loved the humor. But I hated the losing. His principles were always correct. His politics were always right. His causes were always important. His tactics were sound. His legal reasoning always acute. His presentation always direct, impressive.

And he always lost.

Olivia looked again into the mirror and cleared her father from her mind.

Today I will show them all that action is strength. For a moment she envisioned the morning papers. The plan excited her, and she looked into her gray-blue eyes in the mirror, as if searching for a flaw. She smiled in satisfaction.

None.

They had spent too much time watching, waiting, observing.

She knew the route the armored truck drove. She knew the procedure followed when they picked up the cash receipts and when they deposited the cash at the bank. It was always just at the end of the business day, every other Wednesday. Slow time at the bank. She pictured the two guards in her mind. They didn't even bother to unbuckle the straps that held their revolvers. Last week one of the guards had set his shotgun down, when a money bag had slid off of the cart. He was fat and she'd watched him grunt as he lifted it. They had seemed almost bored. Completely relaxed. Oblivious to the one thing that she was going to bring down on them.

And why not? This is a tiny little farming town in wine-growing country. It hardly feels the heat from San Francisco, two hours and one century distant. What's happening on the streets of the cities is just a few bright images on the evening news. Nothing to be overly concerned about.

Nothing until I arrived here.

The plan had two great political strengths. First, the money they planned to seize came largely from a Dow Chemical subsidiary plant. If this small plant made pesticides for farm production, and wasn't connected to the larger plants where napalm and the other chemicals of war were made, well, that was irrelevant. And the assault itself would happen in this small, conservative community. A bunch of tired old Eisenhower Republicans, ripe for the picking. The cops here are all farm boys whose fathers lost their farms to the bank. It will show them that the revolution can spring up anywhere.

That was what she appreciated the most: the shock value.

She looked at herself again, grinning with anticipation. She picked up her pistol and pointed it at herself in the mirror, then held her position for several seconds. The heft of the weapon gave her an electric sensation and she realized that she was on the edge of arousal. Continuing to hold the pistol in front of her, she lifted her free hand to her breast, stroking herself.

All warriors are the same before battle, she thought.

She did not pause as the door opened behind her. It was Emily Lewis. Olivia continued stroking her breast, looking at the other woman in the mirror.

"Tanya," she said. "Can we talk for a moment?"

"Isn't the time for talk over?"

"Yes, that's right. I'm just concerned about one aspect of the plan."

Olivia turned and put her arm around the other woman. For a moment she kneaded the woman's shoulders, then ran a hand through her curly black hair. She moved her to the side of the bed. "Tell me," she said.

"It's the getaway arrangements. I understand about the two vans. I understand about the switch. But what scares me is that on the escape route we'll drive right past the bank. I don't know if we'll be able to stay cool."

"That's the beauty of the escape. We take off in one direction, then, before the pigs know it, just as they all start chasing us, we head right back past them, going the opposite way. You're right. It will take nerve. But we've got strength. It'll be fine. You'll see."

"Do you think she can manage it? I mean the driving? Suppose we get stopped?"

"That's why I let Duncan bring her into the brigade. First off, she's going to do anything her squeeze tells her to. Regardless. The second thing you've got to remember is she's never even had a fucking parking ticket, for Christ sakes. The pigs have absolutely no book on her. And look at her. She looks like your average, slightly far out, kind of dizzy college student. She'd be more trouble than she was worth to some scared cop looking for a bunch of professional revolutionaries. And even if we were to get stopped, and they ran her name and license, nothing would turn up when they checked their computers. They'd have to let her go. And we'd all be in the back, laughing our heads off."

Emily leaned back on the bed. She smiled. "You make it sound so easy."

"It is easy. Kwanzi and Sundiata have done a half-dozen jobs like this. They're cool. Really know the business."

"Yeah, except they got caught once."

"They didn't have the right commitment."

"Now they do?"

"Now they do," Olivia said. She wondered for an instant at how easily she lied. She lied on: "Once they were criminals. Now they are revolutionaries. They just know how to use the knowledge they've acquired on behalf of the struggle."

The dark-haired woman closed her eyes. "Well," she said, "I wish we'd chosen something a little quieter for the first action, but I trust you."

"Good. Think of the money. New weapons. Better quarters. New recruits. The Phoenix Brigade will become a reality. We will become a true revolutionary organization. It will make a mark. Definitely."

Emily laughed. "God," she said, "the pigs are going to be so pissed off."

Olivia bent down beside her and ran her finger along the valley of the other woman's neck. "You must trust me," she said. "You must do what I tell you. Together, we are an army."

"I will. We all will."

Her finger traveled down, undoing the top buttons of the other woman's blue denim workshirt, then tracing the shape of her breasts. Emily closed her eyes. "Bill is jealous when we do this," she said. She shuddered as Olivia touched her stomach, and reached her own hand up to run through Olivia's blond hair. "He'll have to learn I love you, too," she said.

"And I love you," replied Olivia, as she undid the top of the other woman's jeans. "I always have. I always will." She did not say: You're the only one that matters. You're the only one I care for. When this is finished, it will be you and me going away and starting over, rid of all these hangers-on and confused political parasites. We can devote ourselves together to the new world. We are the real Phoenix Brigade. The two of us together.

Emily giggled. "Everyone's excited. I think everyone's going to get it on this morning." Both women laughed together. Then they quickly undressed. As Olivia started to climb on top of the other woman, she noticed the door to the bedroom crack open slightly. She could hear breathing from just beyond her sight. "Enter," she commanded. She waited until she saw the bearded face of her lover's husband.

"You can watch," she told Bill Lewis brusquely. "You can say nothing. Do nothing. Just watch." It was an order, given in tones that left no room for discussion. She jerked her head to the corner of the room. The man flushed visibly, the scar on his neck flashing like a beacon, hesitated, then nodded. He walked quietly to the designated spot, without saying a word.

Olivia smiled, felt the power surging within her, and slid herself up over her partner.

Just before noon, the brigade gathered in the living room. "Okay," Olivia said. "We're going to run through our assignments again. It's important that no one have any questions about their precise role."

Abruptly she pointed at Emily. "What's your job?"

"I'm in the bank first, at the counter filling out a form. I cover the bank guard when I see the brothers make their move on the armored truck."

Olivia wheeled swiftly, and pointed at the two black men.

Kwanzi answered. "We're the ones who start the play. We take down the armored truck guards. Right when they're going through the doors. Sundiata takes the inside, I take the outside."

"Ché?"

"I cover the bank tellers, make certain no one hits the alarm."

She nodded, then swiftly rocked toward Duncan. "And?"

"I drive the first van. I park at the corner of River and Sunset, so I can see the front of the bank. As soon as I see Kwanzi and Sundiata make their move, I pull in front of the bank and open the rear doors."

"And then?"

"Stay cool."

"Right. Megan?"

Megan took a deep breath and, trying to keep her voice from quivering, said: "I stay in the second van parked behind the drugstore, with the engine running. I wait until the first van shows up. Then, when everyone's aboard, I take off. Slowly, and drive down Sunset, past the bank."

"Right."

Olivia hesitated. "What about inside the bank?"

Kwanzi answered quickly. "No shooting. Not if you can help it. And if you gotta shoot, aim at the ceiling. Remember, nothing will bring the pigs faster than gunfire."

Everyone nodded.

"And I don't wanna take a murder fall."

"I think everyone should leave the safety catches on their weapons engaged," Duncan said. "That way we can be certain there'll be no mistakes. We've got to remember our objectives: Get the money, make a statement. If we shoot up the place, then the pig press will just call us a bunch of bank robbers."

The others nodded. Olivia spoke: "The brother is right. Remember why we're there. Nobody get itchy with their gun."

"What if the guards go for their weapons?" asked Emily.

"Won't happen," replied Olivia. "Once we get the drop on them, they're trained to just go along." She laughed. "After all, it isn't their money." There were smiles all around the room. "Look, we'll be in and out before they know what hit them."

Sundiata picked up. "Another thing. Leave the teller drawers alone. They may have a couple of grand there, but they've also got special marked bills and alarms. So nobody get greedy. We're going after the truck's money, brothers and sisters, so let's be cool."

There were murmurs of agreement.

"Could be as much as a hundred grand."

This figure, spoken before, still impressed them. After a moment, Olivia broke the silence.

"Questions?"

"Who's going to carry the watch?" Duncan asked.

Olivia replied: "I am. I'm at the door, watching the street. Four minutes, in and out. Minimum response time, assuming someone is dumb enough to set off an alarm, is five minutes. We'll have sixty seconds to clear the scene, before the first cop car arrives. And the pig will probably just run right into the bank, too, not set out looking for us. So remember, when I say 'Go!' we go. Everyone got that?"

"The sister's right," Kwanzi said. "When Sundiata and I got busted before in that liquor store, it was because we didn't leave when the going was good. Nobody fuck up, man."

"We are an army," Olivia said. "Act like one."

"Right on," said the two black men in unison.

"Remember," said Olivia. "We leave in the order we went in. Right into the back of the truck."

There was nervous laughter.

"All right," said Olivia, glancing at her watch. "It's getting close. We leave in an hour."

The group paused before breaking up. Kwanzi produced a bottle of scotch, took a long pull, then passed it to Sundiata. "Here," said Sundiata, passing the bottle on. "Give you a little jolt to your nerves." The two black men looked at each other and laughed.

Fucking fake macho queers, thought Olivia. Two black prison faggots. And they think I'm dumb enough to trust them. They think they're using us with all their fake revolutionary garbage talk and their new phony African names. I can see through them in an instant. They don't know who they're really dealing with. They don't know about my fire, and they're going to get burnt.

Megan cornered Duncan in the kitchen. He was sitting at a small, cheap table with a linoleum counter top, staring at a pistol and a clip of cartridges. He looked up when she came in. "I don't really think I need this, Meg. I'm just driving, and I'd better keep both hands on the wheel."

He half-smiled, trying to twist his face into a confident grin, but instead simply added lines of worry to his appearance. "You know, this entire past week I've been terrified that I would shoot myself in the leg. Odd, isn't it, how you can wrap all your fears into one specific fantasy? I see myself in front of the bank, by the van, gun in hand, and everything going just right. Then the gun goes off. It's like it's in slow motion. I can see the bullet as it hits my leg. It doesn't hurt or anything, but there's blood, and I can't drive the van anymore, and they have to leave me behind. I break out into a cold sweat, just talking about it."

He shook his head. "Bizarre, huh?"

"I don't know. You've been tossing and turning in your sleep, too."

"Not sleeping well, I'll give you that. I feel like I'm tired all the time."

Megan took a deep breath and quickly looked about. The others were all spread throughout the house; they seemed to have a few precious moments alone. Now, she ordered herself, do it now. Tell him!

"Duncan, are you sure about what we're doing?"

She saw him start to get angry. She cursed herself. She'd picked the absolute wrong way to start the conversation.

"No, no, I know what you're going to say," she continued quickly, screaming commands to herself. "I agree with you about commitment and action. I agree that something has to be done. But look at us. Are you sure this is the right way?"

"I won't talk about it again," he snapped.

Pigheaded man, she thought. I hate him as much as I love him when he acts like this. Makes up his fucking mind, then damn the consequences. Doesn't like to think about anybody else. Well, here's something he hasn't considered.

"Okay," she said angrily. "We won't talk about it. Let's talk about something else, something totally fucking different—"

She took a deep breath.

"—I think I'm pregnant."

A wondrous look of mingled surprise, shock, and a small touch of pleasure fled across his face.

For a moment he just looked at her, then he asked: "You think what?"

"You heard me."

"Better say it again."

"I think I'm pregnant."

"Pregnant? A baby?"

"Christ, Duncan!"

"Well, that's . . . that's—that's—"

"What?"

"Well, that's wonderful. We're going to have a baby. I guess we should actually tie the knot, huh? Make it all legal and everything. Wow! I mean, far out. I mean, are you sure?"

"Not completely. But all the signs are there. I should go down to the free clinic and get checked for sure, but I'm pretty certain."

She looked over and saw what she thought of as the old Duncan. Half boyish delight, half concerned man. She saw his face flash with an enthusiasm that she had not seen for months, and it comforted her. Lost, for just a few seconds, were the plans for the day.

Duncan leaned back in his chair.

"I don't know what to say." He grinned. "I mean, this is really something. You know, everyone always wonders how they're gonna react when they get news like this. Whew! Far out. Far fucking out. This is like jumping on a roller coaster once it's already started . . . Jesus, we ought to call your folks, I suppose. It's been months since you talked to them. Are they ever gonna be surprised . . ."

She looked at him and saw only the Duncan she loved, watching as he rolled this news over in his mind, obviously delighted, confused, proud. Abruptly, however, she saw concern hit his face.

He hesitated. "Hey, I'm sorry. I wasn't thinking. I mean, you want to have the baby, huh? Were you thinking about maybe not having it?"

"Duncan, for Christ's sake!"

"Well, I'm sorry. I thought I'd better make sure, you know." He started to grin again, oblivious to the grimness of his surroundings. "Well, well, well. What a kick in the pants. This is really—"

He stopped in midsentence.

His eyes fell on the weapon on the table in front of him.

"Oh, no," he said. "I get it now."

He looked hard at Megan.

"You're not bullshitting me? This isn't some kind of—"

She interrupted. "Duncan! You bastard! You think I'd lie about something like this?"

The force of her instant anger calmed him.

"No, no, no, I mean, it's just with what you're saying and what we've got to do."

He paused. His shoulders slumped in turmoil.

"This is a mess," he said. "A big mess."

He looked at the gun. He looked at her.

"I mean, what are we going to do?"

"This changes things," she insisted.

"It does. No, does it? I mean, what does it do? We can't back out now. What do we stand for, what kind of commitment have we made?"

She started to answer, words boiling up inside her, ready to leap from her mouth. But she cut them off abruptly at the sound of footsteps hurrying toward where they sat in the kitchen. Her mouth open, her hand reaching across the table for Duncan's, she looked up and saw Bill and Emily enter the room. Ché and Emma, she thought. The big fucking revolutionaries.

What are we doing here? Megan asked herself.

She did not have time to form a reply.

Emily was carrying a pump-action 12-gauge shotgun at port arms. She slammed back on the handle fiercely, chambering a shell. The sound was like an icicle in Megan's stomach. "Time," Emily said in a cold, even voice. "Time to get it on."

"Ready, set, go," said Bill. He had wrapped a bandana around his neck to hide the scar. "Time to start. Let's hit it."

In sudden and almost total despair, Megan watched as Duncan slid the clip of cartridges into the pistol and rose. He jammed the gun into his belt.

Duncan felt dizzy, as if a hundred hands were spinning him in a thousand different directions.

Then, both feeling as if they were being swept violently out to sea by a floodtide, Duncan and Megan followed Bill and Emily through the door.

At the American Pesticide plant on Sutter Road, two men parked an old armored truck near the main entrance and walked inside, heading toward the comptroller's office. One man was portly, red-faced with exertion, and in his late fifties. His companion was wiry and less than half his partner's age. The younger man seemed jumpy, filled with nervous energy. He kept taking off his pale blue policeman-style hat, rubbing a hand through his hair, and then replacing the hat. The older man finally grasped his companion by the arm and slowed his pace.

"Listen, Bobby-boy, take it easy. I wanna make it to retirement, and if you keep racing around, I ain't gonna. I'm gonna fall down dead with a heart attack. And you try explaining that to the boss."

"Sorry, Mr. Howard. I'll take it easy."

"And, Bobby-boy, please call me Fred."

"Sure, Mr. Howard."

They continued down the hallway at a gentle speed. After a second the older man spoke.

"This gotta be your first real assignment. You acting real nervous."

The younger man nodded. "Yup. All I been doing is walking

around inside department stores all night for the last couple of months. Since I got out of the service in April. That isn't much like any real job, like this is."

"That's the truth. You been overseas?"

"Yeah."

"See any action?"

"Well, kinda. I was in a couple of firefights. But mostly I just did what everybody else did, you know—humped around in the jungle without seeing too much, trying not to get dumb and dead, you know what I mean?"

"Sure. So why're you so nervous now?"

"I never got to carry no money nowhere before. Least of all somebody else's."

The older man laughed. "Better get used to it, kid, you wanna stick with this outfit."

The younger man hesitated. "This is kinda like a waiting job for me," he said.

"You gotta application in at the police?"

"Yup. Took both the local police and the state police exams. My uncle was a cop. It's a pretty good deal."

"Good for you, kid. Most kids today don't wanna have anything to do with the police force. Just wanna grow their hippie hair down and smoke dope. Being a cop's a good thing. Help people. Do what's right, you know, for society and all. I was a cop once."

"No shit? I didn't know that."

"Yeah. Military police in Korea, then twenty years on the force in Parkersville. Just me and three other guys. Retired back a few years ago and started working for the Pinkertons. Just another eight months and it'll be three-pension time. The army, the Parkersville force, and this outfit. Every month, just like clockwork."

"Jeez, Mr. Howard, not bad. What're you gonna do?"

"Gonna outfit me a little trailer and take the wife to Florida for a while. Do some real fishing, huh."

"Jeez, that sounds great."

"You bet."

The older man pointed at an office. "In here. Hey, kid, you ever

seen"—he glanced at an invoice—"twenny-one thousand nine hunnert and twenty-three bucks and thirty-seven cents all in one spot?"

"No, sir."

"Well, you're gonna get educated right now. Just don't you go
and start gettin' nervous on me again, 'cause this ain't no big deal.
Not by no account. Wait till you got to carry a million."

He grinned at the younger man and opened the door to the comptroller's office. The two men walked inside.

A young secretary greeted the older guard.

"Fred Howard, five minutes late as usual. How are you today?"

"Just fine, Martha. And who's watching the clock?"

She laughed and asked, "Where's Mr. Williams today?"

"That old fool's come down with the flu."

"Well, won't you introduce me to your new partner?"

The older man laughed. "Sure! Martha, this is Bobby Miller.
Bobby, meet Martha Matthews."

The two young people shook hands.

The young man stammered an embarrassed hello.

"Gotta do better than that, you expect to get this pretty gal out
on a date," said the older.

The young woman and man both flushed. "Fred!" she exclaimed.
"You incorrigible old coot."

He laughed. "Don't even understan' that word," he said.

The young woman turned to the young man. "Don't you pay him
any mind. He's just an old relic that should have been put out to
pasture a hundred years ago."

The older man laughed, delighted at the teasing.

"This going to be your regular assignment?" she asked the younger.

He nodded. "I believe so. At least till my orders come through."

"He's gonna be a real cop, Martha. Good one, too, I'll bet."

"Well," she said, smiling, "that's good. Real good. I'm going to
be right here," she continued. "I guess I'll see you next time."

The older guard hooted before either of the younger people could
speak. The secretary turned to him. "Okay, Fred, you know where
the money is. Sign these, you old buzzard, and get on out of here
before that bank closes."

She smiled at the older man, who scribbled his name on some documents.

In the truck, driving toward the bank on Sunset Street, the older guard said, "I think she liked you. You got a girl already?"

"No, sir. You think she did?"

"No shit."

The younger man laughed. "Well, maybe. Just maybe I'll give her a shot."

"She's a right nice gal," the older man said. "I been watching her for 'bout a year. She started as a dictationist and stock gal, worked up to comptroller's secretary real fast. She's got a good head on her shoulders."

"That ain't all," said the younger.

Both men laughed.

After a moment's silence, the older asked, "So, when you were overseas. Things ever get real hairy?"

"Couple times, in firefights. You know, it was always dark and I'd be shooting away. Had no idea if I hit anything. Scared the hell out of everybody, though." He smiled. "It weren't so bad. What about you?"

"Korea was fucking horrible. At least you guys didn't freeze your nuts off. But the scaredest I ever been was in a high-speed chase after some guys who held up a liquor store. They were driving a 'vette, see, and I was in my cruiser. On the straightaways I could catch 'em, but every time we went around a corner, well, they could downshift that sucker and take off. I thought I was gonna buy it for sure doin' a hunnert and twenny. Hell, it was kinda a relief when they spun out and me and some state boys started to shoot it out with 'em. There mighta been bullets kicking up all around, but at least I had my feet on the ground, you catch my drift."

The younger man nodded and both laughed.

"Just part a growin' old fast," grinned the older man.

He bounced the truck to a halt in front of the bank.

"Okay, here we go, I'll handle the scattergun—"

"Uh, Mr. Howard, if it's okay with you, I'd like to handle the shotgun."

"Something wrong?"

"Well, I just never held that kind of money before, and it really makes me nervous. I think I'd rather just hold the gun."

The older man laughed. "No big deal. But next time, kid, you gotta lift those bags, not me."

The younger nodded, grinned, and chambered a round in the shotgun. Then he unlatched the strap holding his revolver in place.

"I don't usually bother with all that procedure," said the older man. "All we do is grab the sacks, sling 'em on the handtruck, walk 'em through the door and into the vault, sign a paper, and we're out of here."

"Jeez, Mr. Howard, in the training course they were real specific about procedures."

"Tell you what, kid. Just for you, this time we'll do it exactly like the book says. Then you'll see this is a milk run. No big deals, huh? Now, the guard inside is Ted Andrews. Former Frisco cop who took one in the leg a dozen years ago. I don't know how you feel about blacks, but he's an old buddy, so you be real polite."

"Yes, sir."

"You get him to tell you some stories sometime. Learn a lot about being a cop. What it takes."

"Yes, sir."

The older man unstrapped his sidearm.

"All right." He smiled. "By the book."

He hesitated, first searching down the street through the front window, then rotating the exterior mirror to look behind the truck.

"Left side clear."

"Right side clear."

"I'm out. You cover."

"Right."

The older man got out of the truck and walked to the passenger side.

"I'm clear. I'll cover."

"Coming out."

The younger man exited the truck, holding the shotgun ready.

"Going to the rear," said the older man.

"You're covered. I see the bank guard heading this way."

"Doors open. I've got the money. We're on the handtruck."

"Still covered. Let's go, sir."

"Okay, son, here we go."

The older man, one hand on his revolver, the other pushing the small handtruck with three satchels of money, maneuvered through the first bank door. He looked up and started to wave to his friend, the guard inside, when he saw a small black man inside the bank moving toward him. He did not think, he did not compute, he merely allowed his instincts to grasp hold of him, and he shouted, "Maybe trouble!"

The younger guard wheeled swiftly, spotting another black man emerge from around the corner of the bank and stand facing directly at him in a spot barely twenty feet away. This second man paused, reaching for something.

Is this happening? the younger guard asked himself suddenly. But his voice shouted, *"Alert! You! Freeze!"*

The black man in the street did not obey the command. Instead, the young guard saw him lift a shotgun from beneath a raincoat and point it at him.

It wasn't supposed to be like this, he thought. Then he screamed, "Gun!" as the air ripped with the sound of the weapon firing. He fired his own gun as he dove behind the truck. But he was not fast enough to avoid most of the blast from Kwanzi's weapon, which tore into his thigh. He screamed, "I'm hit, I'm hit! Medic! Medic! Ohmigod! Mr. Howard! Help me! Medic!"

The older guard did not turn to look, instead trying to push the handtruck all the way into the bank. He saw a pistol in the hands of the black man who faced him, and he drew his own weapon. He got off one shot before he heard the firing noises, and it was as if a great hand slapped him in the chest and he fell backward amidst the shattered glass of the bank's front door. He was only vaguely aware that something terrible had happened to him, and he wondered why he was having so much trouble breathing. He could not connect this odd thought with the blood he saw washing over the front of his shirt.

Inside the bank, Sundiata turned with his weapon toward the tellers, searching for the bank guard. Everything was noise and panic.

At one counter, Emily swung a shotgun from beneath her coat. It caught on her pocket and she almost dropped it. She started screaming, "Freeze! Freeze! No one move!" She too started searching for the bank guard. Bill, waving his handgun at the bank officers, was screaming, "No one move! No one move!"

No one obeyed their commands. People were jumping every direction, behind tables and chairs, counters, anything. Some were crawling into corners. The small bank branch filled with panicked shouting.

The bank guard had leaped behind a desk in the first second. He had removed his weapon and, taking a deep breath, he rose, using the desk as cover, two hands gripping his gun. From a distance of less than ten feet, he fired four quick shots into Sundiata, who spun like a child's toy and collapsed on the floor.

The people inside the bank started screaming then, their terror mingling with a sudden cacophonous blare from the bank's alarm system. To the members of the brigade inside the bank, the raucous sound seemed to scatter their thoughts and waste their plans.

Emily, mouth agape, staring at Sundiata's body, which had landed virtually at her feet, remembered the guard was her responsibility. She wheeled toward his hiding place and fired a blast from the shotgun. It knocked her backward and smashed through the windows above where he crouched. He fired his last two shots at her, then ducked down, frantically trying to reload his weapon. He had to pry loose spare cartridges from his belt. He had always thought he carried them more for decoration than anything else, and his fingers fumbled with the task. Hearing a noise a few feet away, he glanced up. A striking, tall woman was holding a .45 at him. She was totally pale.

"Pig," she said. She fired the gun. The bullet exploded into the desk next to his head, singeing his ear, throwing wood slivers into his face. The guard was thrown back, as if struck, suddenly deafened by the bullet.

Olivia screamed some incomprehensible curse, aimed, and pulled the trigger again.

The gun jammed.

She tugged on the trigger frantically, her voice wailing.

The guard thrust cartridges into his revolver, snapped the cylinder shut, and raised the weapon at the defenseless Olivia. He aimed carefully, surprised in that instant to be alive, to have a chance, to be able to fight back.

He did not see Emily across the bank vestibule lift her shotgun and, without aiming, fire a second blast, which caught the guard like a wrestler by the head and shoulders and threw him aside, tossing his body across a desktop where he remained, twisted and broken, killed instantly.

Olivia threw her pistol down and seized the guard's revolver. She turned to look for Emily, thinking: Not like this. It wasn't supposed to be like this at all.

Across the street, Duncan was stymied by horror.

He had seen Kwanzi come around the corner by the bank entrance just exactly according to plan, and he had dutifully put the van in gear. But he had traveled less than a dozen yards before the first blast from a shotgun had sliced away whatever normalcy there was on the hot afternoon. He had slammed on the brakes, screeching, as he saw the young armored-car guard fire his own weapon and dive to the side. He could not see inside the bank; the glare from the street seemed to suddenly intensify, erasing any possible vision.

He turned and saw Kwanzi pitched by the blast against a sandy-colored building wall. As Duncan watched, Kwanzi slid down into a sitting position, leaving a great smear of blood behind.

Duncan tried to make a sound, but couldn't.

He turned his eyes away and saw a window on the bank explode in shattered fragments. He heard popping sounds from within. The noise of gunfire seemed about to crush him.

For an instant he gripped the weapon in his own belt, unaware of thoughts, commands, responsibilities. He threw open the van door and started to clamber out.

Suddenly an alarm from within the bank started to ring.

He hesitated, as if frozen by the horrifying sound.

Then he became aware of first one, then another, and another distant noise, growing louder, growing closer.

Oh, God, he thought. Sirens.

They're coming. They're coming.

He thought of Olivia and the others inside the bank, imagining the gunfire tearing into their bodies. He thought of Megan waiting a few blocks away. She's alone, he thought. She's all alone.

He paused, half in, half out of the truck, his weapon still in his right hand, on the top of the steering wheel.

He did not know what to do.

Olivia screamed, "Let's go! Let's go! It's over!"

She heard the sirens approaching, and crossed the bank floor in a single leap. Emily was standing motionless, staring at the body of the bank guard. Olivia grabbed Emily by the arm. "We're leaving," she said. "Right now!"

"Where's Bill?"

Olivia had no idea.

"He's coming! Come on! Now!"

"What happened?" Emily asked. "I don't understand."

"Nothing to understand," Olivia said. "It's over."

She dragged Emily for a few feet, steering her toward the exit, until the other woman's sense of self-preservation took over and she started to run alongside. Both could hear police cars getting closer.

They raced through the first set of bank doors and Emily looked down at the body of the older guard, and came to an abrupt halt.

"Ohmigod!"

She thrust her hand up to her face.

"Don't stop! Don't stop!" yelled Olivia, seizing her arm again. "We must get out now! Come on! Come on!"

She threw Emily over the body and out onto the street. Emily fell to the sidewalk and saw Kwanzi's body. "No," she moaned. "Not him, too."

"Stop it!" Olivia cried. "Don't look! Just save yourself!"

She lifted Emily to her feet effortlessly. She could feel every muscle in her body tense, as if her entire insides were pulled tight. I must get us free, she thought. We will be able to start over.

"Come on, now—time to leave. It'll be okay."

Olivia dragged Emily into the street. She saw the van a block and a half away, Duncan poised half in, half out. For an instant their eyes met. Where are you? What are you doing? You're supposed to be here! Olivia screamed to herself. Come on, Duncan! Save us!

Olivia started to wave to Duncan, but Emily tripped and stumbled forward, and Olivia reached down with both hands.

She looked up at Duncan again. Here! she cried to herself.

The gutless creep, she thought. The coward! The word filled her with anger.

She lifted Emily up again and said, "We've got to run. Come on, we can make it. We can get away. It's not far."

Olivia had just started to haul Emily toward Duncan, when the first police cruiser, all four tires complaining, skidded around the corner, shuddering to a halt a dozen yards behind them. Olivia raised the gun she'd taken from the dead guard and fired at the shape of a police officer as the cop flung himself out of the car, taking cover. Then another cruiser raced into her view, this time blocking her route to Duncan and the van. A third car arrived, then a fourth. She turned back toward the bank, still trying to hold on to Emily. "Come on!" she screamed to her lover. "If we get inside, we can take hostages!" It was not until that moment that she saw the wounded young armored truck guard. He had crawled around the front of the truck, leaving a dirty trail of blood. She fired toward his face, seeing him duck, seeing the bullet smash into a headlight, exploding glass. He had his shotgun pointed toward them.

"No!" Olivia screamed.

Emily turned and lifted her own weapon.

"No!" Olivia screamed again.

The young guard fired.

"No!" she said a third time.

The blast ripped Emily from her grasp.

Olivia cried out, a great shout of anguish, suddenly alone, trying to catch her lover and hold her against the force that had seized her and flung her backward.

She turned and looked down at the street. Emily, gasping, had been thrown down on her back. Her chest was gone, replaced by a great bloody mass of crushed bone and torn flesh. She looked up at Olivia quizzically, as if puzzling some unfathomable question, expecting Olivia to answer her confidently.

Then she died.

Olivia screamed "No! No! No!" and fell to her knees at Emily's side. She dropped her weapon and cradled the other woman's head in her arms. "No!" she cried over and over, pitching her head back like some despairing animal. Rage suddenly suffused her, the first concrete thought that had penetrated her mind in what seemed to her to be hours: *Kill them! Kill them all!*

She reached for her gun.

Then she heard a voice: "Don't do it!"

She turned and stared into the dark barrel of a policeman's revolver.

A guttural cry fled from her as she reached back down for the tattered remains of Emily. She lifted her head once, to try to spot Duncan and curse him, but she could not see past the ring of policemen that surrounded her. So instead, she closed her eyes and gave in to the blackness, agony, despair, and the first few slivers of unbridled hatred that penetrated her heart.

Duncan watched all this happen.

Then he slid from the van and put the gun beneath his shirt.

He fought off the overwhelming desire to run.

Walk. No one has seen me. Walk. No one knows. Walk, damn you. Walk!

He went backward down the street, finally, at the end of the block, turning and pacing swiftly away. He ducked between a pair

of buildings and started to jog. He could hear his breath rasping in
and out through his open mouth, a sound that increased as his panic
rooted and took hold. Finally he ran, down an alley, heart pounding,
as fast as he could, expecting every second to hear the deep roar of
a police cruiser accelerating behind him.

Bill Lewis, too, watched what had happened from the relative
safety of the bank office.

He had seen Olivia seize Emily and drag her out.

We don't have the money, he had thought. We don't have anything. He had looked around at the tellers and bank personnel, the
people spread about, arms lifted in panic and surrender, others hiding
their heads, as if they could hide from a bullet.

What's happened? he wondered almost leisurely.

Everything's wrong.

He had taken three steps toward the front when he saw the first
police cruiser shudder to a stop in the middle of the street.

No, he thought. Not that way.

He retreated, away from the sudden gunfire in the street.

I've got to get out. Out! Out!

Bill turned and grabbed a teller by the arm, thrusting his pistol
up under her chin. He realized that despite all the shooting, he had
not fired his own weapon. He wondered, curious, whether that
would somehow make a difference.

"Give me the money!" he screamed. He was surprised to hear his
own voice, to realize that he was actually doing something other
than sitting stunned by events. He let adrenalin-instinct take over.
He dropped the teller's arm and started shoving handfuls of money
beneath his shirt.

"Out!" he screamed at her. "Back door! Get me out!"

She pointed and he dragged her toward the rear.

He saw a door with a heavy firebar across it and the sign: EMER-
GENCY EXIT.

Well, this sure as hell's an emergency, he thought. He hit the door
and it flung open, activating yet another alarm that joined with the
other noises. He dropped the teller, pushing her savagely away, and

raced into a back alleyway. He could hear more shots from the front.

He ran away, his first thought only of putting as much distance, as quickly as possible, between himself and the sound of those shots.

Then he realized: They're all dead.

For a fleeting moment he thought of his wife and of Olivia and it almost made him stop in the alleyway. He felt a great rush of choking emotion fill his gorge. He breathed in heavily, as if by gulping down air he could restore his reason, reorder the world. He calmed. He saw the alleyway was empty. He thought: There's too much confusion here. You can make it. Escape!

Run, he told himself. Run. Run!

Megan could hear the sound of sirens, and tears raced down her face. Seconds earlier, she had heard the distant noise of gunfire. It had been an odd, unfamiliar sound that had taken her a few moments to process and comprehend. Then, as it had continued, it had plunged her into despair.

I knew it. I knew it. I knew it.

It's over before we even had a chance to start.

Why did I let him? Why did I allow it?

She could not control her sobs.

He's dead. I know it, he's dead.

She wrapped her arms around herself as tightly as she could, rocking back and forth in agony in the driver's seat. I want to go home, she thought. Oh, my poor little baby, I'm sorry. I let him rob you of a father before you even knew him. Oh, God, I hurt so much.

She felt violently sick and managed to push open the door and tumble from the van. She leaned against the side of a building and tried to control herself.

Then, tears still flooding down her face, she straightened up. I'm sorry, little baby. I've made a mess of things, but I'm going to get you out of here. You're not going to be born in some prison cell. You're going home and you're going to have a good life. I promise. Do you hear me?

She stared back at the van. She was wearing thin rubber gloves;

Olivia had made them all wear gloves so as not to leave fingerprints. She stripped the gloves off and threw them into a nearby waste compactor, and felt better as they disappeared.

Megan backed up, still staring at the van, trying to think what connected it to the brigade. It had been rented; the other had been stolen. That had been Olivia's idea, that the first getaway van be hot, and then abandoned, but the second be totally legal, right down to the registration and car rental forms. It was due to be returned to a leasing agency in Sacramento in three days.

It can take us out of here, she thought.

She had to force herself back into the truck. It was as if the insides smelled of conspiracy, of the members of the brigade she was certain were lying dead a few short blocks away.

Megan started the engine, wiping her tears with her sleeve. She put the van in gear and slowly rolled away from the rendezvous location. At the corner, she hesitated, looking both directions before pulling carefully into traffic. The sounds of sirens filled the distant air, but on the street in front of her, traffic was passing normally, as if unaffected by the events so close at hand. She felt oddly invisible, as she headed away. I'm just another person in a car, she thought. I'm no different from anybody else. I could be just like that old lady over there in the sedan, or the businessman in the Cadillac, just ahead of me. She spotted a bunch of long-haired teenagers in a Day-Glo-painted VW camper. I could be them, they could be me. It was as if a sort of shell had formed around her, a bubble that was keeping her safe.

"We're going to make it," she said out loud.

She pulled to a stop at a red light. Then she saw him as he emerged from between two buildings, half-running, half-walking.

"Duncan!" she gasped. She did not think of the risk; all she could see was the person she loved, the father of the child, and she was out of the van, waving at him. She did not consider that there might be a policeman a half step behind him, or that in that moment she might be jeopardizing everything.

She saw his face change when he spotted her. Sudden hope.

The light changed and she jumped back behind the wheel. She

cruised through the intersection, halting in the bus stop on the opposite side. In a second he was at the door and clambering into the seat next to her.

"Where?" she asked. "The others?"

"Just go, please. They're dead, I think. Or the cops have got them. Just go."

She pulled back out into traffic. Within a few seconds she saw the road out of town.

"What happened?" she asked as she drove onto a four-lane highway. She paid no attention to the direction; it made no difference; she knew where they were going.

"It went wrong. It went wrong from the first minute. She said the guards would throw down their guns, but they didn't, they started shooting and all the alarms went off and everything just went to hell so fast, I didn't know what to do."

He pulled up his shirt, exposing the .45-caliber pistol.

"I could have helped them. I could have."

Megan made a shushing sound with her lips."

"It's all right," she said. "You couldn't have done anything. We should have known. That's all. We should have known."

She did not have to lecture him, admonish him with commands to start thinking about the life they'd made in her belly. She understood he probably knew it almost as strongly as she felt it herself, even if he could not put words to it yet. Out of the corner of her eye she saw him lean back and shut his eyes.

"They'll probably catch us right away. Don't do anything. Just do whatever they say. We'll give up nice and easy. It'll be a lot safer that way. I'll say you had nothing to do with it, and they'll believe me. Your dad will get you a good lawyer, and you and the baby will be okay. I don't want you to get hurt . . ." He laughed, without humor, a bitter laugh that betrayed his own despair: "I don't want to die either, I guess."

He paused.

"I could have saved them. I didn't do what I was supposed to do. I let them down. I was a coward."

Megan answered angrily: "They were doomed from the start. We were following some crazy idea. Seduced by that bitch Tanya. You did what was right for me, for the baby. You got away."

"Did I?" he responded. "I don't think I did anything right for anybody."

He leaned back and closed his eyes to all the agonies that warred within him.

After a second he opened his eyes and looked around, as if noticing where they were for the first time. "Where are we going?" he asked.

"Home," she said.

She saw him nod in acquiescence.

The word filled her with a strength she had not known she possessed. She thought hard down to her womb: Don't worry, little baby, it will all be all right. We're going home.

Megan gritted her teeth and let determination fill her.

In silence, they drove east, letting the increasing darkness sweep over and hide them.

3

TUESDAY NIGHT

He wondered why they had not hit him.

The last thing he'd seen when they pushed the black hood over his head was a man's hand holding a pistol right against his grandfather's shrouded temple. As he lay on the floor of the car he was aware of his grandfather's shallow breaths, but he was reassured that they were regular, and they reminded him of times when he'd been younger, holding still in his grandfather's arms for hours on end after the old man had slid gently into sleep while reading a book to him.

He didn't want to move, to shift position in any way, but his legs were starting to cramp and he wasn't sure if he could stand the pain. He tried to think how long they'd been in the car. Surely only a few minutes, but fear had a way of disrupting time, and he couldn't be certain. He could hear the engine, the tires on the highway, feel every bump in the road. No one was speaking, and he did not know how many people were in the car with him and his grandfather. He did not know why they had taken him, or what they were going to do to him. He only knew enough to be scared. He remained still.

Finally, someone laughed. It was a short burst, more of relief than humor.

"Well," said the voice. "It was easier than I thought."

It was a man's voice, Tommy thought. Number One.

"I knew it would be easy. A piece of cake."

Another man's voice. Number Two.

"The best kind of grab is always when you get the subject by complete surprise. It's good to get someone who has no idea it's going to happen to them. The kind of person who doesn't realize someone's interested in them. They're so goddamn surprised, they can't think for themselves. They always pretty much do what you tell them, too. These two were perfect," Number One said.

"No shit. You ever try to take down someone who knows they're a target?" Number Two asked.

"No, but I was in on the planning—"

"Shut up."

Tommy shuddered involuntarily at the sound of the woman's voice. It frightened him.

"Just keep from running off at the mouth until we get home," the woman continued. "Christ! Why didn't you just give the kid and the old man your business card. Don't be dumb."

"Sorry," Number One replied.

"We're not home free quite yet," she said. Then she laughed.

Tommy hated the sound she made. It made him feel dizzy and he could feel tears welling up in his eyes for the first time. He couldn't stop, especially when he pictured his mother and father. I want to be home, he thought. He could feel his lip starting to quiver.

"But we're damn close. Damn close."

Number One and Number Two joined her with short explosions of laughter of their own. He could sense them starting to relax. The car drove on, occasional jolts knocking him about. They were all silent for several minutes. Then he heard the woman say: "Here we are."

The car was turning off the roadway onto a gravel drive. He could hear the sound of the wheels crunching across the stone. He counted slowly from one to thirty-five and thought: It must be a long drive-way, not like our driveway at home. When the car stopped, he reached down blindly, feeling about for his grandfather's hand. When he found it, he gripped it tightly. He was flooded with joy when he felt his grandfather return the grip, holding him. He had to stop himself from crying now.

"All right," he heard the woman say. "Get out slowly."

His grandfather squeezed his hand hard, then released him. He understood, and waited.

He heard three car doors open. In a moment other hands were reaching down for him and he was being half-lifted, half-guided, out of the car. His leg had fallen asleep and he shook it when he stood outside. It was cold and he shivered, his entire body twitching uncontrollably. The hood made everything seem night, and he hoped they would let him take it off soon. He heard his grandfather groan again, and the sound of scuffling feet as his grandfather was aided from the car. He felt the old man's presence next to him. Again he reached for his grandfather's hand and again he found it, recon-necting, feeling the old man's strength. He pushed himself against his grandfather's side, and his grandfather draped his arm around the boy's shoulders. "It's all right, Tommy, I'm right here. Just do what they say. I won't let them hurt you."

"Nice speech," he heard the woman say. "Brave words."

He sensed his grandfather start to say something in reply, then hold himself back.

"We're going inside now," said the woman. "Walk slowly. Old man, you hold on to the kid. I'm going to guide you from behind. Ready? All right, walk straight ahead ten paces and we will come to some stairs."

Tommy walked forward, still gripping his grandfather. His feet crunched for a moment on the gravel, then they found some sort of pathway. He stopped when the old man stopped.

"Good," said the woman. "Now, up three steps, then there's a short porch and up one step through the door."

They did as commanded. Tommy thought it was a little like the game of pin-the-tail-on-the-donkey he'd played at a neighbor's birthday party. He remembered how he'd been spun around and around, then shoved in the right direction.

"Good. Now bear gently to your right. Judge, reach out with your hand and you'll find the banister . . . Good. Up we go. At the top, we go to the left; there's a landing. Then up another short stairway."

The two Tommys climbed the stairs. Tommy stumbled once, but his grandfather's quick hand grabbed him and saved him from falling.

"Good, good," said the woman. "Don't want our prize package damaged in transit." She pushed the old man hard in the back and he had to struggle to keep from falling. They climbed the second stairway. "All right, now straight down the hallway about twenty paces . . . that's good. Wait for me to open the door. Now, up we go again. Careful, this one's narrow." It must be the attic, Tommy thought. "All right," she said, finally. "Welcome to your new accommodations."

Tommy felt her stand next to his grandfather and steer him toward something. He stayed close. "Sit down," she said. They could feel a bed, and they carefully sat.

"All right, take off your masks."

Judge Pearson seized the edge of the black mask, eager to rip the suffocating black away and breathe freely. Inside it, he'd felt only a short step away from death, vulnerable as a newborn child. He had thought: I want to be able to see it coming, when it comes. If they mean to kill me, I want them to have to look me in the eye. He lifted the mask halfway, then hesitated. A horrid thought slid into his head. If we know who they are . . . He left the mask in place for an instant and said, "We don't have to see who you are. We can't make an identification now. Why not leave—"

She interrupted him savagely:

"Take off the masks! Now!"

The judge did as he was told, averting his eyes from the woman's face.

"No, old man, you've got it all wrong!" she said angrily.

The woman reached over and grasped the judge's chin with her forefinger and thumb, turning his head so that they were looking directly into each other's eyes, only inches apart. She was standing over him, like an angry schoolteacher getting ready to chastise an unruly student.

"Look at me," she whispered. To Tommy it seemed as harsh as a shout. "Remember this face. I want you to remember everything about it. Can you tell how beautiful it once was? Do you see the age lines by the eyebrows? See the little crow's feet at the corners of the eyes? See a little extra flesh hanging underneath the jaw? How about the color of the eyes, the shape of the nose and chin? The high cheekbones? See the little scar up under the hair, right at the forehead?"

She abruptly pushed her hair back, showing a small, jagged white line.

"See it? Remember it. I want it frozen in your memories, so you'll never forget it."

She raised herself up, looking down at the two Tommys.

"We're going to get to know each other real well before this is all over," she said. "You've got a lot to learn. Both of you."

The woman bent over and suddenly, frighteningly, pushed the judge backward on the cot. She thrust her hand into his pocket and grabbed his car keys, then stood straight and laughed.

"Especially you, pig. You're going to get re-educated completely."

She smiled. Tommy thought how afraid he was already of her smile.

"Look around, judge. Pace the dimensions. Ever been in one of those cells that you sent people to? Ever been locked away, like the criminal you are? Why don't you make a little scratch mark on the wall? That's what cons do to mark the time. Then imagine six thousand five hundred and seventy little scratch marks. I did."

She paused again, letting her anger ricochet about the tiny space.

She smiled. "I'll bring your dinner shortly." She turned to leave, then added, "It would be best if you went along with the program without complaining."

"We'll do what you say," the judge said.

"That's right, you will," the woman responded. "Because otherwise, you'll die."

She turned and looked at Tommy. "Both of you."

Then she left.

They heard a dead bolt lock slam home, as she closed the door on them.

Judge Pearson instantly wrapped his arms around his grandson, pulling him close and tight.

"Well," he said, "we're in a bit of a mess. Don't worry. We'll get out of it."

"How, Grandfather?" Tommy's words quavered.

"Well, I'm not quite certain, but we'll find a way."

"I want to be home," Tommy said, fighting tears. "I want to be home with Mom and Dad." He started to dissolve.

His grandfather put his finger on the soft skin of the boy's cheeks, wiping away the tears that had started to flow. "It's all right," he said softly. "Don't worry, I'm right here."

Tommy sobbed once, then again, burying his head into the old man's shirt and letting loose with great gasps. His grandfather simply rocked back and forth, holding him tightly, whispering, "I'm here, I'm here," over and over. After a few minutes, the boy quieted.

"I'm sorry, Grandfather."

"It's all right, Tommy. Usually crying like that makes you feel a little better."

"I do feel a little better." He pushed himself closer to his grandfather. "I will be strong, you'll see. I will be a soldier, just like you were."

"I don't doubt it."

"Grandfather, it's hard to be brave when you're scared. She said she's going to kill us."

"She means to scare us."

"She scares me a lot."

"Unhuh. She scares me too. I don't quite see what she's getting at, but I think she wants us to be frightened, that way we'll do everything she wants. If we let her scare us, it makes her more powerful. So we have to not let her scare us too much. That way we can figure out what to do."

"Grandfather, have we been kidnapped?"

The old man smiled and continued to hug his grandson.

"Sure seems that way." He tried to instill as much lightness into his voice as he could. "Where did you learn that word?"

"Dad was reading me the book last year. Is she a pirate?"

Judge Pearson tried to remember the plot, but he could only remember *Treasure Island* and his imagination filled with Billy Bones and black spots and Long John Silver.

"I guess she is, in a modern way."

Tommy nodded. "She acts like one."

Judge Pearson squeezed the boy again. "She surely does," he said. "She surely does."

"Is she going to kill us?" he asked.

"No, no, no, whatever gave you that idea?" the judge answered quickly. Probably too quickly, he thought.

Tommy didn't answer, but seemed to think hard.

"I think she wants to. I don't know why, but I think she hates us."

"No, Tommy, you're wrong. It just seems that way, because she's scared too. What do you know about kidnapping?"

"Not too much."

"Well, it's against the law, that's why she's so nervous."

"Could you put her in jail, Grandfather?"

"I would indeed, Tommy. Put her away so that she couldn't frighten any more little boys."

Tommy smiled through his tears.

"Will the police come?"

"I suspect so."

"Will they hurt her?"

"Only if she tries to fight back."

"I hope they do. She hurt you."

"I'm all right."

Judge Pearson lifted his hand to his temple and felt a swollen contusion. Not too bad, he thought. No real damage.

"There are three of them. Two are men."

"That's right, Tommy. But there may be more, whose voices we haven't heard, so let's be careful. We'll keep ourselves alert and try to figure out how many there are."

"If she hits you again, I will hit her."

"No, Tommy, don't do that." He hugged the boy again. "Don't fight her yet. Wait until we know more about what's happening. The important thing is for us to do what will help us to get free."

"Grandfather, what's happening?"

"Well, usually in a kidnapping they ask for money. She's probably calling your mom and dad now to tell them we're okay and that she'll let us go when they pay her some money."

"How much?"

"I don't know."

"Couldn't we just pay her and go home?"

"No, my darling boy, it doesn't work quite like that."

"Why didn't she take Karen and Lauren instead?"

"Well, I guess she figured out how much your mommy and daddy love you, and she realized they would pay a lot to get you back."

"What if they don't have enough money?"

"Don't worry about that. You dad can always get some at the bank."

The boy seemed to think then, and Judge Pearson awaited his next question.

"Grandfather, I'm still scared, but I'm also hungry. They had baked cheese at the cafeteria today and I didn't like it too much."

"Dinner will be here. You'll just have to hang on."

"All right, but I don't like it. Mom would probably have made stew, and I like that a lot."

Judge Pearson wanted to cry himself. He looked down at his grandson and ran a hand through the boy's tousled hair, then cupped his face in his old hands. He saw the blue lines of old veins and brown age spots on the backs of his hands against the pale young skin of his grandson's cheeks. He breathed in deeply, held his grandson closer, and thought: Don't you worry, Tommy. This old man won't let them do anything to you. He smiled at Tommy and the boy smiled back. They don't know that you have your entire life ahead of you and I will let nothing steal that from you.

"All right, Tommy. We'll be soldiers together."

His grandson nodded.

The old man looked about briefly, starting to survey the attic room where they had been placed. There were no windows, just a dusty low-ceilinged room with a pair of steel-frame cots. It was barely larger than a prison cell, as the woman had said, and just as grim. The ceiling followed the pitch of the roof, giving the room a triangular shape. There was a pile of blankets on one bed, but the room itself was warm. He walked over and stared down the stairway to the only door in and out. He could see a modern, brand-new dead bolt lock had been installed. His quick search through the room showed nothing else of note. But that's not the case, he thought. A room such as this always has secrets. It just takes time to find them out.

He looked down at the barracks beds and the pile of olive drab blankets, and remembered where he'd seen them before. It was another life, he thought. He remembered wading through the warm water that felt like blood, and tasting the sand when he threw himself down on the beach, too busy being scared to think of the death that surrounded him. I was young then, little more than a child, and I did eleven landings under fire. He remembered a drill sergeant screaming, "If Marines die there, then it's worth fighting for!" He had not understood what the man was driving at until he fought for the first forlorn beachhead in the Pacific. The names came back to him: Guadalcanal, Tarawa, Okinawa. He remembered thinking each time that it would be the last, and forcing himself over the side of the troop carrier and into the droning, pitching landing craft. I always thought I would die there, that I would never get home, except in a box. He remembered his surprise at surviving the war. Well, he thought, I didn't fight my way across the Pacific as a kid just to be executed like some stupid cow in a slaughterhouse when I got to be an old man.

He gripped Tommy's shoulder tightly.

"All right, Tommy. We're going to start making some plans."

The boy nodded.

Judge Pearson thought: It's not much of a battlefield, but if it comes to it, it's a good enough place for me to die.

Olivia Barrow shut the door behind her and threw the dead bolt lock. It made a sound that seemed to summon all her years of hatred together and lock them in the room. She cautioned herself: This is only the beginning. Play the hand out.

She felt excitement rush through her.

It's working, she said to herself. All the time and effort and planning, and it's working. I have been thinking about these moments for eighteen years, and now they're here and I love it.

She bounded down the stairs, and found Bill Lewis in the kitchen, making sandwiches. "You suppose they want mayonnaise or mustard?" he asked. Their eyes met and they both burst into laughter. Still laughing, he turned back to the counter to finish making the sandwiches. "I'll make them some soup, too," he said. "It's important that they know we're taking care of them. We have to make them realize that we're completely in charge."

Olivia stepped behind him and pressed her body against his back. "We are in charge," she whispered.

He put the fixings down and started to turn toward her.

"No," she said, moving away. "Later."

She ran a finger down his chest, over his pants buckle and then his zipper. He stepped toward her, but she held up her hand.

"There's too much to do."

"I can't help it," he said. "It's been so many years."

She quieted him with a sharp look. "Where's Ramon?" she asked.

"He walked back down the road a piece, just to make sure no one was around."

"Good. I'm going to go make the phone call. He can drive me."

"What about our guests?"

"You're in charge."

"All right," he said. "I'll see you in an hour or so."

"Probably won't take that long."

She left Bill Lewis, whom she no longer called Ché, by the counter opening a can of tomato soup. She picked up a small duffel bag that she'd prepared earlier, and went outside into the cool early night air. She peered through the darkness, looking for Ramon Gutierrez. She could hear his footsteps moving on the gravel driveway, and waited for him to approach her. He was a wiry, short man, with a glistening, thick black mustache and curly hair. He even moved in an oily fashion, she thought. He had been recruited by Bill, who once had been his lover, years before, when they had both been running underground. Ramon had been with the Puerto Rican Nationalist movement, but had been abandoned by the organization after an incident with the ten-year-old daughter of one of the movement's leaders. He was a nervous man, filled with criminal experience and jail savvy, a victim of his own warring sexual desires. He had once done a stretch for raping an old woman. A child, an old woman, a fling with another man—it had been these weaknesses that had attracted him to Olivia. Olivia knew that as long as she anticipated his eroticism and took pains to control it, she could manipulate him into doing anything. He wants me, she thought. Bill wants me. Now I own them both.

"Ramon," she said brusquely, "get the keys. We've got to make that phone call and we need to go get the old pig's car before someone spots it."

He smiled. "You got this all planned out good," he said.

"That's right," she said. "I've been planning this for years."

In the car, he said, "I did not like hitting the old one, but it just came over me. I was thinking about all the brothers and sisters that he probably sent to prison, and I just hit him. It would be wrong if he was hurt. We'll need him."

"What you did was fine. But you must always remember control. What screws this kind of thing up is lack of control. Everything fits into a plan. We know this, but they don't. That's why we always hold the upper hand. We must always keep them off-balance. Both our guests and our targets."

They drove in silence for a few moments. There were other cars on the roadway, their headlights cutting through the early evening darkness. They are all heading home from work, she thought. A nice dinner, maybe a little television afterward. Perhaps they'll crack a beer and watch a ball game, or else a sitcom or two, then some private eye or cop show. A little violence before the news and maybe some routine bit of spread-legs push-and-grunt under the covers before sleep. They're all so complacent, so ordinary. They don't know who is here, right amidst them.

"You make it sound so easy," he said with admiration.

"It has been. So far. And you know something?"

"What?"

"It will get easier. Like starting right now."

The car was pulling into the town's main street. They passed the post office and the police station, the College Inn and some restaurants. She saw knots of students cruising towards pizza joints and sandwich bars, business men and women, in overcoats, heading toward parking lots, carrying briefcases. It was all so small-town, benign.

She gestured to a phone booth on the corner across from a modest modern office building. She pointed down the street toward a gasoline station. "You drop me here and take care of the car while I make the call."

"This is the place?" Ramon asked. There was an edge of nervousness in his voice.

"This is the place." She laughed at him. "That's right. He's right in there. And he doesn't know what is about to hit him."

Ramon nodded and swallowed.

"I'll fill up the car," he said. "We should always have a full tank."

"Correct," she replied.

She saw her breath vapors in the dark air, looking like smoke. She watched as Ramon pulled the car away from the curb, heading to the self-serve station, giving her a little wave as he drove away.

He has no guts, she thought. When he acts, it is out of fear or weakness. Remember that.

Then she put the thought away and started to concentrate on the task at hand. She walked into the phone booth and put a quarter in the slot. She had memorized the phone number, and dialed it swiftly. It was just five P.M. She was not certain whether the secretary would still be there or not. The phone rang twice, then she heard the voice that she had waited so many years to hear.

". . . Hi. Look—I'm pretty much on my way now," he said, without introduction.

Her reply was out before she could even think:

"Really? I think not. I don't think you're on your way anywhere. Not anymore."

Her heart leaped with delight as the line grew silent.

He knows! she thought. He knows!

I knew it. I knew it all along.

And in those few seconds while Duncan Richards swallowed the instant panic of memory, it was as if eighteen years suddenly evaporated for her. She could scarcely contain herself.

In the attic, Judge Pearson had heard the car start up and then pull down the gravel road. They're going to make the call, he thought. They're smart enough not to use their own phone. He sat on the edge of the bed, holding Tommy close. Then he straightened quickly.

An opportunity, he thought. Maybe.

He stood up rapidly.

"All right, Tommy, we're going to try something. You get down behind the bed. Keep your head down, in case there's some trouble. Quick now."

Tommy nodded and wedged himself down out of sight. The judge moved over to the attic door and knocked sharply on it.

"Hey! Hey, out there! Help!"

He listened for sounds.

"Hey, somebody! Come on! Help!"

He hesitated, then pounded on the door again. He noted that the door lock seemed strong, but the entire frame shook slightly when he knocked. The door itself, he realized, was not solid, but, like many modern doors, pressed wood with an empty space between.

"Hello out there!"

He waited and finally heard footsteps coming up the stairwell.

"What do you want, old man?"

Number Two, Tommy thought. He crouched down further, but

kept his head up so that he could see his grandfather and hear what was going on.

"Listen, I've got to use the can. I've got this bladder condition, and all this"—the judge hesitated—"excitement has made it act up."

"What?"

"I've got to go to the bathroom."

"Christ!"

"Look, one of you can come with me, one can watch the boy, but please—"

"No, no, not right now."

He's alone! the judge realized with sudden electricity. There are only three, and two went in the car. The thoughts tugged at his heart.

"Look, use the damn bucket," Bill Lewis said.

"What bucket?"

"Shit, there's no bucket in there?"

"No."

"Christ!"

Bill Lewis looked around and spotted in the hallway corner the bucket he'd meant to place in the attic earlier that day. He cursed himself quickly. Dammit, he thought, I don't like this at all. I don't trust this old guy one bit. Where the hell's Olivia?

Judge Pearson felt a surge inside.

He's alone, the judge thought with finality. The others did go in the car and they left him. He's inexperienced and scared and unsure of himself.

He took a deep breath. Now, he thought. Now.

If he opens the door to take you to the bathroom, or to give you this bucket, now is the time. No matter what kind of weapon he waves in your face.

The old man coiled himself, talking to all the ancient muscles: Legs, you must spring forward. Arms, seize the man. Hands, choke the life from him. He flexed and poised, crouched over, ready for the door to open.

Bill Lewis hesitated.

It's been so long, he thought. And I've never done anything exactly like this. His heart seemed to contract with sudden doubt. Then he dismissed the thought and told himself: This is what you're here for. You're going to be rich. Don't screw it up.

For one wavering instant he wondered whether he was lying to himself.

Then he swallowed hard and picked up the weapon he had slung over his shoulder when he'd first heard the old man's calls. It was a small machine pistol and he double-checked to make sure the clip of cartridges was properly seated. He flipped the safety catch off and pushed the small lever on the side forward to full automatic. He wished he'd had an opportunity to use the weapon more than once. He fingered the trigger apprehensively.

He put his hand on the door lock.

"Please, I have to go . . ."

Judge Pearson was knotted behind the door, ready to launch himself. He listened to the mock tremor in his voice as if it were coming from someone else. He closed his eyes once, readied himself, and prepared to throw himself upon the person outside.

"All right," Lewis said.

But instead of opening the door, he hesitated once again. "Look," he said after a moment's reflection. "Old man, know this: I'm armed, and I won't allow you to fuck around. I'm going to place the bucket by the door. Then I will unlock the door. You wait until I give you the command, then you open the door and take the bucket."

He took a deep breath and moved the bucket close to the attic door.

"Listen very carefully, old man. I will kill you. I will kill you dead so quickly you will not even have time to realize you're on your way to hell. You make any move that I don't like, and you will be dead."

He paused, letting the words sink in.

"And we'll still have the kid."

Bill Lewis waited, hand on the door lock.

"Let me hear you, old man. I want to hear you."

"All right," Judge Pearson said. He froze in position.

"Listen to this," Bill Lewis replied.

He pulled back on the action of the automatic weapon, fully arming it.

"Do you know that sound?"

"No . . ."

"That's a machine pistol being armed."

He paused again.

"It's a messy way to die. All bullets and blood."

"All right." Doubt crept into Judge Pearson's heart. He could feel a release of his muscle tension. He argued within himself: Now? Is it right? He's alone, can you take him? Do it! No, wait. Wait. No, now is the best time! Do it!

It was as if two unfamiliar voices screamed within him, each demanding his attention.

He straightened up. A third voice, his own stentorian tones, remembered from so many rulings following so many arguments before him, spoke:

No. Not now. Wait.

"I couldn't miss. Not with this weapon."

"I understand," the judge said. For an instant he felt the weight of all his years, a great sad slackening.

Bill Lewis shouted, "Are you ready, old man?"

"Yes."

"I didn't hear you."

"Yes, I'm ready for the bucket!"

As Judge Pearson was speaking, Bill Lewis took his key and threw the dead bolt lock and stepped back. He figured the old man would be distracted by the shouting. He raised the weapon to his hip, pointing it at the door.

"All right. Open the door and take the bucket."

He watched the door swing slowly open, revealing the judge, who looked him up and down. Lewis gestured with the barrel toward the bucket. The judge nodded and grasped hold of the handle.

"Thank you," the judge said. "We appreciate this."

Lewis stared at him.

"No problem. We want you to be perfectly comfortable throughout your stay." He rolled all the *r*'s of the words perfectly. He grinned as the old man nodded.

"Oh, judge?"

"Yes?"

"Mustard or mayonnaise on your sandwiches?"

"Mayonnaise."

Bill Lewis laughed as he locked the door behind the old man. He walked away and did not once remember how scared he'd been in the first moments—which was as great a weakness as the fear itself.

Olivia Barrow let the silence on the telephone line grow until it seemed to admit the entire night blackness. She could imagine the pasty pallor that had grasped her quarry's face.

"Who is this?" she finally heard.

"Duncan, now, really! You know who it is."

She spoke these words like a favorite aunt halfheartedly scolding a beloved child for breaking an ugly antique vase.

"Must we really play guessing games?" she asked him.

"No," he replied.

"Say my name then," she demanded. "Say my name."

"Olivia. Tanya."

"The same."

"Well," she said, "aren't you going to greet your old comrade in arms? It has been such a long time, I expected a nice warm hello, how are you, how the years been treating you? A kind of class-reunion, old-school-tie kind of hello."

"A long time," he replied.

"But we do remember, don't we? We remember everything, even if it has been a long time."

"Yes. I do."

"Do you, Duncan? Do you remember how you left me to die, you cowardly son of a bitch!"

"I remember," he replied.

"Do you remember how Emily died because you weren't there for us? Because you left us alone in that street facing all those pig guns like the sniveling scared rat bastard that you are?"

"I remember."

Olivia couldn't control herself any longer. The phone shook in her hand.

"Do you know how long I've thought of this day?"

"I can guess."

"Every minute of every day for eighteen years."

Duncan said nothing.

Olivia took a deep breath. Then another. She paused, listening to the early night sounds, listening to the anxious breathing on the telephone line. She let the cold air wash over her, clearing her mind.

"Have you got anything to say?" she asked.

He paused, wordless.

"I didn't think so."

She took another deep breath and felt some of the instant rage subside, replaced by the same familiar steady burning that she had known for so long.

"Well," she said, "it's payback time."

She let that word hang in the air.

"What do you mean?" he asked.

"It's a prison word, con language, Duncan, something I know intimately and you don't, because of me. Because I never told them who you were. It's the word you use when someone owes you a debt, and you've come to collect. That's why I'm here, Duncan. I'm here to collect."

She whispered into the phone:

"I've got them, you rat bastard. I've got them and you're going to pay."

"Who? What do you mean? What are you saying?"

She felt his panic and it warmed her heart.

"I've got them both. I took them from the parking lot at that school and I've got them now. You know who I'm talking about."

"Please . . ." Duncan started.

The word infuriated her.

"Don't beg! Don't plead! You coward! You had your chance and you blew it. You should have been there and you weren't!"

Again silence dominated the line.

"What do you want?" Duncan asked, after a few miserable seconds passed.

She hesitated.

"Well, Duncan, it seems you're doing nicely. The years have been kind, profitable. You've done pretty damn well for yourself."

She took a deep breath and paused. "I'm going to take it all."

"Please, don't hurt them. You can have anything."

"That's right. I can."

"Please," Duncan said again, forgetting her earlier admonition.

"You want them back, you're going to have to pay, Duncan."

"I will."

"I don't suppose I have to go through all the same silly threats, do I? Like they do on television. Like don't call the cops. Don't tell anyone. Just be ready to do what I say. Do I have to tell you this?"

"No, no, no, whatever, I'm ready, whatever—"

"Good. We'll talk again soon."

"No—wait! Tommy, my son, where—"

"He's okay. So's the old fascist pig judge. Don't worry. I haven't killed them yet. Not like you killed Emily. They still have a chance—"

"Please, I don't know—"

"But I will, Duncan. I will kill them just as easily as you killed Emily and almost killed me. Do you understand that?"

"Yes, yes, but—"

"Do you understand that!" she shouted.

"Yes." His voice stopped short.

"All right, Duncan. Now just wait. I'll be in touch. I was able to wait eighteen years for this. Surely you can wait a few hours."

She laughed at him.

"Have a nice night. Give my very best to your squeeze, math-man."

Then she hung up the telephone.

Olivia Barrow stepped back swiftly from the pay phone as if it were something alive, and stared at the booth like a surveyor measuring a parcel of land. She spotted Ramon, who had pulled the car into a parking place a short way up the street. She waved, and briskly walked over to where he was waiting. He opened the door for her and she seated herself in the vehicle.

"How did it go?" Ramon asked.

She was flushed. Olivia clenched her fists and slammed them against the padded dashboard, making a sound like a drumroll.

"Is something wrong?" Ramon asked worriedly.

"No," she replied. "It just feels so good I had to do something." Ramon seemed to relax.

"Good, good," he said. "Tell me how it went."

"Later, when we get back," she answered. "I'll run through it once for you and Bill."

"Okay," he said, still edgy. "He's gonna come up with the bread? Right?"

"He's going to pay. Don't worry."

Ramon smiled. "Okay," he said. He turned the ignition.

"Wait," she commanded.

"Don't you want to get out of here now?"

"No," she replied. "One more thing to do."

"I don't get it," he said. But she remained silent, watching out the car window.

"Shouldn't be more than another minute or two," she said.

She watched the front of the bank. Come on, Duncan, she thought. I want to see your face.

As she stared at the bank's front, lights began to switch off inside. There was a second's delay, then the front door opened. She looked across the street and saw Duncan.

"Well," she laughed, "at least he didn't have a heart attack."

Olivia saw him drop the keys to the bank on the ground. She saw him stoop and start over to lock the doors. His raincoat was askew on his back, his hands were moving frantically. His briefcase was unclasped and jammed with papers. She could see the panicked hurry in his actions. She noted that he used two sets of keys, and then he unlocked an electrical panel box near the front door. She saw him punch in a sequence of numbers on what she took to be a keyboard. She wondered how steady his hand was.

"Well, I'll be," she said out loud. "The bastard knows how to arm the security system."

She watched as Duncan reeled away from the bank's front, half-running, half-staggering into a small parking lot.

Ramon grinned nervously at her.

"Shall we go now?" he asked.

"Patience, Ramon, patience. We're learning things."

She saw Duncan's car swing out of the lot and accelerate past where they were parked.

"Okay, Ramon, nice and easy. Let's follow the bastard and his nice, new BMW."

"Why?"

"Just do it!"

He swung out of the parking place and quickly maneuvered onto Duncan's tail.

"Suppose he makes you?"

"What chance is there of that? The poor sod will be lucky if he makes it home without smashing into somebody. But if it makes you feel better, drop back a little ways and just keep him in sight."

"Gotcha."

Ramon let Duncan pull away before sliding the car forward.

"Why are we doing this? We know where he lives. We've seen it before."

"That's right. I just want to make sure he goes home and not straight to the FBI."

"Oh, I get it. Just making sure."

"That's right." The explanation was something Ramon could identify with. He drove along with more enthusiasm for several minutes. They swiftly passed away from the center of town into tree-lined, quiet streets. She watched Duncan's car lights maneuver through the neighborhood.

"He's turning onto East Street now."

"Half a block to go. Give him a minute, and we'll roll by nice and slow."

She turned as they passed the house and caught a glimpse of Megan and Duncan, just as they stood in their doorway, as if frozen by the event that she had brought down on top of them.

"All right," she said with utter satisfaction. "Let's let them think about things for a while. Let's let all that worry and fear build right up till it boils inside them."

Ramon nodded and grinned. "Back to the house?"

"First I need to get the judge's car and ditch it in the woods. Then we'll check on our guests."

She thought: This is like preparing a dish of food. Now it is time to let it stand a bit before turning up the heat.

Megan and Duncan reeled into the living room of their house and sat across from each other, overwhelmed by the flood of questions, unable to ask any. After the initial shock of Duncan's homecoming, and an instant torrent of tears, the two had settled into a lingering state, someplace on the rim of panic.

Megan was trying to control herself, unsure whether an hour had passed or only seconds. It was as if she had lost grasp of time, that it suddenly swirled around her out of control. She tried to force herself to remember a few simple things: It is Tuesday. We are home. It is dinnertime.

But the effort only caused her to dissolve again. I need to grab hold of something, she pleaded to herself. She tossed her glance around the room, picking out familiar objects, forcing herself to recall the history of each: the antique chest purchased at a shop in Hadley, refinished painstakingly by hand; the set of bowls from the craft shop in Mystic; the watercolor of ships at dock done by the friend who'd returned to painting after seeing her children grown. Each of these filled up her life, made her remember who she was that day, who she would be on the next. Yet she felt adrift. There was no comfort in them, and she had been thrust into some different place. This must be what death is like, she thought.

"I don't understand," she said finally.

"What is it that you don't understand?" he snapped.

"All right. This is what I know. Shortly after five P.M., a few minutes after you called me, I got a phone call from Olivia Barrow.

She said that she had taken the two Tommys from the schoolyard and that she's holding them. She said we would have to pay to get them back."

"But I thought she was in prison . . ."

"Apparently not."

"Don't be sarcastic with me!"

"Well, I don't see how she got here has any fucking relevance! She's here! She's got them! That's all that counts!"

Megan jumped out of her chair and leaped across the room, unaware of her actions, driven only by anguish. "You did it! You did it! My Tommy! My dad! It's all your fault! They were your stupid friends! I didn't want to have anything to do with them! Play-acting at being a revolutionary! How could you? You bastard!" She swung hard at Duncan, who sat back in surprise. Her first blow missed and he blocked her second. She threw herself at him, arms flailing wildly, moaning. He gripped her tightly, and she finally collapsed into his arms. He cradled her and together they rocked back and forth.

After a few minutes passed in silence, except for the creaking of the chair as they rocked and her small sobs, she was able to say, "I'm sorry. It just came out. Oh, Duncan."

"It's all right," he whispered. "I understand."

He paused. "We were different then," he said.

She looked up at him through her tears. "Duncan, please, you must be reasonable. All my life, ever since we first met, you've always been the steady one, please don't change now. If you aren't, I don't know how we can get through it."

"I will," he said quietly. "I'll try my best."

They were quiet. She could feel a gasp forming in her throat. "Oh, my poor baby," she said. She squeezed his hand, filling her imagination with a hundred varied thoughts, all charging about within her, unchecked. She swallowed hard.

"What are we going to do?" she asked finally, in an even, flat tone.

"I don't know."

She nodded and they continued to rock.

"My baby," she said. "My father."

"Megan, listen to me. They'll be okay. The judge can handle himself. He'll take care of Tommy. I know it."

She sat up and looked at him.

"You think so?"

"Sure. The old guy's got a lot of moxie left."

She smiled.

"He sure does."

Megan put her hand on Duncan's cheek. "Even if you're lying, it's nice to think so, anyway."

"Look, the important thing is for us not to panic."

"How? Tell me, Duncan, how do we keep from panicking?"

"I wish I knew."

She started to cry again, but was brought sharply to a halt by another voice.

"Mom? Dad? What's wrong?" It was Karen, standing in the doorway. Lauren poked her head out from behind her sister.

"We heard you crying, then we heard you fighting. Where's Tommy? Where's Grandfather? Has something happened? Are they okay?" Both girls' voices were filled with tremors.

"Oh, God, girls," Megan said.

Duncan saw the girls pale. For an instant he couldn't speak, as he watched fear rush through their faces.

"Are they hurt?" Karen asked, her voice rising in sudden loss.

"Where are they? What's happened?" Lauren asked again. "Mom? Dad?" Both girls started to cry in fear, confusion, and apprehension.

Duncan took a deep breath.

"Come here, girls, and sit down. They're both okay, as far as we know . . ."

He watched the two enter the room, moving as always in a sort of unified way, linked invisibly. He could see that they were frightened, hit with something incomprehensible. They sat on a sofa across from their parents.

"No, come closer," he said.

The twins sat on the floor, close to their parents' feet. They were both crying gently, not yet knowing why, knowing only that something had shattered the family's equilibrium.

Duncan just launched ahead:

"Tommy and Grandfather have been kidnapped," he said.

Both girls flushed, eyes wide.

"Kidnapped! Who?"

"How?"

He did not know how to answer. He let silence fill the room. He saw that their tears had been replaced by something other than sadness, different from fear. He could not imagine what was going on in their heads, and it troubled him.

He held up his hand. "You'll just have to hang on for a moment." He felt Megan's hand on his knee. He turned and saw a different concern in her face.

"We have to tell them everything," Duncan said. "They're a part of this, too. We're still a family, and we're all in this equally. They'll have to know the truth."

"What is the truth? How much truth?"

He shook his head. "I don't know."

"Duncan, they're still children!" She reached out and grasped the twins, enveloping them in her arms. They pulled free.

"We are not! We need to know!"

"That's right! Come on, Mom!"

Duncan paused for an instant. "One other thing, Megan, that just occurred to me: How do we know they're not in danger, too?"

Megan collapsed on her chair as if struck.

"Oh no, do you think so?"

"I don't know. We don't know anything."

Megan nodded. She swallowed hard and forced herself to sit up straight.

"Girls, I want you to go to the kitchen and make a pot of coffee. If you're hungry, grab something to eat. Leave your father and me alone for a few minutes while we talk this out just a bit, then come back and we'll fill you in," Megan said in her best mother-knows-best voice, the tones she used when she needed to limit debate.

"Mom!"

"Do it!" she commanded.

Duncan saw Karen tug at her sister's sleeve. They turned toward him, and he nodded. They seemed glum and disappointed, but they stood and went into the kitchen without further complaint.

Duncan turned toward Megan. "So," he asked, "what do we tell them?" His voice gathered momentum. "Do we start by telling them their dad's a criminal? That the police out in Lodi, California, would still dearly love to put their hands on his sorry hide, even after eighteen years? Or maybe we start by saying he's a coward who left his comrades to die in the street when he turned tail and ran. How about the fact that they were conceived before we were married? I'm sure that will rearrange some of their emotions. How do we tell them that the lives we've been living are all a lie, a cover-up for something that ought to be ancient history?"

"They aren't!" Megan shouted back. "Our lives aren't a cover-up for anything. This is who we are. We aren't the people we were. No one is!"

"Olivia is."

That stopped Megan short.

"She is," she repeated with dismay. Then she thought hard: Is she? We don't know. Not yet.

"So," Duncan said, "where do we start? How do we explain it to them?"

"I don't know," Megan said. "I guess we just start."

Duncan's anger fled as suddenly as it had arrived. He paused, then nodded.

"All right," he replied. "We tell them and hope for the best."

But in that instant, both expected the worst, though they couldn't envision what that might be.

Olivia Barrow stood in the parking lot next to the judge's car, feeling the coolness of the night wrap around her. Her eyes searched through the darkness. When she saw no one, she unlocked the door and slid behind the wheel of the judge's expensive sedan. For an instant she stroked the leather seats. Then she fired up the engine and put the car into gear, listening to the transmission's solid thunk.

She drove swiftly, but carefully, across Greenfield's night. The town seemed slowed, hesitant; there were few people out on the streets. Even the neon signs from the fast-food restaurants and stores seemed diminished.

Within a few moments she was cutting away from the center of town, passing through a residential section. She barely looked at the trim houses and suburban order, keeping her eyes dead ahead, as she swept into the greater blackness of the surrounding countryside.

She turned swiftly down one country road, then another, until she saw the turnoff to her house and slowed down. She pulled past it some fifty yards, finally turning onto a half-dirt, half-grass old farmer's trail that cut into the woods. She slowed, letting the big sedan bump and thrust itself through the forest vise. Tree branches and scrub brush screeched against the sides of the car, sounding like so many animals in heat. After a few moments, she found the spot that she'd discovered walking the property weeks earlier. Making certain she did not stick the tires into some bog, she turned the car about.

She shut off the engine and picked up a small duffel bag and checked the contents: a change of clothing, some toilet articles, some false identification, a hundred dollars in cash, phony credit cards, and the .357 Magnum pistol.

Satisfied, she closed up the duffel and slid it down on the floor of the passenger side. Then she got out of the car, leaving the keys inside. My safety valve, she thought. Just in case.

Then she started to maneuver her way through the dark trees and brambles, quickly covering the short distance up to the farmhouse.

Tommy spooned down his soup eagerly, the warmth making him forget his surroundings. His mind filled with thoughts of home, and for a moment he wondered whether his mother and father and sisters were all sitting down around the table and eating dinner. Then he realized that they probably weren't because of Grandfather and him, and he wondered what they were doing. Are they scared, too? He pictured his sisters, and wished they were there with him. He guessed they wouldn't be such good soldiers as him and his grandfather, but they would know games they could play to help pass the time. They always played with me, even when the other kids wouldn't, even when they laughed and called me names, it never mattered to them. He remembered a time when there was a snowfall and he'd stood outside for an hour trying to catch a single snowflake on his hand. The other neighborhood kids had teased me, and said I couldn't, but then Karen and Lauren came out and tried to help me and pretty soon all the kids were trying too. And there was that kid who used to live up the block who used to punch me on the arm so hard, until Karen punched him back and he stopped. The memory made Tommy smile. She really smashed him one, he thought; it made his nose bleed and she wouldn't apologize. He thought of nights when the darkness scared him, and how Karen and Lauren would bring their sleeping bags into his room and sleep on the rug until he'd fallen asleep and they could leave. But I knew it when they left, he thought, only by then the night wasn't so scary anymore. He looked at the sandwich in his hand. They would have made it for me with tomatoes and lettuce and some chips. And Lauren would have snuck me an extra chocolate chip cookie from the high shelf where Mom keeps them.

They will come for me, he thought. So will Mom and Dad. And Dad will hit that woman who scares me and arrest her so that Grandfather can put her in jail which is where she belongs.

I hope that Karen and Lauren remember to bring some cookies.

He paused to drink some milk, which would have tasted better with chocolate syrup in it, and take a bite from a sandwich. As he chewed, he saw his grandfather, sitting on the edge of the other cot, staring out blankly.

"Grandfather, you must eat some soup. It's good," he said.

Judge Pearson shook his head, but smiled at the boy.

"I'm not too hungry right now," he replied.

"But we need to be strong, both of us, if we're going to fight."

Judge Pearson smiled again. "Did I say that?"

"You did."

Tommy put his empty plate aside and moved next to the old man.

"Please, Grandfather," he said, as a slight tremor crept into his voice. "Please eat." He grabbed his grandfather's hand. "Mom always said that you can't run on an empty stomach. You can't play or anything."

Judge Pearson looked down at the child and nodded.

"Everything you say, Tommy, makes eminently good sense."

He pulled his own plate toward him and started to slurp down the soup. To his surprise, it did taste good. He kept eating, as his grandson watched each mouthful disappear.

"You're right, Tommy. I feel stronger already."

The boy laughed and half-clapped his hands.

"Tommy, I think I should put you in charge. You should be the general and I'll be the private. You seem to know what's best for the army." Judge Pearson started chewing on the sandwich. Not enough mayonnaise.

My God, he thought, it has been years since I had milk, soup, and a sandwich. A child's meal. I wonder if they think it will reinforce our dependency—that they can make me less an adult by treating me more as a child.

For the first time, it occurred to Judge Pearson that it might take more than force to find a way out of the attic. He resolved to consider the psychological ramifications of his confinement at a later time. But first, he thought, some action.

"Tommy, do you realize that it has been several hours since we were first captured and we still haven't surveyed our prison cell?" He glanced down at his wristwatch. It was after nine P.M. They weren't smart, he thought. They should have seized the watch. It would have disoriented us further. But now we know the time and we know it has almost been five hours since they took us. That gives us something to hold on to.

"What do you mean, Grandfather?"

"What do we know about where we are?"

Judge Pearson stood up. He could feel energy shifting about within him.

"It's an attic," Tommy replied.

"Where do you think we are?"

"In the country somewhere."

"How close to Greenfield?"

"We can't be too far, because we weren't in the car that long."

"What else do we know?"

"It's a long driveway down to the house."

"How do you know that?"

"I counted to thirty-five when we turned off the highway."

"Good boy."

"So Mom and Dad don't have that far to come get us."

He smiled. "Probably they'll take us to them. Usually that goes with the deal."

"Okay. I wish they'd hurry. Grandfather, do you think we'll go home tonight?"

"No, I don't think so."

"Dad could write them a check."

"They probably want cash."

"I have almost fifty dollars in my bank at home. Do you think they'd take that?"

Judge Pearson smiled again. "No. You'll still have your money. Were you saving up for something?"

Tommy nodded, but said nothing.

"Well?"

"You've got to promise not to tell Mom."

"All right. I promise."

"I want a skateboard."

"Aren't they a little, I don't know, dangerous?"

"Yeah, but I'll always wear a helmet and kneepads, like the older kids at school."

"But you have a nice bike. Remember when your dad and I went to pick it out with you?"

He nodded.

"What's wrong with that?"

"Nothing . . . it's just, well . . ."

"You want a skateboard."

"Yes."

"Well, I won't tell anyone. And tell you what, once we get home, I'll give you a five-dollar bill which you can add to your bank."

"Great."

Judge Pearson glanced around the attic again. There was a single bright light bulb hanging from a center ceiling outlet. They controlled the light with a switch by the attic door. "Tommy, I think it's time we got to know our attic a bit better."

"Okay," Tommy said, getting up.

"Just slip off those shoes," the judge said quietly. "Don't drop them on the floor, just put them on the bed. Then walk real softly, okay?"

"Why, Grandfather?"

"No sense in letting the people downstairs hear us moving around up here."

Tommy nodded and did what he'd been told.

"All right," Judge Pearson said. "Let's start."

The old man and the boy started feeling around the edge of the attic then. "What are we looking for?" whispered the boy.

"I don't know. Anything."

They went down one wall and Tommy found a long, two-penny nail gathering dust on the floor. He handed it to his grandfather. "Good, good," the old man said, putting it in his pocket. They continued around the side. Suddenly the old man stopped. He put his hand on the wood planking. "Feel this."

"It's cold. It's cold all along here."

Judge Pearson pressed a hand against a cold spot.

"We might be able to break through here. There's no insulation. I wonder. Maybe a window once that's been filled in?"

They kept moving. When they reached the attic door, Tommy pointed out that the nails holding the door to the hinges were not seated completely.

They also inspected the two army cots. On one frame, one of the long metal braces was loose. Judge Pearson loosened it further. "I can get that off," he said. Then he sat down on the cot and replaced his shoes. Tommy did the same.

"We didn't find too much," the boy said.

"No, no, no, you're wrong there. You found the nail and we found a weak spot that might lead outside and a piece of metal that we could make into a weapon and we learned something about the door, though it's too early to tell what value it has. We did better than I thought. Much better."

The optimism in his voice buoyed the boy.

"Oh, Grandfather," he said, after a moment, "I'm tired and I wish I were home." He climbed up and put his head in his grandfather's lap. "I'm still scared, too. Not as much, but still a bit."

The boy closed his eyes, and Judge Pearson silently wished him to sleep. He stroked the boy's forehead, and realized that his own eyes were clouding. He wondered where his alertness had gone. He could feel his body tugging toward rest, arguing against the tension and fear. He put his head back.

Suddenly, Tommy bolted upright. "They're coming!" he said.

Judge Pearson threw his eyes open.

He heard footsteps in the hallway and a hand grasp the door.

"I'm here, Tommy. Don't worry."

What a silly thing to say, he thought. But he could think of nothing else.

Olivia Barrow threw open the door and entered the attic. She noted that her charges seemed to have shrunk back against the wall, and she saw apprehension ridged on their faces.

"Have you finished eating?" she demanded.

Both Tommy and his grandfather nodded.

"Good. You must remain strong," she continued, unconsciously echoing Tommy. "No telling how long this will last."

She approached the pair.

"Old man, let me see your forehead."

"It's all right," Judge Pearson said. I'm not going to let her push me around, he thought. Not this time.

"Let me see it!"

"I said it's fine."

She hesitated. "So, you want to play, huh?"

He shook his head.

"Don't you understand at all, you old bastard?"

"What?"

"I asked you a question!"

"Understand what?"

"How terribly vulnerable you are."

"Look," said Judge Pearson, mustering all his irritating reasonable judge's tones together into a lecture. "You've got us. You grabbed us without even giving us a chance. You hit me and scared the boy. You've thrown us into this attic hole. You've probably scared the daylights out of his parents. You're in charge, bully for you. Now why don't you go on about your business. What are you, some sort of amateur operation? Let's get on with it, lady. Let's stop messing around. There's no reason this has to be dragged on one minute longer than necessary. Extort your damn money and let us go home!"

Olivia smiled.

"Ah, judge, you don't understand."

"Stop talking in riddles."

She shook her head, as if laughing at some internal joke.

"Old man, you are so innocent. You think that you can retain all sorts of control by fighting back. Not physically, but intellectually. Argue with your captors. Get them to bring you things—like a bucket. Manipulate the arrangement. Next you'll probably demand extra blankets—even though it's plenty warm enough in here—"

"Well, we could use some more, and some extra pillows—"

"Or complaining about the food—"

"Actually, soup and sandwiches is hardly adequate—"

"You've had five hours and your initial shock has worn off. You've had a bit of time to assess the situation. It doesn't seem too bad. Neither of you is hurt. The attic is not the worst place you've ever seen. Your captors, well, perhaps they seem a little erratic, but you think you can deal with them. You're familiar with the circumstances a bit—you probably listened to kidnap testimony in some trial, no? All in all, things could be a lot worse. So you get to thinking, right?"

"Get to your point."

Olivia took out a large handgun and waved it in the air. "The point is to get me to threaten you again. I know your sort, judge. All jailers are the same. They think that they can outmaneuver force. They know that control is more important. It works that way in prison, judge, although you've probably never been inside one. Hundreds and hundreds of the toughest, meanest, most violent cons follow orders given by a few uniformed guards. It's all in the head— authority, strength, power. It works the same here. I'm the guard. You're the prisoner. I must keep you under control. You seek little ways of maintaining your identity. Really, on this score I'm way ahead of you." She grinned, pointing the gun at them, then moving it away, almost playfully. "But don't you see? I'm an expert."

She looked suddenly down at Tommy.

"Here's a threat, judge. I'll take the boy."

"What?"

"Simple, judge. I can see that the two of you get strength from being together. Maybe I'll split you up. There's a basement, too, you know. We thought of putting you guys down there, but it seemed too cruel. Really. Worse than any hole I was ever put in. No lights. It's kind of cold and damp, musty. Has a backed-up sewer smell, too. Very depressing place, filled with sickness and God knows what else. Maybe I'll just tie the boy down there for a while."

"Please, no! I want to stay here!" Tommy half-shouted. Judge Pearson could feel his grandson's body immediately start trembling.

"That won't be necessary," he said. "We'll do what you ask."

"Your forehead."

"Go ahead, take a look."

Olivia put away her revolver and produced a small medicine box. She dabbed at the contusion on the judge's forehead with Betadine.

"Any headaches?" she asked.

"None other than what you'd expect."

"Well," she said, "let me know if you have any dizziness."

"I will."

She put the medicines away and straightened up. "You've got to understand something, judge."

"What's that?"

"I told you earlier. This isn't a kidnapping. It's not normal. It's not like anything in your experience."

She laughed.

"I'll show you. Watch this. We'll make something utterly ordinary into something terrifying."

He stared at her blankly.

She clapped her hands sharply.

"All right, boys, who needs to use the can before bed?"

Neither the judge nor Tommy responded.

"Oh, now come on. Here's your chance to avoid the ignominy of the bucket. Who wants to go?"

They remained silent.

"Well, you're both going. Judge, you first. Get up, go through the attic door. My compatriot is waiting there, with his little machine pistol—remarkable weapon, judge. Ever use one? You know, they hardly make any noise at all when they kill someone."

Judge Pearson did not know whether this boast was based on reality or supposition.

She laughed again.

"I see what you're thinking, judge. Well, we'll leave that a little mystery for now, won't we?"

She changed her tone abruptly, out of the playful into the harsh: "Now get up on your fucking feet and go to the bathroom. I'll stay and keep little Tommy company."

"Grandfather, please, don't leave me!"

Judge Pearson stood and hesitated.

"Move, judge!"

"Grandfather!"

Olivia stood next to the bed and put her hand on Tommy's shoulder.

"Please don't leave me alone, Grandfather. Please! I don't want you to go! Grandfather!"

"See how difficult all our choices are, judge? Are you torn? What will I do behind your back? What will happen? Maybe you'll go and come back and find the boy gone, down to the basement. Maybe if you don't go, I'll just pick him up and do the same. Come on, judge, make up your mind. That's what judges do, isn't it? Make decisions. Damned if you do, damned if you don't. Come on, judge, guess!

What am I going to do? How cruel can I be? What's the right choice?"

"Grandfather!"

"I'll go. Tommy, stay put. I'll be right back."

"Grandfather! Please!"

Olivia grasped the boy's shoulder. She stared at the judge.

Damn you! he thought. He turned and hurried through the attic door, each footstep seeming to mark another cry or sob from his grandson. The sounds cut through him, and he hesitated, torn between the wails from Tommy and the threats that coursed about in his head. What will she do? Tommy! he wanted to call out to reassure his grandson, whose cries continued unabated. He saw Bill Lewis, grinning, holding the machine pistol, waiting down the hallway for him.

"In there," said Lewis, gesturing. "Leave the door open. You probably want to hear."

The judge hurried, standing impatiently at the toilet bowl while he urinated.

"Hurry up, judge."

He flushed the toilet and raced back to the attic, where he could hear Tommy crying steadily. He felt a sense of relief: At least she hasn't moved him.

"I'm back, I'm back, I'm back, it's okay, Tommy, it's okay."

He threw his arms around the boy and comforted him. He was filled with rage as he squeezed the boy and rocked him.

Olivia let them remain like that for a minute or so.

"Now," said Olivia, "that wasn't so hard. But this will be harder. Tommy! Get up! It's your turn!"

"He can use the bucket," the judge said angrily.

"No, he can't. Not right now. Not allowed."

"Please," Judge Pearson said. "Let me take him."

"No chance."

"Grandfather!" Tommy moaned. "She'll take me to the basement, I know it!"

Olivia smiled. "Maybe. Always a chance, isn't there? Life is so . . . changeable." She grinned. "Let's go!"

"No, Grandfather, no. I want to stay here with you. I don't have to go, I don't! Please, let me stay here, please, Grandfather, please!"

Judge Pearson knew the boy's pleas would have no effect on the woman. "It's all right, Tommy. Be brave. You can be brave. You can do it, and it will be all right. I know it."

He gently helped Tommy to his feet.

"I'll be right here. You go, do your business, and come right back. I'll be right here. Don't worry."

The boy was crying bitterly, shoulders shaking. But his grandfather saw him nod his head. Judge Pearson placed his arms on his grandson and turned him toward the door. He felt a great, sweeping pride come over him. "Hurry. I'll be waiting."

Tommy marched resolutely through the door.

Olivia watched for a moment, then gestured at Judge Pearson.

"Sit down!"

He complied. He expected another bizarre rambling from her. But instead, she turned and walked quickly out.

"Hey!" the judge said.

She disappeared, the dead bolt slamming home.

"Hey, goddammit! Wait! Tommy!"

He heard the boy crying: "Grandfather! Grandfather!"

Judge Pearson was on his feet. He leaped across the tiny space and down the stairs. He started slamming his hand against the attic door.

"Bring him back! Bring him back! Tommy! Tommy! Bring him back, damn you!"

His mind was a raging froth of anger, fear, surprise, and dismay. He was filled with betrayal and instant rage. He could feel his own eyes filling with tears. "Tommy! Tommy!" he cried out.

He started to fall forward, leaning against the wall, defeat mocking his heart.

And just as quickly, the door opened.

He reached out, without thinking, just filling instantly with joy and relief as soon as he saw the boy's little figure. Then he stopped. Tommy was being held by Olivia, with her hand clasped over the boy's mouth. Then she released him, and he threw himself into his grandfather's arms.

Judge Pearson enveloped the sobbing boy, his own tears mingling freely with his grandson's. "I'm here, Tommy, don't worry, I'm right here. I'm going to take care of you, don't you worry. I'm here, here, here . . ."

He whispered the last words into the boy's ear, calming him slowly yet certainly.

Judge Pearson raised his eyes. He stroked Tommy's hair, and held the boy's head to his chest. But his gaze met Olivia's.

"Who's in charge, old man?" she asked brutally.

"You."

"We're learning, pig," she replied. She turned away, locking them into the attic.

4

WEDNESDAY MORNING: KAREN AND LAUREN

At first, the word seemed electric, charged with an energy that threatened to possess them both: kidnapped. They had not known how to react: Nothing like this had ever happened within their experience—they had never been victims of crime, or known anyone who had; they had never been mugged or their house robbed or their car stolen. A man had followed them home from junior high school once, but when their mother had called the police it turned out that the mysterious person had been the retarded adult son of the school board chairman. He had been lost and harmless and the twins had ended up walking him home after fixing him dinner.

So, when trying to absorb precisely what it was that had taken place, they both felt a sense of confusion slide over them. Added to it was a sort of guilt, an anger with themselves, because the excitement and fascination threatened to obscure the idea that they should only be scared for their grandfather and brother. The threat to the two Tommys seemed oddly elusive, however, and so the excitement came to dominate them. They huddled in the kitchen, frustrated with the mundane task of preparing coffee and food, wondering how anyone could be hungry, how anyone could ask them to leave the room, whether this would change their entire lives, but mostly wondering what would happen next.

Karen and Lauren boiled water for coffee and set out some leftovers on a platter in the kitchen. They could hear their parents' voices raised in argument, but they could not really make out what they were saying. They believed that it was wrong to eavesdrop intentionally, but that the seemingly unintentional positioning of themselves adjacent to the open door hardly qualified as intruding.

"It's something about telling us the truth," Karen whispered. "What could it be?"

"I don't know. Do you think they'll tell us?"

Karen shrugged. "They never want to tell us anything, but they always get around to it eventually."

"Do you think they have some terrible secret that they've always hidden from us?" Lauren asked breathlessly. She was the romantic one of the pair.

"Mom and Dad?" Karen answered brusquely. She was the practical one, her voice even carried some of her father's best banking tones. "Come on. Look at them, for goodness' sakes. Do they look like the sort that had some secret life?"

"Well," Lauren replied, only slightly deflated, unaware how close to reality she had guessed, "anything is possible. We didn't know them. And they hardly ever talk about the time before we were born."

"They were hippies, remember, until Dad went to work in the bank. Peace, love, and flowers. Remember the picture where Dad has the long hair and granny glasses and Mom is wearing the flowered dress . . ."

". . . And no bra."

They laughed together.

They were identical twins; willow thin with wiry muscled arms, like their father, with their mother's red-brown hair and blue eyes and gymnastic ability. They played varsity soccer and basketball, acted in the theater club, and struggled with foreign languages. Karen had a way of turning her mouth down at the corners; Lauren would arch her eyebrows. Karen liked to push her hair back from her face with both hands, then shake it hard. Lauren, when pensive, would stroke her chin like some caricature of an ancient philosopher. Each wore a gold chain around her neck with her name stamped from a piece of silver in the center. This was a concession to people outside the family; their parents had never had any trouble telling them apart. Duncan often thought it was simply a tilt of the head, a slight variation in the tone of voice, that let him know which one had come to him. Megan had never even stopped to consider that their sameness could create a confusion for her. They were her children and she would have been able to pluck them out instantly from a hall of mirrors.

However, they were imposing to their friends and to potential suitors, who found their similarity daunting. It was something the twins delighted in. Though they had always traveled in the most accepting groups, right through grade school, elementary and high school, ultimately they had relied upon themselves to entertain themselves. Megan had noticed that the few friends that they truly let into their confidences were almost invariably the loneliest; single children for whom the twins had reached out.

"Do you think Tommy's okay?" Laren asked.

In lives filled with routine there had been one constant that transcended the others: their brother.

They had spoken many times of the moment, years ago, when their mother had come to them and explained that they did not know what was wrong with Tommy, but that he was different.

Their father had come to them with another message. He had taken them out to dinner and a movie, then brought them back and sat with them in the car until they were quiet and listening carefully: "You must always remember that you have each other, and he's all alone, and you must always stand up for him, because he's a part of you as well. All families have challenges, and Tommy will be ours."

Lauren and Karen had never forgotten that.

They also thought that their parents made too much of Tommy's disabilities and vacancies. They had always seen his specialness as something unique and wonderful, "Like being a child in a book where you get carried away to your own special magical land, like Narnia or Middle-Earth," Lauren once said. "He might love all the times he's in space. Maybe he's like the Little Prince and he catches an occasional meteor to take him on a trip."

But if Lauren had been slightly jealous, Karen had been more worldly. When Tommy had thrown tantrums, great wailing, screaming, incomprehensible moments when he'd tossed himself onto the floor and dashed himself against the walls, turning red with rage at the warring elements within him, it had always been Karen, with her soothing practicality, who had calmed him almost as well as his mother. She would simply wrap her arms around him and talk nonsensically into his ear, and he would slow and settle and finally look up, smiling. She could quote Ogden Nash and "Jabberwocky," and tell terrible jokes that always tamed her brother's explosions.

Tommy had never had any trouble either telling the girls apart, even when they tried to fool him by changing clothes. It had been a favorite game of theirs, and he'd never failed.

"Sure. He's really much too tough for any kidnapper. He's a little rock, for goodness' sakes. Remember when he fell from the swing set when he was four and broke his wrist and didn't tell anyone for two days? It wasn't until you saw how black and blue and swollen it was that Mom finally took him to Doctor Schwartzman."

Lauren smiled. "I remember. It's just, you know, when he would have one of those vacant spells, where he would withdraw and not say anything, and just sit there staring at nothing, that I always got worried. Anybody could have hurt him then. Suppose he has another and the kidnappers don't understand? They might hurt him."

"Grandfather's there. He can explain."

"If they let him. And anyway, maybe they'll hurt him, too."

"Boy, you don't know anything about kidnapping. It doesn't do them any good to hurt the people they take. Then they don't get paid."

"I know that. Anybody knows that. But sometimes people get scared. I bet they've got guns. And Grandfather will probably make them angry because he's such a sour old puss, and won't let them push him around. I'm worried about that."

"Where's the cream and sugar?"

"Right under your nose, silly."

"Oh. I got it."

"And anyway, why would anyone take Tommy and Grand-father?"

"I know. That's bothering me, too. Usually it's rich people who get kidnapped. Like oil billionaires' sons. Or movie stars."

"How could Mom and Dad pay?"

"Well, they've probably got enough money."

"How do you know?"

"Well, I saw his checkbook, and he had more than seven thousand bucks in it."

"Kidnappers usually want millions."

"Could he borrow it?"

"From who?"

"I don't know."

"Anyway, what are they arguing about?"

"Yeah. And why haven't they called the police? Did you think about that?"

"Kidnappers always tell you that they'll kill the people they've taken if you call the police."

"Yeah, but on television the cops always get called anyway."

"Yeah. I know. Or some private detective, like Spenser or Mag-num."

"Do you think they'll do that?"

"I don't know. I don't think there are any private detectives in Greenfield. There sure aren't any that look like those guys."

"Do you think we'll have to go to school tomorrow?"

"I hadn't thought of that."

"Poor Tommy. I bet he's scared."

"Yeah, he probably is. Do you think they've tied him up?"

"No. Well, maybe his feet. They probably don't know how fast he can run."

"Yeah. Faster than you, tubby."

"Well, we weigh the same, so speak for yourself."

"No, we don't. I've lost five pounds. I just didn't tell you."

"You haven't."

"I have."

"I bet it was all that grapefruit you've been eating. Yuck."

"Well, he's still faster than both of us."

"Suppose they do kill him?"

Lauren put her hand to her mouth after forming the question. She continued speaking rapidly: "No, no, no, don't even think about it. I can't believe I said that."

"What if they do?" Karen said.

They looked at each other and both felt tears form in their eyes. In a moment they had wrapped arms together.

"I won't let them," Lauren cried. "I won't let them. He's just a little boy and it's not fair."

"We've got to do something," Karen said. "If something happened to Tommy . . . Dammit, I won't either. I won't let them."

"But what can we do?"

"I don't know. But if they hurt Tommy even a little bit, I'll just, I'll just, well, we'll just kill them."

"That's right. They can't screw around with us. Do you remember Alex Williams and the way he used to beat up on Tommy? Well, you fixed him good."

"He never thought I'd hit him."

Karen smiled.

"They never think you'll do that because you're a girl and just a teenager. Well, we're not so young. We could even be in the army if we wanted to."

"You've got to be eighteen."

"So, nine months isn't so long. Anyway, they'll let you join younger if your parents agree. Remember that recruiter who came to the auditorium?"

"That's right."

"Shhh, notice something?"

"What?"

"They're quiet. They're not arguing anymore."

"Should we go in?"

"I think so."

But before they had a chance to move, they heard their father's voice summoning them.

They took seats on the sofa across from their parents. They sat, quietly, waiting for the explanation.

Megan started in first:

"Girls, we don't have a lot of information, but this is what we can tell you: Tommy and Grandfather were taken by some people. We don't know where they are, or what they want. Not yet. They called Dad and spoke with him right before he came home. They said they'd get in touch again soon. That's really what we're waiting for."

"Are they okay?"

"They said they were both fine. I don't think they mean to do anything to Tommy or Grandfather until"—she hesitated—"Well, we just don't know what their plans are. They want money."

"How much?"

"We don't know yet."

"Why don't you call the police?" Lauren asked.

Duncan breathed in sharply. Here it comes, he thought.

"Well, they threatened us, or rather, they threatened to hurt Tommy and Grandfather if we called the police in. So, right now, I think we shouldn't."

"But the cops know how to deal with kidnappers—"

"You think the Greenfield police could help?"

"Well, no, but maybe the state police or the FBI—"

I should tell them everything right now, thought Duncan. He glanced over toward Megan.

"No, Lauren, we're just going to wait first."

"Just wait! I think that's—"

Duncan interrupted: "No arguments."

Lauren slumped back and Karen leaned forward. "This doesn't make any sense," she said. "The police could help us. Suppose we don't have enough money for the kidnappers."

"We'll just have to wait and see."

They were all silent, until finally Karen spoke again.

"Why, Mom, why did this happen?"

"I don't know, dear."

Karen shook her head.

"It doesn't make sense."

The room was silent.

Karen reached over and felt for Lauren's hand. The two of them sat up in their seats. She felt stronger when she touched her sister. Lauren squeezed her hand in encouragement.

"It still doesn't make sense. You think we're just babies, and you can't tell us, but Tommy's our brother too, and we don't understand anything. It's not fair, and I don't like it. You think we don't want to know, but we do. You think we can't handle it, but he's our brother and we want to help, but how can we when we don't know anything?"

Lauren started to cry then, as if her sister's plaint had been her own. Karen's eyes rimmed with tears, too.

Megan felt her own heart stricken. She went and sat between the two girls and put her arms around them each, hugging them to her breasts.

Duncan stood and sat down next to Karen, adding his arms to the entangled family's.

"You're right," he said matter-of-factly. "We haven't told you the half of it."

He looked over at Megan.

"They should know," he said.

She nodded. "I'm sorry—you're right. We'll tell them."

She held the two girls tightly, but she could feel the stiffening of their muscles and their attention spinning toward their father.

"I hardly know where to start," he said, "but I'll give you a few answers first. The reason we haven't called the police for help is because I, we, your mother and I—we know who the kidnappers are."

"You know them?"

"It's a woman we both knew eighteen years ago. Before you were born."

"How?"

"We were in a group of radicals with her."

"What?"

"Radicals. We thought we were revolutionaries. We were going to change the world."

"You guys?"

Duncan stood up and paced about the room.

"You don't know what it was like," he said. "The war did it to us. It was so wrong and so evil, and the whole nation just went crazy. It was nineteen sixty-eight. There was Tet and pictures of the Marines being carted out on trucks, and sappers in the embassy compound and that picture of the Viet Cong being shot. And then Martin Luther King was killed, shot down while he stood on a balcony in Memphis, and there were riots in Newark and Washington and all over. They had to put machine guns on the steps to the Capitol building. It was as if the entire country was hanging by a thread. Then Bobby Kennedy was shot—right there on television, like some terrible television show—and it seemed there was no chance then for anything to ever happen without violence. And then there was the convention in Chicago. You can't imagine what it was like, the police were like storm troopers and kids were bleeding in the streets. It was as if the whole world was crazy. Every night it was the same thing on the news. Bombs, riots, demonstrations, and the war. Over and over again. The war was everywhere. That was what no one realized. It went on here as much as it did over there."

He hesitated, then he quietly repeated: "Nineteen sixty-eight."

Duncan took a breath and gathered his thoughts and rambled on:

"And we hated it. We thought it had to be stopped. We tried to march. We tried to demonstrate. Still, it went on. Nobody would listen to us! Nobody! You can't imagine how horrible it was. No one cared! It was as if the war came to symbolize the whole rotting society. Nothing worked. Nothing was fair. So then we thought society had to change. And then we thought we had to force society to change. And then we thought we had to tear down society in order to start all over again.

"And we believed that. I truly did. It seems so silly and puerile and antique now, but back then it was real and we thought we would have to die to bring about change. We were just slightly more than children ourselves, but we believed. God, how we believed.

"And so you have to understand, that was when we met Olivia."

He paused, as if thinking.

"Olivia had plans. Great plans that appealed to the romantic side in us. Instead of getting beaten and tear-gassed, we were finally going to do something back to them! Worse, she was the sort that could persuade you to do anything. When Olivia suggested something, it just naturally seemed that it would work exactly the way she said it would. She was beautiful and smart and quick. She had us all wrapped up—except maybe your mother. She played every one of us differently. With me, she used sarcasm, shame, humiliation. She baited me into action. With the others, she used sex, argument, logic—everything she had."

The girls had crept forward in their seats, watching their father as he twisted and explained before them.

"We did something with her," Duncan said carefully. "We—no I, mostly, your mother was always against it—went along on what we thought was an act of revolution. A way of striking a blow at the heart of the society that we hated so much. Oh, I had myself pretty damn well persuaded that what I was doing was righteous and correct and appropriate. And surely not criminal. No, you couldn't call us criminals. We were revolutionaries. It was a pure act of revolutionary zeal."

He turned away, but continued:

"I was so naive. I was just a silly student with silly ideals and I got us caught up in something that was way over our heads."

He hesitated.

"No," Megan said. "No, you're wrong about that."

Duncan turned and looked at her.

"It was never silly to want to change things. It was never wrong to want to end the war."

She took a deep breath. "We just followed the wrong leader, that's all. We didn't think for ourselves."

"Olivia?" Karen asked.

"She was very persuasive," Megan said. "You can't imagine how much. Especially when you're ripe to be persuaded."

Lauren spoke: "I still don't understand. Why can't we call the police and have this woman arrested?"

Duncan turned away.

Megan took a deep breath.

"This thing we did, well, she got caught and went to prison. We got away. Eighteen years ago."

"But—"

Megan started to quicken her own speech.

"She never told them who else was involved. If we went to the police, they would probably connect us to her."

"But it was eighteen years ago, and now everything is different—"

"One thing never changes," Duncan said abruptly.

The two girls looked at him and Megan looked away.

"Five people died."

The girls stared wide-eyed at their father.

"Did you—" Lauren started.

"No. Well, not directly. Did I kill anyone? Not with a gun. But was I involved? Yes."

"But what happened?" Karen asked.

Duncan took a deep breath. "We tried to rob a bank."

"You what?"

"We tried to rob a bank. We were going to hit the bank right when an armored car delivered cash and receipts from a chemical plant. You see, the chemical plant was associated with the corporation that made napalm—"

"So?"

"You've got to understand. The napalm was used in the war and—" He hesitated. "It really sounds crazier now than I ever thought."

"But why a bank?"

"To get money. To buy arms and propaganda. To put our group on the map."

"We sure managed that," Megan whispered bitterly.

"But, Dad—" Lauren started.

"Look! I realize all the explanations sound stupid, but there it is."

"But what happened?" Karen asked quietly.

Duncan sighed. "It went wrong from the first minute. The bank guards didn't throw down their weapons like we thought they would. They started shooting. Two of them died, three of the group. It was a disaster. I was driving the getaway truck. I saw what was happening and instead of going to help, I ran away. I was very lucky. I found your mother, and we just came back east, trying to forget it. We hid. We forgot. The world changed. And now here we are."

"But why can't we go to the police now?" Lauren asked again. Her tears had ceased, replaced with an insistent curiosity.

"Because I would have to go to prison."

"Oh."

The entire family was silent for a few moments. Duncan knew the girls were still filled with questions, but would save them for another time.

"Well," Karen finally said with surprising firmness. "I guess that means we have to deal with it ourselves. Can we do that? Give them what they want and get it over with?"

Duncan and Megan nodded.

"I hope so," Megan said quietly.

Judge Thomas Pearson opened his eyes and blinked at the light that filled the room. He was stiff; his neck felt as if it had been wrenched about by some great hand while he'd slept. He shifted position gingerly, trying not to disturb his grandson, who dozed on, mouth slightly ajar, with his head in his grandfather's lap. The boy made a small complaining noise and moved his hands once in front of his face, as if trying to dispel a bad dream or knock away some vision from the edge of nightmare, then he rolled over and slid back into deep sleep. The judge extricated himself carefully, then went and placed a blanket over the boy, who sighed and slept on.

For a moment, the judge considered turning off the overhead light, then decided against it. He did not want the child to awaken in the dark and be frightened.

He glanced down at his watch. It was after two A.M.

I am an old man, who cannot sleep well at night, then catnaps in the day. It is as if my whole body is starting to run down. Things no longer work quite like they once did. He thought of himself as a favorite old clock, one with springs and levers and weights that meshed and rubbed together to guide the time, not like some modern quartz watch, with digital readout and precise movements governed by a computer chip.

He looked about the room for what seemed the hundredth time. Well, there are a few ticks left inside me.

He listened, but he could hear nothing within the house except the steady breathing of his grandson. He marveled at the child's body; so scared, now restoring itself. The boy has been strong so far. But I wonder if the worst is yet to happen. I do not know how much tougher he can be.

He shuddered at the memory of the bathroom fiasco.

She showed me something, he thought. She showed me she can be cruel, that she knows how to play mind games. It was an impressive demonstration of control, one that effectively underscored how tenuous their position was. There probably isn't any basement room, wet and dark and dank like she said there was, but the threat of it was as effective as the reality, perhaps even more so. He made a mental note to be alert for this sort of manipulation; let her deal in solidities, he thought. Force her to deal with real things. Don't let her conjure up terrifying images that merely help her to weaken your resolve.

Judge Pearson shook his head. If it was just me, I would tell them to go ahead and shoot me and to hell with them.

He looked down at Tommy and without thinking ran his hand through the child's hair. But it isn't just me, and I cannot allow them to separate us. That would be the first battleground, he decided, even if they didn't know it. I will not allow us to be put apart, not even for an instant—regardless of how many weapons they wave at us. You can win this little fight, he encouraged himself, and then, when you start to win some small victories, you can figure out how to win the largest one. They are after money. They won't throw their bargaining chips away to prove some small point about control.

Making this decision strengthened him. He found his hand had inadvertently slid onto Tommy's shoulder, feeling the rise and fall of the child's breathing through the rough blanket. He smiled. It is virtually impossible, he thought, to see a child sleeping and not feel the overwhelming urge to stroke the child's head and tuck the blankets around his chin a little more tightly.

Then he sat down on the other bunk and let his mind wander about, daydreaming in the early hours of the morning.

He thought first of his wife, which was natural, because he could see so much of her in the child's appearance. He was glad that she wasn't there to worry about them. That was a selfish thing, but there it was, and there was no stopping it. He remembered her funeral, and how silly he had felt, embarrassed to be alive, to be shaking hands and welcoming all their old friends. It had been an early fall afternoon, and the leaves were just turning, the slightest curl of brown on the edge of green. But the temperature had been hot and he remembered being uncomfortably warm inside his black suit. He had wanted to strip it off, and shout that this was all wrong, and that any damn fool could see that someone had screwed up. The judge hadn't listened to the words from the preacher, or any of the steady stream of condolences from the guests. He had instead watched thick gray clouds form into a great thunderhead over the mountains in the distance, and idly hoped that the rain would move his way, breaking over his head and engulfing him in sheets of water. He smiled: The twins had been the ones who'd seized him by the elbows and taken him away from the gravesite, and he remembered the surge of their youth as it passed through him. It had not rained. The day had grown sunny and strong, and things had gone on.

Still, it had seemed absurd to him that he should survive her and it continued to bother him. He had never considered it a possibility throughout their years together. He had known with a surety born of some silly masculine arrogance that he would die first, and that it was important for her to be provided for. All their insurance payments were designed that way; their wills made only the smallest concession to the idea that she might die before him. He remembered how dumb he'd felt, sitting in the doctor's office, realizing that she was gone. He had looked across the desk at the white-jacketed doctor and thought: This is stupid; certainly this can be reversed upon appeal. He had not seen the absurdity in thinking death was simply another legal matter.

He smiled at the memory.

The problem with the law is that it forces you to see everything in life as precedents and opinions, all subject to review. It is such a cold thing, words and rulings, rigid, trying to force the infinite variations created by humanity into set regulations. She had always seen the impact of those legal words on people and that was what brought the law alive. All those decisions, life and liberty, those years of answering questions of guilt and innocence, and she'd been a part of each until she died and I couldn't really go on anymore.

That was ten years ago, and I'm still here. I thought I was going to just fold up and die, but I didn't and it still surprises me.

I wish she were here. She would eat that bitch alive.

The thought made him smile, even if it was untrue.

The judge lay down on the bunk and curled up under a blanket. It is cold, he thought. There will be a frost tonight and snow soon. It is cold in this room and that is because the walls are weak and the cold air pours through that one spot that I must remember.

He wondered what sort of house it was. Probably an old farmhouse, with two stories up in the center and wings on either side.

And probably isolated out in the goddamn woods with no neighbors and no traffic, he said angrily to himself.

Well, he thought, breathing in deeply, never mind. No place is so far away from civilization that it can't be found. No place is so isolated that the law can't reach it.

For a moment he pictured his captors and he grew angry. They don't even have a guard on the door. They are so confident about what they're doing that they've all gone to bed. They don't fear Tommy and me, they don't fear Megan and Duncan, they don't fear the police who will come storming through the front door and blow their sorry hides straight to hell, if I have my wish.

He was slightly ashamed by the last thought. I should want them arrested and processed. I should want them swallowed up by the system.

But I was thirty years a judge, and I don't trust my own profession. Not one bit.

He was surprised by his own cynicism. He cast his mind back to the situation at hand.

Why are they so confident? They should be nervous, sweating, anxious. They should be pacing about in sleepless tension. Instead, the house is quiet, like some typically suburban family resting up for another routine day.

He did not understand it. They should be on alert. They should be watching everything.

They are not scared to show themselves to us. That's completely wrong.

Judge Pearson shifted about on the cot uncomfortably.

In his courtroom he had heard dozens of kidnapping cases; abductions of all sorts, over thirty years. He started to race his mind back, trying to think what cases he'd had that resembled this, but found he couldn't concentrate, all he could think of was the woman, and the bitter smile that she'd worn when she'd stood in the parking lot facing them.

What have they done? They have taken us, and she acts as if she knows us—or knows about us. Something is going on here that I do not yet understand.

He felt the night chill and gathered the blanket.

She is very dangerous, he thought. The others, despite their weapons, less so. They cannot have her resolve. She will tell me what is going on, that is part of her arrogance. She will create the rules of engagement.

He rolled over on the cot. He could not shut his eyes, instead he stared up into the light, waiting for the morning to come.

Olivia Barrow slid naked from the bed.

The night chill raised goosebumps on her arms and legs and she shivered once, pulled a blanket from the bed, and threw it over her shoulders like a cape. She watched Bill Lewis briefly shift position, and slide back away into sleep. He was a dull lover, filled with grunting, straining, pumping obviousness. He bucks away on top of me as if it were simply an act of reproduction, and collapses after orgasm as if dead. She bit her lip at a sudden piercing sadness, thinking of moments in bed with Emily Lewis.

She walked to the window and stared out through the moonlit darkness. It is a winter moon, she thought; it throws out the light of death. It makes everything seem colder, as if etched by frost. The window faced toward the rear of the house, and she looked down across a small grassy field toward the treeline fifty yards away. It was like standing on the edge of the ocean, with the trees forming the edge of the surf. Once in there, you could lose yourself in an instant.

But not me. I've walked through the property too many times. First with that damn silly realtor, who kept wanting to show me something closer to town. She'd swallowed the fiction so quickly: just-divorced writer needing total peace and quiet and isolation. The sight of cash had certainly eliminated any further questions. And then a hundred times since then until I became completely familiar with my back door.

Olivia let her mind ease back over the events of the day. It seemed oddly segmented; more as if days or weeks had passed, not simply hours.

It had all been so remarkably easy. I've had too long to plan this to have anything go wrong now. Right from the first day they slammed the door on me.

She smiled. She remembered how the police had all thought that when she got her first taste of prison she would crumble and tell them everything they wanted to know.

She remembered an FBI agent, all slick in gray suit and white shirt, hair trimmed military short, his conversation filled with theories of revolution and conspiracy. He'd sat down across a small table from her, giving her a speech about making things easier on herself. "We can help you," he had said. "We can see you do some easy time, then get out into a new life. Come on, Miss Barrow, you're smart, you're beautiful. Don't throw your life away. You think you belong in there with all those whores and junkies? They'll eat you alive. They're going to take little pieces of your beautiful white skin every day, until there's nothing left. You're going to get out old and ugly and wasted. Why? Tell me why?"

The agent had leaned forward, ferret-like, waiting for her response.

She'd spit in his face.

The memory made her grin. He had been so surprised: It reminded her of a moment in high school when she had refused to let the football captain use her body.

Prison had not scared her in the least. She had expected one fight, perhaps two, then grudging acceptance. In her heart, she had known that all those whores and junkies would come to her eventually, and that she would be in command.

In a funny way, though she hadn't been able to say this to the FBI agent—or to her father, whose tears she failed to comprehend, or to the lawyer he'd hired who'd been so upset with her refusal to help defend herself, or the judge who angrily sentenced her after giving her a useless lecture on showing respect for the system—she had looked forward to jail.

The hardest thing about her first days of prison had been adjusting not so much to confinement, but to the physical limits of space. She'd been put in a single-person cell on a tier that was called the "classification" area. She had swiftly learned that this was where she would live until prison authorities determined what sort of prisoner she was going to be. The cell had a bed, a washstand and toilet. It measured eight feet from front to rear, six feet from side to side. She had paced the distance once, twice, then realized that she'd done it a hundred times. She ignored the bars, ignored the sounds of prison, with its near constancy of shouts, screams, footsteps echoing, bars clanging as they opened and shut. In the distance she could always hear electronic buzzers, as sally ports were used. Buzz, clang, clang, buzz, clang, clang. It was the rhythm of prison. It was a noise that measured the size of space and the limits of movement.

She tossed her head to free herself of the memory.

They thought they would classify me, she laughed to herself.

At her first dinner in the prison cafeteria, she'd finished her meal and thrown the empty metal tray crashing to the floor. She'd thrown a cup of coffee in the face of the first guard to reach her, and slugged the second, breaking the woman's jaw.

I classified myself.

She remembered the beating she'd received. It never hurt. She smiled and shook her head at the lie. Actually, they beat the shit out of me. I was all black and blue and bruises for a month afterwards. I thought I would limp forever.

But they could never hurt the inside me. That was the important thing to show them. They never controlled anything except when the doors would open and when they would shut. She thought again of the FBI agent: Easy time. It was all easy time. From the first minute to the last.

Her eyes picked out a slight movement from the forest line, and she watched as a half-dozen deer wandered out into the moonlit field. What a terrible life, she thought. A deer has nothing other than fear. It flees headlong at the slightest sound. It freezes in the winter, endures ticks and flies in the summer. When does a deer know peace? Certainly not in the fall, when it is hunted by every bozo with a rifle from New Jersey to Canada. She smiled. How ignominious a deer's death must be: shot by some weekend warrior who was, in reality, lucky not to have killed himself, his partner, or some farmer's dull cow. Or perhaps dying in flight, trying to escape across a roadway, hit by some half-drunk businessman in his car, staggering broken-legged into the brambles to die alone and in pain while the pig shouted in rage at the damage done to his fender. They live out their entire lives from panic to panic. They are the most stupidly timid beasts, even if they are beautiful in the moonlight.

She watched them graze, every so often picking up their heads, alert to the nuances of the night. Within a few moments the group had grown to at least two dozen collected in the open area in front of her. When something finally disturbed them, they left in a great bounding, leaping rush, flowing across the field like so many dark wavelets driven by the wind across a pond.

When the deer disappeared into the forest, she cleared her mind and thought of the captives in the attic, then of Megan and Duncan.

Are they crying, she wondered? Are they sobbing away the nighttime? Or do they just sit and stare out helplessly? Do they have any idea what's in store for them?

She glanced back at Bill Lewis and made a mental note to tease Ramon, bring his own desires a little closer to boiling. He should want me, she thought. He should want Bill, too. She listened to his snoring and admonished herself to keep his passion on edge.

If I maintain the tension, then they will not be paying attention to what it is I'm really doing. I must stroke them both and keep them churning. They are like all men, unable to see past their stiff pricks.

What I'm really doing is all mine and no one else's. They will help me as long as they think it is something else, and then they will be too surprised to understand what it was that they were part of.

And I will be alone again.

She stood up, dropping the blanket to the floor, and let the moonlight wash over her nakedness.

It was as if she could feel the night penetrate her, slowly pumping away at her with great languorous strokes. Her stomach knotted, her breath quickened, her insides glistened with the rhythm of the darkness within her. She moved her hips forward and spread her legs slightly, feeling the cold air sweep around her, probing her, caressing her. She wrapped her arms around herself tightly, as if to hold this new lover closer.

As daylight started to take hold, Duncan looked around the living room of his house and thought of the problem that the new day presented. Megan had finally fallen asleep on the couch. The girls had been sent upstairs sometime after midnight. They were quiet; he did not know if they'd slept, but he suspected so, the teenage capacity for sleep in the face of almost any event having been previously documented in the household.

Duncan was slumped in an armchair. He found himself watching the slow progress of a shadow across a wall, growing fainter and less distinct with each passing minute. For a moment he thought he would be hypnotized by the sight; then he shook his head and cleared his imagination and tried to focus on the new day.

"So," he said out loud. "What precisely is it that I do?"

He replayed the conversation with Olivia in his head. She had warned him about going to the police, which he had not done. Other than that, her threats had been generalized and her instructions nonexistent. He had not yet been told to collect money; nor had he been asked to perform any other task.

That would come, he told himself.

But what was he to do?

The answer was odious: Nothing but wait.

The idea that he would go up to his room and lay out a freshly laundered shirt and tie, select a conservative wool suit from the rack, shower and dress—just as he did on every weekday morning—nearly sickened him. How could he play-act his way through the day— smiling, shaking hands, going to meetings, reviewing papers?

He looked around the room at all the familiar items. It all seems so normal and well-arranged and acceptable. I have striven so hard for all the externals: the new car, the stately house, a little vacation property in the woods. Providing. That's what I've done, I've provided. I've given my family the fruits of money. They have not lacked for anything.

And it has all been a lie.

For an instant, he thought he envied Olivia. I used to think of her, back in the first years when I thought any day it was all coming to an end. He recalled wondering about her life in prison, imagining with fear that the same confinement, beatings and regimentation awaited him. It had taken him years to understand that she had had the luxury of acting in accordance with her idealism, which was a sort of freedom in itself. And I, he thought, became middle-class and ordinary, which is a kind of prison of its own. She didn't have to look down and see the twins, all newborn and defenseless, and realize that bringing about a new society was one thing, but providing for the children was more important. And then, by the time Tommy came along, everything was different.

He shook his head. But it was never different for her. It was always the same, day after day, in that prison.

Duncan rose from his seat. He paused by Megan's side, reaching down, about to raise her from her sleep, then thought better of it. He wanted to touch her, as if that would be reassuring. But he lifted his hand and let her doze. It is Wednesday, he thought. Time to go through the motions. He went upstairs to the shower. At first he turned the water hotter than normal, letting the scalding flood wash over him. He poured shampoo all over his body, sudsing himself violently, scraping the soap through his hair and across his flesh. Then, as the room filled with steam, he angrily twisted the shower knob to cold, and punished himself with water that could have been ice.

Megan was awakened by the noise from the bathroom, surprised that she'd fallen asleep, unsure whether she was rested. Her emotions tugged at her instantly, like an undertow at the beach.

At first she felt a momentary anger; she hated the idea that Duncan would waste time in such a mundane pursuit. She thought they should all be dirty and bedraggled, as if their appearance should fit the feelings she had.

She kicked her legs off the sofa and sat up, pushing her hair back with her hands and trying to force sleep away from her head. No, she said to herself, he's right. We must be fresh. There's no telling what the day will hold.

She rose and, feeling her way unsteadily, went upstairs.

In their room, she faced Duncan.

"What do we do?"

"I don't know for sure," he said. He was drying himself vigorously, slapping the towel across his body, leaving red striations on the skin. "But I suppose we're expected just to behave as if nothing has happened and wait on them. She'll be in touch. That's what she said."

"I hate that."

"So do I, but what alternative do we have?"

"None." Megan hesitated. "What are you going to do?"

Duncan took a deep breath. "Well, last time she called at the office. So I'm going to get dressed and go to my office and pretend to work and wait for her to call again."

"Do you think they're okay?"

"Yes. Please, Meg, don't think about that. It's just been one night and I'm sure they're fine."

"What about Tommy's school? They'll be expecting him."

"Call them and tell them he's got a touch of fever."

She nodded.

"The twins?"

Duncan thought. "Christ, I don't know. And what about you? Did you have appointments for today?"

"None that I can't cancel, or get someone to take. I'll use the flu excuse."

She paused, then added: "I couldn't stand it if I didn't know where the twins are. I've got to keep them here with me."

"That's fine. Call their school . . ."

"And say they've got the flu. Then what?"

"Wait for me to call you."

"God, I don't know how I can."

"You'll just have to."

"I can't stand it."

Duncan stood, trying to knot the tie around his neck. He tried once, and the thin end was too long. He tried again, and again it was uneven. He tried a third time, but it came out skewed. He tore the tie from around his neck and threw it hard on the floor. "You think I like this? You think I can stand it any better than you? Christ! I don't know, I don't know, I don't know. There! There are all the answers to every question you have. We just have to wait, dammit!"

Megan flared with anger, then bit her tongue.

"All right," she said. "All right."

They were both silent a moment.

"Why don't you get showered and dressed? I'll fix us some breakfast. Wake up the girls after you're dressed."

She nodded and, barely thinking, started to drop her clothes to the floor. Duncan, still struggling with the tie, left the room. He forced himself not to look down the hallway towards Tommy's room as he went downstairs.

Megan let the water stream over her and cried freely.

When she finished, she toweled off quickly and dressed herself in jeans and sweatshirt.

She could smell bacon frying from the kitchen and it almost overcame her. She swallowed hard and went into the twins' room.

"Come on, girls, get up."

"Has anything happened?" Lauren asked.

"Where's Dad?"

"Nothing has happened and he's downstairs fixing breakfast. Get cleaned up and dressed, please."

"We're not going to school?"

"No, you're staying with me."

The girls nodded.

"And make your beds."

"Mom!"

"Listen, dammit, we're still a family and we're still going to do things as if we're going on just like usual. Make your beds!"

Lauren and Karen nodded.

Megan walked slowly downstairs, her head reeling. Still a family. Just act normally. She hated everything she'd said. She hated what she'd done. She could hear the girls in the bathroom, and she hated that they were all clean and ready for the day and that she'd ordered them to make their beds, which, she thought suddenly, was the silliest, stupidest thing in the world to do on the day their brother had been kidnapped.

She walked into the kitchen, wondering if the morning light would hurt her.

Duncan looked at her.

"Steady?" he asked.

She didn't reply.

"There was a hard frost last night," he said. "Everything looks crystal."

"I know," she replied, without looking. She shivered, realizing that the rising of the sun wouldn't warm her in the slightest.

Olivia Barrow kept the engine running, the car's exhaust billowing like smoke behind her. It was sticky warm inside the rental, and she loosened her coat slightly. She bent the mirror toward her and adjusted her hat and her long, red-haired wig. She checked up and down the street, watching the other cars pull from driveways, heading off toward town. Then she looked at herself in the mirror once again, and rubbed a smudge of makeup from the corner of her lip. She was dressed in a nice skirt and white shirt, and wore an expensive woolen overcoat. She had a briefcase on the seat next to her, stuffed with worthless papers. It was part of the disguise. I fit in perfectly, she thought. I look exactly like some typical hausfrau who has seen her kids get into junior high and is now on her way to her job. This place is so wonderfully suburban and predictable. Mortgages and prime rates and stock options and getting ahead. Neo-colonial and white picket fences and foreign cars and private colleges. All they're missing is some drooling golden retriever shedding all over the place.

She glanced down the street toward Megan and Duncan's home. There wasn't even the smallest sign of a police presence. No oddly indistinct cars parked close by. Nobody dressed as workmen outside. No telephone linemen pretending to fix the lines, but actually installing sophisticated equipment that might lead the police to her next phone call. They would stick out in this neighborhood so easily, I would have to be blind not to spot them. Good going, Duncan and Megan. You've followed the first rule. So far, so good.

The sunlight glared off the car's hood, and she slid dark glasses onto her face. She glanced at her watch. Come on, Duncan, she thought. Time to get the day moving.

As she spoke to herself, she saw his car back down the driveway.

"Good morning, Duncan," she said.

She laughed as she watched his car disappear down the street.

"Have a nice day."

She put her car into gear.

"Just have a fucking wonderful day, Duncan."

5

WEDNESDAY
MIDDAY

Duncan waited.

Throughout the morning, he'd felt a surge of anxiety and excitement every time his telephone had rung, only to be thrown into dismay when the caller turned out not to be the kidnappers, but local businessmen and other loan applicants. He'd dealt summarily with every request, performing his job with robotic ease. One person, surprised at his abruptness, had asked him whether he wasn't a bit under the weather, and he'd replied that he thought he was coming down with the flu. He'd repeated this diagnosis to his secretary, who had asked whether or not he was feeling well after he'd acted distracted when she tried to fill him in on some upcoming bank meeting. She had asked him whether he was going to go home, and he'd had the presence of mind to say no, that he had too much paperwork to catch up on, but that he might be a bit erratic with his hours over the next day or so, and that she should cancel any outstanding appointments. She had nodded, all solicitude and understanding, asked if he wanted some chicken soup from the coffee shop down the street.

For an instant he'd been struck by what a wonderful excuse "the flu" was: In the Northeast, people were willing to accept it as the root cause for almost any sort of aberrational behavior. Then he'd returned to his waiting, more anxious than before. As each hour passed, he had grown more concerned. He could not understand why the kidnappers were delaying matters. Wasn't speed their natural ally? He had expected Olivia to move promptly with her demands; by all rights, hers should have been the first call of the morning. For her to stretch the process out even one minute longer than necessary baffled him. Delay was the one thing for which he hadn't prepared himself, he thought, and then reconsidered: In reality, he hadn't managed to prepare himself for anything.

Each minute is the same sixty seconds for everyone in the world, he thought. Time is no slower or faster for any person. But he didn't believe it.

Everything is okay, he told himself.

She will call shortly.

Tommy is fine. Frustrated and scared, but fine.

The judge is angry and cantankerous, but fine.

She is just making me stew a bit, because she wants me to be off-guard and unbalanced.

Everything will be all right.

He rocked back and forth in his chair, letting the squeaking of the springs serve as a rhythmic backdrop for his thoughts. He stared at the phone on his desk. It was one of the modern types, all Italian skinny design. It weighed only a few ounces and had no heft to it. He wished he had an old-fashioned telephone, one with a dialer that went clickety-clickety-click when he turned it and a good solid ring, instead of the tiny beeps and buzzes that he'd grown accustomed to.

They're alive. They have to be.

He heard a slight knock on his door, and it swung open, revealing his secretary.

"Mr. Richards, it's almost one and I'm going out for a sandwich with some of the others. Are you sure I can't bring you back something?"

"Thank you, Doris, but no. Please tell the switchboard I'm still here, and to let any calls ring through."

"All right. You sure? I mean, it won't be any trouble and you're looking a bit pale."

"No, thank you. See you later."

"You should go home and take care of yourself."

"Thank you, Doris."

"All right, but I warned you."

"Thank you, Doris."

"A little flu can turn into pneumonia."

"Thank you, Doris."

"Okay, Mr. Richards. See you in an hour or so."

"Take your time."

She closed the door and he looked outside the window. The morning sunlight had been pushed aside by a thick covering of gray clouds. The wind was steel-hearted and steady, filling the air with a raw dampness that insisted upon winter. He shivered in his seat and hoped that Tommy was someplace warm. He tried to remember what his child had been wearing the day before: jeans and sneakers, with a turtleneck and old red sweatshirt with the logo of the New England Patriots. It celebrated a championship several years past. Tommy had worn a hat and gloves as well, and last year's parka, which was frayed about the edges, but would still keep him warm. No, it had been rainy in the morning and Tommy might have taken his raincoat instead, which was yellow and not very warm. Duncan pounded a fist into his palm and turned angrily in the chair. I don't want him to be cold.

Where is she? He stood up and paced through the small office. Where is she and what is she doing?

He had a sudden vision of Olivia the last time he'd seen her, struggling with Emily Lewis in the street outside the bank, dragging themselves toward the elusive safety of his van.

How she must hate me. All these years in prison, thinking of me and filling herself with hate. The sins of the fathers. He walked to the window. If you are a coward once, he wondered, are you a coward forever? He looked out at the naked branches of an oak tree as they fought against the cold breeze.

Behind him, the phone on his desk buzzed and he jumped across the room to snatch it from its cradle.

"Yes—Duncan Richards!"

"Duncan, it's Megan. I just haven't heard . . ."

"Neither have I," he interrupted. "Nothing yet."

"Oh, God," Megan half-moaned. "Why not?"

"I don't know. Just . . . don't speculate. Try not to let your imagination run your emotions. That's what I've been doing all morning, hanging on and waiting it out . . . Everything will be okay, you'll see."

"You think so?" Megan's voice spoke of disbelief.

"Yes, I do. Just keep a tight grip on yourself and we'll be okay. As soon as I talk to Olivia or whomever she's got helping her, I'll let you know. Are you okay?"

"Don't worry about us. I'm fine, really, just hate the waiting, that's all, and I needed to hear your voice."

"What about Karen and Lauren?"

"They're fine. You know them. They just can't stand being cooped up."

"Well," he replied, "they're going to have to."

"We'll be okay."

"Good. I'll talk with you when I know something."

He hung up feeling worse.

Duncan glared at the telephone: *Where are you, dammit?*

Then it buzzed again. He seized the telephone.

"Yes—Duncan Richards!"

"Mr. Richards?"

His heart fell. It was the voice of the bank receptionist. His secretary must still be at lunch.

"Yes," he replied, defeated again.

"Your one-thirty appointment is here. Are you ready now?"

"My what?"

"Your one-thirty appointment."

"Oh, God, hang on . . ."

Duncan tossed papers about, searching for his appointment calendar. Damn! he thought. I told Doris to cancel all appointments. Damn her! I just can't go through with it now.

He found the small leatherbound book, but couldn't find any notation indicating an appointment. He slammed it shut. I've told her a dozen times she has to keep that book up to date. Dammit to hell!

He took a deep breath. All right. Let's extricate yourself gracefully. Just give them two minutes, then pass them on to one of the other bank officers. He stiffened himself, preparing to make polite conversation, praying that the phone wouldn't ring in the short moments that he had to deal with whatever contractor or developer this was.

"All right," he said to the receptionist. "Send them back."

He grabbed the papers cluttering his desk and swept them all into the top drawer. He straightened his tie quickly, ran his hand through his hair and adjusted his glasses, then glanced around the room, looking for any outward sign of the disaster in which he was caught. Seeing none, he turned toward the door as it opened. He saw the receptionist opening the door and ushering in his visitor and he got to his feet rapidly, his speech set in his mind, halfway out his mouth:

"Hello, I'm sorry, I seem to have misplaced our . . ."

And then he stopped short.

"Hello, Duncan," said Olivia Barrow.

She turned to the receptionist.

"Thank you so much."

The young woman smiled and closed the door, leaving them alone.

Olivia waited while Duncan stared at her.

"Aren't you even going to offer me a seat?" she asked.

Megan paced about the house, finally finding Karen and Lauren sitting in the kitchen, working on schoolwork. Karen was working on a paper about *Oliver Twist* and Lauren was kibbitzing. For a moment, Megan wanted to shout at them, caught up in something so ordinary, when everything else was so disjointed and out of whack.

But instead, she took a deep breath and realized that perhaps they were showing far more sense than she was.

"Mom," said Lauren, looking up, "has Dad heard anything?"

"Not yet."

"What do you think that means?" Karen asked.

"I don't know. The important thing is to realize it may not mean anything at all."

"I'm worried about Tommy. Suppose he gets a cold or something."

"Everything's going to be okay. You just have to believe that," Megan said.

Karen got up from her seat and went and put her arms around her mother. Lauren came and held her mother's hand. Megan felt her daughters' warmth flood her. She thought: Be steady, girls.

"Don't worry, Mom," Karen said. "We're here and Tommy'll be fine."

"I bet Grandfather is giving them hell right now," Lauren said. "Whew! They sure took the wrong guy when they grabbed him. He'll snort and complain and ruin their fun, Mom, you just know it."

Megan breathed in, trying to lift the scent of the girls' confidence and pour it into her own heart.

"I'm sure you're right," she said.

The girls squeezed her, and released her.

"You know, Mom, we're totally out of milk . . ."

"And there's no diet soda left, either."

Megan paused. "I was going to go to the store today. But I can't."

"We'll go," said Karen. "Just give us a list."

"No. I want you girls where I can keep an eye on you. We don't really know anything about these people. If they were to try and grab you girls, well, I don't think your father and I could handle it."

"Oh, Mom, that's crazy."

"How do you know?" Megan snapped.

The girls were both quiet. They watched their mother carefully.

I suppose this is some sort of test, Megan thought. How much do I trust them? How adult do I think they are?

She hesitated. They don't really understand anything. They really are still children. They don't have a grip on what is happening because it isn't real to them yet. All they know is that something has happened and yet they're still here, and life still seems to be going on.

"All right," Megan said, finally. "Milk, soda, some sliced meats and a loaf of bread. That's it. Oh, some instant coffee, too. I'll give you a twenty and you can drive over to the convenience store on East Prospect. Straight there, straight inside, then straight home. Don't talk to anyone or stop for anything. If you think someone's acting suspiciously, I want you just to stop whatever you're doing and come straight home. Got it?"

"Mom . . ."

"Got it?"

"Okay, okay, okay. Can we at least get some magazines?"

"And a newspaper," Megan said. "Sure." She found her pocket-book and extracted some bills from her wallet. "No gum," she said. "Not even sugarless."

She handed the money over and felt foolish for being worried, then foolish for not being more worried. When the girls left by the front door, she jumped over to the window, and watched them get into their car. She saw Lauren get behind the wheel, which comforted her, because the younger was the better driver. Karen waved, and then the car sputtered and rolled off down the street.

Megan turned and went back to the kitchen.

"I'll be damned," said Bill Lewis out loud, though he was alone in the rental car at his vantage point down the street. He watched as the girls' red sports car rolled past where he was parked. "The other kids are going someplace. Well, I'll be damned."

He thought quickly about what that presented: Megan alone in the house. The two twins heading someplace unknown. Olivia had told him to maintain what she called loose surveillance on the house; parking for a few minutes, driving past every forty-five minutes or so. Just frequently enough so that he would be able to tell if something had changed at the house, not so often that someone would pick him out, or think he looked suspicious. He wore a suit and tie, which minimized the chance that anyone walking through the neighborhood would think twice about his presence there. He had known that he was looking for official activity, the cops or the FBI. He had not suspected that the family would head in different directions.

He realized that he had an opportunity, and for an instant wondered: What would Olivia do?

He smiled to himself and made up his mind.

Duncan couldn't speak.

His eyes were fixed on Olivia, standing in front of him. It's her, he told himself. He swallowed hard, and gestured toward a chair, wondering for an instant why he didn't spring across the room, seize her by the neck and throttle her. He watched as Olivia settled into her seat and then motioned at him to sit down. He was barely aware of his muscles responding—one instant he was standing, the next, sitting, watching her across the expanse of his desk. It was as if she were some character from *Alice in Wonderland*, one instant right in front of him, so close he could reach out and touch her, the next, widely distant, as if miles and miles away. His head spun and his mouth was dry, so when he was able to speak, the words rushed forth in a bullfrog croak:

"Where are they? Where's my boy?"

"Not too far," Olivia replied, as if responding to idle small talk about the weather.

"I want . . ." he started, but she cut him off.

"I know what you want," she said. "And it is only barely relevant. Like the hair?" She touched the corner of her red wig.

Duncan blinked. It was the first he'd noticed it.

"It's red," he said.

She laughed.

"That it is."

"It's not how I remember it."

Her smile faded.

"Nothing is how you remember it. Except for one thing: I am in charge and you are going to follow my orders. Only this time, you're not going to screw up—are you, Duncan?—because the stakes are a little higher. It's not your sorry hide this time. It's your son's. And the old man's, too. Don't forget about him. Think about it for a moment, Duncan. Think about how much I must hate everything that that old bastard represents. About how easy it would be to off him, just like the bastard judges tried to off me."

"Where's my boy?" Duncan choked out.

"I told you. Close. In my grasp." She made a little hand motion, as if dismissing his concern.

"Please," he said.

She held up her hand and he stopped immediately.

"Duncan, keep a grip on yourself. It will make matters much easier."

He nodded again and tried to control himself. He could hear his own heartbeat, feel the pressure throbbing in his temples.

Olivia sat back in her chair and settled in comfortably. She smiled at Duncan.

"Time for a bit of negotiation, don't you think?"

"Yes. Whatever you say." Duncan took a deep breath and sat up straight. His eyes narrowed and he put his hands into his lap, beneath the desk, so that she couldn't see how they shook.

"Good."

"I want my boy back. If you so much as harm one—"

"Don't you threaten me!"

"I'm not threatening. I'm promising."

She laughed and leaned forward.

"Got that little speech out of the way? Anything else you'd like to say? Some other little act of bravery? Prove your manhood? Prove your bankerhood?"

"I could have the guard in here in a minute."

"And they'd be dead within the half-hour."

"You're bluffing."

"You think so, math-man? Call it."

Duncan didn't move.

"Come on, Mr. Bigshot Bank Executive. Call it! Call my bluff!"

He didn't move.

"I didn't think you would."

"Why are you here?"

"Now that's the real question, isn't it?"

"Yes. Why don't you leave us alone?"

"Don't be ridiculous."

"What do you want?"

"I told you. Everything."

"I don't understand."

"You will."

He was silent, feeling the depth of her hatred within him.

"Why have you done this?" he asked again.

"Because of what you stole from me. Think of the marker I hold on you. Betrayal. Emily's death. Eighteen years. I can see your profit. Don't you think it's time to share it?"

"Why didn't you turn us in?"

"What makes you think I won't?"

Duncan didn't answer.

"Come on, Duncan! What makes you think I won't?"

"I don't know."

She laughed harshly.

"You see, that's the little wild card in all of this, that's the part I like best. You know, I got to learn a little criminal law during idle moments over the past eighteen years. Prisons are great places for learning law, probably next to Harvard or Yale the best we've got, and certainly with a better clinical program. Anyway, Duncan, I figure technically you were guilty of felony murder—same as me. Conspiracy to commit armed robbery. Conspiracy to commit murder. Bank robbery. Auto theft. Weapons violations. Hell, Duncan, when you ran away you were jaywalking; they'd probably charge you with that as well.

"Now, let's take a best-case scenario: statute of limitations. Not applicable on any of the murder-related crimes. Well, let's say you hire a clever lawyer who argues that you're now a pillar of the community and anyway, you were only the wheelman, et cetera, et cetera. You know, both those men that died were former cops—and they never forget. So what're we talking about? Probation? Sus-

pended sentence? Not fucking likely, Duncan. Maybe for Megan—
let's not forget her little part in all of this—but you, Duncan? A
little bit of hard time, I would guess . . ."

Olivia grinned and hesitated.

". . . Of course, I could be completely wrong about all this. Maybe
the authorities out there will just slap you on the back and say let
bygones be bygones. What do you think?"

"Get on with it."

Olivia's voice seemed squeezed together, compacted into a tightly
wrapped ball of hatred: "That's why I never told them, Duncan.
Even if it would have meant getting out sooner. Because I didn't
want you to be paying off your debt to the state of California. Your
debt was with me."

She hesitated, then whispered, hissing:

"With me, you son of a bitch!"

Again, she paused, sitting back in her chair.

"And you're going to keep on paying. Because even if you get
your boy back—even if you manage that, and personally, I doubt
you've got the stuff to do it—I'll always have that little ace in the
hole. You know there's a prosecutor out there who'd love to have
your name. A couple of FBI agents, as well. And let us not forget
the families of the men who died. I'm sure they'd be interested in
knowing the names of the other members of the Phoenix . . ."

He felt his entire body quiver.

". . . They'll never forget. Not in eighteen years. Not in a hundred
years. They'll never forget."

She whispered again: "Just as I never forgot."

Duncan found himself thinking of a moment shortly after Tommy
had been born; the news that night had been filled with the story of
a toddler who'd fallen into a drainage ditch and become trapped.
Rescue workers had worked through the night to free the tiny child.
Duncan remembered holding Tommy in his arms, feeding his rest-
less son a bottle of formula, watching the footage on the late news
with tears streaming down his face, his insides convulsed. He remembered how surprised he'd been that the child had survived;
usually there are no happy endings, no miraculous rescues. The

world is always trying to kill off our children, he thought. They are such easy targets.

Olivia glanced at her watch.

"I need to make a phone call," she said brusquely.

"What?"

She grabbed the telephone and pulled it toward her.

"I need to make a phone call. You want your son to stay alive, then you'll tell me how to get an outside line."

"I don't get it."

"Duncan, don't be obtuse. If I don't call a series of telephone numbers every ten minutes and tell the person on the line I'm okay, then he—or she—is to assume I've been betrayed again, and to execute the judge and the boy. Now, how much more specific can I be?"

Duncan looked at her in horror.

"How do I get an outside line, Duncan?"

"Dial nine."

"Thank you. One minute to spare."

Olivia quickly dialed a number.

Three blocks away, at a pay phone, Ramon Gutierrez stood waiting, looking at his own watch, unsure what he would do if the phone didn't ring. He was flooded with relief when it did.

He picked it up: "Yes."

"Everything's okay."

"Right. Move to phone two?"

"Right."

He hung up, smiling.

Olivia returned the phone to its cradle. She took her wristwatch off and placed it on the desk in front of her. "I'd better keep a closer watch on the watch," she said, smiling. "Hate to screw up and miss a call."

She fixed Duncan with a harsh look.

"It would be a dumb way to die, no? Because someone forgot to make a phone call. Like being on Death Row and being marched into the gas chamber—or electric chair, whatever—and blocks away, in the governor's office, his chief aide is frantically looking for the piece of paper with the number of the direct line to the execution chamber on it, and realizing damn if he didn't leave it in his other pair of pants."

She laughed.

"Did you know they threatened me with it, Duncan?"

"With what?" he asked, barely able to speak.

"The death penalty. Happily, it was ruled out of my case early enough . . . But not yours, Duncan. Not yet."

When the buzzer at the front door sounded, Megan jumped. At first she thought it was the twins, who'd forgotten something and come back, but then she realized they would have let themselves in with their own key. And then she thought they probably wouldn't bother, relying instead on teenage laziness and the certain knowledge that their mother would let them in: Why struggle with a key when one can simply ring the doorbell? She hurried across the hallway and reached for the door handle without taking a moment to think clearly about what she was doing.

She pulled the door open and froze.

First she saw large sunglasses, out of place on the overcast day. Then she saw the half-grin that hit at the core of her memory. She watched as the man standing before her slowly lifted off the sunglasses. The features that stared at her seemed to rise out of a nightmare that she'd hoped was long past. She stared, open-mouthed, taking a step back, as if she'd been struck.

"But we thought you were—"

"Dead? Disappeared? Vanished? Beam me up, Scotty, I've had enough of life here in the good old U.S. of A.? What did you think, Megan? That I ran away from that bank and never gave it another thought?"

Bill Lewis laughed at the fright in Megan's face.

"Have I changed that much?" he asked calmly.

She shook her head.

"I didn't think so. Well, Megan, aren't you going to ask me in?"

She nodded.

Bill Lewis stepped inside the house and glanced around.

"Nice," he said. "Nice. Rich. Really rich. Solid. Have you become Republicans, too?"

Megan couldn't respond.

"Answer the question, Megan," he said in a low, angry voice.

"No."

"I bet," he snorted.

She watched as his eye took in the substance of the house. He looked down at an antique table in the hallway. "Not bad," he said coldly. "Shaker design, what, eighteen-fifty maybe?" He glanced back at Megan. "That was a question," he said. He ran his finger over the rough wood of the antique table.

"Eighteen fifty-eight," she answered.

"It's a fine piece. Probably worth a couple of grand, right?"

"I guess so."

"You guess so? You guess so!" He laughed, a sarcastic, braying sound.

He wandered into the living room, where he saw some framed pictures and went over to look at them closely. "Duncan has put on some weight," he said. "He looks like I would expect a happy burgher to look like. He hasn't got the fire anymore, has he? No leanness, no commitment, just fat figures and swollen bottom lines, huh?"

He hesitated, looking at Megan.

"No," she said. "He's in good shape. He runs four miles a day."

Bill Lewis let out a hissing laugh. "I should have expected it. The sport of the bourgeoisie. Probably wears a pair of hundred-dollar New Balance sneakers and a three-hundred-dollar Gore-Tex running suit from L.L. Bean. Doing high-tech, high-cost battle with the waistline."

He stopped, looked harshly at Megan and said: "He should try starving. It keeps one very lean and tough. Starving and hiding from the FBI and the cops. It's a great conditioner."

He did not smile as much as snarl. He turned back to the sideboard and picked up another photograph. "Well, I'll be damned," he said.

"The girls are as pretty as you, and they look almost like you did back then. Spitting images." He picked up a photograph of Tommy. "He looks much happier here," he said. "Where we've got him, he hardly ever smiles."

Megan gasped.

"Tommy," she whispered.

Bill Lewis turned savagely toward her.

"What? You thought that this show was just Olivia's? You didn't think there was someone else out there who had spent some time thinking about you and Duncan and wondering when he was going to get a chance to repay you?"

"Tommy," she said again. "Please, my baby . . ."

"He'll die. He'll die unless you do what you're told. So will the old bastard, only he'll die a bit more painfully."

Bill Lewis put the photograph down. He seemed to think for an instant, then he picked it up again and looked closely at it. He looked over at Megan and suddenly, violently, smashed the photograph down on the edge of a table, shattering the glass and frame. The glass breaking sounded to Megan like a shot, and she thought for an instant that she was bleeding.

"We're in control now," Lewis said. "Don't forget it."

He stepped over to Megan and grasped her face with his hand, twisting the cheeks together.

"They will all die, do you understand? Not just the boy and the old man, but then I'll come back and kill the girls too. Think about that, Megan. Then I'll kill Duncan, but I'll leave you alive, because it will be a lot worse for you than dying. Do you understand that? Do you understand!"

She nodded.

"All this, Megan, all these things, all this life, well, kiss it good-bye."

He released her.

"All right, Megan. Turn to the wall. Count to sixty. Then you can go on doing whatever it was you were doing before we took time for this pleasant little conversation. Little housework. Little cleaning. Wash the dishes. Darn some socks. Do something nice and safe and middle-class. Nice seeing you again, after all these years. All these years, Megan."

Bill Lewis pushed her against the wall and started out.

"Oh, hey, give my best to Duncan, too. Tell him he's lucky I didn't kill his wife today, the way he killed mine."

Then he left, leaving Megan sobbing, face to the wall.

She dialed the number of the second pay phone swiftly, and when she heard Ramon Gutierrez's short "Yes" on the other end, brusquely said: "Keep going."

"On to the third phone," Ramon said.

"Right." Olivia replaced the receiver in its cradle. She watched Duncan's eyes, searching for signs of rebellion. "All right, Duncan, let's get on with it."

"Yes," he replied.

"Take out a piece of paper and a pencil."

For a moment he stared at her, wondering what she had in mind, then he complied.

"Good," she said. "Okay, Duncan, how much do you make?"

"What do you mean?"

"Duncan," Olivia said, "don't test my patience. *How much do you make?*"

"My salary is ninety thousand a year."

"And?"

"There are perks, like insurance, car allowance, favorable rates on loans and mortgages, health plan, which are worth something."

"Make a guess," she said.

"Another twenty-five thousand."

"Keep going. Retirement fund?"

"My wife and I have about twenty thousand each in IRAs. The bank contributes to my pension fund, in addition—"

"Write it down."

He scribbled those figures on the pad.

"Good," she said. "Keep going."

"I own a piece of vacation property in Vermont, just the acreage, really, we wanted to build something, maybe next year . . ."

"Add it in."

"Well, it cost me thirty-six thousand for six acres . . ."

"When?"

"Seven years ago."

"I'd guess it's worth what, a hundred? One hundred and twenty?"

"At least."

"Where is it?"

"Close to Killington."

Olivia smiled. "Nice. Real nice. I gather the skiing is great there. Probably will be a real fine season. Do they already have snow?"

"Some."

"Write it down. Stocks and bonds?"

"I have a small portfolio."

"You're too modest. What do you own?"

"Just the blue chips."

"That's what I would have guessed." She motioned toward the pad.

"What else?" asked Duncan.

"Put down your house. And don't forget Megan's real estate work. How did she do last year?"

"She made fifty thousand dollars."

"This is a booming economy here, isn't it?"

Duncan just nodded.

"Who would have thought that the tired old Northeast would make such a revival? Why, back when we were such close friends, Duncan, it seemed like it was simply going to hell in a handbasket, didn't it? Imagine my surprise when I got out and learned that this was boom time, that everybody out here was getting rich."

Olivia reached across and took the paper from him, looking at the line of figures. She let out a long, low, mocking whistle. "Not bad. You've been a busy fellow, haven't you?"

He nodded.

She ripped the paper off the pad and put it in her pocket. Then the smile faded and she leaned forward in her chair. "Listen, Duncan," Olivia said, her voice a single harsh, hissing whisper. "Listen carefully. I'm going to open an account."

"What?" He was confused. "An account?"

"Right, math-man. And you're it."

"I don't get it."

"You will."

He looked at her and waited. He could tell she was savoring the moment.

"Don't you wonder why I came here today?"

He shook his head.

"I had to see you, Duncan. In person. I could have done all this by telephone, and think how much safer it would have been for me. But I wanted to see you for myself, Duncan. I had to see that you had become the enemy. I knew you had. I knew you didn't have the heart. But even I had trouble thinking that you'd fallen so far."

She sat back in her chair and laughed.

"Don't you look in the mirror, Duncan, and feel ashamed? Don't you see everything that is wrong with America wrapped up in your petty little money-grubbing ways? Don't you wake up in the middle of the night and think back to the time when you were important, to when you were doing something! You were part of a struggle. You were dedicated to making the world better, and look at you now. Dedicated to making more money. It's disgusting."

She suddenly reached across the table and grasped his hand. Her grip was iron ice, and he felt her taut, hard muscles pulling and squeezing at him.

"There, Duncan, that's what commitment is. I've never changed. I've never stopped believing in the struggle. I am as tough as I was then . . ."

She released him suddenly, and he slammed backward in the chair.

"I am as strong—stronger. Prison is like being reborn, Duncan. It puts everything into focus. It makes you come out all new and hard."

She looked at him, then she let a small smile flit into her eyes.

"All right, Duncan, you're the banker. You're the expert on loans, values, appreciation and depreciation. You're the one who knows what things are worth in the current market, given the current conditions, economic ebb and flow."

He dreaded where she was going. "Yes," he replied hesitantly.

"Well, you tell me: How much for the boy? How much for the old fascist pig?"

She laughed raucously.

"How much will they bring in the current market?"

Panic flooded him. He felt a rush of heat to his forehead.

"How can I—"

"How much, you bastard! What's a life worth, Duncan? You're the fucking banker, you tell me. How much for the old man? He doesn't have so many years left, anyway. You ought to depreciate him . . . But the boy, well, he's strong, he's got a lot of time left, so I suppose he would fetch a premium price, don't you think, Duncan? Come on, Duncan, don't you think? But shouldn't he be discounted a bit? After all, he's had a few problems so far, hasn't he? A little bit of undetermined anxiety-inducing stress, right? Maybe shave off a bit because of that. Lots of potential, but slightly damaged goods. Damaged in transit, perhaps, huh, Duncan? What do you think, Duncan, what do you think?"

"You bitch!" he whispered.

"Sticks and stones," she said in a mocking voice.

"How can you ask me to put a price on my own child?"

"You did. You put a price on my life, on Emily's, on all the others. You put a price on your own freedom eighteen years ago. It wasn't so hard for you then, Duncan. So you do it now."

She glanced at her watch.

"Time is a-wasting," she said. "Last call."

She took the phone and dialed.

When she heard Ramon's answer, she said: "Almost finished." But she kept her eyes on Duncan. She replaced the telephone receiver, moving with deliberate slowness, all the time letting her anger flow through her eyes and burrow into his heart. Then she reached inside her purse and pulled out an ordinary white envelope. She handed it to Duncan.

"Inside the envelope is a message, Duncan. It will explain to you how serious I am. It will also explain precisely what I will do if I don't get satisfaction. If you"—she froze him with her smile—"default."

She stood up.

Duncan saw her rise and filled again with confused panic.

"But how much, when . . . I don't know . . ."

She raised her hand and cut him off.

"Duncan, here is what I'll tell you. The when part is simple. Today is Wednesday. It will take you the rest of the day, probably, to decipher my little message, which I recommend you get cracking on forthwith. It will clear up any questions about my sincerity . . ."

She glared at him. "I'll give you one day . . ."

"One day! I can't—"

"Okay, Duncan," she said, with her Cheshire cat grin. "I'm reasonable. I'll give you two days. That seems fair. Two business days to come up with . . ."

She hesitated.

"That's what's making this interesting, isn't it? How much will you come up with? Will it be enough? Maybe you'll get back just one, and not the other. Maybe it's going to just be a down payment of sorts, and we'll have to keep at this. Maybe, maybe, maybe. Maybe I'll get scared. You know, Duncan, please don't underestimate how little I want to go back to prison—and how much I will do to avoid it. Do you know what I'm saying?"

"Yes. I guess."

"I'm saying, at the first sign that you're not playing this hand out alone, they die."

She paused.

"Die. Die. Dead. Got it?"

"Yes."

"So, Duncan. Get the money. Get a lot. Get it all. Just do it."

"But you don't understand, it's not like I have cash lying around. It's stocks, property, investments—I can't simply liquidate everything in two days and hand it over. I will, but it takes time. I can't just—"

"Yes, you can, you bastard."

She stared at him.

"You still don't understand, do you?"

"No. I guess not."

"Duncan, I don't expect you to be able to sell your property within two business days. I can't expect you to get the money from stock sales, and cashing in your retirement and all that stuff. That's unreasonable. You couldn't possibly manage that in two days."

She smiled at him. "No, I don't expect that."

"But how?"

"The answer is so simple, Duncan."

"I don't—"

"Duncan. Steal it."

He rocked back in his seat. His mouth opened, but he couldn't speak. She leaned forward over the desk, so that her face was only inches away. Her breath was hot and it poured over him.

"Steal it, you bastard. Rob the bank."

She stood up, peering down at him.

"Finish the job we started eighteen years ago."

She took a step back, and gestured toward the entire bank.

"Steal it," she said.

Then she was gone.

6

WEDNESDAY AFTERNOON WEDNESDAY NIGHT

Duncan remained rooted at his desk after Olivia's departure.

He didn't know how long he stayed locked into position; five minutes, fifteen, perhaps a half-hour. Time suddenly seemed malleable. He felt as if he'd been overtaken by a subtropical fever; his face was flushed, he could feel sweat on his forehead, he looked down and saw his hands palsied and shaking.

Steal it!

His reverie was violated by the telephone buzzing on his desk. He stared at it uncomprehendingly as it summoned him back to reality. He started to reach out to grab it, then stopped, letting it buzz again like an angry hornet. When it persisted, he finally put his hand on the receiver and slowly picked it up.

"Yes?" he said, vacantly.

"Duncan!"

"Yes?" he replied again, as if awakening from a dream. "Megan? What is it?"

"Duncan, he was here!"

"Megan, what is it, who was there?"

He was bolt upright by his desk now, driven to his feet by the anxiety in his wife's voice.

"Bill Lewis! I thought he'd died! He's helping her, Duncan. He's got Tommy, too."

"Bill Lewis?" Duncan felt as if the meager threads of control that held him together were twisting apart, one by one.

"He said he would kill Tommy. He said he would kill the girls, he would kill you, if you didn't do what Olivia asked. He's with her. I couldn't believe it. He looked the same, only different. It was like—"

"Bill Lewis? But I thought he'd disappeared."

"He was here! He was terrible. He wasn't at all like he used to be . . ."

"He's with Olivia?"

"Yes. Yes. They're in it together."

"My God! Who else?"

"I don't know," she moaned.

"Bill Lewis is a savage." Duncan had a vision of Lewis, sitting at the kitchen table in Lodi, pointing an emptied .45 caliber pistol at him and pulling the trigger. He remembered the echoing click of the hammer and Lewis's derisive laugh when he'd jumped, and screamed angrily at him. "Bill Lewis was a psychopath and a coward," Duncan said without thinking of the impact of his words. "He'd shoot anyone, as long as their back was turned."

"No, no, no, he wouldn't, Duncan. He was confused, we all were back then, but he wasn't such a bad guy . . ."

"You just said he was terrible . . ."

"He was, he was. God, Duncan, I'm sorry, I'm so turned around."

"What did he say?"

"He broke a picture of Tommy. He said he'd kill him."

"Not with Olivia there. We don't have to worry about that. She's always had him under her thumb. He always did exactly what she said."

"Duncan, I didn't think I could get more scared, but I am. I don't know what to think anymore."

"Megan, get ahold of yourself. Where are the girls?"

"They went out for milk."

"They what?"

"They had to go out, and I didn't think, it was before he showed up, and—"

Duncan took a deep breath and controlled his racing heart.

"It's okay. When they get back, keep them there until I get home. Don't open the front door to anyone unless you know them personally . . ."

He paused, thinking what a silly admonition that was: That was the trouble; they knew all their tormentors *personally*.

"Are you coming now?" Megan asked.

"Soon. I have something I have to do . . ."

"What?"

Duncan picked up the envelope that Olivia had left on his desktop.

"She left me some sort of message. I have to decipher it. That's what she said. I don't know what it is or how long it'll take."

"Did she tell you how much we have to pay to get the Tommys back?"

"Sort of." He hesitated, listening to the frantic tones of his wife's voice. "I'll explain it when I get home. Just collect the girls and keep a grasp on yourself. I'll be home shortly."

"Please hurry."

"I'll hurry."

He set the telephone down and picked up the envelope. She's on the verge of hysteria, he thought. He did not know what he would do if his wife couldn't handle the pressure.

He shook his head and silently asked himself what *he* would do if *he* couldn't stand the pressure. He took a deep breath.

"All right, Olivia," he said out loud. "I'll play your fucking game." It was easier to act bravely when she wasn't staring him in the face, he noted ruefully. I can always think of the perfect rejoinder after she leaves.

He opened the envelope and let its contents fall onto his desk. First he spotted a photograph. It was of the two Tommys. He looked into his son's scared eyes, and it was as if someone had stabbed him with an icepick. He held the photo unsteadily and forced himself to study it: It was taken with an instant camera. The judge was holding up the morning newspaper. It was posed, like other pictures he remembered from evening newscasts. He tried to decipher what he could about where they were being held; it appeared to be an attic somewhere; he could just make out the brown wooden slats that angled up into the peaked roofline.

At least where they are seems clean and dry, he thought.

He noted the blankets, which reassured him. He studied the judge's face for stress and was relieved to see only discomfort and displeasure. He allowed himself a revolutionary thought: You old, imperious, demanding son-of-a-bitch, give them hell. He was torn between wishing the judge would rip them apart verbally, and on the other hand, knowing how dangerous that would be, especially considering how fragile Lewis's personality was, and how dangerous. Bill Lewis laughed at the wrong moments, he remembered, and sometimes cried at the most ridiculously maudlin things, like unhappy endings in films. He had a psyche that seemed to ebb and flow like a tidal pool.

He rubbed his hand across his forehead, as if trying to feel the lines gathering there. He tried to look at Tommy again, and only allowed himself to see that his son appeared healthy, but apprehensive. He forced himself to be reassured by that observation alone. He would not measure the sadness and lost-little-boy confusion that he could see marking his son's face. But it was too hard for him, and he took a deep breath and said to himself, as if he could transmit his feelings across the airwaves to the room where his son was held captive: I'm trying, Tommy, I'm trying. I'm going to do my best. I will get you back.

He put the photograph down and wondered whether he should show it to his wife or not. Then he picked up the only other item that had fluttered from the envelope. It was an undated newspaper clipping, a death notice cut from the obituary page of an unidentifiable newspaper. He read it through twice, in growing consternation:

MILLER, ROBERT EDGAR, 39, at home on September 5, 1986. Beloved husband of Martha, nee Matthews, and loving father of his two sons, Frederic and Howard. He is survived by his parents, Mr. and Mrs. E. A. Miller of Lodi, his uncle, Mr. R. L. Miller of Sacramento, a brother, Wallace Miller of Chicago, two sisters, Mrs. Martin Smith of Los Angeles and Mrs. Wayne Schultz of San Francisco, and numerous nephews and nieces. Memorial service will be held at Our Mother of the Sacred Redemption Church at 1 p.m. Friday, September 8th. The deceased will lie in repose at the church at noon. The family requests that in lieu of flowers, contributions be made to the Viet Nam Veterans of Orange County Outreach Center. Funeral under the direction of the Johnson Funeral Home, 1120 Baker Street, Lodi.

Duncan did not know who Robert Miller was, and what conceivable connection he might have to Olivia and himself. He could see that the man had obviously died more than two months earlier and that his age made him a contemporary. He was a Lodi man, and that put him in the same town that they'd lived in before the bank job, but it told him nothing else. He gathered, also, that the man had been a Viet Nam veteran, but he could see little else in the notice that linked him to the situation at hand. Duncan rolled the man's name over and over in his mind, trying to find some connection. He stared at the piece of paper and asked: Who are you?

What do you mean to me?

How did you die?

Why?

At first he had no idea how to find out. Then Duncan picked up the telephone and dialed information in California and obtained the number for the funeral home. He hesitated for an instant, trying to invent some fiction that would explain his searching for details. As he dialed the telephone number, he realized that it was the first time in eighteen years he had telephoned the state. For a moment he felt fear, as if, simply from the tone of his voice, someone would be able to tell what he had done there in 1968. A woman's voice answered on the second ring.

"Johnson Funeral Home. How may we help you?"

"Hello," Duncan said. "My name is, uh, Roger White, and I have just been told about a funeral you folks handled back in September, and I, I'm not sure whether this fellow was an old friend or not. I've been out of the country and out of contact for so long, and uh, it was quite shocking—"

The woman interrupted:

"What was the name of the deceased?"

"Robert Miller, back in—"

"In September, oh, yes, I remember that one. What did you say your connection was?"

Duncan guessed: "Viet Nam."

"Oh, of course. Another veteran. Let me just go through my files here. You know, I don't recall that the police have made any arrests in the case."

"The police?"

"Yes. I'm sorry, didn't you know Mr. Miller was murdered?"

"No, no, it's the first I've heard about it."

"Well, I don't really have the details about that part. I know it was a robbery of sorts. You might try calling Ted Reese at the local paper. He covered the case."

Duncan wrote the name down, as he heard the woman shuffle some papers.

". . . Anyway," the woman said, "he was with the One Hundred and First Airborne in Viet Nam from nineteen sixty-six to late nineteen sixty-seven. He won two Purple Hearts and a Bronze Star for valor. He was active in the local Elks Club and both the Little League and the Pee Wee football league. He was a member of the Society of Security Professionals. A lot of former policemen and types like that came to the funeral."

"It was a large service?"

"Oh, yes. He was a very popular man. Very well known hereabouts. The man at the paper could tell you more. Is this the Mr. Miller you knew in Viet Nam?"

"Yes," Duncan lied. "It was."

"Oh," she said. "I'm so sorry."

Duncan hung up, holding his hand down on the hook for an instant to break the connection. Then he called the newspaper office and asked for the reporter. He still did not understand what message Olivia was trying to give him, nor did he see the connection between this murdered man and himself.

"Reese here."

"Hello," Duncan said. "Listen, my name is White and I've just returned to the country after six months, only to find out that an old friend was murdered. The folks at the funeral home said you could tell me what happened to Robert Miller."

"Oh—the security executive?"

"Yes."

"You say you were a friend of his?"

"From the war. One Hundred and First Airborne."

"Oh, sure. Well, I'm sorry to have to fill in the details for you . . ."

"What happened?"

"Just bad luck for him, I guess. Lucky for his wife and kids, though. They had gone away for the last week before school started, so he was home alone. Anyway, as best the cops can figure it, someone knocked on the door and he opened it and let them in. Forced him to open up his safe, which they ransacked. They tore up the house pretty good. This guy had a pretty good collection of weapons, too, including some automatic rifles. Had a damn permit for the things, if you can believe it. You know what the cops say you can sell one of those things for on the black market? Thousands. Anyway, a little bit later, they blew him away with a machine pistol, right inside the house. Made a helluva mess . . . oh, sorry . . ."

"That's okay," Duncan said quickly. "Go on, please."

"Well, not too much to add. He was apparently going for his desk, where he kept a gun hidden. He wasn't the type to go out without trying to make some kind of fight, everyone said that. Guess they left shortly after they tore up the place. Stole a few other things in addition to the guns, including, get this, his wife's red wig. Guess they got almost seven grand. He always kept a lot of cash around, which wasn't smart. But he was an executive with a security firm— hell, he'd worked himself up from being a guard on a truck—and he had state-of-the-art protection on the house. Only thing was, all those electronics don't work worth a damn if you open your front door to your killer. That's what's got the cops so stumped. They can't figure out why he would do that."

"Maybe he knew the killer."

"Yeah, that's what everyone's guessing, but so far all the likely suspects have alibis. Also, he was one of those guys that was worth more to his family alive than dead, you know? He wasn't carrying a lot of insurance or anything."

"Didn't anyone see or hear anything?"

"Well, he lived in a pretty nice subsection and the houses are pretty spread out. And one cop told me that those pistols hardly make a sound, anyway, so they wouldn't necessarily have heard anything. Just a little burping noise, kinda like someone tearing a couple of sheets of paper real fast. It was night, too."

Duncan didn't know what to ask. His mind formed a single picture of Olivia standing at the doorway to the man's house, patiently waiting for him to open up and let her in. She knew he would: Who could refuse a nice-looking, well-dressed, middle-aged woman, even in the middle of the night, even if she was a stranger? You would look through the peephole and then you would open the door, wondering what it was that had brought her to the threshold of the house. You wouldn't think twice about it.

But he still drew a blank as to why she would be there. He heard the reporter's voice droning through the earpiece.

". . . It's a real shame. Imagine that. Making it through a couple of years in Viet Nam, coming home and getting yourself shot up in a bank robbery, finally making it to an executive position, only to end it all because some home-invasion outfit learns you keep cash about. Let me tell you, people were pretty scared when this happened, because if a guy like Miller could get it, then anyone could . . ."

"I'm sorry," Duncan said abruptly, "what did you say?"

"I said it's a real shame."

"After that."

"Well, the guy does his tour of duty in Nam, then gets shot up in a bank robbery—"

Duncan interrupted: "In a bank robbery."

"Sure—back in sixty-eight. Made the headlines for a few days. Bunch of hippie crazies tried to rob a bank and jeez, a couple of bank guards got killed, and Miller got shot in the leg. Couple of the crazies bought it as well. Miller got a Governor's Medal for bravery—"

"I remember," Duncan said.

"Sure. It was a big story for about ten minutes that year. Every story in sixty-eight was bigger than the next. It was that kind of year."

"I remember," Duncan said.

His shoulders slumped and he felt nauseated. For an instant he wasn't sure whether he could keep from vomiting in fear.

I know, he said to himself. I know now. He bit back the bile in his throat and asked: "The police have any suspects?"

"Well, lots of theories. Mostly they think it was this gang that operates out of San Francisco. Apparently there have been a couple of other home invasions in the past few months. But he was in the security business, and who knows what sort of characters he might have run across over the years. You gotta remember: This is California. Anything goes."

"Thanks," Duncan said, his voice a bare whisper.

"Hey, you know anything about the case that might help the cops? There's a twenty-grand reward put up by his company."

But Duncan hung up.

He sat back in his chair and thought about who Robert Miller was: the man who killed Emily Lewis on the street in Lodi in 1968.

And Duncan knew why he had died.

Revenge.

Judge Thomas Pearson watched his grandson.

The boy seemed to have lost some of his nervousness, as his familiarity with his surroundings grew. But Tommy still jumped visibly whenever any sound from the downstairs penetrated the confines of the small room. He could see that the boy was growing increasingly frustrated by the combination of fear and boredom that had descended upon them. He would pace about for a moment, then curl into a ball on the bed, in the fetal position, only to unwrap himself after a few minutes and start pacing again. Tommy had shrugged off all his grandfather's efforts to distract him. They had spent the morning hours alone together, wondering what would happen next; then, after Olivia had taken their pictures, the afternoon had passed with no news, just a complete silence. The judge had wondered several times whether they were alone in the house; but even if they were, had not known what to do.

He stared about the room. What a devilish trap this is, imprisoned by walls and by responsibility, too. If I were to lose Tommy, I could never face Duncan and Megan again. It would kill me to live.

He looked down at his wristwatch and saw that dinner was late. It is night, he thought. Our second night here. Outside it is growing deep black and the sky has covered itself with a shroud. It is growing colder, with the leftover warmth of the day skulking away into the shadows.

He gestured to Tommy to come and sit by him, wrapping his arm around him when the boy took his seat.

"It's so quiet, Grandfather," the child said, echoing his own thoughts. "Sometimes I'm not sure that they're still here."

"I know," the judge replied. "Then, just when you think we ought to take the bed and try to knock down the door, you hear a little noise, and you realize they've been there all along."

"How long do you think we'll have to be here, Grandfather?"

"You've asked that before, and I don't have the answer."

"Guess."

"Tommy, what good will guessing do?"

"Please."

He could feel the boy's tension and didn't know whether to lie or tell the truth. Isn't that always the problem with children? he thought to himself: We are never completely sure whether adult truths will free them or burden them. He had a sudden memory of driving with his wife and children, many years before, on a family vacation. Megan had been close to Tommy's age. "How much farther?" she had asked piteously, over and over. "Until we get there," he'd answered. "But how much?" she'd persisted. "Miles and miles," he'd answered. "But how much?" Finally, after twenty minutes of this, he'd thought: Tell her the truth. "Megan, it's at least another two hours, so just try to relax and look out the window or play a counting game with your mother or something, but stop asking how much farther." She had howled in frustration: "Two hours! Two hours! I want to go home!" And he'd gritted his teeth as she cried.

But that was only a little truth that backfired. What about big truths? Like what are our chances? What about living and dying?

"Well, Tommy, I suspect we'll be here at least another day."

He could see the boy's lip quiver.

"Why?"

The boy's body shuddered massively as he asked his question.

"Well, I suspect they've asked your dad for some money, and it will take him time to collect it. I explained that before."

Tommy nodded his head, his body still shaking.

"I want to leave," he said. The judge saw tears welling up in the boy's eyes. "I want to go home," he continued, his voice rising, punctuated by sobs. "I want to go home, home, home, home . . ."

His grandfather wrapped his arms around him tightly.

But the boy, instead of dissolving into the comforting arms, exploded, knocking Judge Pearson back.

"I want to go! I want to go! I want to go!" Tommy started screaming. He stamped his foot in rage on the floor. Then the boy jumped across the attic floor and started pounding on the door with his flat hand, making a resounding crash, like a bass drum. "*I want to go!*" he screamed.

The judge jumped up and seized the boy by his shoulders. He tried to pull him away, but Tommy fought free.

No, Judge Pearson thought, no, please, Tommy, not now. Please, not now.

The boy tore himself from his grandfather's grasp a second time and threw himself against the locked door, which creaked with the great smash of the boy's body.

"Out! Out! Out! Out! Home! Home! Home!" Tommy screamed.

When Judge Pearson tried a third time to grasp him, Tommy wheeled and flailed away at the old man with his fists: "No! No! No! Mine! Mine!"

The judge fell back, surprised by the strength of the boy's assault.

Oh, my God, the judge thought. He's losing it. I can't hold him, I know I can't hold him. It used to take Duncan and Megan both to hold him when he went wild. I can't do it alone.

Tommy was slamming his fists against the door again. The noise seemed to shake the entire house, booming like thunderclaps through the old wooden boards.

The judge could hear the sound of feet running through the hallways and stairways toward them. Oh, my God, he thought, they're coming!

"Tommy, stop! Stop! Please, stop!" he pleaded, trying to hold the boy back, but as successful as if he were standing holding his hands up against the winter wind.

"Let me go! Let me go!" the boy cried hysterically.

"Tommy! Tommy! It's me—please—Grandfather . . ." Judge Pearson tried again to tear the child away from the door. He saw Tommy's hands were bleeding and the sight of blood terrified him. "Tommy!" he shouted. "Tommy!"

"No! No! NOOOOO!" screamed Tommy, as he felt the judge's hands on his shoulders again.

The judge could hear the sound of the dead bolt lock being turned, and he tackled the child, pulling him momentarily back from the doorway.

Tommy let loose a long, drawn-out cry that seemed barely earthly and which echoed in the tiny room, overpowering the small space and filling it with terror. The cry reverberated throughout the entire house.

Olivia Barrow and Bill Lewis, both brandishing handguns, stepped through the door, their faces riven with their own confusion and a touch of panic. They stared down at the twisting, struggling child, locked in his grandfather's grim hold.

"I want! I want! I want!" screamed Tommy. "Let me go! Go! GO! GO!"

"Shut up!" shouted Bill Lewis.

"Quiet!" Olivia yelled.

It had no effect upon Tommy, whose eyes were closed and whose body arced like an electric current.

"I can't hold him," the judge suddenly called out, as he felt the boy slipping from his grasp.

He released his grandson rather than break the child's arms. Tommy flung himself toward the door, oblivious to the two adults with their pistols who blocked his path.

"Jesus!" yelled Bill Lewis, as he caught Tommy, staggering backward under the child's assault.

The child continued screaming, trapped by this new set of arms. Tommy fought madly, wildly, punching and kicking away with demonic strength.

"I'll shoot him! I'll shoot him!" Lewis screamed at the judge.

"He can't help it—just hold him!"

"Don't move!" yelled Olivia, training her gun on the judge.

"Christ! Give me a hand!" shouted Lewis, who let out a yelp of his own as he tumbled over onto the floor, trying to hold back Tommy's rage. His weapon clattered to the corner, as Lewis tried to keep the boy from biting him. "Jesus, Olivia!" he screamed.

"Nobody move!" Olivia yelled again.

"Fuck you," said the judge, throwing himself onto the tangled, twisted pair on the floor, trying to help Bill Lewis control the boy. Within a few seconds, each adult had hold tightly of Tommy's limbs, and together they had him pinned to the floor.

"Nobody move," Olivia called again, but this time it was a moot command, as they were all frozen in position, locked by the straining child's muscles.

The judge looked down and saw that Bill Lewis's pistol was on the floor within reach.

My God, he thought, the gun!

He hesitated. His hand twitched slightly forward.

But he heard Olivia's steady, even voice, spoken now in normal tones, which after the screaming seemed a whisper: "You'll die, old man. I see it and you'll die."

The judge closed his eyes for an instant and thought, How many opportunities will I miss?

But he said, "What the hell are you talking about?"

Bill Lewis, oblivious to the moment that had passed between Olivia and the judge, looked at Judge Pearson and whispered, "Thanks. I couldn't have held him." He gritted his teeth as Tommy surged again.

Then, abruptly, Tommy's body suddenly went limp in their arms.

"Christ!" Bill Lewis exclaimed. "What the hell is it! Have I hurt him? Is he dead?"

"No," Judge Pearson said, slowly relaxing. "It's a sort of fugue state. He goes into it after an episode like this. Help me get him onto a bed."

Tommy's eyes were wide open, his breathing slow and shallow.

"Come on," the judge said. He looked at Olivia. "Clear the way—hurry up."

She hesitated, then jumped up and arranged a space on one of the cots.

"Will he be okay?" Bill Lewis asked. "Christ! That was something . . ."

"He'll be okay when he gets out of here."

Judge Pearson looked over at Olivia, pointing a finger at her. "Now, get some Betadine and Band-Aids for his hands, which are all cut up. You knew this, didn't you? You had all this planned out and you knew he had these spells, didn't you?"

"I knew he was a special-education student, but I didn't—" she started. Then she glared at the judge. "Tough. Sorry, but it's just tough fucking luck. It's your job to keep him under control."

"I'll do what I can," snapped the judge.

"Well, does he need some medication or something? I mean, we can always get him whatever he needs . . ." said Bill Lewis. He stood by the bed, staring down at the boy. "Shouldn't you cover him with a blanket?" he asked.

"Yeah," said the judge, still glaring at Olivia.

"I'll get it," said Bill Lewis. "Never seen anything like that."

Olivia looked at Lewis. "You go get the medical kit," she said. "Fix up the kid."

Then she turned and exited, leaving the judge sitting by the bed, waiting for Lewis to return.

Ramon Gutierrez parked some three blocks away from Megan and Duncan's house and stepped out into the dark and cold. He pulled his parka closer to his body when he felt the first touch of the evening on his skin. He thought of winter nights in the South Bronx when he was young, where the cold mingled with misery, and he imagined that those times were much worse because they had no hope. He tried to remember Puerto Rico and imagine the tropical warmth that covered the island, but he was unable to. He had come to the United States as a child, and only returned to the island once, when he was a teenager, for a visit with his uncle. The movement to make the island independent had grown up in the ghettos of New York City; he had joined first out of a sense of curiosity, then because he discovered that he would be accepted by the group if he performed a particular political role. Having felt ostracized through much of his teen age, first by family, then by the neighborhood, it had come as a pleasant surprise to him. He had embraced the political rhetoric of the movement wholeheartedly, without even the slightest amount of sincerity.

As he walked briskly past the dark trees and well-lit houses toward Megan and Duncan's home, he thought of his old neighborhood. It was always too warm or too cold. He thought of a young junkie who'd inhabited an empty shell of a building on the end of his street. The man had frozen to death one night when the temperature had plummeted and the wind had stormed through the holes and gaps in the building. Ramon and some of the other boys had found him, curled around a broken washstand, stiffened by death. The man's brown skin had turned a lighter color and looked like mud that had frozen on a field. His face had seemed like a Halloween mask.

He shook his head.

I will never go back there.

I will never have to go back when this is over.

He paused to admire a Cadillac in a driveway, then paced on, remindful of Olivia's admonition simply to check on the family, make sure they were all at home, and that, once again, there was no police presence. A six-block walk, she'd said: Park, get out, don't hesitate, simply walk by, keep walking, go around the block, back to the car, get in, drive by once more and return to the farmhouse.

He forced himself to think of the money that they would get, as if that might keep him warm. He wished she had let him take one of the weapons with him, but he understood her reasons against it. Still, he thought, I wish I had my gun.

He wondered for a moment whether any of the people whose shapes and forms he could see moving behind the windows of the houses he passed had ever been inside a prison. Life is always a prison, he thought. When I was in Attica it was no different from where I grew up in the South Bronx. He laughed to himself: The only change was that at Attica the locks on the doors worked; at home, they never did.

If the lock had worked, I wouldn't have had so much trouble.

The embarrassment of his memory almost made him stop. She said she was thirteen. How was I to know she was only ten? For an instant he remembered the smooth olive skin that had fluttered beneath his hands. I did not know she was retarded, he thought angrily, and what difference was that, anyway? He dismissed the memory from his mind, clearing away the picture of his mother screaming in Spanish, a torrent of obscenities and abuse, and his father, unbuckling his garrison belt and winding it ominously around his fist.

He breathed in the air, the cold made it seem like he was inhaling the edge of a knife. He paused in front of Megan and Duncan's house and caught a glimpse of the twins as they moved through the living room. He felt a familiar pulse-quickening, and for an instant he allowed himself the fantasy of catching them alone. She says she wants to make them all pay, he thought, and what better way is there? He shivered, but not from the cold, and clenched his hands together. He looked at the house and thought: Maybe we can have a date, huh? Before all this is over.

He wanted to laugh out loud. I don't hate you, he told himself. I want to love you, because of what you are going to give me. I only hate who you are.

The rich think money is bravery, but it is not. It only buys new fears. They think it buys safety, but it only buys new dangers.

His mind filled with the image of Olivia some ten weeks earlier out in California. She had sat patiently in the front seat of the car, checking the action on the machine pistol, before turning to him and Bill Lewis and saying: "Watch. The pig will open the door. I will knock, and he will look though the peephole and open the door. He will be polite and solicitous and friendly and he will invite me in. I will give you a signal when I get the drop on him. Stay down until then." He had been filled with fear and admiration; he understood why she wanted to kill the man, he had only wished that she had done it without him. But she had insisted, saying: "This will be our bond. We are all together in this and in all things from now on." Ramon remembered how confidently she had walked to the front of the car and raised the hood, pretending that the car was disabled. Then she had marched right up to the man's house and rung the doorbell. He had wondered for only a few seconds whether the man who quickly showed himself in the lighted entranceway had any idea that his death waited outside.

And it had happened exactly as she said it would.

He saw the girls again, and his reverie changed abruptly.

We will have a party, he said to himself. A party you will never forget. One that someday in the future you will be unable to explain to your new husbands.

He smiled to himself. I wish I had my knife.

The headlights of a car pulling out from another house suddenly cut across where he was standing, and he felt a momentary panic. He thrust himself into the shadow of a tree and watched as the vehicle rolled past him.

She is right, Ramon thought. She has been right about everything. This town hasn't the sense to know fear. We can do anything here.

He looked back at the house. The twins were out of sight.

"Good night, ladies," he said out loud. "We will see each other soon."

He walked on, through the night. He thought of money, and wondered how much it would be. Enough to go wherever I want and start over. He wondered whether Bill Lewis would come with him. He doubted it, which made him sad for just an instant. He will trail after Olivia, who will never love him the way I would. She will only use him forever and break his heart over and over. He has her bitch smell in his nostrils and he will never be able to get it out, and someday, it will kill him. He would be much happier with me, in Mexico maybe, where I can pass for a native, and where we would be rich because they have so little. We would live together like kings, down by the ocean, where it is always warm and not ever dark like this night. He does not understand, Ramon decided. There is only pleasure. But he has pleasure all wrapped together with guilt and that makes him sad and vulnerable.

But I am not, he thought proudly. I am free.

He buried his hands in his coat pockets and pushed them against his crotch. He strolled through the night, vaguely aroused, which warmed him against the darkness that surrounded him.

Tommy could feel his grandfather's hand as it stroked his forehead, but it was like a memory, as if it were not happening right then. He stared up at the attic ceiling and imagined that the roof disappeared, opening up to a great black expanse of space, dotted with diamond stars and washed with soft moonlight. His eyes were fixed open, but his head swirled about in the vision; he had the sense of being lifted up into the night sky and flying free. He could feel the wind on his cheeks and it was warm, comforting, like being wrapped in an old and familiar blanket. As he spun up into the endless darkness, he could hear his mother and father calling to him and he could see his sisters waving, beckoning him to their side. He smiled, laughed, and waved back, then started to swim through the blackness in their direction. But as he tried to steer toward them, he could feel the winds shift, and suddenly he was battling against a hurricane blowing hard in his face, tearing at his clothes, pulling him away fom his family. He reached out, but they grew distant, increasingly small, their voices fading, until they disappeared.

He gasped and shivered.

Then he heard his grandfather's voice:

"Tommy, Tommy, Tommy, I'm right here, right here with you. Everything is going to be okay, I'm here, I'm here."

He shuddered and turned toward his grandfather.

He saw Bill Lewis's face, peering over the old man's shoulder, but this time he wasn't scared.

"He's coming back," Lewis said. "Jesus, that's scary."

Tommy reached out and grabbed his grandfather's hand. But he saw Lewis's face break into a grin.

"Hey, kid? You feeling okay?"

Tommy nodded.

"You need anything? Hungry? Thirsty, maybe?"

Tommy nodded again.

"I brought your dinner up. It's right outside."

Lewis dropped from his sight, and Tommy looked at his grandfather. "I'm okay," he said. "I'm sorry, Grandfather. It just came over me."

"Don't worry about it," the old man said.

"My hands hurt," Tommy said.

"You cut them when you pounded on the door."

"I did?"

The judge nodded.

Tommy lifted them up so that he could see his hands.

"They're not too bad," he said. "Just a little sore."

Bill Lewis walked in, holding a tray.

"I made some stew. It's out of a can, but it tastes pretty good. I'm sorry, son, I'm not too much of a cook. But I brought you a soda, as well. And a couple of aspirin, in case your hands hurt."

"Thank you," Tommy said, sitting up. "I'm hungry now."

"You too, judge, might as well eat. I'll stay and help the boy if he has trouble."

Bill Lewis sat on the edge of the bed, taking Judge Pearson's spot.

The judge watched as Tommy spooned down some of the stew, then started to eat as well. He realized suddenly that he was famished, and he tore into the food.

"Take your time, Tommy," Bill Lewis said. "There's bread and butter, too. I put a couple of cookies on the tray for dessert. Chocolate chips okay?"

"Yes, thank you."

Tommy hesitated. "I don't know your name," he said.

"Just call me Bill."

"Thank you, Bill."

"Don't mention it."

"Bill?"

"Yes?"

"Do you know when we can go home?"

The judge stiffened and thought: Not now!

But Bill Lewis just smiled.

"Tired of it up here, huh?"

Tommy nodded.

"I don't blame you. I had to spend a month, many years ago, inside one room of a house. I didn't dare go out, didn't dare do anything. It was pretty terrible."

"Why?"

"Well . . ." Lewis hesitated, then thought: What the hell. "Well, I was pretty sure the police were after me, and I was waiting for some people to help me. I was underground. Do you know what that means?"

"Like a groundhog?"

Lewis laughed.

"Not exactly. It means hiding out."

"Oh," Tommy said. "Are we underground now?"

"Sort of."

"Did they ever catch you?" Tommy asked.

Lewis grinned. "No, kid, I always stayed one jump ahead. And after a while, I guess they just stopped looking. At least, it felt that way. So, after a few years, well, it just seemed to slide."

"When was this?" the judge asked.

"Back in the sixties," Lewis answered, without thinking.

"Why don't you just tell him everything?" Olivia Barrow said harshly.

Her voice seemed to break the air in the room, shattering the moment of peace, putting everything back on edge. She stood in the doorway, glaring at Bill Lewis, fingering a revolver.

Lewis jumped to his feet.

"I wasn't saying anything. Nothing they aren't going to figure out anyway."

"Sure," she replied.

Lewis looked down at Tommy. "Sorry, kid."

"It's okay," Tommy answered. "Thanks for the dinner."

"Hey, keep the cookies. You can eat them later."

"Thank you."

Lewis collected the dishes on the tray and paced past Olivia, who fixed him with a sharp glance. She remained behind, staring at the judge.

"He is an emotional man," she said after a few moments passed. "Very mercurial. Capable of extreme tenderness one instant"—she paused—"and extreme violence the next. Please consider his instability when you deal with him; I'd hate to see something awkward happen."

Judge Pearson nodded.

"Maybe I should let Ramon come next time with the food. He loves little children, judge. But not in the kind of way you'd be very comfortable with."

The judge did not reply.

Olivia walked over and stood above Tommy.

"Boys this age are always disarming," she said. "They drive you crazy with love or crazy with frustration."

"Do you have children?" the judge asked quietly. If you did, he thought to himself, you would never do this.

Olivia laughed.

"No, no chances. Prison isn't the best place for conceiving children. No, the only things conceived in prison are plans and hatred and the need for revenge. Those are my babies."

"You're bitter," he said.

She laughed again. "Of course I'm bitter. I have a perfectly good right to be bitter."

"Why?"

She smiled. "Now look who's getting ready to shoot her mouth off."

The judge didn't reply.

Olivia shrugged. "Why not?" she said. "Judge, haven't you wondered why we haven't taken any pains to conceal ourselves?"

"Yes. It's bothered me from the start."

"You must have handled a bunch of kidnapping, extortion trials while you were on the bench."

"I did. Not like this, though."

"Right. I said that earlier. You see, there is one single element of genius to all this, judge, one little thing that makes it all work."

"I don't understand."

"It's your daughter and son-in-law, judge."

She hesitated.

"What do you know about them?"

"What do you mean? They're my—"

"What were they doing eighteen years ago?"

Judge Pearson cast his mind back: 1968. I was younger then, he thought, stronger. My wife was alive and we were worried. We didn't have any idea what they were up to. They wouldn't tell us anything. I was too rigid and demanding, and they just left us waiting. For what? There was the war, which we all hated. There were riots and long hair and demonstrations and they were a part of that. I was on the bench and we were part of the system and the system was evil. He remembered a dozen shouting matches with Duncan— arguments that had faded almost entirely from his memory—that dissolved into months of quiet when they moved to the coast. Then everything changed. He pictured Megan and Duncan's arrival back in Greenfield, unexpected, late at night. Megan was pregnant with the twins. It was magical. They had been so lost, and then they came home so suddenly, and all our fears dissipated overnight. They wanted our help, they wanted to start a new life, a normal life, right in Greenfield. No more mad political rhetoric, no more accusations about the evil system and the rotten society. We never asked, we were so glad to have them back. And then when the twins arrived, it was like everything had started over, we were all a family again, without anger and sharpness.

"What were they doing back in 1968?" Olivia asked again, her voice carrying a tinge of demand.

"I don't know what you mean. Megan had finished art school and she went out to California to be with Duncan while he finished his master's at Berkeley. They were living out there . . . that's all I remember."

Olivia snorted.

"What about their politics?" she asked sarcastically.

"Well, Duncan was active in the antiwar, antidraft movements. He'd been in SDS as an undergraduate at Columbia, and he took part in the demonstrations there. I think he was connected in some vague way to the Weathermen faction. But he left it all behind. He dropped it when they came back east."

Olivia interrupted. She snorted.

"Port Huron and the Weathermen came later."

"I didn't know. Well, it's just all titles, anyway—"

"Don't be so dumb."

"I didn't know, dammit. What are you saying?"

"They were more than a little involved in the movements," Olivia said, her voice an edge of anger. "We all were. And he didn't just 'drop it' like you say. No, sir, not at all."

"Yes?"

"Don't be so dumb!"

"I'm not, goddammit. We never asked. We were just glad to have them home."

"They were running around in the mountains in Marin County with weapons, practicing for the revolution. They were learning to build bombs and propaganda. That's what they were doing."

"Well . . ."

Judge Pearson didn't know what to say. He was suddenly over-come with the sensation that he didn't want to hear what she was saying.

"That's where I met them. And things got more intense. We were a band of revolutionaries. We were committed. We were armed. We had split off from all the others, which was perfect, because everyone else ended up surrounded by FBI infiltrators and informants. But not us! We were together and we were ready!"

Olivia had started pacing about the room, gesturing with the re-volver. The judge could feel her passions filling the small area.

"We were going to rip the heart out of this rotten country and start anew. And they were part of it, just like me and Bill and Emily and the others. Only they fucked up, judge, they fucked up and ran. They were cowards! In an army, you get shot for battlefield cowardice, for disobeying an order in the face of the enemy. Well, that's what they did when they panicked and ran. They ran right back to your silly little bourgeois society, where they hid. They had the perfect disguise, too: They became ordinary. They blended in. They became interested in things like mortgages and new cars and PTA meetings and United Way fund drives and getting promotions and making more money, more fucking money all the time. And you helped them to become invisible, judge, anonymous, just like all the other traitors in our generation, except they were a bit worse, wouldn't you say? I went to jail and Bill went underground and Emily died. And time passed. They liked being anonymous, so they got happy and fat and rich and ordinary, judge, they got so fucking ordinary!"

She spat out: "They were traitors!"

He saw her stop, clenching the pistol so tightly that her knuckles showed white on the grip.

"But I wasn't. I never got fat and happy and bourgeois. I just got leaner and tougher and all I did for eighteen years was wait for this time, when I would pay them back for leaving me. I did eighteen years hard time, no slack time, no minimum security easy time. And then I got paroled. That's the way the system works, you know that, don't you? They give you a parole officer's name and a new clothes outfit and one hundred dollars. And then I got out and here is where I came. I knew they would be here, judge. They may have been invisible to everyone—but me!"

She looked at Judge Pearson.

"They owe me eighteen years. And there's not a damn thing they—or you—can do about it. They were just as guilty as I was, of the same crime."

She sat down abruptly on the cot next to him and drew her face close to his.

"You think they're willing to go to prison for eighteen years?"

He shook his head. "It doesn't work like that."

"No?"

"They've changed. Everything has changed. They wouldn't even be charged—"

Olivia drew back.

"No? You don't think so? You tell me, judge. What's the statute of limitations on felony murder?"

He swallowed hard. Oh no, he thought. No, not possible. They couldn't have.

"There is none," he answered.

She tossed her hair and leaned backward and roared.

"What a fucking sharp legal mind you have, judge."

Olivia leaned forward then, lowering her voice to a sort of conspiratorial whisper:

"So, now you know something you didn't know about your darling children. Maybe you suspected something, but the reality is much worse than any fantasy, isn't it? And you, you cute little boy, now you know something new about your nice mommy and daddy, don't you?"

Olivia stood up sharply and quick-marched across the floor to the door. She paused before speaking:

"They're killers. Just like me."

She slammed the door shut behind her.

*   *   *

Duncan picked up the picture of Tommy with the shattered glass still trapped within the frame. Without thinking, he touched the edge, where one crack ran across his son's face, slicing his finger open. He did not instantly summon an expletive, as he would have on almost any other occasion. Instead, he simply let this new pain roll together with all the other hurts that had bonded together within him.

He put his finger into his mouth and tasted the sweet salty blood.

"Oh, Duncan, do you need a Band-Aid?" Megan asked.

He shook his head. I need a lot more than that, he thought. He glanced over toward Karen and Lauren, who sat in the corner quietly.

"If something happened to you two—" he started, but they interrupted him.

"We'll be okay!" Karen said.

"We're not going to let some stranger threaten us," Lauren continued.

"You girls don't understand," Megan said. "You're too young to understand how vulnerable we all are."

They had been arguing about this since Duncan's return home. Megan had told him and the twins about Bill Lewis's visit. Their reaction had been one of defiant stubbornness—traits that Megan assumed they had adopted whole cloth from their father. In a way, angry as she was at them for their persistent failure to feel the same fear and panic that she did, she was infinitely proud: They have the immortality of youth flowing through their veins. She remembered when she and Duncan, barely older, had thought the same: There was no comprehension that the weapons they practiced with up in the mountains could rip and tear and leave someone lifeless. There was no sensation of danger, only a heady feeling of living close to some undefined edge.

Megan looked across at Duncan and the girls, who had grown quiet, and realized that everyone would think that they had won this argument. That was the way the family operated: Everyone stated their position, and believed that because they were undoubtedly correct, everyone else would go along—when, of course, no one really did. All families are established on the same sorts of illusions, she thought. Everyone creates the same kind of workable relationships. Even Tommy knew that.

She heard Duncan say, "Well, let's be careful. Anyway, I don't think Bill Lewis is our biggest problem. It's still Olivia."

"But what does she want?" Megan said.

"That's what's so difficult," Duncan said. "She won't say how much money. I don't think the numbers are important to her, really, it's how she wants me to get it."

"Well, how?"

"She wants me to rob my own bank."

The room filled with silence. Megan's head spun, and she tried to seize hold of any single idea, to form into words and speak, but she could not. She heard the girls' voices, as if echoing from a great distance.

"What?"

"But how?"

"I can do it," Duncan said. "I'd have to work out the details, but I can do it."

"But, Dad! If you got caught—"

"You could go to prison! What good would it do us to have Tommy and Grandfather back if you just go to jail? And anyway, why would she—"

"It makes perfectly good sense from her point of view. She thinks I failed her in one bank robbery. Now she wants me to complete the job. That's what she said. It has a kind of symmetry to it."

"Duncan!"

"Well, it does. Olivia isn't dumb."

"But suppose—"

"Suppose what? Karen, Lauren, suppose what! What alternatives do we have?"

"I still think we should go to the police. Then they'd give you the money."

"We can't, we just can't. Look, let's go over it one last time. One, if we go to the cops and Olivia finds out, she might just decide the hell with it, and kill them both. Let me tell you one thing: She's capable. Don't think for an instant that she's not. But at the moment, she's feeling pretty confident and in control, and we can't do anything that makes her worried, because then there's no telling what she might do . . ."

Duncan hesitated, aware of the envelope in his pocket and of what he had learned that afternoon.

"She's a killer, we've got to remember that."

He paused, watching for reaction about the room. He saw the effect the word had on the three women. He persisted:

". . . Two, if we go to the cops, your mother and I will then have to face charges in California, so what good is that? Three, even if we go to the cops, there's no guarantee that they can do any better at getting the two Tommys back than we can by playing along. Think about it!"

"What do you mean?" Megan asked.

"Well, the girls don't remember, but we do: Think about all the kidnappings you've ever heard about. The Lindbergh baby, for example: The cops got called and the baby died. How about Patty Hearst? Every damn FBI agent in the entire nation was looking for her and it was only after she became a revolutionary herself and robbed her own goddamn bank that they found her. She even called herself Tanya."

"I remember," Megan said softly. "That's what Olivia used to call herself, long before Patty Hearst."

Duncan half-smiled. "She even lost her nickname when she went to prison."

He went on: "Anyway, I just don't think the police would be much help. Do you?"

Megan shook her head.

"Lauren? Karen? Do you remember reading anything in the daily papers that might suggest confidence in the Greenfield police?"

It was an unfair question, but he posed it anyway.

They remained quiet.

"All right, then. Just maybe, after we've got them back, then we'll call the cops. But not until we've got them back."

"But, Duncan," Megan heard her voice, as if it was coming from someone else, "if you rob the bank to get the money, the place will be swarming with police. How can we get away with it?"

"We don't have to."

"I don't understand."

"Look," Duncan said. "All we need is the money and a little time. If I do this, say, Friday night, it won't be discovered until Monday. We can get the Tommys back over the weekend. Then, on Monday, I can go to Phillips and tell him the truth—or enough of it to explain why I did what I did. Remember, he's one of your dad's oldest friends. We can make restitution to the bank—we'll sell everything if we have to. You dad will help us. But, given the circumstances, I don't think I'll get prosecuted—"

"That sounds ridiculous."

"You got any better ideas?"

"I mean, it's filled with—"

"Sure, chance. Luck. Goodwill. Christ, I know. But what else can we do?"

"We could—"

"What? Tomorrow I'll call our broker, sell all our stocks. I'll call a realtor up in Vermont and put the property on the market. We can cash in everything, but it will take time. More than two days, and that's all she's given us."

"Do you really think you can?"

Duncan laughed bitterly. "It's probably a more common fantasy then any banker would like to admit. And usually they embezzle the money. But what I'm going to do is rob the fucking bank. Just like some goddamn Jesse James or Bonnie and Clyde."

"They all got caught," Megan replied abruptly. "And killed." She ignored Duncan's obscenity, thinking it was somehow pertinent to the tone of the conversation.

Duncan frowned.

"Two days. That's all we've got. And anyway, what are we gambling with? Our son's life. The judge's. We have to go along with what she wants, even if it seems wrong, or it screws everything up in the future. We have to deal with these things right now! And anyway, Megan, you've got to see what's really going on here: It's not the money that she's interested in. Maybe for the others, like Bill Lewis and whoever else she's got helping her, but for Olivia, I'm sure: It's not the money . . ."

He looked around at the faces of his family.

Slowly he pulled the envelope containing the death notice and the picture of the two Tommys from his pocket. He dropped them on a coffee table in front of his wife and daughters.

"It's us."

7

THURSDAY

Megan spent the day utterly at the mercy of renegade emotions, unable to control the visions that rose up within her. It was like being caught in a fast-running river, dragged one moment beneath the suffocating white-green froth, the next, thrust upward, gasping for breath, into the clear air. One instant she hallucinated Tommy swinging in the tire hanging from the great oak in the front yard, and she'd give a cry of pleasure, and start to rush outdoors to hug him—only to pull back sharply when she saw the empty tire. The next second, she'd turn, cocking an ear, realizing she could hear the familiar, unmistakable tread of her father's steps creaking on the house's stairway. She'd have to hold herself back from running to the foyer to greet this ghost, bitterly forcing herself to recognize he had not returned, except in her mind.

Megan thought about her father's footsteps. He has the lightness of age in his walk: It is a mistake to think that elderly people always walk heavily, as if burdened by their time on earth. For some of them, there comes a time when suddenly they are lighter, as if the brittleness of their years is finally lifted by removing the humdrum responsibilities of life. That is why the two Tommys always seemed to race a foot or two up in the air. It is we in middle age who walk with stolid, thumping determination, stuck in mire and routine.

Megan stared out into the gray late afternoon sky. A gust of wind swirled a last dry bunch of leaves down across the lawn, and for just an instant, they seemed alive as they jumped and tossed about, following the dictates of the breeze.

She placed her hand against the windowpane. She could feel the steady cold through the glass.

When Mother died, it was warm. Indian summer filled the tree leaves with a deceiver's hot wind. She wondered whether her mother had fought against death, or accepted it with the quiet ease with which she'd accepted most things in life. She died quickly, in her sleep, her heart just stopping one morning as she rocked on a porch swing. The mailman had found her and called the ambulance, but it was far too late. He was a young man with a beard, who always had a nice word for Tommy. He stopped by and said that when he found her, she was smiling, and he thought at first she was simply sleeping, but then he'd seen that she'd dropped her glass of lemonade, and there was something in the limp way her arm hung down which told him he was mistaken.

I wish I'd had a chance to say goodbye, before she snuck away like that. But that was her style; quiet, efficient.

I wish she were here right now, Megan thought suddenly, because she would know what to do. She wouldn't be crying every minute and wringing her hands together. Instead, she would be filled with plans and ideas. She would take charge of all her emotions, and put them in order. And then she would figure out what she should do, instead of simply waiting for the next awful thing to happen, like I am.

She would never let them die.

All those years acting as the judge's alter ego had given her the confidence of her strength. He has always been filled with a combination football-lawyer-Marine-judge bluster. In a fight, he would never waver for an instant. He approaches life like he did all those beachheads: He throws himself forward, shooting dead ahead, picking out the straight path.

But she was subtle.

She saw all the small ramifications, the tiny effects of each action, and she measured all those things together. She picked her way across the minefield of life gingerly, walking lightly, so that all the dangers never knew she was there. I was so blind, when I was young, thinking she had given up too much when she didn't remain in law school herself, but instead dropped out to support her husband.

Megan walked away from the window and went over to the wall where the family pictures were hung. She saw the photograph of Tommy with its broken frame. Duncan had cut his finger, then been unsure whether to hang it on the wall again or not. Finally, he had plucked as many shards of glass as possible from the frame and then returned the picture to the wall. She had felt a great sense of relief at that; she had not been able to stand the idea that Tommy's picture—even broken—would not occupy its customary place on the wall, next to the twins and a little above a portrait of the entire family. She glanced across the pictures until she came to one of the judge and her mother. It had been taken a few years before her death. Her hair had turned a silver-white, but her eyes were wild and filled with life.

I will be more like you, Megan thought.

I will be stronger.

Megan looked into the eyes in the picture and thought:

I know what you would do.

What is that, dear?

You would fight for your child.

Of course I would. That is what women are here for.

We're here for lots of things.

Of course, dear. We're here to be lawyers and doctors and realtors and whatever you want to be. But when all is said and done, we're here for our children. You may think it sounds silly and traditional, but it's true. It is we who bring them into the world, and it is we who must guard them.

But Duncan . . .

Oh, Megan. I know, you're very modern. But he is a man and doesn't know.

Doesn't know what?

That the pain of childbirth is only the first, and then we endure many others.

I know that.

Then you know the other thing too, dear.

What's that?

That when we bring these children into the world, they never stop being the part of us that they once were. And that is why we fight for them so hard. We must fight to bring them out, then we must fight to see them grow. We never give this up, no matter how many other things occupy us. Never.

You're right.

Of course I am. Do you know what else?

What?

This is what makes us far stronger than anyone, even ourselves, ever realizes. This is why we are always being underestimated, mostly by men. Look inside yourself. There is steel and iron, sinew and muscle. Look deep. You will find it. And when you need this strength, it will be there.

I'm scared. I'm scared for both Tommys.

There is nothing wrong with being scared, dear. As long as we don't let it get in the way of doing what we must.

What we must. How will I know?

You will know.

Are you sure?

Totally.

"Then I am sure too," she said out loud.

She took a deep breath and sighed. Then she heard Karen and Lauren calling from the kitchen: "Mom! Are you okay? Is someone there?"

"No," she called back. "I'm just talking to myself."

She picked herself up and went in to where the girls were seated.

Duncan sat at his desk, figuring out how to raise money for Olivia.

He had spent much of the day on the telephone with his stockbroker in New York, a realtor in Vermont, and assorted other people connected to his assets. Each had been dismayed when he used the single word: sell. They had tried to dissuade him, yet he had persisted in a jocular way, worried that some of his panic would emerge, and someone would guess his needs and his plans. Consequently, he made jokes, told anecdotes, laughed and acted unconcerned—always trying to give the impression that he was doing something normal, as opposed to the actuality: liquidating his life's profit in order to buy another.

By noontime, he was starting to estimate how much, in theory, he had raised. He knew he would have to take a quick offer on the property, so he was ready to take a loss there. And the sale of the stocks and other investments would likely bring a check from his broker of more than $86,000. But it would take several days for that to arrive, and weeks before he would see any money from the sale of the land. His house was already mortgaged, but the mortgage was more than a half-dozen years old and he had a line of credit based on the equity he had established within it. He did not want instantly to exercise that money—he figured when it came time, he would need those funds to make good on what he would steal. That's the trouble with cash in this era: You can't get it unless you're willing to stick up a liquor store some ghetto night. Cash is outdated. Money is all on paper now, in plastic cards and computer banks. If you want some, you need to fill out forms in triplicate, undergo processing and examination, and then wait. He was mildly aware of the irony it presented: I have made so many people do exactly that, he thought. Now it is my turn to wait. But he guessed that, at least, he would have a check from his brokerage house by the following week, which would be enough to make a minimum down payment on what he would owe the bank.

I should take the money to Las Vegas or Atlantic City. Play blackjack or the slots and try to walk away a winner. I would have just as much chance there. Because that is what I'm doing—gambling.

Duncan shrugged. He would do what she asked. Then, afterward, he could try to work his way through whatever the consequences might be.

First, he told himself, get Tommy back.

He kept his mind on the problem of stealing the money and then trying to outguess how she would want him to hand it over. It must be a direct transfer, he thought. I must force that on her—I'll hand her the money and take Tommy from her. Don't trust her for an instant. He continued trying to anticipate Olivia's maneuvering, although he did not expect to hear from her or any of the other kidnappers, that day.

She will let me stew. She knows how much pressure she's created already, and now she will let her silence simply build. The more tension she is able to deliver to me, the more willing she expects I will be to do precisely what she asks, without question. She recognizes that it is equally terrible to hear from her as to not hear from her.

For an instant he was pleased with his understanding. I know Olivia, he thought, better than she thinks. I must use that knowledge. Somehow I've got to put her off-balance, just a little, not so much that she panics but just enough so that she begins to realize that this arrangement has two partners, who will have to cooperate to succeed. I must make her recognize that she calls the shots only just so far— and that ultimately we are sharing this thing.

She must be made to deviate, just a little, from her design. Just enough so she recognizes this is a business deal.

And then I will have a real advantage, because I know how to make a deal, and she doesn't. I know how to squeeze her, cut her loose, and finally, cut her out.

I understand money: How to make it. How to steal it.

He felt a sudden surge of confidence that evaporated almost as swiftly as it arrived. Sure, he thought, I know about banks and stocks and bonds, playing the float, and all the accessories to money. But she understands the commerce of revenge.

He shrugged away fear and concentrated on robbing his own bank. It was ironic—if he merely wanted to embezzle money, he would use the bank's computers, setting up phony accounts and channeling money through them. That's the way things are done now: a little bit of creative mathematics with a few interest charges from large accounts, slide the money electronically into some dummy account, then retransfer it into a branch of some offshore Bahamas bank. He'd known a competitor who'd been caught in a similar scheme. He'd been caught because he'd made one fundamental mistake: He'd gotten ambitious. Like all things connected with money, success was the father to greed. If you were more modest, if you thought of simply becoming comfortable instead of becoming rich, then it wouldn't be so hard to avoid detection.

He had a sudden memory of going into a five-and-dime store as a child, with one of his neighborhood friends. The boy had been a magnet for all the other children; a little older, a little wiser, filled with the runaway sophistication of youth. A wild child. Freckle-faced, red-haired, wiry tough, the son of a local police officer, which gave him a sort of license in the other children's eyes, he was the one who always rode his bicycle down dead man's hill, and the first to try to smoke a cigarette. He was the one who walked on the ice on Fisher's pond first, even when it made little creaking noises beneath his feet. He would be first into the quarry in the summertime, splashing about in the cold black waters, laughing at the other kids, who were troubled by the mundane considerations of the huge NO SWIMMING—DANGER sign posted there by the town fathers. And I was always second, Duncan thought. I always hesitated that one instant that kept me from being first—but I threw myself in, right away. It was as if everything was a dare, once done, to do again. I was always next in line, turning my momentary reluctance into a sort of guilt that drove me to prove myself immediately.

He remembered the boy had wandered one aisle in the store and up the next, as if searching for something specific, but in reality, as he passed a shelf filled with candy bars, looking only for the right moment. His friend pocketed several, then, with the bravado born of wild youth, walked up to the register and asked the women behind the counter if they had any get-well cards for his sister, who was in the hospital. The woman pointed out the proper aisle, where the boy hesitated only an instant before saying thank you, but those aren't what I had in mind, and exiting. In the street outside, he showed the others what he'd stolen. Then he had looked at Duncan and said: Now you do it.

And so Duncan tried.

He saw the woman behind the counter eyeing him, as he did what his friend had done, walking up and down the aisle. When she turned away, he seized a single candy bar from the shelf and slid it into his pocket.

Then, as his friend had done, he approached the woman. I suppose you want a card for your sister, too? she asked sarcastically, and Duncan knew, in that moment, that she knew everything, that his friend had gotten away with nothing that the woman had not allowed for whatever reason. Instead of speaking, he dug into his pocket and pulled out a quarter, which he slapped down on the counter. Then he started to run, although he'd paid for what he'd thought he was stealing, but the woman called after him, Hey! You've got change coming. No, he'd said, no, we owe it, we do, thinking of the candy his friend had taken, and then he ran from the store.

He had been nine.

A failure of nerve, but it was a small town and my father would have punished me if he'd learned. Duncan thought of his parents for the first time in many years. They had both been teachers, though his father had risen to administer the junior high school in their upstate New York town before his death. They both died in the midst of their old age, when he was just starting his senior year in college, in a car wreck on a wet fall night.

A state trooper, all clipped and emotionless, had called him that evening in his dormitory. He had taken the call on the telephone in the hallway, where a half-dozen other students had idly walked by, eavesdropping shamelessly, wondering whether it was a date he was talking with and whether she was pretty and had he gone to bed with her—then doubly curious when they realized it wasn't.

Hello, is this Duncan Richards?

Yes. Who is this?

This is Trooper Mitchell of the New Paltz barracks. I'm afraid I have some difficult news for you.

Oh.

Your folks have been killed in a car wreck on Route 9 near here.

Oh.

A tractor-trailer heading the other way jackknifed on some wet leaves in the rain. They were killed instantly.

Oh.

I'm sorry. I'm sorry to be the one to have to tell you this.

Officer, I don't understand. What do I do now?

Son, I can't answer that question.

Duncan remembered when his uncle called him, an hour later. A flighty man, whom Duncan had known only vaguely, he was near hysterics, calming only when he realized he had to make the arrangements for burial. It had all seemed so hurried, so quick. One instant they were there, the next gone. It was the only time in his life when he truly had wished for a brother or sister. The funeral had seemed so stiff and formal. There were no real tears, no real emotions, just a steady line of acquaintances who showed up out of duty. School officials. Teachers. Local politicians. It wasn't like when Megan's mother died. People loved her. But people didn't know my mother and father, so they had a handshake approach to their death.

I don't think I knew them much better, either.

That was why I decided I would be there for my children. I wasn't going to put things between them and me. Even if I stole a little time for extra work, or perhaps a tennis game on a summer morning, I repaid it. I always carried markers with me. I understood the debt that parents owe their children. We are like the banking window that never closes, constantly open for withdrawals. It never ends, and it shouldn't.

Duncan pictured Tommy again, in the small room. I could lose you, he thought. He saw all the times when he had spoken sharply, or denied him something, and thought: All those times and no way to make them up. All the little robberies where I've stolen some pleasure from my son—even if in the guise of teaching him something, or keeping order in the family.

With Tommy, I gave him things, I took away things, I tried to show him life, I took him when he felt his lowest and tried to restore him. That is what being a father is all about. And now there's a chance I won't be able to restore him again.

I won't let it happen. I won't hesitate.

He saw himself as a child again, always hanging back, just that single instant. Not now, he said to himself. It was as if he was ordering his heart with a precise, military command. I will not hesitate this time. Not for one millisecond.

Duncan rose, and walked to the doorway to his office. He looked through, out across the bank. It was rapidly approaching quitting time, and he saw the accelerated energy of the employees as they went through their day's-end routine.

Tomorrow, he thought, the bank will stay open late, to accommodate the Friday rush of weekend customers. Evening hours, five to seven P.M.

Only on this occasion, he knew it was going to stay open a bit later.

Judge Pearson and his grandson played paper, stone, and scissors in the attic room, trying to pass the time. They counted together, one, two, three, shoot! and thrust forward with closed fist, or spread fingers or flat hand. Paper covers stone. Stone breaks scissors. Scissors cuts paper. Tommy won, the judge won, Tommy won again. Time dissipated slowly. Over and over again, one, two, three, shoot.

The day had passed in fits and starts. At lunchtime Bill Lewis had promised to try to find them a pack of cards, but he had returned later, apologizing that he couldn't discover any. He told them he would get some at the store, if Olivia sent him out again, but only if she would allow it. He reluctantly told the judge that Olivia had decided against allowing them any reading material, or bringing a television set up to the room. Tommy had asked if there was a pencil and paper, so that he could draw, or write a letter, but Lewis shook his head. They were simply to occupy themselves as best they could. He was sorry.

Consequently, the two Tommys had spent as much time as possible playing word-association games. It reminded the judge again of being cooped up in a car for a long time. At one point he had Tommy do some calisthenics, to try to limber the boy up and burn off some of the energy that the judge knew was being stored to the breaking point within him. He joined the boy in the stretching routines, realizing that it would do no good to stiffen and slow himself.

He hated the boredom probably more than he hated the confinement. He despised himself for allowing their circumstance to become so banal, so passive. I must force myself to think, to come alive, he insisted, but he couldn't rise from the apathy of waiting.

It felt almost like a physical pain, like the gnawing discomfort of an aching tooth or the steady hurt of a twisted ankle. He realized that he was exhausted, but had done nothing except watch the time drain slowly from the day. It was as if the tension of their situation was, if not diminished, thrust backward. He hated the idea that Olivia or one of the others could walk into the attic room at any point and simply execute them. Then how bitter these last hours would seem, wasted in steady dull boredom. It would be a great evil to die after yawning away one's final minutes.

He looked over at Tommy, who had taken the nail they'd discovered in their first search of the room and was idly scraping away at the wood slats of the wall. The sound was like a tree branch scratching against a windowpane, thrust there by the wind. He saw Tommy cut his initials into the wood, then add his grandfather's, which made the old man smile.

"Put the date, as well."

"Okay," said Tommy. "Anything else?"

"No," the judge said. "Yes, wait. Put something down that's like a message."

"For somebody to read?"

"Yes. Like your mother and father."

"Oh," said Tommy. "That's easy."

He carved away rapidly, yet carefully, with a little boy's singularity of purpose. After a moment, his grandfather asked, "What did you write?"

"I put down: We miss you and we love you. Is that okay?"

"That's perfect."

"It's sort of like the letter they won't let me write."

"Absolutely."

Tommy handed the nail back to his grandfather, who hid it under one of the pillows. He wanted to ask what was going to happen next, but he realized no one knew, and was able to hold back. He looked at his grandfather and thought that the old man's face seemed paler, his hair whiter, and his skin almost translucent, and he worried that he might be getting weaker somehow. For an instant he shuddered and quickly pushed himself close to the old man.

"What's wrong, Tommy?"

Tommy shook his head.

"Come on, what's wrong?"

"I just got scared for a minute. I was scared of being alone."

"I'm here."

"I know. I was scared that maybe you weren't."

Judge Pearson swept his arms around the child. He laughed a little bit. "Come on, Tommy, I'm not going to disappear on you. I said at the beginning, we're in this together, and we'll see it through to the end. Don't you worry, I'll bet that pretty soon we're sitting in your mom and dad's house eating a pizza and telling them about our adventure."

"You think so?"

"Sure. And imagine how much fun it will be to see Lauren and Karen, too. I'll bet they'll want to hear everything about what has happened to us."

"They will, I know."

"So don't be discouraged. I know it's hard sitting around here. But it'll be over soon, and we'll have some stories to tell."

Tommy sighed and relaxed next to his grandfather. After a few seconds he spoke up again:

"Grandfather, tell me a story, please."

"Sure, Tommy. What sort of story?"

"A story about yourself, when you were young. A story about being brave when you were a Marine."

The old man smiled. "Once a Marine, always a Marine," he said.

"That's the motto of the corps: Semper Fidelis. Did you know that?"

"Yes." Tommy smiled. "You've told me that before. Always faithful."

"I've told you that before?" The old man laughed and poked the boy in the ribs. "You mean to say I've repeated myself?" He teased and tickled and Tommy squirmed about, finally breaking into a grin.

"Yes, yes, no, no, please, Grandfather. We shouldn't be laughing."

"Why not?"

"They might hear us and get angry."

"Well, that's their tough luck. We shouldn't let them scare us all the time. And anyway, a laugh is good for you. Did I ever tell you about the time laughter saved my life?"

"No. What happened?"

"Well, it was on Guadalcanal—you know about that place, right?"

Tommy nodded. "Unhuh."

"Well, my platoon was in the forward element. That means we were in the front of the whole battalion, and we were moving through the jungle. We didn't know where the enemy was, and we weren't sure whether he was going to attack us, or we were going to attack him. It was dark and scary and hot when we finally stopped for the night. We all dug in and stared out into the nighttime, waiting for orders, trying to get some sleep, worrying about what was going to happen. Did I ever tell you this before?"

"No, no, what happened?"

"Well, we all thought for sure we were going to have trouble. We knew the enemy was out there, and we knew he was waiting for just the right moment, so we were pretty nervous. Not so different from you and me up here, and the way we get nervous because we don't know what's going to happen at all."

"What about the laughter?"

"Well, I'm coming to that. There was this one man in the platoon, Jerry Larsen from New Jersey, so we called him Jersey Jerry, and whenever he got pretty scared, he would always tell a joke. Same joke, every time—"

"What was the joke?"

Judge Pearson had a sudden vision of himself hunkered down

behind some sandbags, young, sweaty, covered with the sandy dirt of some island battlefield and hearing about the Lone Ranger and Tonto, and another bunch of wild Indians and Silver the Wonder Horse. And he remembered the punch line: I said posse, not pussy, you dumb horse. He smiled. Posse, not pussy. He looked back at his grandson and wondered whether he knew the word. Maybe, maybe not. It was always hard to tell what children knew and, more, what they understood.

"Well, it was an adult joke."

"A dirty joke?"

"Yes. Who told you that phrase?"

"Karen and Lauren."

"What else have they told you?"

"Oh, not that much. They tell me I'm too young."

"Well, you are."

"Oh, come on, Grandfather, please."

"You are."

"Will you tell me the joke?"

"When you're older."

"Oh, Grandfather."

"When you're older. As old as Karen and Lauren."

"Okay," Tommy said reluctantly. "So what happened?"

"Well, anyway, we'd all heard the joke a million times, because we'd all been scared at least that much. But the really strange thing was, the joke was always funny. Even if we knew the punch line, even if we knew exactly, word for word, every bit of the joke, it was always funny. And it wasn't such a great joke to begin with, either. But for some reason, I don't know why, but I guess it had something to do with tension, it always made everybody in the platoon break out in laughter and giggles . . .

"Anyway, it's 'round about three in the morning and most of the platoon is trying to sleep, except for Jerry and me and a couple of other guys, who are on guard and right nervous because it always seems like the jungle is moving all around us, no matter what time it is, and it's really hard to tell whether the sounds are animal sounds or people sounds. It's hot and we're tired and suddenly I can hear

Jersey Jerry a few feet away start to tell the joke. I'm kinda mad, kinda scared, trying to get him to shush up, but he goes right ahead and tells the joke and I start to laugh. Not real hard, mind you, just a little bit. But it wakes up the man next to me, who rolls over and says: 'What is it?' and I say, 'Jerry told the joke again.' And he groans, but because he knows the punch line by heart, like everybody else, he kinda laughs too. And that wakes up the lieutenant, and a few others. And within a few seconds we're all awake and whispering and getting angry with Jersey Jerry for getting everybody up, when I hear something that's a little different, right in front of the platoon—"

"What's that?"

"Well, it turned out to be an enemy squad, moving in front of our position."

"What happened?"

"We had a fight, and we won."

"Really?"

"Really."

"Shooting and everything?"

"Yes. We called in for artillery, too, so there were great big explosions. It was like being caught right in the middle of the fourth of July fireworks. Scary and beautiful all at the same time."

"Did you shoot anyone?"

"Yes and no."

"What do you mean?"

"Well, it was so dark it was hard to see. I was shooting my rifle like everybody else, but I don't know if I hit anything or anybody. But that's not the point. The point is, if we hadn't all been awakened by the joke, then we would have been taken by surprise and maybe we wouldn't have won."

"Oh. I see. Well, what happened next?"

"By morning we were in a big battle. But that's another story. But I'll say this. After that night, we had a rule: Jersey Jerry told the joke every time the going got tough. It was like a good luck charm, because it saved all our lives that night."

"Like a magic saying?"

"Right."

"We should think up something like that."

"All right, let's try."

Judge Pearson felt a sudden harshness inside. It wasn't the best magic saying, he remembered. He had an abrupt vision of walking past his friend's body, months later, on a different island. He had been shot through the forehead by a sniper, and his body was rigid and mocking in death, as if sneering to hide his jealousy at those who lived on. Judge Pearson remembered how much he'd hated seeing those men who were killed by a single shot, or a single piece of anonymous flying shrapnel. In an odd way, he preferred to see the men whose bodies were ripped and torn apart by great explosions, shredded by machine guns, blasted by mines. It was as though their deaths were less capricious, less specific. If Jersey Jerry had ducked his head a millisecond earlier, he would have lived. In a battle where murderous hunks of metal were filling the air, death was somehow logical and understandable. How could one expect to live through the firestorm? But he despised the idea of someone sighting down a rifle barrel at his heart or his brain and uniquely stealing his life.

But even after he died, we still told the joke. And it seemed to work for us, if only a little bit.

"Grandfather? Here's a riddle I learned in school: What walks on four legs in the morning, two legs at noon, and three legs in the evening?"

Judge Pearson knew the answer, although he had not heard the saying in decades.

"I don't know, Tommy. What, some sort of bug?"

"Man!" said the boy. "When he's a baby, he crawls on his hands and knees. When he gets a little older, he walks on his two legs, and when he gets to be old, even older than you, Grandfather, he uses a cane to help him walk. That's three."

Judge Pearson laughed. "That's a fine riddle," he said.

"How shall we make it into a magic joke?" the boy asked.

"We'll just say, tell the walking riddle, and then we'll both know what we mean. How's that?"

"The walking riddle. Okay."

Tommy reached out and took his grandfather's hand in his. The two of them shook with mock solemnity. Then they both smiled and laughed.

"Do you think it will work like magic?" he asked.

"Why not?" Judge Pearson replied.

"That's right," Tommy answered firmly. "Just why the hell not?"

"Tommy!" the judge said. "Who—"

"Well, that's what my dad says when he gets a little mad and wants to sound a little strong and angry, like, 'Tommy, why the hell won't you get into the bath,' or something like that."

The judge laughed out loud at the boy's perfect imitation of his father's voice. We forget sometimes that we are raising little mirrors, on which we etch everything, he thought.

Tommy smiled and stood up.

"Grandfather, one thing has bothered me all day. It's the first time I've ever spent an entire time, like a whole day, without seeing the sky. I don't know what sort of day it was outside. I mean, even when I was sick at home, I still had my window. And even when I was younger and I would have to go to the hospital and have all those tests, I still would know somehow. Somewhere I would see out and I could think about what sort of day it was and what it would be like if I were outside playing. But here I can't tell whether it rained or snowed or if the wind blew or the sun shone, or maybe it got a little warmer and I could have gone to the playground at school with just my sweater on. We can't tell anything in here and that sort of bothers me." Tommy shook his head. "It's just like we were in prison."

The judge got up and stood next to the boy. Prison, he thought. An odd combination of ideas started to form within him.

"Well, let's see. Let's try to guess. What do you think?" he said, but all the time he was mentally chewing over what his grandson had said.

"All right. But how?"

"Well, if it had rained, we would have heard the rain hitting against the roof and running in the gutters. They must be right outside the attic, so right away, we can rule that out."

"Okay. No rain. But what about snow?"

"Good question. But when it snows, there's a way that you can feel it lying on the roof. It makes it colder. Here, let me hold you up and you feel, and tell me if you can sense it."

The judge was guessing about this.

Nevertheless, he reached down and lifted his grandson up, so that the boy could stretch and touch the ceiling.

"It's cold," Tommy said, "but not so cold."

"So, what do you think?"

"No snow," said the boy.

The judge put the child down and Tommy went over to the weak spot in the wall. He put his ear up and remained there silently for a few seconds. Then he shivered.

"But real cold. I could hear a bit of wind, too."

"So, let's figure the temperature has continued to go down and the wind is blowing a bit."

"Now, how about the sky? Cloudy or clear?" Tommy asked.

"That's got me stumped," Judge Pearson replied. "Sometimes the wind will clear out the clouds. Sometimes it blows strongly and they seem to collect."

Tommy shivered again. "I think cloudy," he said. "I think there were lots of big gray clouds overhead and people took their boots to school and work because they were afraid it would snow. The cold air feels damp, like that little bit that gets inside you right before it starts to really come down hard."

"Well, last year we had six inches of snow two weeks before Thanksgiving, remember?"

"And Christmas we went sledding over at Jones Farm."

"So, it could be getting ready for real winter."

"I hope so," Tommy said. "This year I'm going to play ice hockey in the peewee program."

The judge turned away. This year, he thought. He had an overwhelming desire to hide his head from the reality of their situation, but instead he sat and saw Tommy walk to the weak spot in the wall. The boy touched the wood gingerly, pushing at the planks.

"Grandfather," Tommy said, "I think we should start trying to get these free. Maybe take the nail and scrape away at them, like you thought. It would give me something to do."

Judge Pearson saw the boy's look of doubt, and thought suddenly: Why the hell not?

He stood up and said, "Dammit, Tommy, we've sat about too much. Let's try that."

He stepped over to the wall and knelt down to inspect it. "Okay," he said. "We're going to start. Quietly."

But as he stood up and turned to get the nail from its hiding place, he heard footsteps in the hallway outside their locked door. "Back to the bed, Tommy!" he whispered urgently. But his head was churning with another thought: She has put us in this prison consciously. But she has also told us, without thinking, how to act. What did she do? She slugged the guard her first day. She plotted out all the terrible details of what she's doing. But what she didn't do was what I have been doing: sitting around and feeling sorry for myself.

Tommy jumped across the attic and the judge followed behind him as the door opened and Olivia Barrow walked through. She carried a small tape recorder in her hand.

"Hello, gentlemen," she said briskly. "Keeping ourselves amused, are we?"

The judge just glared at her. He noticed that Tommy, too, frowned instead of shrinking.

"During my eighteen years of paid government vacation, I spent precisely six hundred and thirty-six days in what was called administrative segregation, which is bureaucratic-speak for something any person familiar with old Jimmy Cagney movies would know as The Hole. It wasn't nearly as nice as this, judge, but you're probably getting the idea."

"So what now?" Judge Pearson asked angrily.

"I just need to steal a little part of you, judge. And a little bit of the boy there, as well . . ."

"Forget it," the judge said.

She paused and let the silence between them grow for an instant.

"Do you remember the Getty kidnapping, judge? The billionaire's grandson? Not that long ago, now, was it? Anyway, those kidnappers had their sincerity doubted. They ran into extraordinary reluctance on the part of the old moneybags to come up with the bucks. Very bad move. Bad business, all around. They had to demonstrate quite graphically the sincerity of their intentions. Do you remember how?"

Judge Pearson felt as if he'd been struck in the stomach. Images flooded back from the evening news and the newspapers, all of the same horrific event: The kidnappers had lopped off the boy's ear and sent it to the reluctant billionaire.

He squeezed all his muscles together and felt a rise in anger. I won't have it anymore, he thought. I won't allow her to twist and threaten. No more.

He realized he was on his feet, and had pushed Tommy behind him.

"You won't touch anyone," he said coldly, evenly.

Olivia put her face a few inches away from him.

"Don't give me orders," she said.

"You won't touch him."

"Who are you to say what I can and can't do?"

She suddenly thrust a revolver barrel up under the judge's nose. He didn't move. He didn't acknowledge the presence of the weapon.

"You won't touch him," he said again.

For an instant, the two remained frozen in position. The judge was aware of the barrel pressing cold against his face, of her finger on the trigger.

Then she lowered the weapon.

"Very tough, judge, very tough. Good show."

She stepped back. Then she mockingly clapped her hands together.

"Very strong showing by the underdogs. I admire will and determination, judge. Probably the only things I do admire."

She let out a small laugh.

"We probably have more in common than you think," she said.

The judge relaxed suddenly, but he narrowed his eyes and continued to glare at her.

"Yes," he said. "We're getting to know each other a little bit better now, aren't we?"

She paused, not answering directly, but nodding slowly.

"But still, I need something from you," she said. "And now you will cooperate. I will even ask nicely: Please. Pretty please."

She tried to bait him with the sarcasm in her voice, but for the first time was unsuccessful, and for an instant he thought he saw a different anger flashing in her eyes, one with perhaps a small element of doubt at its core. Then, just as swiftly, it was gone, replaced by the steady burning determination that he'd come to anticipate.

The judge looked down at the recorder in her hand and envisioned himself more than forty years younger, waiting for the dawn's fake promise of security with his friend in the jungle foxhole. Posse, not pussy, you dumb horse. He said the joke to himself and felt stronger and alert, as he had on that awful, clammy night in the past.

Megan called Karen and Lauren: "Girls, come on!"

They were at her side in a moment, their voices raised with instant questions: "Is something wrong?" "What is it?"

Megan shook her head. "No, I just need some fresh air. We all do. I took the phone off the hook and we're all going to go outside and get some air for a couple of minutes. Get your coats."

The twins nodded in unison and started throwing on winter clothes. Megan looked at them and for an instant thought about how she loved each differently, although she always thought of them together. Karen has her father's sturdiness and cool, appraising eye. Lauren is more emotional, more willing to give in to fantasy and adventure. More like me.

She gestured at the girls. "Come on, we need to look at something."

They followed her out, quieted by curiosity.

Megan saw the last moments of day skulk from the gray sky and felt night chill pull at her. She shivered away the discomfort and saw the twins pull their coats closer to their bodies. She walked down the path to the sidewalk, then turned and looked back at the house.

"How long have we lived here?" she asked.

"Mom! Come on, you know," said Lauren quickly.

"Eight years. Since right after Tommy was born, remember?" Karen said. "I remember nothing worked at first and the house seemed too big."

"And the furnace went out the first winter, and we almost froze that one night. Brrrr, I'll never forget that," Lauren said quickly, "because Karen looked like a Martian wearing socks on her hands, and that silly old red hat. And there wasn't enough room in the downstairs closet for all the winter coats, and it got lousy television reception, so we couldn't watch our shows. I mean, now it's okay because of the cable, but I thought it was crazy when we moved in."

"Do you know why I loved this house?" Megan asked.

"The neighborhood?" Lauren tried.

"It's got good schools," Karen pointed out.

"No," Megan said. "Because it was the first house that I really felt was mine. When you guys were born, we were still living with Grandfather and Grandmother. Then we moved into a rental house in Belchertown, then a ranch-type house in South Deerfield, which we bought because Duncan got a good deal on the mortgage. But I hated those places, because they weren't like me. This house was. I know things didn't work quite right at first, but I always felt like this was our home, more than any other place. It was where you guys really grew up. It was here Tommy got started, and where he had all his struggles. Because this was the place where Duncan and I were home. You know, the first Christmas after your grandmother died, when instead of going there, Grandfather came here, do you remember?"

Both girls nodded.

"I wanted to cry that Christmas. Not because my mom was gone, which was sad and terrible and made me lonely, because I still miss her, but because I had finally, I don't know, stopped being someone's child and started being myself. She would have understood that. You won't understand it for some time, but someday you will. It's not wrong to have your own life, or to want to be on your own. But it's hard to find your way sometimes."

"Is that what happened with you and Dad?" Karen asked. "I mean, back in the sixties."

"Sort of. We were looking for something. Everyone was. It took a long time to figure it all out."

Megan thought of peace signs and long hair, American flags burning, bell-bottom jeans and ragged leather vests. The music of revolution thumped in her head, heavy bass beat and screeching guitars. Columbia. Berkeley. Haight. The summer of love. Woodstock generation, followed by Altamont and Kent State. Up against the wall. Her pulse quickened.

"It wasn't wrong, what we did," she said. "It may seem like it now, but it wasn't wrong then. No—" She hesitated, then continued. "Well, the robbery was always wrong. But it was hard to see it that way, back then. And it seemed like such a smaller wrong, in comparison with all the others that were happening all over the world, every day."

"But you changed?" Lauren asked.

"Well, yes and no. The world changed. We went along with it. It was as if the whole world wanted to forget about all the things that happened then, and we wanted to be forgotten right alongside. Maybe that was a mistake, you know. Maybe people should have kept worrying about all the things that we worried about then. But it was such an intense time, and I guess the world couldn't stand it. So things became calmer, more sedate."

"But Olivia, she didn't change?" Lauren asked.

"That's right."

"How could she?" Karen said. "She was in prison. All she could see was how the prison changed. Not her."

"That's right, too," Megan replied softly.

"That's probably why she hates us so much," Lauren said.

Megan nodded. She was about to say something, but instead she paused, looking up at the sky. She could see the moon hanging over the treeline, shedding wan light through the stark branches. "The year you guys were born, 1969, a man landed on the moon. It probably doesn't seem so remarkable for you, what with the space shuttle and all that you've grown up with. For Duncan and me, too, it was pretty much what we'd expected. We'd grown up with the bomb ourselves, and technology was something we were all used to. But I remember sitting with Grandmother and Grandfather, nursing you two, watching it on television. The incredible thing was not that we landed on the moon, but the way your grandparents stared at the television screen in amazement. They said it was because they were born back in the twenties, when the world was so new to technology. They were children of a depression. Airplanes were barely invented. They had grown up on Buck Rogers and they had never thought it possible that they would see man go to another world. That was something reserved for science fiction."

She looked at the house again. "I grew up in this town," she said. "Just like you and Tommy have. This is our place. It always will be. Even if you two and Tommy grow up and move away, you'll always be able to come back here and feel, I don't know, right, maybe. At ease. No matter how much it changes and you change."

"Mom," said Lauren, with a somewhat bemused tone, "you sound like Scarlett O'Hara."

Karen stifled a little laugh and added, "Or Judy Garland in *The Wizard of Oz*. There's no place like—"

She looked over at the two girls and saw them share a quick glance between themselves and inwardly she smiled. *They must think I'm crazy or senile. The tension has gotten to me and I've stepped over the edge.*

Maybe they're right.

She shook her head, clearing her mind. She let the frigid air fill her lungs and seep through her body.

She remembered her father taking her on a camping trip into the Maine woods when she was about ten. She and her mother had wandered away from the campsite, picking wild berries in a field. As they stepped through the brambles, they'd spotted a mother black bear and her two cubs, two dozen yards distant. The bear had risen up, freezing its position, staring at Megan and her mother. The two families had watched each other momentarily, sharing the same meadow, picking the same fruits. Then the bears scuttled off in an unhurried and unafraid fashion. Megan remembered her father warning them later never to get between a mother bear and her cubs, because then the she-bear would suddenly turn savage and dangerous. She recalled her own mother's soft, matter-of-fact response: So would I.

Megan turned to the twins and said, "You must know something. We are not going to lose it. We are not going to lose our family. I will not allow it."

"Mom!" Lauren said. "Of course not!"

"Don't worry, Mom," Karen jumped in. "We're not going to let it happen. None of us are."

"You know, Mom," Lauren said, "there's nothing wrong with the way we live. Nothing at all. You guys tried to do what was right. You tried hard."

"Why should we feel guilty?" Karen asked.

"That's right," Megan said. She suddenly threw her arms around the twins and hugged them close. She noticed that for the first time, Lauren's eyes were red with the first moments of tears and Karen seemed to have set her jaw with a bulldog tenacity. She watched as the elder half-punched her sister on the arm, as if to tell her to shake loose from emotionalism and straighten up. My daughter the drill sergeant, Megan thought. And my daughter the poet. She saw Lauren stiffen and nod, and she sensed a small moment, as if the heat from the girls' closeness had abruptly thrown back the evening cold.

She was filled with an indefinable mother-pride and she put her arms around her daughters, and they walked back into the house linked together by the first few strands of defiance.

Duncan sat at his desk and went over his checklist.

I am an organized person, he thought. Even when it comes to an act of considerable desperation, I still draw up a list of items to be attended to, down to the smallest details. Be prepared. He smiled. I was a good scout, a patrol leader. I reached Star. How many merit badges did I get? A bunch. For knot-tying and canoeing and semaphore-signaling and woodsman's skills. He shook his head at the memory. Those were the only medals I ever deserved. He looked again at his list. Would I get a merit badge for bank robbery? He smiled. Maybe this time. Certainly not for the first.

The list was written on a yellow sheet of legal paper and was headed with: INSIDE THE BANK with subheads for ALARM SYSTEM, MAIN VAULT, AUTOMATIC TELLER MACHINES, and RED HERRINGS. He scribbled an admonition at the bottom: Destroy this paper/Destroy six sheets beneath. The FBI had spectrographic machines that could read the minuscule impressions made by the weight of his ballpoint pen on the clean sheets beneath his list.

I make good lists, he thought.

It was no different when the family went on vacation. It was always up to Duncan to make certain that there was a bag with dry shoes and socks and extra sweaters, that extra juice and crackers were placed in the car for the children. He was always in charge of making certain that the bills were paid on time, and on Saturday mornings he would set out for the grocery store and stock the house with fundamentals. He wondered why he took such satisfaction in preparation. He always knew what the weather report was, knew precisely whether an invitation required a jacket and tie, or jeans and a sportshirt. It was always a shock to his wife or to the children when it rained and he hadn't packed raincoats.

He stared again at the paper. He had a single bitter thought: I should have planned the fucking robbery in Lodi. I would have anticipated the guards' reactions. I would have had run-throughs and trials, and spent weeks observing the bank. I would have pulled it off. Then none of us would be in this mess.

Duncan stopped his train of thought when he realized what he was concluding: I would have made a better damn criminal than she.

He stood up and went to his door, looking out over the bank. The inside of the main room seemed to glow with light and activity. He could see closing preparations under way. The tellers were totaling their drawers and sorting receipts and checks. Everything was routine, which is the way bankers like it, he thought.

He watched as one of the assistant managers went to the passageway that led to the automatic tellers. Duncan knew what the man would do: He would open the back of each and check to be certain that it contained enough funds for overnight. The same man would walk the same route the next day, only this time he would ascertain that the machines were full. There were four out in the lobby. Each carried $25,000 in ten- and twenty-dollar bills. On a busy weekend, like homecoming at one of the colleges, or Labor Day or Columbus Day, each would dispense almost half that amount in small twenty-dollar to two-hundred-dollar transactions.

Not this weekend, he thought.

As he watched, the assistant manager returned from the corridor and walked into the president's office. There was a drawer there where keys were kept. Just about everyone in the bank knew about the duplicates in the office and that was the beauty in Duncan's plan. Just about everyone in the bank knew how it operated, knew where the alarm system shutoff was located, knew where the master keys were kept. We are still a small, friendly organization, he thought. That is what makes us vulnerable.

The security here is designed to prevent three things: someone breaking into the computer system from within or without; someone, a stranger, breaking into the bank after everyone has left; some wild-eyed bank robber walking through the front door and pulling out a gun.

He remembered when the bank officers had talked things over with the security analysts who'd put the alarms in, and who had programmed the computers to recognize the most common kinds of frauds. It had been the major concession to the larcenous nature within everyone, bank managers included. It had never been contemplated that someone who knew the bank would rob it like some Jesse James or even Willie Sutton.

He went back to his list and looked at it carefully. He added a category: CLOTHING. Under this he wrote: Gloves. Sneakers. Jeans. Sweatshirt. At the Mall.

His secretary knocked on the door and walked into his office. He did not try to hide the list. Instead, he picked it up, fingered a pencil, and rocked back in his chair, so that she couldn't see what he was writing.

"Mr. Richards, I'm taking off now. Anything I can do before I go?"

"Thanks, Doris, but I'm leaving in a minute myself."

"Are you feeling better?"

"No, not really. It just sort of comes and goes. Could be a virus of sorts, I guess. I've been running a little temperature all day."

"You should stay home."

"Well, tomorrow's Friday, so maybe I'll take off early and spend the weekend in bed."

"Doesn't sound like much fun."

"Well, Doris, when you get as old as I am, you don't think of the weekends for fun as much as to recuperate, anyway."

"Oh, Mr. Richards, you're not so old . . ."

"Thanks, Doris. Flattery will always get you ahead in this organization."

She laughed and gave a little wave, and left.

How old am I getting? Duncan considered. Closer to the end than to the beginning? He thought of his own parents; they were old when I was born, older still as I grew up alone in that quiet, stolid house. They were forever tired and slowed by life. He tried to remember some moment of unencumbered happiness, some Christmas-morning childish joy and abandon, some birthday awakening that was without care and caution, but he could not. It was always a house where everything was in place, where all times were set and all moments planned. I took that with me forever. I became a man of numbers. Did I hate that? he asked himself. Was that why I sought out the spontaneity of revolution? Olivia was always so vibrant. She took ideals and actions and rubbed them together and they became a sort of combustible mass in her hands. The rhetoric, the enthusiasm, the struggle; he remembered how intoxicating the entire time had been. I was really alive.

Duncan hesitated and thought: I was also terrified.

He looked outside, through his window, and saw some of the bank workers walking down a pathway toward the parking lot. They were laughing, but walking quickly, with their coats pulled tightly around them. He wondered what was so amusing. As he watched, he saw them march past the first row of cars in the office's parking lot, where he and the other officers had marked spaces. His stomach clenched with tension, as he recognized an omission. He immediately grabbed at his planning pad of paper and wrote: CAR.

When he looked up again, the group was gone. Purple-blue light from the streetlamp frustrated the darkness.

He realized abruptly how much he owed his own children. I could have become just as quiet and steady and boring as my own parents, but I didn't, and they are the reasons why. It was as if I traded a revolution of ideals for a revolution of responsibility.

And now, am I old? he wondered again. Do I still remember how to fight?

He did not know the answer to this question for certain, but he was absolutely sure he was going to find out in the next days.

The mother and two daughters stripped off their outerwear and headed toward the kitchen. The girls were chatting about the cold and wondering whether it would snow soon, and getting ready to make some hot chocolate, which sent a hook through Megan's heart when she remembered how much Tommy loved it. She paused to replace the telephone receiver in the hallway, in case Duncan wanted to call. She glanced at her watch and guessed that he would be heading home soon. She tried to relax, but couldn't.

Tommy should be here, she thought. It has been forty-eight hours now that I haven't been able to hold him.

"Mom! Do you want a cup?" Lauren called.

"It's good," Karen added editorially.

Megan did not trust her voice to answer, but she swallowed hard and replied: "Sure. Why not?"

As Karen handed her mother the cocoa, the telephone buzzed.

"That's our line," Lauren said. "I'll get it."

She went over to the wall phone and punched a button and lifted the receiver.

"Hello," she said. "This is Lauren."

"And where is your equally beautiful sister?" Olivia Barrow asked, without introduction.

For an instant, Lauren thought she couldn't breathe.

She knew who it was, but forced herself to answer:

"She's right here next to me. Who is this, please?"

Megan saw the color flee from her daughter's face and dropped her cup to the floor. The cup broke with a crack that was lost in the sudden smothering tension that filled the room. The chocolate spread quickly across the floor, forgotten.

Karen seemed to hesitate, her own cup posed halfway between table and lip, then she whispered to Lauren: "I'm coming!" and dashed to the hallway, grabbing that telephone from its cradle.

"Who is it?" Karen demanded.

"Ah," said Olivia. "I can hear your father's voice. You have his tones, his inflections. Are you like him in other ways, as well?"

Karen didn't reply, but nodded her head.

"What do you want from us?" Lauren asked. She was struggling hard to control the quavering tones in her voice. She looked about wildly, first for her mother, then for her sister.

"I just wanted to hear your voices," Olivia said. "I just needed to know what you sound like."

Karen could not control herself. She thought it was as if she could see the words forming in her head, then bursting out from between clenched jaws.

"Give them back!" she near-shouted, her voice a quivering octave higher than usual. "We want them back! We want them back!"

Olivia simply laughed.

"All in good time, children. All in good time. Isn't that what the wicked witch is supposed to say?"

Megan felt the strength of Karen's loud demand and the ice within her shattered. She seized the phone from Lauren's hands.

"I'm here, goddammit."

"And Megan—good to hear your voice again."

"What is it, Olivia?"

"It's been so long, you know, and I've been thinking about you so hard. I just knew you would turn into the perfect little surburban matron, Megan. You always had that written all over you."

"What is it, Olivia?"

"And here I'd spent so much time talking with your squeeze, and neglecting you. But he's become such a *nice* fellow," she said. "Everything has become so *nice*."

"Olivia, please. Why are you doing this?"

"I would think that would be abundantly clear by this point."

Megan was silent for an instant.

"You think that revenge will make you feel better? You think that by torturing us you can restore all those years? You really think you can get some peace by doing this?"

Megan was shocked at the words that plummeted from her mouth. Lauren stepped back, looking oddly at her mother. She gave a small whoop, made a power fist and shook it in the air, and then charged to the downstairs library to pick up the telephone there. The questions surprised Olivia, and she hesitated before replying:

"Well, Megan, perhaps you're right. Perhaps revenge is a silly and inadequate way of dealing with this—"

Then she cackled.

"—but it sure beats whatever is in second place."

Olivia laughed and Megan swallowed hard.

Both women grew quiet for an instant. Olivia finally spoke.

"You got away with everything, didn't you? You got away with your life perfectly intact. Without ruffles, without creases. Your life wasn't bent, folded, spindled, or mutilated, was it? No way. You escaped, scot-free, just like it was some little kid's game. Only it wasn't, was it?"

"No."

"I was the one who remained true," Olivia said. "I was the one who never wavered. And look what we have today. A government that can't follow its own laws. A nation that lets people wander about mad and hungry on its city streets. Where getting rich is a religion. The ghettos are just as bad today as they were twenty years ago! You've done a helluva job with social change, Megan. A helluva job! You're just another complacent, what's-in-it-for-me suburban bitch."

Megan started to protest, but stopped.

"You think I'm evil and criminal," Olivia said. "But I'm not. That hasn't changed, Megan, and it never will. One person's commitment is another person's crime."

"Please," said Megan. "Please give them back."

"Win them back," Olivia said. "If you're brave enough."

Then she added: "Buy them back. That's the way you people think now, isn't it? Everything has a price. So, buy them back. What can you afford?"

"Anything."

Olivia didn't reply.

"What do you want?" Megan asked, after a moment.

"I told you. I wanted to hear your voice. I wanted to hear the twins' voices."

"You've heard them. What else?"

"A little message."

"Well, give it to me, then. You've already shown you can terrify old men and little boys. Now leave my daughters alone!"

She surprised herself with her vehemence.

Olivia was slightly taken aback as well.

She allowed the silence to grow on the line, before replying pedantically, "Terror is the most legitimate expression of anger. That has been shown over and over again."

"Old men and little boys," Megan repeated.

"And why should they be immune?" Olivia suddenly demanded. "Are they really so innocent?"

Megan was silent, but Karen jumped into the vacuum.

"They are! They never did anything to hurt anyone!"

"Karen!" Megan shouted. She had forgotten that both girls were listening. "Get off the line! I'll—"

"No! Let them stay on," Olivia said. "They should hear as well. Is Lauren there, too?"

"Yes," came her younger daughter's voice. It seemed a bit smaller than her sister's. "I'm right here."

Megan was about to interject something, but stopped herself. Olivia took a deep breath and asked:

"How is Duncan proceeding?"

"On schedule," Megan replied briskly.

"Good. It's always wisest to keep to a timetable," Olivia said. "Leaves less room for screw-ups."

"He will do what he has to."

"I know. At least, I think he will. But you must admit, Megan, that my experience with Duncan does not automatically lend itself to confidence." She laughed bitterly. "Especially where banking is concerned."

"Say what you mean."

"You know what I mean. He screwed up before. People died. He screws up again. People die. It's that simple."

Megan heard one of her daughters gasp, but she wasn't certain which. She shut her eyes and nodded her head.

"We understand that."

"Good. I thought it might be helpful if the twins understood it as well. Girls?"

"We heard you," Karen said quietly.

"I understand," Lauren added.

"Good," said Olivia.

"You'll never be happy, will you?" Lauren whispered.

"What?" Olivia asked sharply.

The girls were silent. Olivia was about to press them, but then decided to let it slide. It bothered her, but she forced herself to concentrate on the task that had prompted her phone call.

She fingered the small black box in her left hand. It was cold in the telephone booth outside the convenience store where she was calling. She watched as a car with a young-looking, but harried, man pulled up sharply to the curb, and he rushed inside. Probably needs milk for the baby, or diapers. She felt a disquieting sense about the conversation.

"All right," she said. "Listen carefully."

She lifted the small tape recorder up to the receiver and pushed the Play button.

Megan could hear the judge's voice, coming as if from some great and unattainable distance.

". . . Hello, Megan, Duncan, and the girls, too, if they can hear this. We are both fine. We are being treated adequately. Tommy is okay, except he misses all of you. So do I. He had one bad spell, but he seems to be over it now and is fine. We would like to come home. She hasn't told us what she wants you to do, but we hope you will do whatever it is and we can come home . . ."

There was a small pause on the tape, then Megan could hear her father snap, ". . . All right. Is that it?" and she heard Olivia's reply: "That was sufficient. Tommy?"

Another brief delay followed, before her son's voice scratched through the receiver.

"Hello, Mom and Dad and Karen and Lauren, too. I really miss you guys and I want to come home. Please, I want to come home because I miss you all so much. Grandfather is fine and I am okay. We play some games, but it isn't like home up here and I want to be home . . ."

She could hear her son's voice shake slightly and it was as if black ropes were thrown around her own heart and head.

". . . So bye for now and I really love you and I hope I'll see you soon because I miss you so much . . ."

On the tape, she could hear Olivia say, "That's fine, Tommy. That's enough now. Thank you."

She heard a clicking sound and then there was a small silence before Olivia came back on the line.

"Did that hurt, Megan? Was that painful?"

She did not reply.

"Girls?"

Karen and Lauren each had the sense to keep their mouths shut.

"I thought it might," Olivia said.

Megan took a deep breath.

"You've made your point," she said. "Let's get on with it."

"Tell Duncan," Olivia whispered. "Make him understand."

"When will you call?"

"When I know he has the money."

"How will you know that?"

"I'll know."

"But—"

"Goodbye, Megan. Goodbye, girls. Think about this, won't you: They've only been in prison for forty-eight hours. But I was there for eighteen years."

Olivia hung up the telephone, crashing the receiver down onto the hook.

Damn! she thought. Dammit to hell! She had a wretched feeling that she had done something wrong and she was at a loss to figure out what. She walked slowly through the early evening black and cold to her car, replaying everything in her head and thinking: I must keep control.

Megan held the telephone for an instant, listening to the emptiness before replacing it on its cradle. Her son's voice echoed through her and she could hardly stand. She slammed a fist onto the table in anger. She pictured him sitting alone in a tiny room and she desperately wanted to be able to reach out her hand to him. She had an odd memory, one that leaped unexpected into her head. It was of learning from her physician that she was pregnant, as she suspected. The news had arrived with a mixture of excitement and consternation; her life with Duncan and the girls had been so settled and ideal, and she was afraid that a baby would disrupt the magic symmetry of the family. She wanted to smile, thinking how naive she had been. She had had no idea what a disruption Tommy would prove to be. But the girls were the children of my youth, she thought, as the twins walked back into the kitchen. Tommy was the child of my maturity. He is the one who signaled my real beginning. He was the product of a steady, solid adult love, not the heady, wild passion Duncan and I had when we were electric young lovers. And if I lose him, I lose all I've built.

She turned toward the girls, who both seemed pale, but unbowed. She nodded to them, then put her arms around them.

Megan felt as if something within her had cracked and broken, like an eggshell, only to reveal something different inside.

She hugged her two daughters close to her and let black murderous ideas fill her to bursting.

8

FRIDAY

Shortly before dawn, Duncan sat on the floor in Tommy's room and for the hundredth time went over his checklist. The house around him was quiet, save for the ordinary clicks and creaks of darkness, the heating system starting up, the wind rattling some tree branches against a window, a sigh from the twins' bedroom, where their sleep seemed edgy and out of synchronization with the waning night rhythms.

"I can do this," he whispered to himself.

Duncan placed the list on Tommy's bed and stood up. The last hours before morning are always the most difficult. He remembered moments with his son, rocking him through the pre-dawn blackness, holding him in a wrestler's grip, as if all the boy's problems tugged and pulled at him, threatening to carry him away to some unreachable spot. Sometimes it had felt like a physical battle, holding off the stresses that clawed at his son.

Duncan's eyes drifted to his son's bureau top. He picked up a spotted brown and white turtle shell and held it in his hand, turning it over and over, rubbing his fingers across the dry, rough exterior.

Where did he get this? he wondered. What does it mean to him? He put the shell down and picked up a rock that seemed cut in two, exposing a quartz-like purple and white interior. And what secret does this hold? Two dozen toy soldiers had been lined up in opposing rows, knights mingled with Civil War figures and army commandos in some historically preposterous confrontation. Which side were you on, Tommy?

Duncan felt all the tensions and exhaustions of the last few days gather within him—then just as suddenly recede, like a wave running across the sand. He held his hands out in front of himself and asked, Who are you?

I am a banker.

No, you're not.

I am. I am a businessman and a father and a husband.

And?

That's it.

And?

That's it!

Liar.

Right. I'm lying to myself.

He looked down at the sheet of paper on the bed with his checklist. He examined all the details of the crime that he'd planned. I am a criminal, as well. I have been since that day in Lodi. It has always been within me, waiting to come out.

Then he shook his head. They've stolen my child. It is up to me to get him back. Why should I let anything stand in my way?

He thought of his own mother, then of Megan, and finally of Olivia. The three women in my life. My mother was impersonal and distant, ordered, spinsterish, without enthusiasm. Megan was filled with color and art and spontaneous, vibrant. She was everything my mother wasn't. And Olivia, what was she? Danger, rebellion, fury, direction.

Duncan remembered seeing her for the first time at a campus demonstration against Central Intelligence Agency recruitment. She had led a phalanx of students down a street, chanting slogans, waving banners, then finally breaking into a rush and throwing themselves

forward, filling the lobby of the administration building, disrupting
secretaries, admissions officers, and university personnel with screamed
imprecations. Vials of sheep's blood were splashed across desktops.
Papers were strewn about in the hurricane force of the takeover.
Chaos littered the scene, then redoubled with the arrival of the police.
She had been driven, possessed, he thought. Everything that she
touched seemed to burst into flame, as if she were some combustible
liquid. And I was drawn to her, irresistibly, at meetings for the
SDS, antiwar teach-ins, demonstrations, concerts, and finally, at
smaller, clandestine gatherings, in post-midnight darkness, grouped
around wine bottles and Marxist tracts, the air filled with cigarette
smoke and revolution.

Duncan sat back hard on Tommy's bed, thinking about the sim-
plicity of that time. There was right and there was wrong. We were
our parents' worst nightmare come true. Then he shook his head.
Wrong. This is a parent's worst nightmare. He thought of the first
time he'd seen Megan. He'd been wandering through the art department at college, looking for a quiet place to read through a physics
text, when he walked past a life drawing class. Megan had been
posed at the front, naked except for a towel thrown across her lap
in minimal modesty, her breasts jutting outward as if in defiance,
daring anyone to snicker or laugh. The students were sketching her
silently. He had stood in the doorway, stricken, eyes locked onto
her, until the professor went over and closed the door in his face.
The class had tittered, but instead of fleeing in embarrassment, he'd
waited outside, waylaying her as the students flooded out. He tried
to apologize, but instead stammered something silly and disjointed,
which she had listened to with a half-smile that spoke partially of
invitation and which caused him to bluster and trip on his tongue
until he was thoroughly ashamed and confused, more naked in his
desire to meet her than she had been without her clothes.

He warmed with the memory. He was always amazed at her
interest in him. It always seemed to him that she was a hundredfold
more exciting, that his work, his academics, his doggedness, was
dull and boring. His head was forever filled with theorems and
figures; hers with colors and bold pen strokes. She was filled with

confidence, he with doubt. He had never quite believed her devotion to him, the way she had followed him through his own academic wanderings, steady in her love, while he searched miserably for something elusive.

I would never have been brave enough to take off my clothes in front of a drawing class. I never had that freedom. I had to hunt for what was missing inside me.

He took a deep breath.

Instead, I found Olivia.

He settled back on the bed. She is right about one thing. It is a debt. You thought you would escape. But you were wrong. You have never escaped. A part of you has been waiting for this day for eighteen years.

All right, Olivia, he said silently. You've come for your pound of flesh. I will steal it for you. And then we will end this.

Duncan understood that after this night, nothing would ever be the same for him. It did not bother him nearly as much as he thought it would.

He rose up, overcome by a need to see the twins. He maneuvered through the darkened house to their doorway, peered in, and saw them flung into their beds, clothes strewn about the floor. There was just enough early morning light filtering through the window for him to make them out. For an instant he simply admired the way their hair fanned across the pillowcases, the way their limbs seemed supple, yet relaxed. He wondered if they had any idea the joy they had brought to his life. Probably not. Children do not understand what they are until they become parents themselves. Joy, terror, worry, and delight all wrapped together into an impossible knot of emotions. He shook his head, took one last look at the sleeping forms, remembered them, in that moment, as babies, as toddlers, as children, and now, as the near-adults they were. He made his way through the darkened house to his bedroom, and saw his wife where she had tossed herself in exhaustion a few hours earlier. He walked to her side and gently stroked her arm. Megan's eyes fluttered open and she reached out for him, still half-asleep. They embraced, and she blinked herself awake.

She said nothing, but surprised herself by pulling him down on top of her, forgetting, if only for a few seconds, everything that had happened, everything that would happen.

At breakfast Duncan announced that this day was going to appear completely routine: The twins were to go to school, Megan to her real estate office, him to the bank. Karen and Lauren squealed their objections immediately.

"But, Dad! Suppose something happens?" Karen said.

"We won't be home. No one will!"

"That's the point," Duncan said. "Go to school. Talk to your friends. Act as if nothing out of the ordinary has happened. Come home at your regular time. Do everything just as if it were a regular Friday."

"That's going to be impossible," Lauren muttered.

"No," Megan said, after getting over her initial surprise at her husband's request. "Your father's right. Today we must act as if nothing unusual is happening. I'll go to work. I'm going to smile and act just as if I hadn't a care in the world. We've got to keep what's happening to ourselves, and the best way to do that is to do nothing out of the ordinary."

The girls looked dismayed, and Duncan tried to cheer them up: "Look, we're going to be over this soon enough. I know you two can act it out for a day. You've fooled me enough times—"

"Dad! We haven't!" Karen said.

"At least not that often," Lauren added.

"You two have always said you wanted to be actresses—" Duncan said.

"But not like this!" Lauren interrupted.

"I don't see what this has to do with acting," Karen said.

"It has everything to do with acting," Megan replied swiftly. "We're all performers throughout this whole thing. So far, we've been acting like the victims we are. Well, starting today, we're going to begin behaving a little different. We're doing something, for goodness' sakes! That's different, right there."

The twins nodded slowly.

"You know," Lauren said suddenly, brightly, "there's a dance at the gym tonight. The annual Winter's Here/Mukluk and Parka dance . . . I think Teddy Leonard is expecting me to be there. And I know that Will Freeman has been trying to hit on Karen—"

"Lauren! He has not! We just were both interested in the same physics problem and got to talking."

"Well," Lauren drawled, "he *is* on the basketball team, and he *is* handsome and he *does* follow you around everywhere, and he *does* call every chance he gets, so I must be completely insane if I think he's interested . . ."

"Well, what about Teddy? Wanting to drive you home every day? What's that all about?"

The twins weren't bickering as much as teasing each other. Megan let them continue as they volleyed back and forth. She smiled over at Duncan, who shook his head in mock consternation. When there was a momentary lull, Megan interrupted.

"Karen. Lauren. I don't think going to a dance is the right idea right now."

"Oh, Mom, I didn't really mean it. I just was, well—"

"She was just being a bother," said Karen quickly, sticking out her tongue at her sister, who frowned at her.

"Well, it's okay. Just tell those boys that you've been grounded."

"They'll believe that," said Lauren.

"And remember: Be careful."

"How?"

"I don't know," Megan continued. "Just be alert. Anything out of the ordinary, even a little bit. Stick together and keep quiet, and be aware of what's going on around you."

Duncan broke in. "If you're scared, come home. Or call me or your mom. Or stick with some friends, but don't tell them what's going on. Use your judgment."

The girls nodded.

Megan wondered for an instant whether she was making an awful mistake. She fought against the urge to turn to Duncan and refuse to let the twins from her sight. But she understood the strength in what he was suggesting, and she forced herself to go along.

She watched them get ready and her doubts pulled her to the front door after them. She waited outside in the cold while they climbed into their car and pulled away from the curb. She continued to stare after them as they disappeared around the corner. She could see Lauren waving from a half-block away, and then they were out of her sight.

Olivia Barrow sat in an overstuffed armchair in the small living room of the farmhouse, burrowing about, trying to find a comfortable group of lumps. For a moment or two she remained staring out the window, across the back field, down to the woodline, in the direction where she had parked the judge's car, just beyond her sight. She made a mental note to go down to the hollow where she had stashed it and turn the engine over a few times, just to make absolutely certain that it was in good operating condition. A shaft of sunlight burst through the windowpane, bathing Olivia in a warm glow, and she shut her eyes and contemplated her design. For an instant she felt the heat of satisfaction, but then, as the light faded, shut off by a passing gray cloud, so did her sense of accomplishment, replaced by her own doubts. What did I do wrong? she asked herself.

She went over the conversation with Megan, in her head.

It was not the actual words that bothered her. Megan had responded just as she'd anticipated—her vulnerability has always been her emotions, Olivia thought. She has always placed a high premium on loyalty and honesty, and that is a great weakness.

But there was something—not defiance—Olivia was sensitive to that, but something within the tones of Megan's responses that bothered her. Something that insinuated an angle not anticipated, a direction not covered.

She shrugged it off, and looked about the room, surveying the blank walls, the empty fireplace, the threadbare furniture. She could hear Bill Lewis and Ramon Gutierrez moving in different parts of the house; this place has worn thin, she thought. We've been here two months getting ready for these few days and now it's almost time to leave. She wondered where they would head. Someplace warm. The house was always drafty; New England blasts of cold air creeping through the hallways, lurking in the corners.

In prison, it was always warm. Massive institutional boilers pumped out great surges of heat when the weather turned, which mingled freely with all the stored-up hurts and angers of confinement.

What will you do when you get out?

The question was at the core of everything in prison; it was the center of every conversation, every bad-tasting meal, every slow-passing day, every sleepless night. Getting out. Even the women doing time for murder were preoccupied with the idea, even if twenty, thirty years distant. I'm gonna find a man who'll love me right. I'm gonna get out of this fucking state. I'm gonna find my kids and settle down. I'm gonna live my life without bars. I'm gonna be free to do what I want. I'm gonna get me a little place and go back to living day to day. I'm gonna be a secretary, an office worker, a construction worker, a cleaning lady, a whore, a drug dealer. I'm gonna make some money hustling on the street so I can retire someplace comfortable. I'm gonna go back to what I was doing, only I'm gonna be smarter and I'm not gonna get caught. I'm gonna make just one more good score then get out for good.

She remembered a hundred, thousand, million conversations. I'm gonna this. I'm gonna that. None of the gonnas ever really came true. Too many I'm-gonna-go-straights came back in a couple of years, with a few new tattoos and a few new scars and some new plans and some new I'm-gonnas. There had been one woman, a tall, statuesque black woman, whom Olivia recalled with a small pang of grief. I loved her a little, she thought, not as much as I loved Emily, but a little. She was the only one to whom Olivia had admitted her own fantasy: I'm gonna get the people who put me here. The woman had nodded, and said, Remember, they won't be the same as they were when you came in here. So you're gonna have to find some different way of getting them back.

Did she die? Olivia wondered. Did the streets swallow her up? Probably. But she remembered the woman's advice, storing it away next to all the conversations she had had with Megan and Duncan in the early days of the Phoenix Brigade, conversations that had always started benignly, with some offhand question like: "So, where are you from?" and "What about your family?" or "When was the last time you went home?" But she had stored away all this knowledge and much more, and knew where to go when she got out, just as she would have known where to find any member of the brigade, even after eighteen years.

Olivia took a deep breath and blew out slowly.

It is all working. It is all on schedule.

Keep control. Keep control. Keep control.

She felt better, and went off in search of Ramon Gutierrez, wondering whether she should let loose a little of his unique brand of terror.

Tommy happily scraped away at the built-up dirt and plaster between the attic's wooden slat walls, feeling with his bare hand the cold air that blew against the side of the house. He thought for an instant that things were reversed, that the chill wind that awaited outside was caged and that he was trying to free it from captivity, loosening its chains and allowing it to soar skyward again.

Since morning, with his grandfather leaning over his shoulder and kibbitzing frequently, Tommy had worried free a half dozen wooden boards. Each time he reached a point where the board seemed ready to come loose from the framework, his grandfather had stopped him, gone to the metal cot, and retrieved the strut they had found earlier. Judge Pearson would then wedge the strut behind the board and gingerly tug at it, loosening nails and cracking the wood, until the two were sure that a single hard tug would strip the board out.

It was slow going. Whenever they heard any sound from the rest of the house, they would stop, clean up the area as quickly as they could, and retreat to their cots. Then, when things had grown quiet again, Tommy would be back at the wall, making steady inroads with the nail, fighting off fatigue and cramps, tearing away at the confines of their prison. As he worked, he fantasized about escaping. He could see himself leaping through the hole in the wall, jumping down to the pitched roof he knew waited for him outside. Then he would prance down the peak, swinging off the edge onto a porch, then leaping the final story down, alighting on the cold ground. He could see himself racing across the fields, down the roads, jogging steadily through the winter day, blowing icy breaths in front of him. The woods would give way to cleared land, then isolated houses, finally the outskirts of town. In his mind's eye, he could see Green-field's streets. He would cruise past his school, past his mother's office, past his father's bank, past the high school where Karen and Lauren went, no longer breathing hard, no longer fighting the cold air, no longer scared or tired, his feet barely touching the earth as he flew toward his own street.

He scraped harder. Stroke in, stroke out. Tug and pull. Gnawing like some determined rodent at the wall. I am a mouse, he thought, I will make a mousehole.

He saw his house, his family waiting for him.

Tommy gritted his teeth. His hand slipped briefly, and he felt a splinter jab into his finger. He bit back the sudden sharp pain.

I am a soldier mouse.

He pried a last particle of wood from the wall, and felt the rush of pleasure that he knew awaited him when he tumbled into his mother's arms. He thought, too, of the great bear-hugs that he would get from his father and the warmth he would feel from his father's body. Karen and Lauren would hug him and kiss him too many times, but he smiled and decided he would let them this time, though ordinarily he was too big and too grown-up for that sort of thing.

"Grandfather, I think I've got another one loose enough. Bring the metal thing."

Judge Pearson freed the metal slat, hefted it in his hand, allowing himself the fleeting thought of bringing it squarely down on one of his captor's heads, and approached the wall.

"Good boy, Tommy. We'll be out of here in no time."

"Try it."

The judge wedged the metal behind the wood and gave a short pull. There was a muffled cracking sound and then a creak, as the wood gave way.

"That's good," the judge said.

"Shall I keep at it?"

The judge straightened up. "Why don't you take a break—" he started, speaking easily. Then he stopped and held up his hand. "Shhhh!"

Tommy paused.

"Someone's coming!" the boy said. He felt as if someone had robbed him of his wind and he wheezed harshly.

They both heard a door squeak, and footsteps.

"Hurry!" said the judge.

Tommy frantically wiped the floor around the area with his hand, shooting dirt and wood chips into the corners of the room. He burst across the room and hid the nail beneath the cot's mattress. The judge had maneuvered the metal slat back onto the bed. They heard the dead bolt lock turn and they both looked toward the door. It was Bill Lewis, carrying a luncheon tray.

The judge relaxed, and stood, pausing to put his hand on Tommy's shoulder, trying to slow the boy's rapid breathing.

He won't notice, the judge thought. Olivia would immediately see in our eyes that something was amiss. But Lewis is not as alert.

"Sandwiches again, I'm afraid." The familiarity growing as each hour of confinement passed had put some jocularity in Lewis's voice. "I put some extra jelly on yours, Tommy. I'll try to whip up something hot tonight. Or maybe go out for pizza or chicken. What would you prefer?"

"Pizza," said Tommy, his head dizzy, responding by rote.

"Chicken," said the judge.

Bill Lewis smiled.

"We'll see." He pushed the tray toward them.

The judge took a sandwich from the tray, grimaced at the choices of cold cuts or peanut butter and jelly, then settled back, munching on bologna and mayonnaise. He pushed the tray toward Tommy, who reluctantly plucked peanut butter and jelly from the offering. The judge saw the boy take a tentative bite and glance fearfully at the spot on the wall where they were working. A sliver of fear raced through the judge, but he thrust it aside, reaching over and patting his grandson on the knee, trying to seize the boy's attention without being obvious. He turned away, and smiled at Lewis, thinking: Get out of here! But Lewis sat back on the bed across from the captives and stretched out. Damn! thought the judge. Leave us alone!

Instead, he asked, "How are things progressing?"

Lewis shook his head.

"She gives out all the information," he replied.

"Give me a break," said the judge.

"Look, Olivia makes the rules. This is her show, and so far everything has gone exactly the way she said it would. So why would I screw things around now?"

"Well, I don't see the harm."

Lewis shrugged. "Sorry."

"I mean," the judge continued, "what's the big deal? All I wanted to know was whether things were progressing. Surely you can answer that with a yes or no. Look at us. We're stuck up here without any contact with anyone except you guys. I don't see what the harm is in giving us a little bit of encouragement or whatever."

"I'm sorry. I said I was sorry. Give it a rest." He glanced around, as if making certain they were alone, then whispered, "Look, she says it's all going okay, so I guess we're getting closer to the end. But that's all I know and you'll have to settle for that."

The judge nodded. "It just doesn't seem fair to keep us in the dark so much, especially the boy."

"Life isn't fair."

"Now you sound like she does. You're not like her, really, are you?"

"What do you mean?"

"Just what I said. You're not like her."

"Sure I am."

The judge shook his head.

"I am!" Lewis protested. "I always have been, since we first met."

"When was that?"

"Back in sixty-five. A few years before the Phoenix Brigade. We were always together. You know—solidarity. All that sort of stuff."

"But she went to prison—"

"Yeah, and your daughter and son got rich. And I went underground."

"For how long?"

"I still am," Bill Lewis said, slightly boastful.

"But surely—" the judge started, then stopped.

"Surely what?"

"No, it's nothing, I didn't—"

"What?"

"Well, there must have been a point where you figured they'd stopped looking. No one gets pursued forever."

"Sure they do. Come on, judge. . . ."

Lewis lounged on the bed. He seemed to settle in, anxious to talk. Tommy watched him stretch out, and nibbled at his sandwich, each bite tasting dryer and harder to swallow. The dizziness in his head threatened to overtake his entire body. Not again! he yelled to himself. Stay here! But his emotions tugged and jerked at him, and he felt himself slowly but steadily drifting away.

"You know what it is, judge, living underground. There comes a terrible point when you don't know whether they've given up looking for you or not. It's the worst moment by far. You see, running isn't so bad. Your adrenaline is always pumping out, you're always alert, ready, prepared for anything. It's really like some intense upper, an amphetamine high. It's the best part of being what you would call a criminal. You're just constantly on edge, and it's exciting and sort of fun. But after a while, a few years maybe, perhaps a decade, you start to wonder. Everything around you has changed, but you haven't. Even if you're working, teaching high school math or building houses— I did both of those—or working on an oil rig in the Gulf of Mexico— now that was hard work, judge—even if you're doing these things, you know inside that it's all a lie. Really you're who you were and still running. And that's the terrible time. Because you don't have any idea anymore that there's someone out there actually looking for you. You see, without those anonymous cops or feds or whatever, the underground wouldn't exist. It would be irrelevant. So you wonder whether you've suddenly become irrelevant, too. Wasting your life only to end up as a footnote in some damn poly-sci major's master's thesis."

"So what happened to you?"

"Well, when I hit that wall, Ramon and I were together. I figured there was no way really to find out for certain if they still were after me. So I did the next best thing."

"Which is?"

"I got in touch with Olivia."

"I don't get it," said the judge.

"You've seen her, Judge. Haven't you figured anything out? They'll always want Olivia. They'll always hunt her. She's just got that sense about her that authority hates and fears, and they'll always hate her for it. Think about it. If she came in front of you, say for jaywalking or maybe littering, what would you sentence her to?"

Judge Pearson didn't hesitate:

"The max."

Bill Lewis threw back his head and laughed.

"So would I. So would I."

The two men were silent for a moment.

"You see," Bill Lewis finally continued, "that's what she gives me. A re-entry to a real life. I feel alive again. I'm doing something. Not just going from job to job, wondering all the time, watching everyone else build their own little futures while knowing my own was all in the past."

Judge Pearson shook his head, suffused with thoughts. He didn't know which way to bend the conversation, so he guessed.

"So you got in touch . . ."

"I wrote her a letter."

"A letter?"

"Sure. Prison authorities are always dumb, judge. They couldn't decipher the simplest code. I remember the opening lines: 'Dear Olivia, thanks for your note. Cousin Lew is fine. Bill is, too. They want to hear from you . . .' Lew is and Bill. Didn't take her too long to figure out who was writing."

"And you came up with this plan."

"Well, we stayed in touch."

"You don't seem like the sort of guy who'd get involved in this kind of thing."

"Hah! Shows how much you know."

"I mean, I can understand some of her hatred, she's spent so many years behind bars. But you've been out and . . ."

The judge let his voice trail into nothingness when he saw Bill Lewis's face contort.

He straightened up abruptly. He had a lanky basketball player's build, which made him seem to be towering above them. He suddenly pinched forward at the waist, leaning his face inches away from the judge's. Judge Pearson rocked back, almost as if he'd been struck. Lewis's face twisted, a mocking sneer and grin mingling frighteningly with a barely controlled rage.

"Your fucking children, pig! They cost me as much as her. You think my prison was any different! You think running and living underground is any different from being in jail? You know who died out there, on that fucking street in Lodi? She was my love, too. She was my wife! And we both loved Olivia! When Duncan fucked up, it cost me my future! Goddamn his eyes! My whole life, judge, my whole life! Do you know that I was a single dissertation away from a doctorate in applied engineering? I could have been a builder! I could have been something in the new world, if only that son of a bitch hadn't chickened out and left us! I ran, judge, I ran right from the moment he killed our future, right to this moment. Now, I'm collecting the toll for all those miles."

Lewis's force of recollection drove his arms into the air and he windmilled about above Tommy and the judge. His neck scar flashed red, as if keeping time with his clenched fists.

Tommy first recoiled, then thrust himself against the judge.

Judge Pearson recovered from his initial surprise and then remained sitting, ramrod straight, staring, unblinking, at Lewis's tirade. He could feel Lewis's rage and anger filling him and thought it strengthened him. He recalled a hundred moments on the bench when men just sentenced had lashed out at him. He had stared all those criminals down, and he fixed Bill Lewis with the same steady, unafraid glare that had quieted a thousand courtroom outbursts. He could feel the narrowing of his eyes, the set to his jaw, and it was like discovering a favorite old pair of slippers at the bottom of the closet and sliding them onto his feet. Olivia had told him how erratic Lewis was. She'd underestimated him.

Bill Lewis threw back his head.

"They owe me!" he shouted.

"Why? Because things turned out differently for them? The hell they do!"

"You don't know anything, you old pig! You've got no idea."

"I know that what you did was wrong and that what you're doing is wrong."

"Tired old pig ethics."

"Tired old rhetoric."

For an instant, it seemed Bill Lewis would smash his fist into the judge's face. Then he pivoted and pounded across the attic room, stopping directly in front of the wall where they had been working. Judge Pearson felt Tommy stiffen and make a small gasp.

Lewis seemed to be staring directly at the loosened boards. From his seat, Judge Pearson could see the scratch marks and telltale splinters of wood that rendered their plan obvious. He froze, not knowing what to say.

There was one terrible second, then Tommy spoke up:

"But why didn't you just go home?"

"What?" Bill Lewis pivoted away from the wall, still shaking with anger.

"Why didn't you just go home?" Tommy insisted.

"I couldn't."

"But why?"

"Home! Just go home! Why not?" Lewis laughed and shook once, his entire body convulsing. For an instant he seemed to be glowing with rage. Then, just as abruptly as the storm had blown up, it fled. He sighed, like a balloon releasing air. The judge thought he could actually see the man's anger dissipate in the hot attic.

"I wish I could have," Lewis said quietly. "I didn't have a home like yours, Tommy."

Lewis dragged himself back to the bed. He stared disconsolately at the plate of sandwiches. "Can I have one?"

"Sure," replied the judge.

Lewis took a large bite, then looked over at Tommy.

"I didn't have a home like yours," he repeated.

"You didn't?"

"Nope. My folks didn't want to have too much to do with me or with Emily. They pretty much kicked us out. My old man was career army, you know. A drill sergeant. He didn't like hair and he didn't like education and he didn't like radical politics, and I had a lot of all those things."

Lewis smiled.

"Especially hair."

He fingered the red scar on his throat.

"The old bastard gave me this when I was seven. About the same size as Tommy, there. I didn't follow some order quite fast enough, and he was standing there with an old garrison belt. Wham!" Lewis clapped his hands together suddenly, startling both Tommys. "My old lady even called the military police when she saw all the blood. They carted me off to the base hospital, stitched me up, and that was that."

Lewis smiled.

"We all have our scars," he said. "This is just the most obvious."

That, Judge Pearson agreed, was true.

The two men continued eating the food, as if oblivious to the explosion that had just taken place. The judge relaxed and said, "Well, you make good sandwiches, at least. I suppose one ought to be grateful."

Bill Lewis nodded. "I really apologize about all this, you know. I mean, I've got nothing against you or Tommy, really. But a plan's a plan, judge. You know, you got to stick with the procedure. You know that better than anyone. That's what a courtroom is, right? Procedures."

Judge Pearson chewed and swallowed.

"You've got that right. Ever been in one?"

"Nope. Except for traffic court, down in Miami. I've been lucky."

Bill Lewis smiled.

"You know the really stupid thing about all this? Back in sixty-eight, when we were all together in the brigade, I wanted Duncan and Megan out. I didn't think they had the right stuff, to borrow a phrase. I didn't think they were really committed to the plan or to the philosophy. I wish I'd insisted."

"That's life. I'd guess that in maybe sixty percent of the cases I handled there was something, some moment, where the people could have changed everything, if maybe one thing had happened. But it did or it didn't and so they ended up in front of me."

"Capricious fate," Bill Lewis said. He grinned.

The judge nodded.

As the two men were talking, Tommy put his half-eaten sandwich down. He slid away from the judge, moving gingerly to the end of the bed. His mind was divided into two sections, the first screaming instructions to him, the other shouting at him to ignore those commands. Do it! said the first. Sit still! called the other. Go! Stop! Go! Stop!

He was unsure if he was the only one aware that Bill Lewis had not locked the door behind him when he delivered the luncheon.

Tommy turned and wondered whether he could make himself invisible, whether he could rise so silently that no one would notice his parting, and tread so lightly that his footsteps would make no sounds.

He saw Bill Lewis stretch toward the tray of food, turning his back ever so slightly away from him.

Now! The command seemed to startle him with its force. *Now! Go now!*

Tommy could feel his muscles twitch. His head spun dizzily, as if he were caught in a sudden undertow at the beach, pulling him beneath the waves, his breath deserting him.

Now!

He jumped up.

"Hey!"

"Tommy!"

His grandfather's and Lewis's surprised voices seemed distant. He was aware only that he thought himself flying across the attic space.

He dove toward the stairs, nearly falling down in his flight, bump-

ing savagely against the wall to regain his balance. He threw himself
at the attic door, scrambling for the handle, only vaguely aware of
the two men leaping up behind him.

"Stop!"

Bill Lewis's voice was high-pitched and panicked.

"Stop, stop, stop right there! Goddammit, Tommy, stop!"

Tommy seized the door handle and flung open the unlocked door,
a few feet ahead of the hands that reached for him.

"Christ! Olivia, Ramon! The kid! Help!" Lewis bellowed.

Tommy thrust himself through the door, trying to outrun Bill
Lewis's cries for help. He heard his grandfather yell behind him:

"Go! Go! Run for it, Tommy!"

"Get him! Get him! Help! Help! Goddammit! Stop! Stop!"

Lewis was a half-step behind and Tommy swung the door back
hard, crunching down on the man's outstretched arm.

"Shit! Goddammit! Help!" Lewis's powerful voice seemed to fill
the air around Tommy, buffeting him like a wild wind.

"Run, Tommy, run!" he heard his grandfather calling far behind
him. "Just go! Go! Get away!"

Tommy dashed down the hallway, past doors, past the bathroom,
heading toward the stairway. Things flashed in and out of his vision,
a washstand, a bedroom, a pile of dirty clothes, some weapons and
ammunition on a bed. He disregarded them and flew on, hearing
only the scraping sound of his feet as they fought for purchase on
the wood floors. He could sense Lewis behind him, knew, without
seeing, that the man's arms were reaching for him frantically. He
dodged back and forth, grabbed the banister, and swung himself
around the corner, feeling Lewis's fingers rip free from his sweater.
There was a thudding sound and more obscenities as Lewis slipped
and fell. He looked down and saw Olivia and Ramon, weapons
drawn, racing up the stairway toward him. He turned and saw Lewis
scramble back to his feet and bear down hard on him from behind.
He ducked and slithered past Lewis, who pivoted, slipped again,
and continued screaming obscenities. Tommy headed back down
the hallway toward a bedroom, slamming the door as he passed
through, angling for the window.

Behind him he heard Olivia yell, "I'll shoot, dammit! I'll shoot!"

But he ignored her and fought for the window. He reached it and frantically tried to throw the sash up. He could see down to the next roof story, then caught a glimpse of a distant line of dark trees and a wide, gray, overcast sky. He could hear his breathing, loud, panicked, as if it were coming from somewhere else. He realized that bodies were piling up behind him in the doorway and he felt their rage precede them.

Then there was an immense explosion as one of the weapons was fired. Tommy recoiled, knocked to the floor by the sound, as plaster and wood chips exploded in the wall next to his head, raining down upon him.

I'm dead, he thought, then instantly realized he wasn't. He could hear his grandfather roaring in fury: "Leave him alone! You sadist! I'll kill you if you hurt him!" And he heard Olivia's measured shout in reply: "Out of my way, old man, or I'll shoot you instead."

All the voices seemed jumbled, screams of pain and rage and insult all filling the small room, mixing with the cordite smell and the reverberations of the shot. He suddenly realized that he too was shouting, a single high-pitched word that penetrated all the rest: "Home!"

He scrambled to his feet, dodging the hands that reached for him, and picked up a chair. He aimed it at the window, thinking: Break it! Jump! But he felt a hand seize his collar and jerk him back. Another set of hands grabbed at his arms and pinned them down, the chair slipping from his hands and crashing to the floor. Hot angry breath ran over his face like blood.

He was aware he was being shaken, pummeled about, tossed like an unwanted rag, punched and kicked.

Tommy caught one brief glimpse through the window of a sliver of blue sky that seemed to break through the cloud cover for just the barest of moments before being swallowed up. And he thought it worth it, just to see that, no matter how hard and terribly they beat him. He curled up, trying to protect himself from the blows flailing at him, shutting his eyes, closing his hands over his ears, so that he could not hear all the voices screaming at him. He said to himself, They'll kill me now. He hoped that his grandfather would tell his family that at least he had tried to escape, and he figured they would be proud of him. In the midst of all the noise and tumult, he picked out his grandfather's deep voice, trying to defend him, which comforted him just a tiny amount, as his eyes rolled back and he slipped away into a darkness of his own creation.

Megan rocked in her chair at her office, unable to sit still, thinking of Olivia.

She remembered Olivia's voice, which had an unusual depth to it, a throaty masculinity which intimidated the women and entranced the men. She remembered her leonine mass of hair, and imperious beauty. She understood Olivia's true genius: She could concoct the most harebrained plot and make it seem routine and simple and something you would want, no, need to be a part of.

Megan wanted to pound on her desk in sudden anger. How could I have been so obtuse? she thought.

Because I was still a child.

She pictured their house in Lodi. I should have walked out and made Duncan follow me. I should have spoken up. But Olivia had all the answers and she always knew all the questions ahead of time. It was as if she never contemplated anyone else having any input into her scheme; it had to go precisely as she planned it or it wasn't worth doing. Megan remembered going with Olivia over the escape route, back and forth, once, twice, a dozen times, until she knew everything, even the timing on the stoplights. She had tried, feebly, once, to suggest a different street, but Olivia would hear nothing of it. But, Megan thought, it was all wrong. We practiced the wrong things. We studied the wrong designs. We really didn't know what we were doing, no matter how well planned and careful Olivia made it seem. It was all an illusion.

There was a knock on the door, and it swung open. A pair of the other realtors in the office were pulling on overcoats in the hallway. One spoke up: "Meg? Would you like to join us for lunch?"

Megan shook her head.

"No, thanks. Just yogurt here at the desk today."

"You sure you don't want to come along?"

"Thanks, but no."

The door closed and she sat in the quiet with her memories. She thought again of the house in Lodi. It was a hateful place, dirty and decrepit and wretched, and we all thought it was someplace special because we were able to deceive ourselves constantly. She remembered driving with Olivia to the landlord's office, where Olivia had paid him two months' rent in cash and behaved slightly coquettishly. Megan remembered how Olivia had insisted on appearances; they were to seem to be a couple of hippie girls with hippie boyfriends. She had insisted that Megan remove her bra and wear a loose-fitting paisley shirt to the man's office. Harmless children, all caught up in benign peace, love, and flowers, with their most dangerous act perhaps smoking marijuana or dropping the occasional tab of acid. It was part of the disguise. She recalled how Olivia had lectured them all on pretending to be something other than what they were. It was the keystone of the scheme. She remembered the landlord, a middle-aged, friendly man, who blushed right up to his bald pate when they flirted with him, and who seemed to adore the attention of a pair of jiggling young women. He was completely bamboozled.

Megan sat up suddenly in her chair.

Fragmented memories and bits of conversation stampeded through her head.

Why Lodi? Why was staying there so important?

That was where the bank was.

Why that house?

Because Olivia insisted on being located where the robbery was going to happen. She demanded a base of operations close to the scene.

Why?

To study. To learn everything she could about the bank and the money delivery from the chemical plant.

Why?

So that Olivia would always be in control. She would be able to anticipate everything. It was of critical importance to her.

What does that mean?

It means she knows everything. She's been planning right here. She knows Duncan's routine at the bank and when the twins come home from school. She had to know when the judge picked up Tommy at the end of the day and which days he rode the bus. She knows where my office is and where I go to lunch. She knows all these things because she hasn't changed. She's the same Olivia. Only we're the bank job this time, and she's been studying us.

So where is she?

She's in a house like the one in Lodi. A house she rented two or three months ago, and paid cash for, and where she pretended to be someone else.

She's close. Not quite close enough for us to see her, but close enough for her to see us. She's in a house where she can reach out for us when she wants to, and feel safe when she doesn't, where the judge and Tommy can be hidden, but not far, not far at all.

Megan stood up, as if in a trance, overcome by the obviousness of it all. She walked over to the bookcase in the corner of her office and pulled out several large loose-leaf binders. Each was embossed with gold block writing: GREENFIELD MULTIPLE LISTING SERVICE— Greenfield, Westfield, Deerfield, Pelham, Shutesbury, Sunderland and rural areas—JULY/AUGUST, SEPTEMBER/OCTOBER, NOVEMBER/DE-CEMBER. RENTALS AND SALES.

She sat down slowly at her desk, opened the top drawer, and reached in for a detailed area map, which she spread out on her desktop. Then she very carefully took a sharpened pencil from a holder next to the telephone. She touched the point gingerly, imagining it was a sword. She slid a yellow legal pad in front of her, paused, poising the pencil above the pad. For an instant she waited, letting the quiet surround her.

You're right here, Olivia. I know your mind like I know my own, I just didn't realize it. You haven't thought of everything, like you think you have. You haven't factored in one element of the equation:

This is my territory.

She opened the book and started in with the available rental listings for late in the summer just past.

*   *   *

At their last free period of the day, Karen met Lauren in the high school library. It was a low-ceilinged room, with fluorescent lights and long, uncomfortable tables. The only person in the room was the assistant librarian, a middle-aged woman busily sorting books behind a central counter. She looked up and smiled at Karen as she came through the door, and whispered, probably out of habit, because there was no one else to disturb: "Your sister's back in the stacks." She gestured to the rows of shelved books that surrounded her.

Karen walked back and saw Lauren weighted down with a half-dozen thick books. Lauren jerked her head toward a table in the corner. Karen hurried to her side.

"Do you think you've found it?" she asked excitedly.

"I don't know, but if it's anywhere, it'll be in one of these."

The two teenagers spread the books in front of them. Karen picked one up and opened it haphazardly. A photograph sprung out at them: six helicopters in formation angling low over rough jungle terrain. The choppers were outlined against a dull gray dawn sky. They could see a green-suited soldier hanging out the side of the lead helicopter, firing a machine gun down at the ground. The tracer bullets appeared as red-yellow streaks in the photograph. Karen turned the page and saw another picture, this time of a helmeted police officer lifting a truncheon above his head, ready to bring it crashing down on the skull of a demonstrator. She stared at the picture for an instant, caught by the look of madness in the policeman's eyes. Karen saw that the demonstrator was a young woman, probably not much older than herself. She handed the book to her sister, who turned the page to a photograph of a city street burning behind a flak-jacketed National Guardsman; then a long-haired student, wearing sunglasses and smoking a cigar, sitting at a university president's desk. She kept flipping through the pages, past photos of Russian tanks rolling through Czechoslovakia and athletes at the Olympics standing with their heads bowed and their fists raised during the national anthem; past pictures of swollen-bellied babies, dying of starvation in Biafra, and stricken leaders, dying of assassins' bullets.

After a moment, Lauren sighed. "You know," she whispered, "I see these and I just don't understand."

Karen didn't reply. She picked up a large, thick reference book entitled: *Book of the Year—1968*. "It will have to be in here," she said. She glanced up at a clock on the wall. "We don't have much time," she whispered. "Mom's expecting us."

Lauren nodded. "You look in there. It should be late in the year. I'll keep checking, see if I can find some pictures."

For a few moments, the two of them were silent as they searched through the pages. Karen finally stiffened, and nudged her sister with her elbow. She pointed down at a small block of text. Lauren leaned over and read:

> Throughout the nation, there was a variety of smaller demon-strations and acts of radical civil disobedience. California became a focal point for self-styled "revolutionaries" particularly in the San Francisco area, who engaged in sporadic acts of violence. A bomb was exploded at the Bank of America offices in Berkeley. A group broke into the Selective Service Headquarters in Sac-ramento and poured blood over files. There was a rash of bank robberies, which were seen as the preferred method of raising cash for further action. One such robbery, in Lodi, California, resulted in the deaths of two security guards and three radicals, when the robbery erupted into gunfire.

"That's it?" Lauren asked.

Karen snorted. "I want to know more. I want to understand what they were doing."

Her sister glanced down at one of the picture books open in front of them. She saw an unsettling photograph of a tightly packed group of students, their mouths open, as they shouted in rage. In the center of the picture, one student was making a violent, obscene gesture toward the camera.

"What's that?" Karen asked.

Lauren read the caption. "Chicago. The Democratic National Convention." She sighed. "I look at these pictures and it seems like ancient history, like looking at things that happened a million years ago."

Karen shook her head. "Everything went crazy. They just went crazy along with it. That's all."

"Except that it's still with them."

"It's probably still with a lot of people," Karen replied. "They just hide it better."

"I wonder," Lauren said quietly, "if we really believed in something, I mean, *really* felt strongly—whether we would do the same."

Karen started to reply, then stopped. The bell rang then, and they hurried to return the books to the stacks and get home, leaving the last question shelved alongside the words and photos that they'd inspected.

Shortly after three P.M. Duncan buzzed his secretary and said: "Doris? I'm going to run over to the pharmacy and pick up a few things. Hold down the fort here until I get back, please."

"Oh, Mr. Richards, why don't you just head on home? We can handle—"

Duncan cut her off. "Well, I think I will, but I've a few more things to do. I'll let you know after I get back."

He hung up the telephone and gathered his overcoat from a coat-hook in the corner. He slipped it on and wondered whether the heat he felt building within him was excitement or fear. Then he concluded the two traveled together and shrugged it off. He picked up his large briefcase, which he'd already emptied, and headed out the door.

His first act was to move his car from its assigned spot in the bank's parking lot to a space in a public parking area about three blocks away. It was an enclosed parking garage, only partially filled. Duncan drove the car far past the first available spot, onto a level where only a pair of other cars was parked. He placed his car in the darkest corner he could find.

Taking the elevator down to the street, he spied a cigarette butt crushed on the floor. He picked it up carefully and deposited it in an envelope, which he placed inside his suit pocket.

He stopped next at a hair salon which catered to both men and women, mostly students. The receptionist looked up at him and smiled.

"Can we help you?" she asked.

He took a deep breath and smiled.

"Sure," Duncan replied. "I'd like to get my hair spiked."

The young woman was taken aback.

"Really? Okay," she said, "we can—" Then she noticed Duncan's smile and said, "Oh, come on, you're kidding me, aren't you?"

"Maybe some other time," Duncan said. "Actually, I just came in for some shampoo that my daughters use. The trouble is, I can't remember the name—"

"Redken? Natural Wave? Is it amino free? What sort of hair do they have?"

"It comes in a red and white bottle."

"Like this?"

"Uh, maybe."

The young lady smiled. "Why don't you take a look back in the bath area, where we shampoo hair. Maybe you'll see it." She gestured toward the rear of the room. Duncan nodded. He was fingering his car keys in his pocket, waiting for the right moment. He started across the room, and as soon as he spotted what he was looking for, he brought them out and let them drop. He bent down carefully to pick them up, at the same time grabbing several strands of newly cut hair. He stuffed keys and hair in his pocket, walked back, glanced at the shelf of shampoos, then returned to the reception desk.

"I think it's that stuff there," he said.

"Great." She took a container and put it in a bag. "Twelve dollars."

Duncan looked stricken. "For eight ounces?"

"Actually, six and one-half."

"I'm in the wrong business," he said. "I ought to sell hair products."

The young woman laughed and took his money. She waved as he went out the door.

Out of sight, in the street, he took the hair strands and added them to the cigarette butt in the envelope. Then he proceeded to the corner pharmacy, where he purchased two pairs of surgical gloves, a box of plastic garbage bags, some large rubber bands, and a variety of cold remedies.

It did not take him long to find a taxi which drove him to the nearest shopping mall. He paid the driver and headed inside rapidly, checking his wristwatch, making certain he wasn't spending too much time away from the bank. The mall was an older one, enclosed, spread over dozens of acres of what Duncan remembered used to be gently rolling farmland. It had been green and beautiful once, dotted with grazing cows and horses, cornstalks rising in the warm summer sun. But now it was profitable. Eighteen years earlier this realization would have made him sad, and he was ashamed that it no longer did. The bank had written the purchase loan, and helped with the construction financing. It had been one of his first major projects. He had spent nights driving past the site, checking the number of cars in the lots. At holiday times he had walked the corridors, counting the people, allowing himself to feel a sense of relief as he was buffeted about by crowds.

He hurried through a small side entrance and ducked into a sporting goods store. He found a clerk, dressed in a striped referee's shirt, and gestured to him.

"I need a pair of high-top sneakers for my nephew," he said.

"What size?"

"Ten and one-half, with a D-width."

"How much were you looking to spend?"

"Thirty bucks?"

The clerk shook his head.

"Canvas. Real hot on the feet. Not much support."

"Forty bucks?"

"We've got some leathers on sale for fifty."

"God. When I was playing the game, the shoes cost about ten."

"When was that?" the clerk asked.

"Prehistoric times. Dinosaur days."

The young man laughed and went to get the shoes. Duncan thought: They'll be fine. They are a full size smaller than my normal shoe size. They'll be just fine.

Duncan paid cash for the shoes, and added a gray sweatsuit to his purchases.

At a clothing store a few paces away, he purchased a blue and red knit sweater. It was cheap acrylic and polyester, the sort of thing that a student would buy, wear until it fell apart, which it would do rapidly, then buy another just like it. As with his other purchases, he paid cash.

In a large chain drugstore, he went to the wall where they kept automotive and electrical equipment and purchased several small electrical clips and wires, tape, a set of screwdrivers, and a small hammer. It will be dark inside the bank, he thought, and he grabbed a small flashlight and batteries, as well. For an instant he paused outside, looking at the flow of people, thinking how anonymous he was, how everyone lost their identity within the mall. No matter how well-lit, everyone was invisible. He headed for the side exit.

Outside the mall, he ripped all the tags from the clothing and threw them in a wastebasket, then placed all the items in his briefcase, squeezing it shut. He looked up at the sky. The gray was slowly being overcome by the darkening night sky. It gets so dark so quickly, he thought. It is as if the light isn't strong enough to battle the evening, and just gives up and dies. He sucked in air and blew out slowly. He could see his breath in front of him. Time to start, he thought. He could feel his muscles contract around his heart, tighten across his stomach, and for an instant his knees felt weak. He stood still and let the cold air wash across his body. He felt like a sprinter coiled at the starting line, bent to the earth, waiting to leap forward at the sound of the starter's gun. He lifted his hand into the air, forming a pistol with his fingers. "Bang," he said softly.

Then he pulled his coat tightly about him and flagged another taxi for the trip back to the center of town.

For once, Ramon Gutierrez did not feel the drifting late afternoon cold. He remained completely preoccupied with waiting for the twins to come through the school parking lot. He kept his collar high, though, and his hat slouched down, watching anonymously from an adjacent street as the students jumped into the typical variety of teenage vehicles, spinning tires, squealing across the black macadam surface of the high school parking lot. It wasn't much different from his high school in the South Bronx, except that everyone there had been heading toward buses or the subway instead of sports cars and motorcycles. It had been a dangerous, exuberant moment, a time when gang members squared off or people made dates for the weekend. Now he was making his own sort of special assignation. They just didn't know it.

He saw the twins get into the red sports car and he smiled. They managed to pull only partway out of the parking space before being stopped by a pair of gangly teenage boys, who hung on the windowsills, leaning over toward them. He did not know what they were talking about, but he let his imagination roam about freely.

He was enjoying himself for the first time in days.

Olivia had given him his orders in the angry aftermath of the attempted escape. Ramon pictured the boy, curled into a fetal position on the floor of the attic. He had never seen a child die, and he wondered if that was what it was like. Whatever happens, happens, he thought. As long as we get the money. The grandfather had struggled momentarily as well, mostly out of shock and panic, until quieted by Olivia. As the old man had yelled in protest, she had cocked the hammer back on a revolver and placed it up against the side of the judge's head. Ramon recalled what she had said: "Do not tempt me, judge. Do not force my hand, because I will not hesitate." After seeing the captives locked away, her anger had exploded, uncontrollably, shaking the walls of the old farmhouse. Ramon was unsettled by it. As he sat behind the wheel of the car, he pictured her, contorted by rage, as she screamed imprecations at Bill Lewis. He had remained stock still, hangdog, listening without reply.

Well, he should be ashamed, Ramon thought. He almost blew the whole show. After all the planning and preparations and finishing all the dangerous stuff. Christ!

For a moment he had been worried that Olivia would shoot Bill, then he thought she would shoot the hostages. She had paced across the living room, waving one of the weapons, her entire body twisted by fury. What had surprised him was that she seemed to take the boy's escape attempt personally, as if he was doing something to her, instead of just trying to help himself.

Ramon had trouble with that. If I were caught, he said, I'd do the same. At least, I'd want to. He remembered trying to shinny down a drainage pipe at a youth detention center, only to fall and sprain his foot and be captured, trying to limp to freedom.

He had to admit a sort of grudging respect for the child. He hated the moments in his childhood when people had done things to him, and he'd never fought back, never run away, never battled.

His train of thought was interrupted. The twins were maneuvering their car into the street.

He remembered Olivia's command, after she had regained the slightest control of her anger: "Go pay the twins a little visit. Megan's at work. The house is empty. Give them a little something to be scared of. Fuck them up a bit."

"How?"

"Just any damn way you want!"

The memory of his momentary discomfort at twisting the strands of rope around the thin arms of the captive child dissipated. He put the car in gear and accelerated.

Karen and Lauren did not notice the late-model sedan that cruised past them on Pleasant Street, nor did they notice the occupant's quick, leering glance in their direction.

They were on the verge of an argument.

"I still think we should be doing something," Lauren insisted, while her sister continually shook her head.

"We are doing something. We're doing what they said to do."

"I don't know if it's enough."

"Well, we can't tell, can we?"

"No, and that's what's bothering me. I can't believe you can just sit there and not want to do anything."

"Well, I sure don't want to do something that's going to make things worse."

"But you don't know!" insisted Lauren. "You can't tell that what they're doing is right. And what do Mom and Dad know about dealing with these people, anyway? It could all be wrong!"

"Yeah, but it could all be right, too," answered Karen, sliding easily into her most practical tones.

"I hate it when you sound like that. You're trying to sound grown-up and we're not."

"So what do you want to do?"

Lauren remained silent.

"It just all seems so crazy," she said after a momentary hesitation.

"So, what's important is for us not to act crazy, too."

"Remember when Jimmy Harris spotted that guy breaking into the cars in the school lot? Remember what he did? He got the guy's license and called the cops and they came right away."

"I can't believe what you're saying. Yesterday it was me that wanted to call the police and you were saying the opposite."

"I was not."

"You were."

Lauren nodded. "You're right. All right. I'll be quiet. I just wish we could do something." She sighed. "I miss Tommy."

"So do I."

"No, I mean different than what we're supposed to. This morning I woke up and I couldn't believe the little creep wasn't there beating us to the bathroom."

Karen laughed. "And leaving the cap off the toothpaste."

"And leaving his socks and underwear on the floor."

Karen shook her head. "We've got to believe he's coming back. Tomorrow. That's what Dad said."

"Do you believe that?"

"I'm not letting myself believe or not believe anything. I'm just waiting."

"I felt like I wanted to cry all day."

"Me too, except for a couple of moments when everything seemed normal, and I realized I'd forgotten everything and then it would hit me."

"I saw you talking with Will again."

"He wants to go out."

"What did you say?"

"I told him to call me next week."

Lauren smiled. "He's neat."

"Yeah." Her sister gave in to a giggle. "I like him."

"He's sexy, too. I heard that he and Lucinda Smithson were a real item last year."

"I heard that, too. But it doesn't bother me. And what about Teddy Leonard, huh? He went to Paris last summer on that exchange trip and I heard they went to a real whorehouse."

"I don't believe that story."

Karen laughed. "They'd probably be too scared."

Both twins smiled.

"You know why I like Teddy?" Lauren asked, then continued without waiting for her sister's reply. "Because when he came over, he took the time to play with Tommy for a while. I worry sometimes that Tommy doesn't get to see how older guys act. He just sees us. Remember, Teddy took him out and they threw the football around for a half-hour? Tommy was just glowing. Did I ever tell you what he told me later that night? I went in to give him a glass of water, just after lights out, and he said, 'Lauren, I like that guy. You can marry him if you want.' Can you beat that?"

Karen laughed out loud, joining her sister's giggle. But within a few seconds their mirth had slipped from the car, as if it had flooded through an open window, replaced by an iciness that cracked and shifted about within them.

"If they hurt him, even a little—" Karen started.

"We'll kill them," her sister completed. Neither thought for an instant how they might accomplish it.

Instead, they drove on in determined silence.

As Karen rounded the corner and cruised down their street, she said, "I can't believe it—Mom's not home yet."

"Do you think—" started Lauren, but her sister cut her off.

"No, she's probably on the way."

Karen parked the car in the driveway, but neither got out. They looked up at the house uncomfortably. It was dark on the inside. "I wish Dad had installed that automatic light system," Karen complained.

"I never thought I'd think the house looked creepy," Lauren said quietly.

"Stop it!" Karen snapped. "Don't make it seem any worse than it is. I hate it when you get into these gloomy, scary moods, like you're some sort of fragile flower or something. Come on, let's go."

She slammed the car door shut, and Lauren half-skipped to keep up with her. Karen thrust the front door key into the lock and threw the door open. She stepped inside and flipped on a light switch, which broke apart the deepening gray of the house's interior. Both girls shed their coats and hung them in the hall closet. Karen turned to her sister and said, "See? No big deal. Let's make a cup of tea and wait for Mom. She should be home soon."

Lauren nodded, but hesitated.

Karen watched as her sister stood still, listening.

"What is it?" she whispered.

"I don't know," Lauren said.

"If you're kidding around with me—"

"Shhh."

"I won't hush!" Karen said. "You're just scaring me. We can't let our imaginations just play games."

Lauren ignored her sister's small outburst and said, "Why is it so cold in here?"

"How the heck should I know?" Karen answered quickly. "Probably they turned the thermostat down when they went out this morning."

"Can't you feel the chill? It's like an open window."

Karen started to respond, but stopped.

"Maybe we should wait outside," she said abruptly.

"I think we should look around."

Karen looked at her sister. "I'm supposed to be the practical one," she whispered. "I think we should just get the heck out of here."

"Not yet."

Lauren took a few steps toward the living room. Her sister followed.

"See anything?"

"No, but I can feel the cold air coming in."

"So can I."

"What should we do?"

"Keep going."

"Where?"

"The kitchen."

Moving gingerly, they stepped toward the back of the house. "Hold my hand," Lauren said abruptly, and her sister seized her wrist.

"Do you hear anything?"

"No."

Cautiously, they entered the kitchen.

"Anything?" Karen asked.

"No. But it's freezing—"

Karen suddenly gasped: "Oh, my God!"

Lauren jumped, startled.

"Where?"

"Look!"

Karen was pointing across the room, toward a small pantry area. Lauren followed her gesture and gasped as well.

They both stood still, staring at the small alcove. A window was thrust upward, and a screen pushed in and dropped to the floor, bent by the force of the break-in. The storm window on the exterior had been shattered, and shards of glass had landed on the linoleum.

"We've got to get out of here!" Lauren said.

"No. We should check the house."

"Do you think—"

"I don't know."

"Well, it could be—"

"I don't know!"

Karen tiptoed over to a drawer next to the sink and pulled out a large kitchen cleaver. She handed it to her sister and grabbed a rolling pin for herself.

"Come on," she said. "Let's check the upstairs."

They maneuvered back through the house, climbing the stairs

quietly. Twice they paused to listen, then they proceeded onward, once again holding hands, and brandishing their weapons. At the top of the stairs, they quickly glanced into their parents' bedroom.

"Seems pretty straight to me," Lauren said. She was beginning to feel more confident. "I bet whoever it was got scared off when we drove up."

"Shhhh!" said her sister, restoring some of the fear of the moment. "Let's check Tommy's room. Maybe they came to get something for him."

They walked quietly over to their brother's doorway.

"How could we tell if something was missing?" Karen said. "Look at all this stuff."

They crept down the hallway to their own room. The door was slightly ajar, and Lauren pushed it open further with her foot.

"Oh, no," she cried out.

Karen jumped back, then stepped forward, next to her sister, so she could see into their room.

"Oh no," she echoed.

The room was a mess; clothes and bedclothes were strewn about. Drawers had been dumped out. Books were scattered everywhere. Knickknacks and bric-a-brac were shattered.

Lauren was pale and started to cry. Karen's hands shook.

"They did this to us!" she said.

"Why?"

"I don't know."

"But—"

"I don't know." She too felt her eyes start to fill. Karen walked over to the pile of clothing and picked up an item from the top. It was underwear. "Oh no," she half-moaned.

"What?" Lauren asked.

"Look." Tears started to run down her face. She held up the panties. They had been sliced and cut with a knife.

Lauren put her hand to her mouth. "I think I'm going to be sick," she said.

Then they both heard a noise. Something indistinct, yet alien. They could not tell whether it was distant or near at hand, whether it was nothing or something threatening. It was merely a noise and it catapulted them into terror, replacing the fright in their eyes with something unknown and awful in their imaginations.

"They're here!" Lauren said.

They looked at each other.

"Run!"

Both girls turned and sprinted for the stairs. They thundered down, all stealth and caution forgotten, just trying to get outside into the increasing evening darkness. Lauren stumbled on the bottom step and almost fell, her sister catching her and thrusting her forward. Both girls were groaning with effort. Karen reached the front door first, grabbing the handle and flinging it open.

Megan stood outside.

Both girls shouted, half-screams of fear that turned to relief with recognition.

Megan, stricken instantly, reached out and seized the twins, grabbing them and pulling them to her. She dropped her keys, her briefcase, her coat, and spun them away from the front door. "What is it?" she cried. "What's wrong?"

"Someone's there!"

"They wrecked our room!"

"They broke in!"

For a few moments the three of them, wrapped together, remained on the front porch. Megan comforted the twins, all the while staring past them into the house. After the two had finished sobbing, and their breathing had returned to normal, Megan said, "All right. Show me."

"I don't want to go back in there," Lauren said.

"We heard something," Karen pleaded.

"No," Megan said. "This is our house. Come on."

With the twins trailing her, she entered the front vestibule. She picked up the knife and rolling pin where they had been abandoned in their rush to exit. "All right," she said again. "Now, what did you see, and where?"

"It started back there," Lauren said, gesturing toward the kitchen. "We found the open window—"

And then she screamed.

Megan jumped and Karen cried out.

Lauren stepped back, grabbing for her mother, who had just enough time to catch a glimpse of a man's grinning face, looking in at them through the kitchen window from the backyard. Then, as quickly as it appeared, the apparition vanished. Megan felt a surge of violation, anger and protectiveness, and uttering a half-shout, charged the kitchen, waving the knife above her head.

The girls followed, their mother's assault surprising them so that their own shouts and tears abruptly ended.

Megan's heart was pumping, her head reeling.

She peered through the window, but could see nothing.

She could feel her stomach tightening, her insides draining tension. Outside, the night had taken over, covering everything with its perfect camouflage. It's over for now, she thought. Then she realized how wrong she was: It's still beginning.

She pulled the two girls close to her, and settled in for the long wait until her husband returned home.

A few moments before six P.M., an hour before the bank closed for the weekend, Duncan stood in his office and readied himself. He had drawn the drapes to close off the glass front wall so that no one in the main office area could see in; it wasn't typical, but it was ordinary. He wore his overcoat, and had his hat on his head. His briefcase was closed, ostensibly holding documents and memos, but actually stuffed with the items he'd purchased earlier that day. Through his open door, he could see a dozen people in line for the two remaining tellers. An assistant manager passed by, carrying a sheaf of papers for storage. There was a hum to the core of the bank, as it did its usual steady weekend business; all the folks who needed cash or who got their paychecks on Fridays, trying to make deposits. It was always a busy time, handled by a skeleton crew, a little confusing, a little hurried, as people worked quickly to get back on their course for home. It was a time when things were easy to slip. The only guard on duty was an elderly watchman whose job it was to set the alarm system when everyone had cleared the building.

Duncan saw his secretary getting ready to depart. He paused, just long enough for her to get her desk in order, then he buzzed her on the intercom.

"Doris? Still here?"

"Just getting ready to go."

"So am I. Can you just do one thing for me?"

"Sure."

Carrying a loan application form, he left his desk and met his secretary in the doorway. He wondered whether his hands shook, whether his voice had some telltale quiver to it. He could feel sweat dripping under his arms. She'll smell it, he thought in panic. She'll recognize it as fear.

He closed his eyes, breathed out slowly, and stumbled on.

"Doris, I think we're supposed to take this thing up on Monday morning early, so could you just run the top page through the copy machine a half-dozen times? You don't have to distribute them, just have them ready so that we can pass them out first thing on Monday."

"Sure, Mr. Richards. Anything else?"

He handed her the papers, then, as he talked, walked back to his desk.

"No, I don't think so. Sure hope I can shake this damn cold over the weekend. Sometimes I worry that I'm going to spend the entire winter, from December through March, sniffling and sneezing . . ."

He buttoned his overcoat and picked up his briefcase. He glanced around, like a man preparing to leave.

"You should take care of yourself."

He forced a laugh and smile.

"Maybe Megan will make enough money selling real estate that we can move to the Bahamas or somewhere. Then I could run one of those little illegal banking operations where it's warm and profitable. What d'you think, Doris? Ready to come along?"

His secretary grinned. "Weather report is for it to drop into the twenties tonight with plenty of frost. I think you could tempt me, as long as I can bring my cats."

Duncan gave another laugh and stood with his secretary in the doorway. He half-closed his office door and made a big show of reaching beneath his overcoat for his keys. As he brandished them, he turned to Doris.

"You take off as soon as you do that. I really appreciate it."

"Okay," she said. "See you Monday."

"Whoops, left the desk lamp on. I'll get it. See you Monday."

He watched as she turned and headed away across the bank to the copy room. He took a swift glance about to make certain that no one was watching him, then, taking a deep breath, he slid back into his office. He closed the door quietly and locked it. Then he crossed to his desk, turned off the lamp, and stood for a moment in the darkness, thinking, What she'll remember is me standing there in coat and hat, on my way out the door.

The watchman will walk through the office, checking each door before arming the motion detector. Then he will hurry through the front door, double-lock it, and activate the perimeter guard. He won't even look back at the building as he walks away, because he'll know it's secure. Even if someone were to beat the exterior alarm, they would still have only a half-minute to locate and disarm the interior system. Bad odds.

But no one ever suspected it could be done in reverse.

He could feel a thin line of sweat on his forehead.

It'll work. I know it.

He took off his coat and hat and tossed them into a corner. Then he dropped to his knees and crawled into the footwell behind his desk. He wedged himself in as far as he could fit, balancing his briefcase on his lap. By the luminous dial on his watch he could see it was only a few minutes after six, and he settled in to wait. He thought of the irony of hiding in his office: I have been hiding here for eighteen years.

Then he shook his head and filled his imagination with alternating visions of what he was about to do and of his son. That galvanized him, clearing his mind, so that when his legs started to cramp after some thirty minutes, he felt only pain and no guilt.

He tried to distract himself by listening for the last few minutes of bank activity, but he couldn't hear anything. He was afraid to move; he did not know whether the security guard would open his office door and then relock it, or just try the door handle. He guessed that would depend on whether the man had dinner waiting for him or not. He was also scared that someone outside might catch a bit of motion as they walked through the parking lot and stared back into the darkened office. He tried rubbing the cramps, then concentrated on relaxing the muscles. The pain surged, then dissipated slowly. He stared at his watch and tried to imagine what was going on outside. The last customers would be leaving and the two remaining tellers would be locking their cash drawers after running the figures through their computers. After they were finished, the head teller would close down the computer system. Then the assistant manager would double-check the locks on the safe. This would all be hurried; no one liked it when it was their rotation for Friday night. There was an impatience to the hour, as if the start of the weekend was being held off capriciously. The security guard would survey all this, then, sweeping the last people out, begin his final check.

Duncan wondered what was keeping him.

Then he froze. He could hear a hand on his door handle. The door rattled in the frame as the guard pulled on it and checked the lock.

Don't come in, Duncan prayed. Don't come in.

He held his breath and tried to keep his legs from twitching. He thought his heart beat so loud that it penetrated the soundproofing, echoing across the bank, bringing the guard to him.

The door stopped shaking and Duncan released his breath.

All right, now check next door. Then old Phillips' office.

He waited, letting the time seep around him, enveloping him in a sort of liquid embrace. It must be like drowning, he thought.

He pictured the guard standing in the center, sweeping the bank with his eyes. Then he would move to the wall where the interior alarm was set.

In his imagination, Duncan could see the man punching in the seven-digit code on the key pad.

Now, hurry! Duncan said to himself. You've only got thirty seconds to get to the first set of doors, out to the automatic teller area.

The lights would switch off automatically when the system was armed. A master switch turned them on again at seven A.M.

Duncan waited. Lock the door. Check it. Good. Now, head outside to arm the perimeter system.

He stared down at his watch. Seven-twenty.

Wait, he said to himself. Keep waiting.

He tried to think of nothing for ten minutes.

It will be done now, he thought. The guard will have found his car and driven off. I am alone inside. Now I can move.

But he didn't. He waited another ten minutes.

A singular calm came over him then. He wondered for an instant whether he would be able to move, now that he was certain he was alone. He tried to give orders to his legs, to unfold and emerge from hiding, but they would not respond. He wanted to laugh. This is where they will find me on Monday morning, he thought. Unable to move, with no suitable explanation.

Slowly he extricated himself from beneath his desk, then, crawling, he made his way to the front of his office, to the curtain he'd drawn earlier. He pulled it back gingerly, peering out, like an adolescent boy spying on his sister's bath.

The bank was dark and empty.

For a moment he stared up into the corners, to the electric eyes that covered the tellers' windows and to the infrared beams that detected motion. The electric cameras were not a problem, he knew. They operated on the same circuit as the bank's lighting system. They were shut off at night. But the motion detectors were another matter. They are my enemy, he thought. He took a deep breath. They only cover the main area. But they are formidable. He knew they were equipped with sensors, so that they would sound an alarm if tampered with. The only way of beating them was to shut them off. He crawled back to his desk and found his briefcase. Sitting on the floor, he stripped off his shoes and suit, slipping into the sweatpants and shirt. He left his feet bare for traction. He rolled over onto his back and stretched his legs, trying to shake the cramps and stiffness out. You must work, he said savagely to his muscles. You must behave and do what I ask you.

Satisfied that most of his limberness had returned, he crawled back to the door.

He paused there, allowing himself to fill with one last wave of fear, tension, and dismay. Then he steeled himself and thought: There is only this way. Now, think of nothing. Just do it.

He turned the lock.

Ready, he said to himself.

Set.

Go!

Duncan thrust open the office door and sprinted across the floor. His feet made a slapping sound in the dark room. He counted to himself: One—one thousand, two—one thousand, three—one thousand, four—one thousand. Gray-blue lights from the streetlamps outside gave the interior of the bank a haunted, otherworldly glow. As he cut past one desk, his hip caught the edge and he stumbled, pain shooting through his body. He steadied himself and continued hurrying to the wall; fifteen—one thousand, sixteen—one thousand, seventeen—one thousand. He crouched down next to the electronic key pad. He stopped his hand abruptly before touching it: Get it right, get it right. He breathed in, twenty-three—one thousand, twenty-four. In the dim light it was hard to see the key pad, and he realized he'd left the flashlight back in the office. He didn't even have the time to curse himself. He screamed inwardly: Do it! And then he punched in the code.

For a terrible instant he thought he'd done it wrong.

He closed his eyes and leaned against the wall, biting his lips, waiting for the alarm to sound.

A minute passed, perhaps two, before Duncan realized that he was free. He stood up dizzily and marched back to his office. He slumped down into his chair and tried to control his racing emotions. He commanded himself: Concentrate! and felt better. Do not think about what this means. Do not think about anything except stealing the money. He blanked his mind. Follow the plan, he thought. Follow the plan.

All right, he told himself. First, deception.

He unlaced the sneakers and tucked his feet into them. They were uncomfortable, but tolerable. He pulled two surgical gloves on each hand. He seized his briefcase, first pulling the cheap sweater out. All right, he said to himself, let's get started. He walked down to the women's bathroom at the back of the bank, flipped on the light switch inside and entered the stall. By climbing on top of the toilet, he was able to reach up and dislodge a ceiling panel. He clambered up higher, onto the top of the stall, and peered into the darkened area. He remembered the spot, from the design sessions before the building was constructed. The women's bathroom ran adjacent to the heating/cooling ducts, and there was a small crawl space above, which was buttressed sufficiently to allow workmen inside and gain access to the area. Leaning in, using the small flashlight to illuminate the area, he took out a few strands of hair and left them on the floor. Then he added the cigarette butt, scrunching it down and shredding it. On the edge, where he'd pulled down the ceiling panels, he rubbed the sweater until he was certain that enough fibers had come loose.

He climbed back down and thought: There. That will give some forensic scientists something to work on.

Next, Duncan went into the bank president's office, using the screwdriver and claw hammer to rip the door lock open. He was shocked and surprised at how easily he was able to force the door.

He felt a wave of embarrassment come over him, thinking how hard it would be to explain himself to old Phillips when it became time. But he recognized the critical importance of making the robbery appear to be something other than what it was. He needed time more than he needed friendship. He jammed the screwdriver into the locked desk drawer and began rifling through the papers. After creating enough diversion, he forced another drawer open, discovering the set of keys that he knew the bank president always kept on hand. He reached behind the drawer and found the piece of paper taped on the back of it. It was a list of combinations. Just like some high school kid trying to hide something from his parents. He is an old man, and he remembers a different era, Duncan thought. It was commonly known at the bank that the president kept the keys and the combination list.

Duncan left the office and walked over to one of the desks in the main office. He turned on the typewriter and swiftly rolled a sheet of paper onto the platen. Then he wrote down the seven-digit number for the interior key pad, as well as the four-digit number for the external perimeter defense. He crumpled this paper up and stuck it in the pocket of his sweatshirt.

All right, he thought. Now for the money.

Duncan went to the safe where the tellers stored their drawers, and opened it. There were eight drawers with cash, averaging about five thousand dollars. In addition, each drawer had a robbery stash: a pile of ten hundred dollar bills marked with infrared signatures and whose serial numbers had been recorded in the bank's computer system. These were designed to be handed to any wild man who might stick a gun in a teller's face. Duncan took them as well, thinking bitterly: Let the bitch chew on these, maybe they will put the feds on to her.

He stuffed all the money into his briefcase.

He went to a second safe, which kept the bank's cash reserve, and opened it. Fifty thousand dollars in various denominations was stacked neatly on three shelves. His hand started to shake as he loaded the money into the briefcase. He felt an acid taste in his mouth and he wanted to spit, but his tongue was too dry and he fought off the urge.

Duncan stood and looked at the collection of cash. All right, he said to himself, keep going.

He walked down and unlocked the door to the automatic teller machines. These he opened, one after the other. Each could hold up to twenty-five thousand dollars in cash, but the bank customarily kept something less inside. They were restocked on Monday, after the weekend rush. In the first, he found seventeen thousand, in the second, twelve, in the third, fourteen, and in the fourth, only eight. That was reasonable, he thought—it is the one closest to the door and gets the most traffic. In each machine he left two thousand dollars, giving him forty-three thousand dollars. He knew that when the machines were empty, a shield automatically lowered over the area where cards were inserted. He did not want that to happen all at once. Someone from the bank might come in over the weekend and be suspicious.

Duncan walked back into the bank. He searched about for an instant, wondering whether he would ever be able to come back again. Then he shook the thought from his head and went back to his office.

He did not look at the money. He hoped it would be enough. He remembered: How much? and Olivia's reply: What's a life worth? He closed his eyes. Mine is worth nothing.

Depression and dismay seemed to suck him down for an instant, as if pulling him beneath some dark surface. It's all wrong, he thought. Then he toughened himself. So? What of it? Tommy comes first.

Then he stripped off the sweatsuit and replaced his regular business suit. He left one sneaker on one foot and put his own shoe on the other.

He put the used clothes in a plastic bag, tore off some electrical tape and wire, and went back to the security key pad. He unscrewed the pad and pulled some of the wiring out, then bridged over a few random circuits and taped some back down. Further confusion, he thought.

Duncan returned to his office and put on his coat and hat. He took the time to tape a plastic bag over his sneakered foot. Then he collected money, clothing, equipment, locked his office door, and headed out. He paused for one instant, surveying the brightly lit vestibule and the darkness just beyond it. This is the most dangerous time, he thought. If someone were to enter now, all would be over. He hesitated for a second, then put his head down and surged forward, thinking: No sense in stopping now. He used his own key to leave the bank, then pushed himself past the automatic tellers and out. For the moments he was caught in the light, he felt sick; then, as the cold dark surrounded him, he felt relieved. The external alarm box was adjacent to the front door. He took the piece of paper with the security digits typed onto it and dropped it into the mud of the shrubbery. Then he took his sneakered, bagged foot and squashed it down, leaving an indistinct footprint.

He stepped back and swiftly tore the bag from his foot and jammed sneaker and bag into another plastic bag. He pulled on his own shoe and stepped quickly away from the front door.

Suddenly, he was aware that he was out, that the night surrounded him and embraced him in its cold arms.

Duncan looked up at the streetlights, and felt their glow curl around him like a mist.

He started to walk up the street toward the lot where he'd hidden his car. The bag of items he carried in one hand and the briefcase in the other seemed to be gleaming, neon electric signs that shouted out what he had done. A car rolled past him in the street and he wanted to scream. Another's headlights caught him briefly, and he thought it was like being tossed by a wave in a stormy sea. He hesitated, then walked on. Greenfield's streets seemed alien, unfamiliar. He stared at stores and shops that he'd known for years and could not recognize them, as if they came from some different space of time. He hurried on, forcing his steps, picking up speed, finally breaking into a run, which lasted only a few yards before he slowed, winded, gasping for breath. He stopped, sucked in freezing air, and then continued at a steady pace. A funeral march, he thought, with slow, deadly cadences, walked by a ghost.

He thought: Now it is complete. I have betrayed everyone.

Except my son.

With the weight of what he'd done pressing on his mind, Duncan slid through the night.

9
SATURDAY

Judge Pearson sat on a bunk with his grandson's head in his lap, stroking the child's forehead with slow, rhythmic caresses. Tommy slept, occasionally moaning slightly, as if his dreams lapped the shores of nightmare. But his breathing was deep and steady, apparently normal, and far different from what it had been earlier, when Olivia had locked them away, and the child's wind had been shallow and wheezing, filling his grandfather with fear. The judge glanced down at his watch and saw that it was well past midmorning, and hours since his own eyes had finally nodded shut for a few brief moments. He let Tommy continue to sleep, imagining that his grandson's body was steadily restoring itself. Grow stronger, he thought. Rest and recover. He let his hand wander over one of the bruises on the child's arm, which was already turning an ugly purplish-blue. He gingerly touched a red scrape on the boy's forehead, wishing somehow that he could transfer all the hurts and pains to himself.

We're lucky, though, he thought. He has no broken bones, concussion, or internal injuries that I can discern. He has no bullet wounds. He was not certain whether it was because Olivia was a poor shot or because she had hit what she was aiming at.

He whispered to his grandson, "We're going to be okay. You're going to be just fine. Don't worry."

Tommy's eyes fluttered, and he awakened.

For an instant he looked panicked, and his grandfather hugged him tightly. Then reason returned to the child's eyes and he sat up, looking about himself with a curiosity that encouraged the old man. Judge Pearson smiled at him, feeling the child's vitality surge through him as well. Last night I thought they'd killed him. Children are always stronger than adults give them credit for. They always know more, see more. He admonished himself to keep that in mind.

"How long have I been out?" Tommy asked.

"Almost sixteen hours. It was a long night."

Tommy tried to stretch, but caught himself midway.

"Ouch! Grandfather, I hurt."

"I know, Tommy. It'll pass, trust me. They knocked you about a bit. Me too . . ." He ran his fingers gently over his own bruised forehead. "But nothing serious. You're just going to be stiff, I think. But tell me if anything really hurts."

Tommy rubbed at his arms and at his legs. He stood up gingerly and shook his arms and legs out, like an animal after a lengthy nap. He looked about the attic room.

"I'm okay." He paused. "Well, here we are again."

"That's right," his grandfather replied, encouragement racing through him. "Here we are again. Listen, now, I need to know: Any pain in the stomach? In the head?"

Tommy hesitated, as if running an internal inventory. "No, I'm okay."

"I thought so," his grandfather said. He smiled. "Boy, it's good to see you."

"I thought they were going to kill me."

His grandfather started to say, So did I, then thought better of it.

"Nah, I don't think so. They were pretty angry and they wanted to teach you a lesson, but they need you. They really do. They're not going to do anything to you, don't worry."

"When the gun went off—"

"Yeah, that was scary, wasn't it?"

"I almost made it. I could see the treeline and forest for just a minute. If I could have gotten through the window, they never could have caught me."

"I think they knew that."

"It looked real cold and real gray outdoors. It looked like the kind of day where you would never want to go out to play, no matter what your mom and dad said. But I wanted to be out so bad. I guess I just wasn't thinking."

"No, you did right."

"You know, Grandfather, it was all sort of like it was happening to someone else. Like it wasn't me that jumped up and ran, but someone faster and stronger and smarter."

"I can't imagine anyone being those things. Or braver."

"Really?" Tommy winced as he moved about. But he smiled.

"No. Nobody."

"Anyway, I'm sorry."

"For what?"

"For leaving you."

Judge Pearson forced a laugh.

"You did great. You took everyone by surprise. It was the best damn sneak attack I've ever seen. You were really something. You showed them what you're made of. Tommy, you're a whole hell of a lot stronger than they are, and don't forget it. I was proud of you. Your mom and dad and sisters will really be proud of you when I tell them how you almost made it."

"Really?"

"Really."

Tommy dropped his head against his grandfather's chest and asked, "How much longer?"

"Not too much."

"I hope not."

The two were quiet for an instant. Tommy's eyes caught a pile of clothesline coiled in a corner and he looked toward his grandfather.

"They tied you up."

"But how?"

"Well, after they left, I untied you. They said not to, so they will probably be pretty angry when they come in to check on us. I don't know why they didn't tie me up as well. I think they were just as confused and scared as we were. Maybe they actually wanted me to untie you. We'll see."

Tommy nodded. He realized that nothing made much sense anymore.

"Why do they hate us?" he asked.

"Well, Bill probably got chewed out something awful—"

Tommy smiled. "I'll bet he did."

"—and the little one just seems slimy and angry all the time. He kept hitting you, slapping at you really, after you covered up your head. Actually, it was Bill who pulled him off."

Tommy nodded again.

"He probably hates everyone who has had a better life than he has."

The judge hesitated, then continued:

"And Olivia? Well, her bitterness knows no end, does it?"

Tommy shook his head.

"How do you think she got that way, Grandfather?"

"I don't know, Tommy. I wish I did." A dozen different psychological profiles slid into the judge's mind, but he discarded them all. "It seems to me that everyone grows up with love and hate and all sorts of other emotions inside them. Well, somewhere along the line, she lost all the good emotions and just kept the bad."

"Like the Grinch."

The judge burst out laughing.

"Precisely. Exactly like the Grinch."

Tommy smiled. "Born with a heart two sizes too small."

He hugged the child.

After a moment, Tommy pulled loose.

"I think we should work on the wall," he said with a military confidence.

The judge nodded. "If you're up to it."

The boy rubbed his arm where the bruises were forming.

"Might as well," he said. He walked over to the spot where they'd been scraping the day before. Then he turned and smiled at his grandfather. "You can really feel it," he said. "The air coming in. We're gonna get free yet, Grandfather. I know it."

The old man nodded, and watched as Tommy began to worry away at the joints. Judge Pearson slid down next to where Tommy was working and put his back against the wall. He closed his eyes and rested, suddenly suffused with exhaustion. The boy's resiliency strengthened him and comforted him at the same time. He wanted to sleep, but knew it would be impossible, that he needed to keep his eyes on Tommy and to protect him in case they tried to tie him again. He blinked his eyes open, fighting fatigue. Tommy turned to his grandfather and gave a little wave.

"Why don't you take a rest, Grandfather. I'll be okay."

The old man shook his head, but relaxed. He closed his eyes again and thought of his own youth. He recalled a moment when he'd fought a neighborhood bully. How old was I? He couldn't remember precisely. He could see himself, thin, wiry, perpetually dirty, clothes usually a bit tattered, his own mother's millstone. He smiled. What was the kid's name? It was a good bully's name, like Butch or Biff or some such. They'd fought in the playground after school. It had been springtime and warm; he remembered the light breeze moving the new greenery about. His tongue could taste the blood and dirt. Butch or Biff had thrashed him easily, knocking him down a half-dozen times, bloodying his nose, loosening a tooth. He'd absorbed so much punishment that the older and larger boy grew weakhearted, finally apologetic. The judge remembered the tears that had streaked down his face as he rose and kept flailing away, until finally Butch or Biff had pushed him down and departed.

He blinked open his eyes and saw his grandson.

The judge wanted to laugh out loud. It must be in his gene pool, he thought.

The judge thought of hundreds of criminal cases that had landed before him. The problem was that victory or defeat in the courtroom rarely paralleled real life. I dealt in degrees of guilt and innocence, levels of success or failure. The man charged with first degree, convicted of second, thanks to an impassioned speech by a defense attorney: It is a success for him because of what he could have faced, a failure for his victim's family. The same was true of the drunk driver acquitted of vehicular homicide because the state trooper failed to read him his rights before administering a sobriety test; justice handed on a platter to the guilty man, but stolen by neglect from the survivors. The robber convicted of burglary because his weapon was discovered during an illegal search; one reality changed into another by dogged adherence to rules. Those were the ordinary moments of the criminal court, distinctions of degrees. It was all a theater where each side was trying to promote one version of the truth versus another. It was a cold, heartless place, filled with hundreds of little lies conspiring to make a single truth.

He looked about himself, his eyes traveling across the attic confines: This is truth, he thought. It's nothing at all like the stately, removed reconstructions of the courtroom. He shook his head. All those years, I heard all those people talk of all those horrors, and I never really knew what it was like. He remembered the wave of fear that had swept over him as Olivia raised her gun and fired it at Tommy's back. Guilt flooded into the pit of his stomach: I should have jumped on her before she shot. I should have thrown myself in the bullet's path. His heart shook with the thought of how close he'd stepped to the abyss of failure. He steeled himself.

I will be ready next time.

I have been seduced, he thought. I have grown accustomed to my little prison, to thinking that someone will magically appear and free us. What has come over me? Tommy was right from the start. We are soldiers, they are the enemy.

He looked over at Tommy. You're completely right. We must save ourselves.

The judge picked his head up suddenly. He heard footsteps approaching the attic door, and turned toward Tommy. But the child was already moving swiftly to cover up the signs of digging.

Together they returned to a bunk and awaited their visitor.

*   *   *

Megan drove quickly through the outskirts of town, her mind awash with barely contained anger: We've done it. Now, where the hell are they? Why don't they call?

She tightened her grip on the steering wheel and muscled the car through an S-curve, accelerating on the exit, letting her anxiety flow directly into the car's engine, fueling it with a speed to which she was unaccustomed. She gritted her teeth and listened to the car's tires squeal as she negotiated another sharp turn. She pictured Duncan's pale face, when he'd come home the night before, and remembered her momentary fear that he'd failed, then the subsequent, equal fear that he'd succeeded. He had placed the briefcase with the money on the kitchen table and slowly counted out the proceeds of the robbery. "It's done," he'd said.

"No, it's not," she'd replied. "Nothing is done until we get the two Tommys back."

He had nodded and said, "Well, at least we've started."

Then she had told him of the violation of the house and the shambles made of the twins' room. They had spent most of the previous evening straightening it up while waiting for Duncan's return.

He had hugged the girls, who were past the point where they needed comforting, and said, "We must get this over with."

Megan agreed. She simply doubted it would happen.

She could think only of Olivia, her imagination a minefield of conflicted emotions; she knew Olivia had sent her henchman to ransack the twins' room. It was part of Olivia's design: disrupt and disorder the routine, and then destroy our complacency, make us think we are completely vulnerable, at any moment, at any time. That was the political thrust behind the bank job in Lodi. She pictured Olivia standing in the house before they set off to the disaster, arrogantly and confidently lecturing her troops.

Megan smiled despite herself: I heard that speech too many times, bitch. I heard it every morning, noon, and night, at every clandestine gathering, every public meeting. You haven't even had the sense to change your tune.

Megan almost missed the entrance to the town dump. She had to turn the car sharply and for an instant she thought she might lose control as it fishtailed in the loose gravel drive. Then Megan straightened it out and headed toward the dump. There was a little shack, with an elderly man sitting inside. He was smoking a cigarette and reading a copy of the *National Enquirer*. He waved Megan through when he saw she had the proper sticker in the corner of her car window. He paid little attention to her, which was good. She drove as far as she could toward the trash area. The stench seemed to hang in the solid cold air. She breathed through her mouth when she stopped the car and stepped out.

She had three green plastic bags in the trunk. One contained the clothing and paraphernalia Duncan had used during the robbery. The next held all the items of clothes that the twins had found on the floor of their room. Megan had instantly agreed with their request to throw out anything touched by the invader. The third bag was filled with regular garbage; she had gone through it carefully to make sure that there was nothing, an envelope or mailbox handout, that might connect them to the other bags.

She took each bag, double-checked to make certain it was sealed tightly, and then flung them, one after the other, as far as she could into the mass of garbage. The exertion made her breathe hard; she was satisfied with the distance she'd obtained with each. They seemed swallowed up by hundreds of similar stinking bags.

All right, she said to herself. She brushed her hands against her coat. Now let's go home and wait on Olivia.

She had not told Duncan or the twins of her research. She was not sure of it herself; she knew only that the hours spent poring over the rental listings of a few months earlier, and then matching them against those still active, had produced a dozen potential homesites. She had located each of them on a detailed map of the area, but she was not certain what she was going to do with her list now that she had it. She refused to let any of the possibilities enter into her mind. She forced herself to believe that Olivia would arrange to get the money and the Tommys would be returned and that would be that.

But the harder she forced herself to think it, the less she thought it would happen.

Duncan met her at the front door. He answered her question before she had a chance to ask it:

"No, nothing yet. Not a word."

"Damn," Megan replied. "What do you think they're waiting for?" She looked down at her watch, then out at the afternoon. "It's after three-thirty. It's almost four. There won't be much light left soon. Do you think they'd try to make the switch at night?"

"I don't know. Probably she just wants to screw around with us some more. She's a sadist and she thinks all this waiting is funny."

"Dammit to hell."

"I know."

Megan had an awkward thought: "Do you think she knows? I mean, how does she know you've got the money? How does she know we're ready?"

"She said she would know. Maybe she staked out the bank and saw me come out last night. Maybe she's just guessing. It makes no difference; today is the deadline she set. We've met it."

Duncan paced about. Megan watched him.

"Do you think—" she started.

"I don't know."

"I mean, she's got—"

"What?" said Duncan. "Who can tell what she's got in mind? All I know is that she'll arrange some way to get the money, and I'll demand she exchange the Tommys at the same time. That's it. That's the extent of my current planning! Robbing my own bank took some thinking," he said sarcastically. "But now that I've done it, what can I do? We wait!"

Duncan stomped into the kitchen where he peered about uncomfortably. Megan trailed after him.

"I'm sorry," she said.

He clenched his fists, then unwound slightly.

"Nothing," he said. "No fault. I'm sorry."

She nodded.

"What have we done?" she asked abruptly.

Duncan looked surprised.

"What do you mean?"

"What have we done? Have we lost everything?"

He nodded. "And nothing." He looked at her and then laughed. "It's only money."

"What do you—"

"That's it. Just money. We'll repay it, or maybe I'll go to prison or something, but it's only money. That's the one thing Olivia has had wrong from the start; she thinks this still is important to us."

Duncan smiled wryly and continued:

". . . But let's let her think that all we are is money and cars and vacation properties and stocks and mutual funds and whatever. It makes things a bit simpler, really. Let's just get the Tommys back. Then go on from there."

Megan nodded.

"It's all changed, anyway," Duncan said. "I realized that walking out of the bank. We are no longer what we were in sixty-eight, nor what we are in eighty-six. We're something different. If we just get the family back together, well, I think things will be fine."

Megan nodded again.

Duncan looked at her.

"You don't believe me?" he asked.

She shook her head.

He smiled.

"It's okay. I don't believe me either."

They sat down at the kitchen table.

"Isn't it funny how you can make some completely crazy speech and it both makes you feel better and worse at the same time?" For an instant Duncan dropped his face in his hands, as if hiding, and Megan remembered how he would hide behind his hands and play peek-a-boo first with the twins, then with Tommy, patiently, for hours it seemed. She bit back a sudden flood of tears.

Duncan lifted his head.

"It seemed like a dream last night. Alone in the bank. Stuffing the cash in the briefcase."

He leaned back in the chair, letting his eyes search skyward.

"I feel like something has broken inside of me. Broken in two."

He was silent for a moment, as if thinking about what he'd said. Then he added:

"I feel like I should make a speech about sacrifice and change and duty and love and all that crap. But I can't. I just want the phone to ring."

Megan didn't respond. The two sat wordlessly, watching the telephone, occasionally staring out at the quickly fleeing daylight, as if with the passing of the slate-gray sky, their hopes were darkening.

Olivia Barrow looked down at Judge Pearson and his grandson and said, "I would apologize and say I was sorry for having to do it this way, but I know you wouldn't believe me, so I won't."

Judge Pearson simply glared at Olivia. His hands were tied in front of him, knotted securely to a second loop that had been tightened around his ankles. He could feel his muscles and joints stiffening quickly. Tommy was similarly trussed beside him.

Olivia held up a roll of white masking tape.

"This could go over your mouth, judge."

"It's not necessary," he said quickly, perhaps a bit too quickly. He instantly wished he had the words back.

Olivia pulled a six-inch strip from the roll and tore it off. She held it up so that they could see it. She placed it over her own mouth, an inch away from making contact. She made a face. "Smelly," she said. "Unpleasantly sticky."

"It's not necessary. We'll wait quietly."

Olivia grinned. "No? I have your word as a judge on that?"

He nodded.

"How about you, Tommy? Scout's honor?"

Tommy nodded, but shrank against his grandfather.

"All right," she said. "See? I'm not such an ogre after all." She rolled the strip up into a ball and tossed it away in the corner. "I wouldn't want one of you to gag and choke. Come back here and find one of you dead. And so close to the end, as well. It would be a shame to have made it this far and then blow it, wouldn't it, judge?"

He grunted in agreement.

"You especially, Tommy. Don't think I've forgotten about those quick little feet of yours. In prison there were always a few people who had rabbit in them. It's a good expression. Kind of captures the essence of the desire to escape."

She looked at Tommy. "No more rabbit in you, is there?"

"No," he said. "I promise."

She smiled.

"And I don't believe you for an instant."

Olivia continued to grin. "Well, don't blow it. Think about it. You're almost home free."

"You're saying you're going to get your damn money and we can go home?"

"More or less, judge. Just got to put old Duncan through a few more hoops and then we'll be closing down this little show. Make you feel a little better? Tommy?"

"I want to go home," he said.

Her false smile faded. "You little bastard, you've made that abundantly clear."

Tommy shivered, but Olivia returned to her mocking self, glancing down at her watch as she said: "Well, time to go. Now you boys stay nice and quiet and safe and we'll be back in a little while to say our farewells, huh?"

The judge didn't reply. Tommy merely looked at Olivia. She means none of it, he thought abruptly. The force of his recognition almost startled him. His eyes widened and bore down on Olivia. She locked in on him, and he saw that she was taken aback by the strength of his gaze, if only for an instant.

Olivia turned away. She marched down the stairs and slammed the attic door shut. She locked and then checked the lock twice. For a brief moment she allowed herself to fill with a disquieting rage. She thought about the look of hope that had scorched across the judge's face. He's been mine, almost from the start, she thought.

I've always known what he would say, what he would do. But the boy sees through my every lie. All that innocence is extremely dangerous.

She picked up a small hand-duffel bag from the floor and unzipped it. She checked the contents: a revolver, a pair of binoculars fitted with night-vision lenses, a compass. She slid the roll of tape inside.

Olivia looked over at the two men.

"Armed and dangerous," she said.

They smiled and she led them out into the quickening cold.

"It's showtime," she said. They fell in behind her.

When the phone rang, it was as if an electric charge ran through both of them. They reached for the receiver simultaneously, but Megan pulled her hand back abruptly and let Duncan answer the call.

He put the phone to his ear and said, "Yes?"

"Hello, Duncan," said Olivia.

"Hello, Olivia," he replied.

"Have you got the money?"

"Yes."

"Does anyone know?"

"No."

"You haven't been dumb and called the cops, have you?"

"You know the answer to that question."

"Good. Good going, Duncan. We're ready to go on to the next step. A higher level, so to speak." She made a small laugh.

"Look, dammit, Olivia. I have the money. A lot of money. Now I want my boy back. And the judge. I'll hand over the money when I see they're safe."

Olivia was quiet for an instant. She was standing in a Burger King restaurant on the edge of the same shopping mall that Duncan had visited the day before. Ramon and Bill sat at a nearby table, nursing cups of coffee. Bill had the remains of a hamburger on the table in front of him.

"Don't give me orders, Duncan. You do what I say, you get them back. Assuming you've come up with enough long green."

"Listen, it's more than—"

Olivia interrupted. "Let it be a surprise."

"I'm tired of these games, Olivia."

"Really? But I'm not and I'm the only person whose vote counts."

"I'm warning you, Olivia. You've pushed things a bit too far!" As soon as he spoke, he realized how hollow and clichéd his words were. He felt adrift and stupid. Olivia responded with a short laugh.

"Tough words. But I don't think so. Anyway, in this game, Duncan, I hold the aces."

They were both silent for an instant. Duncan finally broke through, exasperation clouding his voice, filling his head and fogging his reason.

"All right. What next?" he asked.

"Good. That's a bit better attitude. Look at your watch, Duncan."

"It's a little before four."

"Better be more careful."

He looked again.

"It's three minutes of four."

"Good," she said. "Now for the excitement. Do you know the telephone booths outside of Smith's Drugs on East Pleasant Street? You ought to, that's where you get your prescriptions filled."

Duncan thought, then replied: "Yes, I guess so."

"Great. This is just like they do it on television. Third booth from the wall. You've got to be there by four-oh-five. And all by your little lonesome, remember. Bye, bye."

"What!"

"Better hurry, you son of a bitch. Better do what you're told. Exactly what you're told, Duncan, or else it all ends. Prematurely. Do I need to spell things out any clearer?"

"No."

"Good going, Duncan. You've wasted thirty seconds already."

Olivia hung up the telephone. She turned to the two men at the table. "Here we go," she said. "He's off."

Duncan threw down the telephone and grabbed the briefcase with the money. Megan looked frightened: "What is it?"

"I've got five minutes to get to a phone booth in town."

Karen and Lauren had entered the room as the telephone had rung. "We'll come with you," Karen said. She inadvertently stood in the doorway and Duncan barreled past her.

"No, no, no," he insisted.

He grabbed his coat from the hall rack.

"Someone should come with you—" Megan started, but he cut her off, struggling to get his arms into the sleeves.

"No, no. Alone—I'll do it alone."

"We'll follow you," Lauren said. "In our car."

"No!" Duncan shouted. "Alone! She demanded I go alone."

"But what about us?" Megan cried.

"I don't know! Just wait. Please, my God, just get out of the way." He was rushing through the door. The three women stood and watched as Duncan threw himself into his car and fired back down the driveway.

"Oh, God," Megan said, as she saw him spin the tires and race up their street. "Oh, what have we done?"

"What is it, Mom?" Karen asked.

"I don't know. I just don't know."

She turned to the twins and adopted a half-smile of encouragement that she knew they would disbelieve. They went back into the house to wait. She was filled with things to say, but said none of them, realizing that every word that might fall from her lips was more foolish than the next. For one horrible instant she wondered whether she would ever see any of her men again. Then she forced the thought away before it sickened her. She gratefully accepted the steaming tea from Lauren's hands, trying to let its warmth fill her and obliterate the cold that was spreading within her so steadily.

Duncan didn't look at his watch, but knew his time was probably gone. He pulled the car into the back of a bus stop, praying that none of the local policemen spotted him as he rushed across the sidewalk. As he approached, he heard the telephone ring and he threw himself into the booth, grabbing the receiver.

"Yes—"

"Hey, Duncan! Good going," Olivia said. "I didn't think you'd make it."

She and the two men had moved inside the mall. There were telephones at a half-dozen different locations, which she'd staked out.

"What next?" Duncan asked. "Dammit."

"Impatient, huh?"

"I want my boy."

"All right. At the other end of town, in front of the Stop and Shop. That's where Megan buys your groceries. You've got eight minutes. But, Duncan—"

"Yes!"

"First reach under the telephone stand and take what you find there."

She hung up and checked her watch.

Duncan thrust his hand beneath the telephone and found something taped to the underside of the stand. He ripped it free. It was a compass. He jammed it into his pocket and dashed back to his car.

Duncan thought of nothing except his son, and speed. He ran a yellow light and passed another car in the breakdown lane, causing the cold air behind him to fill with blaring horns. He could feel sweat on his forehead as he pulled into the parking lot of the grocery store. He saw the phone stand, and slammed on his brakes. He ran toward the booth. Lights from the front of the store made the area seem gray and lonely.

The phone was quiet.

Duncan looked down at his watch. Seven minutes, he thought. I'm sure it took no more than seven minutes to get here. He waited. He watched the second hand sweep up towards the eighth minute and he reached out his hand.

The phone remained quiet.

His hand shook as he placed it on the receiver.

Ring, damn you, he thought.

There was no sound.

Panic filled him. He could feel his heart tripping. He searched about frantically, wondering whether he was at the wrong phone. He couldn't see any others. He stared at his watch.

Nine minutes.

Oh, my God, he thought. What's wrong?

He was aware of the cold and increasing darkness. It was as if he was caught in the last of the day's light, while Olivia worked from the shadows. He looked about wildly. The town around him seemed misshapen and bloated, as if he was looking at a hundred familiar locations and yet seeing them for the first time.

Ten minutes.

Tommy, he thought with despair.

Then the phone rang. He ripped it toward his ear.

"Hey, thought I'd give you a little extra, what with all the traffic and everything," Olivia said pleasantly.

Duncan gritted his teeth.

"Do you think we're watching you, Duncan? Don't you realize that somewhere along the road, we're keeping an eye on you? That's the purpose of this little dog and pony show. Got to see if you can take orders. I know you couldn't. Not eighteen years ago."

"Where next?"

"Harris Farm Supplies on Route Nine. It's five miles, Duncan. I know you're familiar with it. Like to get seedlings there, and probably your Christmas tree as well. Mulch for the shrubbery. You like a little gardening, don't you? You know where you're going. Oh, yeah, you've got, oh, how about six minutes. The phone's right in front, but you know that."

He ran to the car.

Duncan saw the sign for the farm store, and maneuvered across traffic, accelerating into the parking lot. Six minutes, he thought. Six minutes have passed. He slammed down hard on the brakes and jumped from the driver's seat, only to stop in his tracks. He felt his heart plummet through his body: There was a woman talking on the outside phone.

He raced toward her. The woman looked up as he approached.

"I'll just be a minute," she said.

"It's an emergency," Duncan replied.

The woman was middle-aged. She wore a parka against the cold. "Look, Mom, there's a problem here. I'll be by to pick up the kids as soon as I finish here and at the grocery."

"Please," Duncan said. He stared at his watch.

The woman glared at him. "Someone says they need the phone. I'll be there as quick as I can."

Duncan reached for the phone. "Hang it up!" he shouted.

"I'll remember the broccoli," the woman said.

Duncan seized the telephone and slammed it down on the hook. The woman took a quick step back. "I ought to call the police!" she said. "You rude bastard!"

Duncan turned his back on her and heard her stomp across the gravel drive. He looked at the telephone.

When it rang, he reached out in relief.

"Olivia? It wasn't my fault, there was someone on the phone— I'm sorry," he said.

She laughed.

"Close, math-man. Real close. Hadn't really expected to get a busy signal at that phone. Who would want to stand in the cold talking? Ah well, onwards and upwards. Now, how long a drive is it to Leverett?"

"Twenty minutes."

"Okay. On the way into the center of town, there's a Seven-Eleven convenience store, right next to the Mobil station. The phone's in front. Twenty minutes."

Duncan drove quickly. Within seconds he had passed out of Greenfield and was enveloped by intermittent light and shadows, as bare stands of trees rose against the sky. He turned on his headlights, which blocked a bit of the falling night away, but he felt alone, as if at sea. The road to Leverett was a winding, two-lane back road. He had driven it many times, yet on this occasion it seemed eerily unfamiliar. For a moment or two, he had trouble keeping his car in the lane; despite tugging at the wheel, it seemed to drift on him. He lowered the electric window on his side, flooding the car with frigid air. Still he felt warm, and he could feel dampness on the back of his neck, rubbing against his jacket collar. He saw his hands on the wheel and they were white and ghostly.

He spotted the gas station and the convenience store next door with a minute to spare. He cut past the pumps and pulled in front of the telephone. He jumped out and leaped to the phone. Then he stood waiting, wondering what was next. He fingered the compass in his pocket and imagined that Olivia was watching him.

The phone did not ring.

I'm here, he thought. I'm here.

The drive had quieted his jangled nerves some. He glanced at his watch. All right, dammit. Here I am.

The phone remained quiet.

He waited, as he had before. At first he thought Olivia was just playing another head game with him, so his concern was limited. Then, as each minute passed, he increased his anxiety, stepping swiftly from discomfort to worry, to sweaty fear and finally reaching the ledge of panic.

The phone remained quiet.

He did not know what to do.

As before, he cast about, wondering whether he'd reached the wrong location.

His eyes swept across the neighboring gas station. He spotted a single exterior phone booth, located by the road, midway between the convenience store parking lot and the exit for the station.

He looked back at the telephone in front of him, which remained frustratingly silent.

No, he thought, she said this one.

He looked at his watch. Five minutes over deadline.

Duncan refused to allow himself to think of consequences. He knew that Olivia was doing something, but he was unsure what. He tried to imagine, but drew only a blank.

He was again aware of the grayness of the afternoon. He could just make out the edge of night in the sky. He could see his breath steaming from his mouth like smoke.

Ten minutes over deadline.

He looked over again at the other telephone.

She mentioned that gas station.

Duncan stared at it. There was a lonely, brief moment when no cars or trucks were passing, and the air grew quiet.

He froze. He strained his hearing.

It's ringing, he thought. He felt dizzy with fear.

He stepped away from the front of the convenience store, toward the solitary phone booth. A car rolled past, obliterating the sound, but he took a quick step, then another, and the ringing sound became clearer, more insistent.

He began to walk tentatively toward the phone. He glanced back over his shoulder at the phone at the convenience store. Indecision ricocheted about within him.

He started to walk briskly.

The ringing seemed to grow louder in his ears.

He quickened his pace. He started to jog.

As he watched, he saw one of the station attendants head toward the phone booth. No! Duncan thought. No!

He broke into a sprint, dashing across the parking lot.

He saw the attendant swing open the door and pick up the phone, staring oddly at it, after a second.

"No!" Duncan cried. "Here! Don't hang up!"

He could see the man looking quizzically at the phone.

"Here! Here! Dammit, I'm here!" he shouted, running flat-out now, sprinting for all he was worth, waving his arms wildly.

The man swung halfway out of the booth, looking at Duncan. "Hey," he said, "you Duncan?"

"Yes!"

"Well," the attendant said. "I'll be damned. There's a call here for you."

Duncan seized the phone.

"Yes. Yes! Here I am!" He shut the door on the slightly bewildered attendant, who shrugged and moved away.

"Good going, Duncan. I didn't figure you'd manage this one. Really, I didn't . . ." Olivia said with mock enthusiasm.

"You said the Seven-Eleven!"

"Hey, got to be a little flexible."

"You said it and I was there!"

"Duncan, Duncan, calm down. I just wanted to see if you were into it or not." She snorted a brittle laugh. "I'd have called the other phone in a couple of minutes. I just wanted to see if you could figure it out." She laughed again. "Maybe I would have."

Duncan took a deep breath. He tried to steady himself, but realized it was futile. He managed only to remove the quaver from his voice.

"What's next?" he asked.

"Directions. I'll only say them once. Ready?"

"No—yes—go ahead."

"Ready!"

Duncan took another deep breath.

"Yes."

"Take out your compass. Go north three point three miles. Go east two point six miles. At the fork, go northeast one point one miles. Stop the car. There will be a field to the west. Go into the field until you find a marker. Then wait for instructions. Got it?"

"Repeat them, please, Olivia."

"Duncan, Duncan, I'm trying to be so fair, and yet I sense you don't appreciate my efforts." She laughed mockingly. "All right. I'll repeat them: north three point three. East two point six, northeast one point one. Go, Duncan. Get going."

She hung up the phone. She turned to Bill Lewis and Ramon Gutierrez and said, "Like a lemming headed to sea. He is disoriented, scared, and acquiescent. One might even say ripe." She smiled. "Mission accomplished," she said. "Let's go."

They were both too nervous to do anything other than smile awkwardly. They're weak, Olivia thought, and had to fight off a momentary disgust. They get close to a bit of money, and it gets to them, bad. I still need them, she thought. Not much longer, but just a little while. She quick-stepped from the mall, trailed by the two men, who had to hurry up to keep up with her.

Duncan climbed behind the wheel of his car and reached over the dashboard to set the odometer to zero. He placed his hands up along his head, to try to steady the dizziness that trapped him. He thought it must be like being caught in a whirlpool. He felt his heart racing within him. To try to calm himself, he repeated the directions to himself, like some devilish mantra, and picked the compass out of his pocket. For an instant the needle bounced about, as confused as he was, then it settled and Duncan realized that he could take a side road and head due north. He put the car in gear, blew a long breath of whistling wind out between his clenched lips, and headed out.

Once again, within a half-mile he had been enveloped by countryside. He drove slowly, looking up at the old New England farmhouses that he passed. They were a uniform clapboard white, frayed by time and hard winter, and all the barns seemed swaybacked with age and duty. The earth seemed brown and the tree stands black. Tree branches hung starkly against the last light. The world seemed suddenly ancient, primeval, and frightening. The road became a slippery gravel surface, and the car started to bounce in and out of potholes. He was cutting between fields and hills; alone but for the occasional farm vehicle that he passed heading in.

His first turn was easily found and he proceeded, keeping an eye on the odometer.

He found the fork in the road, checked the compass, and turned to the northeast. Excitement swept over him, and he allowed himself to think, if only for an instant, that he was about to see his son. He battled against false hopes and watched the odometer. Nine-tenths of a mile; one mile; one point one miles.

Duncan stopped the car.

What little light remained to the day was precious. The sky was a gray-black blend, fading toward night with each passing second.

He stepped out and surveyed the field that opened up before him. There was a hedge, and an old stone wall, which came up to his waist. Beyond that, perhaps a half-mile away, was a line of forest. The field rolled toward the woods, like a placid ocean toward the shore. He stepped to the stone wall and scrambled over.

Duncan cleared his thoughts, thinking only of the money in the briefcase and his son. He started to walk across the field, only to sink up to his ankle in mud. He pulled his foot free with a whooshing sound and continued, fighting against the loose, slippery ground, feeling the dampness seep into his sneakers and socks, chilling his feet. There was some thin ice in the field, as well, and Duncan heard it crunch beneath his shoes.

He stumbled once and dropped the briefcase. He kept going.

What am I looking for? he wondered. He kept his eyes wide, roving from side to side, trying to find some marker. The light was almost gone, and with it came despair.

Duncan struggled on. He turned and looked back toward the road. He realized he was nearly midway across the field.

It's got to be here, he thought.

The night cold seemed to fill him.

"Where is it?" he cried out loud. "Where?"

He pushed on another twenty yards and spotted a wooden stake pushed into the earth. It had a Day-Glo orange band painted around the top. That's it, he thought, and he picked up his feet, half-running, half-falling to reach the marker.

Then he stopped.

He stood next to the stake and peered at it. There was no sign, no message, no indication that it was anything other than a stake in the midst of a field. For an instant, confusion and pain pummeled him.

Duncan breathed in. His soaked feet sent waves of cold through his body. He shivered and thought he could sense the remainder of the day's warmth blowing up into the overcast sky.

He talked to himself: "She said to wait for instructions. All right, Olivia, instruct me."

The silence grew about him.

He leaned up against the marker and breathed out slowly. Unbidden, tears started to flow down his face. What's wrong with me? he wondered, but he was unable to check the surge within him. I am strong, I am prepared, he told himself, but the words were scant comfort. The flood of darkness around him carried only more despair, and he felt his hopes dwindle. He clutched the briefcase to his chest, as if it were a child, and he rocked back and forth a bit, trying to warm himself, trying to imagine what had gone wrong, what was happening, what he was supposed to do. His mind filled with pictures of his son, which crushed down further on his heart. He let out a sob, but he remained standing by the marker, realizing in that horrible instant that he had no other plan, no other idea of what to do.

A hundred and fifty yards away, hidden in the treeline, Olivia watched through her binoculars. Satisfaction filled her entire body and she shivered, but not from the increasing cold.

"So, Duncan, how long will you wait? How long will you stand there in the middle of nowhere? Will you wait all night for your son? Will you wait a few minutes? How much patience do you have? Can you stand the cold? Can you stand the pain? All by yourself? How long, Duncan? Eighteen years," she whispered. "Eighteen years."

She watched and waited.

After an hour, Duncan knew Olivia wasn't coming, but he felt powerless to move. He waited a second hour, until his feet lost all sensation and he was afraid he wouldn't be able to find his way back through the inkiness that surrounded him.

He finally stood up.

For an instant his head spun about, and he felt a drunk's insecurity.

The tears on his cheeks had dried.

The hollowness inside him seemed vast, endless.

His mind was a blank of despair.

Duncan moved steadily, robotically, across the field, back to where he hoped his car remained. It was as if the time spent dashing across his town, then finding this particular lonely spot, had happened years before, somewhere in his memory, not mere hours beforehand.

He slipped and fell headfirst once, lying for an instant in the damp, scraggly field. He could taste blood on his lip. Then he picked himself up and tried to wipe some of the wet mud from his body. He stumbled on, finally picking out the stone wall, which seemed at first to be a dark wave rushing toward him. Clutching the briefcase, he scrambled over the top. He spotted his car a hundred feet up the road, and trudged toward it.

He did not know what he would do when he got home.

For a few moments, as he opened the door and strapped himself in, he thought: This was just like her. A test, just to see what I'd do. His anger was so immense that he felt not rage but a great vacuum inside.

He started up the car and put it in gear. He did not have any idea what he would say to Megan and the twins. The car's tires spun momentarily, as he turned it around, and he thought: That's all I need, to get stuck out here. He drove slowly back down the road.

I wonder if she'll call tonight. Or tomorrow. He tried to imagine what sort of arrangement she would want to make to get the money, but was unable to invent a scenario. This time I will insist, he thought, I will demand the trade take place. The Tommys for the money. Perhaps that is what she has intended all along, but he doubted it.

He slowed down as he approached the fork in the road. He thought of the disappointment that Megan would have, and he tried to think of something to say to her that wouldn't mimic the despair he himself felt. He wondered what Karen and Lauren would think. They've been through the wringer, too. I've got to do something for them. He breathed out slowly, and started to turn to his left, keeping the directions in mind, backtracking from oblivion.

Then he screamed.

Headlights blinded him suddenly and he threw the wheel hard to avoid an onrushing car that emerged from the darkness like a wraith, heading right at him. He could hear the sound of the car's engine, and the noise of its tires fighting for purchase on the loose-packed gravel as it swooped in attack toward him. He plunged his foot down on the brake and felt his car swerve, fishtail, and finally slam to a halt. It stalled with a shudder.

He held his hand up, trying to ward off the light that flooded his windshield. Then his door was ripped open.

He twisted in the seat and saw Olivia.

She thrust a revolver into his face and cocked the hammer back with a solid, sickening click.

"Money, Duncan. Give me the money."

He could hardly speak, and he croaked, "My boy . . ."

"Give me the money, Duncan, or I will kill you right here."

"I want my boy," he said, voice quivering.

"Kill him!" came a voice from the darkness. "Just kill the pig now!"

Duncan grabbed the briefcase.

Olivia's voice remained absolutely calm.

"Think, Duncan. Get a grip on yourself. You could die out here and it would all be over and they'd never get home. You could fight or refuse and die and it would all be for nothing, wouldn't it? Give me the money, Duncan, just hand it over and live. It's your only chance. It's the boy's only chance."

Another voice cut into the blackness: "Come on! Olivia, hurry!"

Duncan knew the voice. It was Bill Lewis and he stared out into the darkness, wildly, searching for him.

"Just blow the fucker away!" said the other voice.

"Duncan, use your head," Olivia said quietly. She did not grab at the briefcase, but she pointed at it deliberately. "Just hand it over. Can't you see that I can just take it if I want to?"

He handed her the briefcase, and she dropped it behind her, keeping the gun trained on him.

"Good," she whispered. "Smart, Duncan."

She reached past him and snatched the keys out of his ignition. "I'll drop these about fifty yards up the road," she said, "when you see me tap the brake lights. They'll be right in the center of the road, and you'll be able to find them if you're careful."

"Tommy . . ." Duncan moaned.

"I'll count the money and be in touch. Just stay cool, Duncan. You've almost made it. No one's dead yet. No one has to die. Think about that. Think about it real hard. No one has to die . . ." She emphasized the word "has."

She hesitated. "But they might," she whispered.

Olivia stepped back, picking the briefcase up from the spot where she'd dropped it. Duncan half-fell from his car, trying to keep up with her. She whirled and brought the pistol to bear on his chest.

"Play the game, Duncan," she said.

He stopped in his tracks, hands outstretched, in half-supplication, half-despair. Olivia abruptly turned her back on him, with a snort. He watched as she got back into her car. The headlights that had blinded him were suddenly extinguished, but the engine surged and Duncan had to leap backward as it roared toward him, scorching past where he stood. He pivoted and saw it stop fifty yards away. As she had said, she tapped the brake lights. He could see that the headlights were turned on past the spot where he might have read her license number or made out the make of car. Then it accelerated into the darkness. Duncan started to run after it, his breath coming in gasps and gulps, but the car disappeared around a corner, the lights vanishing. Duncan stood for an instant, staring at the endless night.

Then, with absolutely nothing else to do, he got down on his knees and started to hunt for his keys.

10
SUNDAY

It was well past midnight, but Duncan continued to search through the basement, muttering to himself as he delved into the dusty accumulation of boxes, old tax returns, bundled magazines, and scarred furniture that littered the shadowy room. Megan sat on the steps, beneath a bare hundred-watt bulb, watching her husband, not precisely certain what he was looking for. She felt drained and wretched; in the hours since he had returned home muddy, half-frozen, and alone, they had passed through tears and shouts and recriminations to a stunned silence that had been interrupted when Duncan abruptly rose and said, "Well, I know one thing that isn't going to happen again." Then he had tromped down to the basement, without explaining his cryptic statement. She had been watching his search for half an hour, without speaking—scared to speak, actually—because every word seemed to insist on the horror of their position.

"Dammit, I know it's here somewhere," Duncan said as he shifted a box. "Christ, what a mess!" As he moved, his misshapen shadow slid across the floor.

Megan put her elbows on her knees and cupped her chin in her hands.

"Duncan," she said quietly, "do you think they're still alive?" She wanted to snap the words back as soon as she said them.

He paused, shifting a cardboard container, then in a sudden, violent move, threw the container against the wall, where it crashed and exploded in dust.

"Yes! What kind of question—"

"Why?" she whispered.

"What reason would she have to—" he started.

"One hundred and forty-one thousand seven hundred and eighty-six reasons," Megan said glumly.

Duncan stopped and stood, waiting for his wife to continue.

"She has the money. She's probably ruined our lives, as well. What's to prevent her from killing them and simply walking away, richer, satisfied, and free as a bird?"

Duncan did not answer for several minutes. He stood thinking, preparing his words carefully.

"You're right," he said, "It makes absolutely no sense for her to leave witnesses. It makes no sense for her to hang around here for one more instant than she has to. She knows that Monday morning the bank will be swarming with cops. She knows that she's pushed us to our limits. Sticking around only endangers her more. What would make sense is to shoot the Tommys and get the hell out of here."

Megan fought tears.

"Which is why," Duncan said, "she won't do it."

"What?"

"She won't do it. She won't do what makes sense."

"But—how—I can't see—" Megan stuttered.

Duncan took a deep breath. "You know, it's funny, I said it the other day. Was it Thursday? Wednesday? God, it seems like it was forever ago. Anyway, I said it and then I forgot it and I shouldn't have: It's not the Tommys. It's not the money. What she wants is us."

Megan opened her mouth to respond, then stopped.

They both remained quiet for a moment. Then Duncan said it again: "Us. Understand? That's why she's still here. That's why she won't leave, not quite yet. No matter how much sense it would make to get out. Not while there's still a card or two left to play."

"What cards do you think are left?"

"Just two," Duncan said softly. He pointed first at Megan and then himself. "King and Queen of trumps."

Megan nodded.

"Do you think she means to kill us?"

"Maybe. Maybe not. Make us suffer? Torture us? That's what she's been doing. I don't know; I just feel sure that she means some crushing act, something she can see and taste and feel. Something she can savor for years. Maybe she means to kill us. But maybe it's something else, something that we would have to live with every day, the way she did." Duncan shuddered. "I'm not sure. But I know the Tommys are alive."

Megan realized that she was again dipping her head in agreement. She'd wondered why Olivia hadn't killed Duncan earlier, out in the lonely countryside. She'd had a perfect opportunity. Except I wasn't there.

"Do you think there's any chance she might just return the Tommys? After all, if it's us she really wants—"

Duncan cut her off. "No. Absolutely none."

Megan nodded. "You know, it'll sound crazy—"

"Nothing sounds crazy right about now."

She smiled wanly. "—but I think if he were dead, I would feel it somewhere inside of me. Like something would break or go off."

Duncan nodded. "I think so, too. Whenever he's been sick or troubled, I always thought I could feel it inside . . ." Duncan let his voice trail off. He spotted something in the corner of the basement and suddenly reached down for it.

"So," Megan said with an abrupt firmness that surprised even herself, "what do we do? Where do we go from here? How do we fight back?"

Duncan straightened up, holding a shoebox-sized metal container.

"I knew I could find it," he said. He shook his head. "I don't know why I didn't think of it earlier."

"Do we go to the police now?" Megan asked.

"I never knew what to do with it," he said.

"No," Megan answered her own question. "No. I know what we do." She thought of the list up in her briefcase, with the area map. "It's what we should have done at the beginning."

She realized that she was on her feet, that her voice had an unfamiliar tone. There was an edge and harshness to her words that she barely recognized, but it was welcome.

Duncan paced over to where she stood. The bare light bulb threw their shadows across the basement, making their images on the wall seem gigantic. He tugged at the latch on the tin box and it came free. Megan craned to see what it held, and then remembered as she spotted the piece of stained oilcloth that had covered the contents for so many years.

"Will it still work?" she asked.

"It did in nineteen sixty-eight," Duncan replied. "I never knew what to do with it," he repeated. "I suppose I should have thrown it away when we first ran back here, but I didn't and then I just never got rid of it. We've hauled it everyplace we've moved."

He held the .45-caliber pistol up to the light, inspecting it for rust and age. He slid a clip of cartridges from the handle, then reached up and snatched back the chambering action, cocking the empty pistol with a harsh, metallic noise.

"Do you remember how she would call us?" Duncan asked. "What did she call it? The morning prayer."

"We are the new America," Megan intoned.

She took the pistol from Duncan's hand and sighted down the barrel. "We are the new America," she repeated. She pulled the trigger, and the hammer clicked down on the empty chamber with a sharp sound that echoed in the basement and resounded in their imaginations.

Megan let Duncan sleep.

He had paced the floor of the living room until past three in the morning, wound up with a hundred ideas, finally falling exhausted into one of the armchairs, nodding off with the .45 in his lap. The twins had discovered him in that position when they awakened; Lauren had gently lifted the weapon from his hand, while Karen put her hands on his shoulders so that he would not awaken startled. Moments later Megan had joined the twins in the kitchen, where they'd placed the weapon in the center of the kitchen table, and were staring at it as if it were something alive.

"Where did we get that?" Lauren asked.

"And what are we going to do with it?" Karen added.

"We've had it since sixty-eight. We just never had a need for it . . ." She was only slightly taken aback by the twins' attitude, spoken in matter-of-fact tones; they seemed neither shocked nor scared to discover the handgun in their house.

"Until now," Lauren finished her mother's statement.

"Until now," Megan repeated.

"Are we really going—" Karen started, but her mother held up her hand.

"Is there a plan?" Lauren asked.

"None yet. No."

"Then what are we going to do?"

"Right now?" Megan looked at the twins. "You guys are going to stay here and keep an eye on your father. No one is to do anything. If the phone rings, wake him up. It could be them. They said they were going to be in touch."

"I hate this waiting," Lauren said with sudden force. "I hate this always waiting for things to happen to us! I want to do something."

"We'll have our time," said Megan. "I promise."

Lauren nodded, satisfied. Her sister eyed her mother.

"What are you going to do now?" Karen asked.

Megan took the pistol off the table and put it in her briefcase.

"You're not going to do anything silly all by yourself, are you? I'll wake up Dad," Lauren admonished. "We're all in this together."

Megan shook her head. "No, I won't. Don't worry. All I'm going to do is look at some real estate," she said. "That's what realtors do on Sundays. They inspect properties."

"Mom!"

"Mom, you can't just head off alone. Dad will go crazy."

"I know," Megan said abruptly. "I know he will. But I'm going to do this myself."

"Why? And what are you going to do?"

"What I'm going to do is take a stab in the dark," Megan replied carefully. "I've taken a guess at some possible places that they might have rented. Maybe I'll get lucky and find the Tommys."

"Yeah. And maybe you'll get unlucky and get in trouble," Karen muttered.

"Mom, this is crazy—" Lauren started.

Megan nodded slowly. "Yes, I suppose so. But at least it's something and that's better than nothing."

"I still think you should wait for Dad," Karen insisted.

"No." Megan shook her head. "He did what he had to do, by himself. Now I'm doing what I have to do, by myself."

She looked at the two girls carefully. She wondered for an instant why she was so dogmatic—but she knew that she had to get out of the house before Duncan awakened. He would be reasonable and practical, she knew, and he would be frightened for her. He would prevent her from taking this chance, and that would be worse than all the danger she might face. She felt her insides churn with conflict. I have done nothing, she thought. And now it is time for me to do something.

"Mom, are you sure you know what you're doing?" Lauren asked.

"Yes," Megan replied. "No. What difference does that make?"

She put on her jacket, a hat and scarf. "When your father gets up, tell him I'll call in an hour or two. Tell him there's nothing to worry about."

She left the twins, neither of whom believed her for an instant, hovering protectively about Duncan, who slept on, driven by exhaustion.

Outside the front door, Megan paused, breathing in a draught of cool air, letting the damp cold seep into her head, clearing her thoughts. She allowed herself a single twinge of guilt, thinking of how furious Duncan would be when he awakened. Then she dismissed the sensation and forged ahead. She walked steadily to her car, searching the area for any signs of Olivia or her crew. She peered up and down the street and saw no one except the neighbors. She watched as one family took seats in a station wagon and backed gingerly out of their driveway. They had loaded up the car with hockey sticks, and skates, and wore bright red and blue jerseys. She saw another neighbor sweeping some dead leaves out of a pathway. Up the street she saw an elderly couple packing mulch around a flowerbed in anticipation of the first snow of the season. For an instant she was almost overcome by the normalcy of it all. A car cruised by and she recognized one of the other realtors from her office, who lived down the block. Megan waved with a jocularity that sickened her. But she used the opportunity to let her eyes follow the neighbor's car, inspecting the street. When she was satisfied that there was no one waiting for her, no one watching the house, she slipped behind the wheel. But before starting the engine, she checked her supplies: Map. Addresses. Paper and pencil. Binoculars. Instant camera and film. Gun. She wore tall waterproof boots and a dark parka, and she had one of Duncan's knit ski hats, which she could pull down over most of her face. She turned the ignition, took another deep breath, and headed out.

She drove quickly across Greenfield, constantly checking the rear-view mirror, each time wondering whether the dark sedan, or the station wagon or the sports car or the delivery van that cruised behind her was tailing her. I must know for certain, she thought. Twice she pulled into gas stations and paused, letting traffic sweep by, but she wasn't persuaded that it was a successful way of losing someone following her. Finally, she hit upon another course. She drove to the entrance to Greenfield College, on the outskirts of town. It had a long, circular driveway in front of the admissions office. She pulled quickly across traffic, into the drive, accelerating around it, and coming out heading in the opposite direction. Then she paused, searching in the mirrors for any vehicle that might make a U-turn. When she saw none, she went on, not exactly certain how she was going to approach her task, but sure that she was going to try.

*   *   *

In the farmhouse, the kidnappers argued.

The previous evening's money-counting euphoria had given way to debate over what their next course of action should be. Olivia, settled in a large armchair, listened intently as Bill Lewis and Ramon Gutierrez snapped out their desires. It was odd how a little bit of money changed people, how quickly it caused them to lose sight of what was really important. She wanted to laugh at the change in their attitudes. Twenty-four hours earlier, they had both been shaky and indecisive, hamstrung by tension. Now, with success in their grasp, they were filled with bluster and bravado. She had nothing but contempt for them both, but she was cautious not to display it. It was time for the next step in the plan.

"I don't understand," Ramon was saying, "why we don't just get the hell out of here right now. What's to keep us? We've done what we came for. Every minute we wait is a mistake."

"Have we?" Olivia asked coldly. "Are you sure we've accomplished what we set out to do?"

"I have," Ramon answered. But then he turned silent.

"Ramon's right, Olivia. Why should we hang around here? Why don't we just jump in the car and split?"

"You think they've paid enough?" She had to play this carefully now, make them believe one thing while she did another.

"It's almost fifty grand each. It's more than I've ever had. It's enough to get started somewhere new."

"You don't think they've got more?"

"Where? He robbed the bank. What's left?"

"What about all the money he's cashed in? Stocks, bonds, trust accounts, real estate, all that shit Duncan owns and which he's selling like crazy. Don't you see, he probably figures he can pay back the bank, I know that's what he thinks he can do. Well, that money should be ours."

The two men thought about that. Olivia watched them closely.

"How do we get it?"

Olivia smiled. Got them! "We could always come back for it."

"How do we do that?" Bill Lewis asked.

"We just do it. We leave. Time passes. We get broke. We come back. Simple as that."

"How can we be sure he'll cooperate?"

"Because he has no choice. He will never have a choice. Cooperating with us will always be the safe and expedient thing for him."

Lewis nodded.

"I don't know," said Ramon. "How far can we push them?"

"As far as I like," Olivia replied.

"You're crazy," he sputtered. "Suppose he thinks he's had enough and calls the cops."

"He won't."

"Yeah—but suppose he does?"

"He won't. I know him. He won't."

"I don't like it. I don't ever want to come back here again. I want to take the money, cover our tracks, and leave. We shoulda just killed him out there. We shoulda done what I said. Then maybe you'd be happy."

Olivia nodded. "I thought of that. It wasn't the right moment."

"What about the guests?" Bill Lewis asked. He pointed upstairs. "They're getting pretty antsy. I wonder how long they can hang on. Especially the kid. It doesn't seem fair."

"Fair?" Olivia asked. Her face filled with sarcastic surprise.

"Well, you know what I mean," Bill retreated.

"What should we do with them?" she asked.

"Kill them," said Ramon.

"Let 'em go," said Lewis. He glared at Ramon. "I didn't think you were like that," he sneered.

Ramon shouted back at Lewis: "They aren't worth my life! They know who we are. They can describe us. I don't want to spend my next ten years like you have, always looking over my shoulder. I want to be free. That means no witnesses. It's pretty damn simple."

"Yeah, real simple. Like you. We kill them," Bill Lewis said calmly, sarcastically. "And what's to prevent Duncan or Megan from spending the rest of their lives hunting us down? If we could find them, what makes you think they couldn't find us? Christ, are you stupid."

"If they have a rest of their lives," Olivia interjected.

"Jesus!" Bill Lewis said, his voice filling with exasperation. "What are you saying? Pull some Charlie Manson? This isn't getting us anywhere. I'm not murdering old men and kids, got it? I'm just not doing it. I didn't want to do that guy in California, but that was your show, and I went along. But not some kid. He's a good kid, too."

"You don't have to," Ramon said. "Maybe others don't have the same feelings. Maybe others aren't so scared—"

"I'll tell you what I'm not scared of, you bastard—I'm not scared of you."

"You ought to be, you damn fool. Can't you see that you're going to get sentimental and screw this up for all of us? This is my big chance and I'm not going to let some faggot ex-hippie screw it up!"

Lewis started across the room toward his former lover, his hands clenched. Ramon jumped from a chair and reached for a revolver.

"Stop it!" Olivia yelled.

They both hesitated and looked at her.

She pointed at the two of them. "You're going to do what I say when I say it. This is my show and I'll tell you when it's over."

The two men stood staring at her.

"So what are we going to do? Kill them all?" Bill Lewis spat.

"Whatever we're going to do, let's do it and get the hell out of here," Ramon said.

Olivia assessed each man's will to struggle against her. They are scared and strung out, she thought. Give them both what they think they want. Then do what you want.

"All right," she said, as if lecturing children, "you're both agreed that you want to wrap this up, right?"

Both men nodded, still glaring at each other.

"And I think Duncan owes us a bit more." *Much more*, she thought.

They continued to stare at her uncomfortably. She noticed that they did not look at each other. Spring the trap, she thought, and smiled.

"Now take it easy, you two. Has anything gone wrong so far? Haven't I spent years figuring every angle?"

The two men glanced at each other, then back at her and nodded.

"Hasn't everything happened exactly as I said it would?"

They nodded again, appearing slightly relieved.

"Well, this is one of the angles I've spent the most time working out. It's the final twist of the knife—and it's foolproof. Here's the plan: I'll contact Duncan tonight, just when he's ready to go completely crazy. I'll tell him to meet us tomorrow morning. Someplace nice and isolated. And I'll tell him he's not through paying. We'll be out of here by eight-fifteen. On a plane by noon. That good enough for you?"

Olivia looked at the two men. They were still fidgeting a little, but just a little.

"I still think we should just kill them and go," muttered Ramon.

"Real smart," said Bill Lewis. "It sounds fine, Olivia. But why wait until the night?"

"Because that's when he'll be most vulnerable. People are always more twitchy when darkness falls. The world seems smaller, closer, more dangerous."

"But look, we could take off right now and do it from some pay phone far away. We don't have to be here."

"Yes, we do," said Olivia. "Don't you think he'd be able to tell? It's being here that puts the edge on it, the knowledge that we could still go up and blow them away. With everything combined, the waiting, the dark, the threat—Duncan will do whatever we say."

"How's it going to work?"

"Simple," Olivia said. "What I plan to do is send him out to some Godforsaken place and then just leave the two hostages upstairs. They'll figure it out eventually, and we'll be long gone. We'll simply sneak out, leave the door unlocked. It will take the old bastard some time to get up the nerve to try the door. Then he's going to have to figure out how to get out of here. We'll cut the phone line. Maybe take their shoes with us. By the time he manages to contact Duncan and Megan, we'll be at Logan airport in Boston and flying somewhere warm. Then, when we get short, we'll just take a little holiday to Greenfield and visit our personal banker. He won't want to go through all this again. I know Duncan. The math-man will want to take the easy and expedient way out. He'll get us the money. End of story. Until we need a bit more. And more. And more."

Ramon shrugged, but Bill Lewis appeared relieved.

"You're right," he said. "The bastard will pay forever. And we're not leaving witnesses, we're leaving reminders. He'll always remember how easy it was for us to snatch them. How we could do it again."

"Ah," said Olivia with a small laugh, "you're learning."

"I'd still rather leave no witnesses," Ramon said.

Olivia hesitated, then responded.

"Are you going to make me insist?" She fingered a revolver.

Ramon shrugged.

Olivia narrowed her gaze at the small man.

"No," he said. He pouted.

"Good," Olivia said. She stood up and walked over to Bill Lewis. She ran her fingers down his cheek, then patted him. "You're getting soft," she said, smiling. "We knew beforehand that there might be deaths. We knew that and we agreed." She jabbed her finger into his stomach, hard. "You must be strong. Not soft." He shook his head, but she reached up and grasped his chin tightly with her long fingers and turned it into a nod, forcing his head up and down.

Ramon laughed, and Olivia smiled. Bill Lewis smiled, too, but he rubbed his skin where Olivia's fingers had dug in.

"I guess you're right," he said. "I should just listen to you."

"That would make matters easier," Olivia replied. She gave him a playful slap on the cheek. "All right, now take lunch up to the guests. You can tell them that they've only got a little time to wait. Don't be too specific, but tell them you think they can go home tomorrow or the next day. Give them a little bit of hope and tell them to keep in line. It'll do wonders for their patience."

Lewis nodded and pounded out of the room. Ramon started to follow after him, but was frozen when Olivia turned, all jocularity instantly vanished, eyes narrowed, jaw set, mouth compacted into a tight frown, her gaze insisting he remain where he was. After a moment, they both heard Bill Lewis's heavy tread on the stairs.

"Yes?" Ramon said.

"The plan will work with your solution as well."

"It will? But I thought—"

"Money is one thing," Olivia said. "Revenge is another."

Ramon nodded and smiled.

Olivia stepped over to him. She slid a hand through his tangled mass of hair.

"You think more like I do," she said. "You're tough enough. You see things for the way they really are. I wonder why I haven't noticed that before."

He smiled.

"But when? I mean, Bill thinks—"

"Not until tomorrow morning. Right when we leave. Right then. Bill will go crazy, so we have to be careful."

His head bobbed up and down in agreement.

"Fuck him. He doesn't know about these things. Fuck him."

"You did once upon a time."

"A long time ago. He's changed. He's soft. I've changed. I'm hard."

Olivia smiled.

"Suppose he doesn't make it?" she asked.

Ramon grinned. "Then we will split the money two ways."

"Okay," she said. "Now, do me a favor and check all the weapons."

Ramon snapped quickly to attention and hurried out of the room, filling with an unfamiliar, yet narcotizing warmth. Olivia shook her head as she watched him leave. That was easy, she thought. Now all I have to do is let Bill know that I don't trust Ramon, and stand back out of the way and watch the fireworks. She was impressed with how malleable people were under stress. But I am in control, she said to herself. I have been from the very start. She found herself idly whistling a tune as she settled back into her chair. She did not see the pressing need to split any of the proceeds of Duncan's efforts with anyone, which, of course, had been the real plan, right from the start.

*　　*　　*

Megan sat in her car, warming her hands around a cup of coffee. She had parked next to a convenience store, wondering for an instant whether it was the same store outside which Duncan had hovered the day before. She looked down at her list of potential homesites and shook her head. She stared up into the overcast sky, as she sipped the coffee, thinking that she had only two or three effective hours of sunlight left. She sighed and spread the map out on the dashboard.

Where are you? she wondered.

She was impatient with the time it took to approach each house. She couldn't really barrel up the driveway; consequently she was forced to locate the house, then park some distance away and reconnoiter cautiously. So far she had come up with nothing. The first house she'd seen had children playing out front, which had cracked her will for just an instant. She had remained rooted out by the roadway, staring in at a passel of kids as they raced around in some free-form game that seemed to combine cowboys and Indians and tag. All she could tell was that some children were "it" and there was a great deal of mock shooting going on. She had turned reluctantly away from the scene, remembering times when she'd watched the same games from her own window.

Another house had an elderly couple raking leaves from the front yard; she'd moved away swiftly from that one. A third had been eliminated when she'd spotted a baby seat in the rear of a battered station wagon parked in front.

Two houses had been empty of life. She had forced herself up to their front porches and stared in through the darkened windows, checking for any signs of activity. All she had seen had been cobwebs and dust.

She looked at her map. Four houses remained. She thought of all the possibilities that would keep the house off her list. She recognized that it was possible for Olivia to have rented the house through a newspaper ad—not a realtor. But it wasn't her style; Olivia would hate having to deal directly with an owner. An owner might require a reference, or look carefully at her, but a realtor would see only

her cash. Megan wondered whether Olivia might have moved out
of the Greenfield multiple-listing service area. It was possible she
was in Amherst or Northampton. Both those communities catered
to students, and there were dozens of rentals available. But would
she want to drive that far? Megan doubted it. She remembered what
she'd thought the other night: Close enough to watch us, far enough
to be just out of our sight.

She's here, Megan thought. She's on the list.

But her confidence wavered.

Megan had traveled progressively farther into the countryside, as
she had checked the houses. She stared up into some green pines
that swept up a nearby hillside. An occasional group of stark white
birch trees broke up the wave of dark green, like death's bony hand
reaching up through the surface of the ocean. Megan shuddered,
finished her coffee, and stepped from the car. She saw the telephone
and decided to call home.

Lauren answered on the second ring: "Richards residence."

"Lauren?"

"Mom! Where are you? We've been worried."

"I'm fine. I'm still out hunting about."

"Dad was fit to be tied! And when he realized you took the gun,
he was ready to go out after you!"

"Everything's fine. Is he there?"

"Yeah. He's coming. I told him not to worry, but it didn't do any
good, because we were all really sort of worried anyway. Why don't
you come home?"

"In an hour or so. Just one or two more."

"What the hell's going on?" Duncan asked abruptly. Megan had
not heard him take the telephone from her daughter's hand.

"I'm just checking some properties."

"What are you doing? Checking *what*?"

"Just a hunch."

"What the hell are you talking about? The girls said you were out
looking for the Tommys."

"Duncan—don't be angry."

"I'm not angry. I've just been scared silly." He paused. "Of course I'm angry. I'm fucking furious! Suppose, suppose—"

"I'm okay."

"So far. Why didn't you wake me?"

"You wouldn't have let me go."

He was quiet for an instant. She heard him sigh and regain some sense. His voice finally picked up again, modulated and even. "You're right. I wouldn't have."

"I just felt like I had to do this. Alone."

He was quiet again. "Look," he finally said. "Please just be careful. And don't stay out much longer. I don't think we could stand it after dark."

"I'll be home soon. Keep an eye on the girls."

"If I haven't heard from you by, say, seven, I'm coming looking for you."

"I'll be home by then," she said.

"Seven," Duncan insisted.

Megan got back into her car and checked the next address on her list. Something quickened within her, some sense of internal impetus, and for an instant she had to fight a dizzying sense of fear and excitement. You're here, she thought again. She reached over swiftly and checked the pistol, which she moved underneath some papers on the seat next to her. She worried wildly that the old ammunition might not fire properly. But then, she realized, if she had to use the weapon, all was probably lost anyway. She pulled Duncan's watch cap down on her forehead and pulled out of the parking lot.

Within a few moments she was tucked away in the folds of the wooded countryside. She drove a few miles through the intermittent light and shadows, finally spotting the first of the remaining houses on her list. It was set back fifty yards from the quiet road. Possible, she thought immediately. Very possible. She slowed her car. Are you there? She couldn't see any activity as she cruised past, so she pulled her car to the side. I've got to check, she thought. I must be certain. She turned in her seat and saw that the road seemed empty, so she got out of the car and walked a few yards back to the entrance-way to the drive. She stared up at the house, past some bushes and a large oak tree that reminded her for an instant of one in her own yard back in Greenfield. Are you in there? she wondered again, hesitant to go closer, driven to know for certain. She took a small step toward the house, trying to spot some way of approaching it stealthily, aware suddenly that she was standing out in the middle of the road. Then, as she hesitated, she heard a car approaching.

It took her a moment to decipher the sound, but when she did, it threw her into panic.

She quickly searched for a place to hide, and saw none.

She took a few tentative steps toward her car, then broke into a headlong run, scrambling for the safety of the vehicle. Behind her, she could hear the engine noise growing in her ears. She grabbed at the door and threw herself behind the wheel, not knowing whether she had been spotted or not.

If they have, she thought, end it here.

She gritted her teeth and fought for control.

Megan reached for the pistol, lifting her eyes up so she could see into the mirror, expecting to see Olivia and a gun. But instead she saw a gray sedan pull into the driveway behind her. She could not see the occupants.

She pivoted in her seat, to try to catch a better glimpse, but could not. She turned back and started the engine, jamming the car into reverse, backing up with a flurry of spinning tires and rattling gravel. She slammed on her brakes by the entranceway to the house and searched the location quickly.

Her heart fell instantly.

The first thing she spotted was a pair of young women carrying bags of groceries. She saw two young men taking more packages from the trunk of the car. They were laughing, oblivious to her presence. Students, she thought abruptly. Probably two graduate couples sharing the house.

She realized that her hands were shaking on the wheel.

She calmed herself, glancing over at the house and then the car

long enough to see a large, red University of Massachusetts decal on
the window.

She breathed out, both relieved and frustrated.

Go on to the next, she told herself.

And keep control. And keep hidden.

But the next house was right on the roadway, and she could see
immediately that it was occupied by another family. The front yard
was littered with toys, all in various states of disrepair. In a way,
she thought, this was fortunate. She stopped the car on the country
road and waited. In the few minutes she was there, she managed to
regain her composure.

She drove on, aware that the day was fleeing about her. The wan
sunlight that penetrated the trees seemed to have lost its edge and
she could sense the cold gathering for its evening assault. Come on,
she said to herself. Come on.

She checked the addresses and the locations on the map. Two
remained. She drove swiftly in the direction of the closest one,
turning down one country road, then another. She came to a cross-
roads, and followed an old, faded sign.

She found herself cutting down a beaten road, swaying from frost
heaves in the highway, occasionally dipping the car into a pothole.
No tax money spent on this road, she thought. It was a realtor's
observation, and it froze her. She saw it then with another set of
eyes. No traffic. No prying eyes. Rural oblivion. No neighborhood.
No contact with anyone. She slowed the car and started checking
the numbers on mailboxes. Her pulse speeded up as the number
approached the one she was hunting.

She spotted the gravel drive curving into the woods, before she
saw the mailbox number, and she knew it was the one. This time,
however, she pulled quickly past, not even daring to glance through
the woods toward where the house might be. Some fifty yards past
the drive, she spotted a secondary road, a sparse, rutted dirt path,
cut through the brush, leading back into the woods. An old fire road,
she thought. Or maybe a farmer's tractor trail down to a lower
field. She fought off the urge to pull in there, thinking: Too close.

She kept driving. A mile away, she saw another empty track, this time leading off into the opposite direction. She pulled her car in there, hiding it from the road.

Megan swallowed hard and collected her kit. She took the sketch pad, camera, and binoculars and put them into a haversack. The gun she tucked under her coat.

She got out of the car and walked back to the roadway. She wedged her cap down and started jogging slowly back up the road.

When she reached the secondary road, she ducked off it and slid into the forest. She could see her breath in front of her. For an instant she paused, letting the darkness seep over her. She maneuvered along the edge of the forest, sticking close to the farmer's trail, hoping it was leading her toward the other drive and the house. She had no way of knowing this for certain; but the angles felt right to her, and she could sense her heartbeat beneath her coat. Underbrush snagged at her parka, but she tugged free, moving as quietly as possible. She thought she was making a racket; each broken twig sounded to her like a gun blast, each sucking step in a mud hole, like a missile launch. She pushed on, pressing through the pines, searching for the house.

She hesitated when she spotted light. She crouched down and stepped forward stealthily.

She had a sudden fear of dogs, but then dismissed it. She thought: If I'm wrong, I'll surely owe some poor farmer an explanation. But she crept on.

She could see an old stone fence, bordering the edge of the forest, and she got down on her knees and crawled to it. She laid her cheek against a moss-covered rock, letting the cool sensation calm her. Then, slowly, she lifted her head.

She looked up at the old, white clapboard farmhouse. The evening mist seemed to gather about it. She could see no activity. For an instant she cursed the growing darkness, aware that it both helped hide her and helped hide what she was searching for.

She pulled out the binoculars and focused them on a car parked in front of the house. Her heart raced when she spotted a rental sticker. No farmer drives a rental car, she thought. No student, either. But I remember one person who does. That's just like her.

She swung the glasses around and trained them on the house. She could see little that distinguished the farmhouse. Like so many, it had three stories up, Cape style, with each level looking out over the others. She thought: Living room, dining areas downstairs, bedrooms on the second floor, then attic up top. It would be right.

Megan quickly put the glasses down and sketched what she could see of the location, making a rough map. She was situated by the side of the house, able to see the front and back. She could see a long, sloping field that ran away from the rear of the house, down to a line of trees. She wondered whether that was where the secondary road went and suspected it was. She could see that the drive curled into the front of the house, where there was a porch. There was a bit of old lawn, so that anyone approaching the house from the front would have to cross fifty yards of open space. She picked up the camera and took several quick pictures. They were dark and blurry, but they were something she could show Duncan.

She put the camera and sketch pad away, and lifted up the glasses. The darkness was closing in and she worried for an instant that she might get lost trying to make it back through the woods. Then she dismissed the fear and again trained her eyes on the house. *Are you there, Tommy?* She tried to concentrate, to see within the walls, to feel her son's presence. *Give me a sign, dammit. Show me something.* She wanted to call his name, but she fought it off, biting her lip hard, until she could taste blood. She saw a bit of movement in one room and peered in that direction. A light was switched on inside and for a millisecond, she saw a figure.

It was Bill Lewis. She knew it instantly: the man's unmistakable, gangling shuffle. Then, just as quickly, the figure passed from sight.

She wanted to scream.

She dropped the glasses, grabbed the pistol, and started over the stone wall, oblivious to anything except the certain knowledge that her son was inside the farmhouse.

I'm coming, her heart shouted. *I'm coming!*

But she stopped herself just as she flung her leg over the wall. She pitched back and forth for an instant, rocking in a firestorm of desire and reason. Then she pulled back and threw herself down behind the wall again. She was hyperventilating, and it took her a moment to calm herself. She tried to rationally assess her chances against the three armed kidnappers, and realized, even with the element of surpise, they would be minimal.

She closed her eyes for an instant, searching for the will to leave. She wanted desperately to find some way of telling her child that she would be back for him, but knew there was none.

She opened her eyes and saw her pictures and her sketches and picked up her pencil. Stay calm, she warned herself. Take things of value. You will be back here. She raised her head and drew in every detail of the surrounding land she could make out, sketching a map as accurately as her excited hand and encroaching night would allow.

Then Megan picked up the binoculars and searched the house another time. She couldn't see anyone moving inside, but that told her nothing. I know you're there, she thought.

She whispered this to herself: "Tommy, I'm coming."

She tucked the gun back under her parka and collected her things. She forced herself to start crawling backward through the scraggly underbrush and near full darkness. But as she moved, she spoke quietly to herself, hoping the force of her words would rise through the sky, and penetrate the walls of the jail, slip unheard past his captors, and search out her child and echo gently in his ear: "Tommy, I'm coming. Do you hear me? I'm going for Daddy and we're going to come back and bring you home. We're coming."

Megan retreated through the woods, alone, determined, and filling swiftly with the juices of battle.

11

SUNDAY
NIGHT

Duncan paced angrily through the house. His feet felt as if they were mired in quicksand. He wanted to pull free, to do something other than remain waiting. He felt waves of dread tug at his stomach. He glanced at his watch, at the idle telephone, out the window at the fleeing daylight and the encroaching night blackness, then back toward his daughters, who sat wordlessly watching him.

"Where the hell is your mother?" he said.

Karen and Lauren didn't reply.

"I can't stand it," he said. "She's left us hanging here, and Christ knows what's happened."

"She's okay," Lauren said. "I know she's okay."

"Don't worry, Dad," Karen said. "She'll be back."

And where the hell is Olivia? he thought. He was struck by the irony. I'm waiting for the two women left to me: Megan and Olivia. Trapped between the two.

He felt something unraveling inside of him, as if the tension were suddenly about to break loose. He breathed in deeply.

And then the phone rang.

Both twins jerked, startled.

Duncan picked up the receiver.

"Yes?"

"Ah, Duncan, so good to hear your voice."

"Olivia. I want—"

She ignored the start of his plea, rambling on in a mock-friendly voice.

"So, math-man. You've probably been toting up the seconds into minutes and the minutes into hours. Figuring the interest on time. Your waiting compounded daily, huh?"

"Olivia—"

"I guess in this case, math-man, time really is money."

She laughed hard at her joke.

"Olivia, I held up my part of the bargain."

"Spoken like a moneyman, Mister Banker. You've been counting up minutes. I've been counting up dollars."

"I want them back now!" Duncan shouted into the telephone.

"Stay cool, math-man," Olivia replied softly. Menace, as always, swirled around her voice. "Maybe I should just hang up and make you wait a bit more."

"No!"

"Duncan, you have no patience. You should learn to control yourself. I have. I'll call back later. Maybe."

"No, please!" Duncan cut his voice in half. "I'm here. What now?" He was immediately angry with himself: Every time we've talked she's pulled the same threat, to cut me off and leave me hanging. And every time I fall into her little head-trap without thinking. He gritted his teeth, grinding them angrily.

But in the moment he waited, with the silence growing between them, he realized that she hadn't mentioned Megan. That meant that his wife was okay. Somewhere, but okay. The thought filled him with relief.

After a few moments he heard her breathe out slowly. When she spoke, her voice hissed barely above a whisper:

"It's not enough," she said.

Duncan's heart felt as if someone had grabbed it and twisted it.

"I can't believe—"

"It's not enough!" she insisted.

"I'll get more," he replied instantly.

"That was fast," Olivia said, laughing quietly.

"I don't know how. I'll get it," he said. "Just let the Tommys go."

"You don't understand, do you, Duncan?"

Duncan didn't know what to say and remained quiet.

"Perhaps what we need is a relationship," Olivia said.

"Olivia, please, what the hell are you talking about?"

"What I need is a banker. My own personal banker and my own private account. Just like I said the other day. Well, math-man, you're going to be my account. When I want more, I'm going to come back and get it. And you'll just give it to me, won't you?"

He thought: It will never end.

But he said: "Yes."

Olivia burst out with a raucous, unforgiving laugh.

"That was too quick, Duncan. Much too quick."

He took a deep breath. "Yes," he said slowly.

"You won't know, you see. It could be six months. It could be six years. But I'll be back. A long-term debt relationship, I suppose. Isn't that what you'd call it? A mortgage on your life, Duncan, that's what."

Duncan thought again: It will never end.

"I agree and?"

"You get them back."

"Then I agree."

"So quick and easy," Olivia said. "Don't think that you can prepare for me, Duncan. You'll never know when. Don't you see the beauty of it all? You make money, and occasionally I take some. Your family gets to live in peace. No bullets in the back. If I wanted to, it would be so easy. Perhaps one of the kids walking out of school one day. A high-powered rifle fired from some distant car. Or Megan off to some realty appointment that turns out to be something else. Assassination is simple, Duncan. It's a real American tradition. Surely you remember that? Our year together was quite a famous one for murders."

Is this real? Duncan thought.

"Whatever you want. How do I get my son and the judge?"

"You sure you want the old bastard back, Duncan? He's been the most contentious guest. What about inheritance? Don't you stand to make a bit of cash when the old guy checks out? Wouldn't you rather have me waste him now?"

She laughed again.

"I want them home."

"That's up to you."

"How?"

"Remember the field you waited in?"

"Yes."

"Think you can find your way back there again?"

"Yes."

"All right. Tomorrow morning at eight A.M. Don't be early. Don't be late. Someone will be watching you. Don't screw up. I see any other car, any other people at all, even some lost fucking farmer on a tractor, and terrible things will happen, Duncan. And let's make it the two of you, okay? You and Megan, in the middle of that field at eight in the morning."

"Why her? I'll come alone."

"The two of you!" Olivia whispered with sudden force.

"But—"

"Both of you where I can see you!"

"I don't see—"

"Dammit, you don't have to see why. You just have to do it. Can't you understand that? Or maybe you'd prefer the alternative."

Duncan's head spun in the silence that stretched over the telephone line.

"All right," he said quietly. "Whatever you say."

"Right." Olivia breathed out harshly. "Got it now? Don't screw up."

"Yes. I understand. I understand completely."

Olivia laughed. "That way you'll have enough time to get changed and get over to the bank before it opens up for business. And won't that be an exciting time, Duncan? Think you can handle it? Cold blood running in your veins, Duncan? No quiver to the hands? How's the old pokerface?"

For an instant she listened to the silence on the line, delighting in it. She felt the spider's satisfaction as it spins the final strands of its web.

`Then she hung up the telephone.

Duncan replaced the receiver on the hook.

"What is it?" Karen asked. Both twins were standing up, watching their father for some sign.

"Are they okay? Are they going to give them up?"

"I don't know," Duncan replied. He exhaled slowly, as if coming up for air.

"She's mad, you know. Crazy with hatred." He said it in a matter-of-fact tone that contradicted the terror of their situation.

"They're awful," Lauren said.

Karen shook her head. "The worst."

Duncan felt a hardening within him, as if all the seas of his emotions had iced over from a great winter wind. He stared at his two daughters, his eyes narrowing with his own immense anger. And I'm crazed, too, he thought.

"Well, there's one answer to that," he said.

"What?" asked Karen.

"To be worse than them."

Megan, electric, drove hard and fast through the darkness, pushing the car through the variegated shadows of the back roads, then through the settling night in town. She traveled in a vacuum, shutting out everything but the image of the white clapboard farmhouse rising through the evening shadows in front of her. She was oblivious to her surroundings, to the other cars and the few people walking on the sidewalks, their coats pulled tight against a freshening wind. She hurried against the encroaching night, her decision made, her needs blistering her heart. She made an illegal U-turn to get onto the highway from a side street and accelerated until she saw the glowing lights of the mall parking areas. She arrived fifteen minutes before closing time.

For an instant she said a small, hypocritical prayer of thanks for the mall. Duncan's mall. When it was built she had teased him endlessly, with a touch of malice, singing: ". . . They paved paradise and put up a parking lot . . ." Now, the bright lights beckoned to her.

She had made up her mind in the first moments of retreat from the farmhouse. She had been bothered that she couldn't telephone Duncan and tell him what she had found and what she was going to do. She knew that delay would be impossible. He would understand when she presented him with the results.

Megan left her car and ran across the macadam. She pushed her way through the wide entrance doors, dodging the last few shoppers straggling out into the parking lot and quick-marched through the corridors, hearing her shoes click insistently against the polished floor. She was breathing hard, like a swimmer fighting against the waves. The lights from the shops—a never-ending variety of boutiques and clothes stores—glared at her, as if spotlighting her panic and desperation. I must control myself, she admonished. But a voice inside her recognized that she should be keening a dirge for her lost soul. What I am going to do is not wrong, she told herself. She saw the eyes of the store window dummies, fixed and wooden, staring out at her as she half-ran past, and she wondered whether that was what dead eyes looked like. She swept the thought from her mind and hurried on.

When she walked into the sporting goods store, she was relieved to see that she was alone, but for a solitary clerk totaling up receipts behind a register.

He was a young man, and he glanced at Megan, then the clock on the wall—saw that it was a dozen minutes before closing time—and then turned back to Megan. He walked out from behind the register and Megan saw that he was wearing blue jeans, a white shirt, and tie, and that he sported an earring. He did not look like the outdoors type.

Then, she acknowledged ruefully, neither did she.

"Hi," the young man said, pleasantly enough. "Just got in under the wire. How can I help you?"

"I'd like to see your hunting equipment," Megan replied, trying not to let anxiety slide into her voice.

The clerk nodded. "No problem," he said. He led Megan to the rear of the store, where one wall was devoted to an array of weaponry: wildly curved bows and brightly colored arrows that seemed like crazily futuristic weapons, and an arrangement of shotguns, rifles, handguns, and crossbows. The racks on the floor carried parkas and hunting pants in contradictory fluorescent orange or muted camouflage colors. The countertop was glass, and the display shelves were lined with an assortment of hunting knives—serrated, gleaming, wicked-looking things. There were a few magazines displayed as well: *Field and Stream, Guns and Ammo,* and *Soldier of Fortune.* For a moment, Megan felt utterly lost and foolish as her eyes traveled over the available arsenal. But then the thought was replaced by the reality of her mission, and she settled her mind on the task at hand.

"So, exactly what sort of hunting gear were you looking for?" she heard the clerk ask. "Are these gifts or for your own use?"

She took a deep breath. "For my family," she replied.

"Gifts, then. So what do you have in mind?"

"Hunting," she replied abruptly.

"Well, what will you be hunting for?" the clerk asked. He was patient and seemed mildly amused.

"Beasts," she replied under her voice.

"I beg your pardon?" The clerk eyed her oddly.

She ignored his stares and tossed her mind back to the house in Lodi. She remembered sitting around in the murky living room, thick with smoke and enthusiasm, listening to Olivia discuss weapons with Kwanzi and Sundiata. The two black men had had a ghetto appreciation of guns: Saturday-night specials and sawed-off shotguns. Olivia's knowledge had been more sophisticated; she spoke about firing velocity and range, and dropped brands and calibers easily into her conversation, showing off. Megan pictured Emily joining the group, showing them all how she planned to hold her shotgun under her long raincoat; she pictured the shotgun in Emily's arms. She could see the black barrel and brown wooden stock. Megan lifted her gaze up to the rack of weapons in front of her.

"Like that," she said to the clerk, pointing.

"That's not really much of a hunting gun," the clerk replied, turning to the shelves and examining the weapon she indicated. "That's a twelve-gauge riot pump. It's the sort of weapon that policemen carry about in their cars. Farmers use them for shooting woodchucks and other varmints. You see, the barrel is shorter, much shorter, which reduces accuracy at distance. Some people use them for home protection, though—"

"May I see it, please?"

The salesman shrugged. "Sure. But most hunters usually want something a bit more—"

He stopped himself, frozen by the look in Megan's eyes.

"Let me get it down for you." He took a key and unlocked a bolt that secured the weapons. He grasped the gun and handed it to Megan.

For a moment she held the shotgun at port arms, wondering what she was supposed to do. She tried to recall all the lessons they'd had, after dark, shades drawn, in the house in Lodi. She seized the pump action beneath the barrel and tugged back hard, listening to the shotgun's arming mechanism click soundly.

"That's right," the salesman said. "But a little more gently. You don't need to slam it quite so hard." He took the weapon from her and pointed it toward the rear of the store. Then he dry-fired the gun. "Watch," he said. "One, two, three, four, five, six. Then you have to reload—here." He pointed at the slot in the side of the gun's magazine.

Megan took the weapon and mimicked the salesman. The heft of the piece was satisfying. It wasn't nearly as heavy as she thought it would be. The sensation of the wooden stock against her shoulder was almost seductive. But she recognized the deception. When it fired, it would be a leaping, twisting, wild thing, and she wondered whether she could handle it.

She breathed out hard and thought, We'll just have to.

"Fine," she said, putting the gun down on the counter. "I'll take that one and another one just like it."

"You want two—" the clerk started, surprised. Then he stopped and shrugged. "Sure, ma'am. Whatever you say." He reached up and grabbed an identical weapon from the rack. "Ammunition?"

Megan again searched through her memory. She remembered Olivia's lecture: "You must always use what the pigs use, or better. Never be outgunned."

The recollection forced a bitter smile to her lips.

In as friendly a voice as she could muster, she said, "And a couple of boxes of double-ought buckshot, please."

The salesman's eyes widened slightly and he shook his head briefly. "Ma'am, I hope you're hunting for elephants or rhinos or whales." He reached beneath the counter and came up with two boxes of shells. "Please, ma'am, these things will blow a hole through double-thick sheet metal. They'd knock down a wall in your house. Take them out to the firing range and give them a try, please, just so you know what you're getting into."

Megan nodded and smiled. She looked back up onto the shelf and saw another weapon, one that seemed familiar from a hundred nightly newscasts. "What's that?" she asked.

The clerk turned slowly, and again examined what she was pointing at.

"Ma'am, that's a Colt AR-Sixteen. It's a semiautomatic rifle and it fires an extremely powerful slug. It's the nonmilitary version of the rifle the army uses. It's not really a hunting weapon, either. You know, I just sold one the other day to a couple who were planning to sail their boat around the Caribbean this winter. It's a good weapon to have down there, on board ship."

"Why is that?"

"Well, it's very accurate at distances up to a thousand yards and it will blow a hole in something a mile away. It fires very rapidly and it comes with an optional twenty-one-shot clip of bullets."

"Why the Caribbean?"

"A lot of smugglers and hijackers still operate down there. They sometimes like to grab a luxury yacht and use it for a single drug run. An AR-Sixteen can go a long ways towards dissuading someone from approaching you in a hostile manner. You see, with a shotgun or a handgun, you have to wait until your trouble gets too close. Not with this weapon."

He held the rifle up and demonstrated the firing technique.

"This is how it works. Not much kick, either."

He looked down at Megan, still holding the rifle to his shoulder.

"I guess you want this one, as well?"

"That's right," she nodded. "No one wants their trouble to get too close."

"For hunting, right?"

"Correct."

"Okay." He shrugged again. "Whatever you say. Anything else?"

"Ammunition."

"Of course."

"An extra clip."

"Got it."

"A box of forty-five caliber bullets for a pistol."

He looked at Megan and smiled.

"Right here."

"An extra clip."

"I should have guessed."

Megan spun around and eyed the racks.

"Do those camouflage suits come in men's and ladies' sizes?"

"They do."

"One man's large. Three women's mediums, please."

The clerk went to the rack and picked through it swiftly. "These are real good quality," he said. "Gore-Tex and Thinsulate. Keep you warm under any circumstances, back of any duck blind. Hats, gloves, boots?"

"No, I think we're set on those."

"Hand grenades? Mortars? Flamethrowers?"

"I beg your pardon?"

"Just joking."

Megan didn't return the man's smile. "Wrap it up," she said. "Oh, and one of those, too, please." She pointed into the display case.

The salesman reached down for a black-handled hunting knife. "Very sharp," he said. "Carbon steel blade. You could stick it right through the hood of a car, no trouble—"

He shook his head slightly. "—but you're not hunting for cars, right?"

"Right. We're not."

The salesclerk started to total up the items. When he reached the end, Megan handed him her American Express Gold Card.

"You want to use a credit card?" the clerk asked, surprise tingeing his voice.

"Yes. Is something wrong?"

"No, no," he said, grinning and shaking his head once again. "It's just that, well, when people buy the, uh, selections you have in bulk, they generally pay cash."

"Why is that?" Megan asked, trying to sound equally jocular.

"More difficult to trace."

"Oh," Megan said. "I suppose that makes sense." She felt embarrassed for an instant. Then she shook her head. She didn't care. She thrust the card forward. "I suspect that stores like this are generally discreet?"

"You bet," he replied. "And we're a big chain. The sales all get sort of lumped together into the computers. But discretion doesn't really help when you see a court order in some detective's hand."

Megan nodded. "You shouldn't concern yourself," she said. "This is all for recreational use."

"Sure," the clerk said, with a small, snorting laugh. "Recreational use in Nicaragua or Afghanistan."

He took the card and ran it through the electronic verification machine. Then he started putting the clothes and ammunition in one bag. "The guns should really be in cases," he said.

"That's all right," Megan said. "Just wrap them up."

"Please," the salesclerk said quietly. "Please, lady. I know it's none of my business, but whatever you're hunting for, please be careful."

Megan offered a thin-lipped smile.

"You've been very helpful," she said. "This will take me two trips to the car."

"Can I give you a hand?"

She shook her head. He smiled. "I didn't think so," he said.

Tommy heard the lock turning in the door and hurried over to his grandfather's side. "Maybe this is it?" he whispered, a half-question.

"I don't know," Judge Pearson replied. "Don't get your hopes up."

He knew the kidnappers had received the money from Duncan; their self-congratulatory laughter had seeped through the old wooden floors. Then Bill Lewis had told them that it was almost over, that they were going to arrange for the exchange. Then hours had passed without anything happening, except having their hopes soar and plummet with each passing minute.

Judge Pearson had racked his imagination for some plausible, non-terrifying explanation for this delay, but had come up with nothing. He knew, though, that Olivia was still using the two of them to get something. Which meant that even though the money had been paid, a debt was still owed.

In the few seconds that Olivia took to climb the stairway, he felt more unsettled than at any moment since the start. He worried that his hand might shake, his voice quaver—and that any of these little things would tumble his grandson into a panic. As much as anything, he hated the way she made him feel old and infirm.

"Hello, boys," Olivia said warmly.

"What's the delay?" he asked.

"Just straightening out a final piece of business," she answered. "Tying up a few loose ends, that's all."

"Do you really think you're going to get away with all this?" the judge demanded. The force of his words surprised him.

But Olivia laughed. "We already have, judge. We were always meant to get away with this. I'm surprised at you. You know that most crimes go unsolved. This one's not exactly 'unsolved,' of course. Maybe 'unresolved' is a better word."

She walked over and cupped her hand around Tommy's chin. She spoke to the judge, but stared into the boy's eyes, as if searching for something.

"The best crimes, judge, are the crimes that have no end. Where threats and possibilities continue to exist. The crimes sort of take on a life of their own. They take over people's lives completely. That's what's happening here."

"You're crazy," he said.

She laughed again. "Maybe, judge. A lot of the women in prison went crazy—from confinement, from boredom, from tension, from hatred. Maybe I did, too. But you better get used to it. I'm going to be part of the family from now on. What do you think, Tommy? Like some eccentric spinster aunt, perhaps. You know—childless, a little mean, a little weird. The type that always gets invited to all the family functions, but everyone hopes won't show up."

Tommy didn't respond and she dropped his chin and moved away.

"You haven't seen anything up here. Think about what has happened: I've put you in one prison, put them in another. What did you think, that I was going to let everyone out on parole after one little week? That's not how the system works, judge. They're in for some hard time."

"Is that what I'm supposed to tell them?"

"No." Olivia shook her head. "I don't need a messenger for that."

"Then why tell us?"

"For him, judge." She pointed at Tommy. "So that he never forgets." She stared down at Tommy. "I told you at the start how important you were to all this," she continued. "You're going to be their reminder. So they'll never forget."

The judge had a terrible thought: A living reminder? Or a dead one?

"When will you be finished with us?" he asked quietly, trying to slide demand into his voice.

"Soon. Hours, maybe. Tomorrow at the latest. Keep your hopes up. Maybe they won't screw up. So far, they've followed every order like the good little soldiers they are."

She ruffled Tommy's hair.

"Just think positively," she said.

Olivia gave a little wave of her hand and left the two Tommys in the attic alone. Tommy waited until he heard the dead bolt click home and listened carefully for the soft sound of her steps receding down the hallway.

"Grandfather," he said shakily, biting his lip to keep from crying. "She's lying. She doesn't mean any of it. She hates us too much. She hates Mom and Dad too much. She'll never let us go."

Judge Pearson pulled his grandson close.

"That's not what she said," he reminded the child.

"She never does what she says. She only wants to scare us more. When she says she's going to let us go, I don't believe her. I want to, but I can't." Tommy straightened out of his grandfather's grasp, wiping away tears from the corners of his eyes. "She couldn't stand to see us get home and be happy again. Can't you see that?"

Then the child plunged his head back against his grandfather's chest, sobbing softly. After a moment, he raised his head again.

"I don't want to die, Grandfather. I'm not scared, but I don't want to."

Judge Pearson could feel his own throat closing with emotion. He stroked his grandson's hair, looking deep into the boy's eyes, past the fear and hurt, the troubles that had dogged the child for so many years, seeing instead only an intensity of light. Then he said the first thing that jumped into his mind:

"Tommy, I won't let them. You're not going to die. We're going to get out of this. I promise."

"How? How can you promise?"

"Because we're stronger than them."

"They've got the guns."

"We're still stronger."

"What are we going to do?"

Judge Pearson stood up and surveyed the attic, just as he had in the first moments of captivity. He reached down and stroked Tommy's soft, little boy's cheek, letting a smile run across his face, trying to transmit some confidence to his grandson. He remembered something he'd thought in the first few minutes of life in the attic. It was perhaps not a great and glorious battlefield, but if it came to it, it was a good enough place to die.

He took a deep breath, sat down on the bunk, and pulled Tommy close.

"Did I ever tell you how the Twentieth Maine held Little Round Top on the second day of the battle of Gettysburg? They saved the Union. Have I told you that story?"

Tommy shook his head. "No, you haven't."

"Or how the One Hundred and First Airborne held Bastogne?"

Tommy shook his head again. But he smiled and he knew that his grandfather was answering his question.

"Or how the Marines retreated from the Yalu?"

"You've told me that one," Tommy said. "Actually, a bunch of times."

The judge lifted his grandson from the cot and bear-hugged him close. "Let's talk a bit about bravery, Tommy. And then I'll tell you what we're going to do."

"Megan! Where have you been?" Duncan yelled, as she hurried through the front door.

In a second he was at her side in the vestibule. She could see the strain of the day in his eyes, diffuse, barely under control. "We've been scared sick," he said. "We had no idea. Dammit, don't ever do that again!"

She held out her arms and seized him, holding him at arm's length, her fingers gripping his muscles tightly. She was pale, herself, and for an instant she could not speak.

"Are you okay?" he asked, calming down.

She nodded.

"What happened?"

She took a deep breath. "I've found him," she said quietly.

Duncan stared at her, his eyes widening.

"Where?"

"In one of the rentals I told you about."

"Are you sure?"

"I saw Bill Lewis."

"Where is it?"

"Not too far. A dozen miles out of town in the country."

"My God!"

"I know."

"My God," Duncan repeated.

This time Megan merely nodded.

"I've been so worried, since you called this afternoon. I thought—I don't know what I thought. All I could do was worry."

"I'm okay," she said. She did not actually believe it.

Duncan spun away from her, pounding a fist into his palm. "Damn! We've got a chance!"

He turned back to Megan.

"She called," he said, abruptly turning quiet.

"And?" Megan felt her heart surge.

"She says she'll give them back—but that we still owe her. It wasn't enough, she said. She said she'll come back for more. Someday. She says it will never end."

Megan stood frozen. For an instant she thought she could not stand any more pain, any more hurt. She tried to breathe in slowly, collecting herself.

"It will never end?" she asked.

Duncan said: "Yes." For a moment, the weight of the words made his shoulders sag, then he gathered himself.

"Come on," he said. "We need to talk."

He led Megan into the living room.

The twins were there, uncharacteristically silent. They have had to find strength and bravery that they had no idea they owned, she thought. It saddened her. It's hard to be thrust into adulthood. Then she went over and hugged each of them.

"I think it's time this ended," she said to her daughters.

"But how?" Lauren asked. "What alternative do we have?"

"One," said Duncan. "One alternative. We go and get the Tommys."

"But how do we *do* that?" Karen asked.

"I don't know," said Duncan. "But we know where they're being kept now. So we just go. We've got a pistol. It's not enough, but maybe we could figure out some way . . ."

His voice trailed off as he watched Megan rise. She walked out of the living room, through the vestibule, and out to her car. She seized one of the packages from the sporting good store, then, oblivious to the night wind and cold, quick-marched back inside.

Duncan was staring at her. "Megan, what is going on?"

Before he could say anything more, she unwrapped the semi-automatic rifle, ripping away the paper cover. She held it up where they could all see it. The weapon seemed to glisten in the living room light.

"Before I came home," she said, "I went shopping."

Olivia Barrow went to the bedroom window and stared out into the darkness. She could hear Bill in the kitchen cleaning some of the mess of paper plates and cheap crockery that they had accumulated in their stay. She knew Ramon was in another room, nervously cleaning weapons. She wondered if he had the nerve to do what he said he would. She frowned, uncomfortable with the idea that she could not predict at any moment what her companions would or would not do.

She thought: It finishes tomorrow.

Olivia turned away from the window and glanced at the pile of money sitting on the bed. She walked over to it and grasped a handful. She felt oddly conflicted, as if the sight and feel of the cash left her unsatisfied, like the moments after a failed lover had finished making excuses.

Methodically, she began stuffing the money into a red satchel, idly counting as she did so. Her mind wandered to Duncan and Megan, and she wondered whether they would sleep that night. She laughed slightly: I doubt it.

Olivia finished storing the money, put a revolver on top, and closed the bag. She went back to the window. The sky was an onyx black, dotted with the light of stars. It stretched out away from her endlessly, and she thought: The night starts here with me.

She pictured the same night closing in on Duncan and Megan, swallowing them. What will I do with them? she asked herself.

I can kill them. I can wound them. I can ruin them.

Just as they did to me.

She wrapped her arms around herself, as if trying to contain the success of her design. Then she unfolded slowly, stretching her arms wide. She lifted one leg, ballet-like, holding it out in front of her. She remembered her mother at night, dancing with subtle grace, before being robbed of energy and beauty by disease. Olivia lifted herself up onto her toes, as her mother once did. Then she released herself slowly.

What will happen to the guests? she wondered.

Bill Lewis was like a faithful bloodhound, Ramon Gutierrez an erratic terrier. Where will you put your money when they clash?

She smiled. It makes no difference.

Neither of them gets out alive.

As for the two Tommys—well, she shrugged, whatever happens, happens. She searched through her heart for compassion and found none. She recognized that any result was fine. She could not see how she could lose in the morning. If they all die, that was fine. If they live, well, then she would be able to return—just as she had lied to Duncan she would.

"I can do anything," she whispered to the window and to the vast night. "I can do whatever I want to, when I want to."

Then she uttered a small laugh, and turned her imagination to warm beaches and spending the money. A fast car, she thought, a really fast car. And some expensive clothes. And then we'll see what the future holds. Smiling, she retreated back into the room to pack the remainder of her things.

Duncan was on the extension, holding his hand over the receiver, while the number rang. Megan caught his eyes with her own, nodded, and took a deep breath to steady herself. The twins sat quietly, listening.

In a moment, the ringing stopped, and Megan heard a familiar, breezy "Hello?"

"Barbara? It's Megan Richards of Country Estates Realty."

"Megan! My dear! It's been months and months."

"Oh, Barbara," Megan barreled on, her voice filled with false jocularity. "It's been such a tough couple of months for us. Have things been better over at Premiere Properties?"

"Oh, I had one great sale, you remember the Halgin house that was so very, very overpriced? Couple of transplanted New Yorkers swept it up."

"That's terrific," Megan said. She pictured Barbara Woods. She was in her early fifties, with silver-gray hair that she pulled back in a bun, giving her a schoolmarmish look that contradicted the designer clothes she wore, with jewelry that clanged and jangled as she walked. She's not an attentive person, Megan thought, she's not aware of detail and dimension. Megan sighed and launched ahead.

"I'm really sorry to bother you at home so late at night, but I just got a call and thought I'd touch base with you. Do you remember a listing you had this past summer and early fall for an old farmhouse off Barrington Road . . ."

"A sale?"

"No, a rental."

"Let me think. Oh, sure, of course, the old whooziwhatsit place. Brr, gave me the chills just going inside. But that writer sure seemed to adore it."

"Oh, you mean you rented it?"

"Yes, to some poet from California who wanted to write a gothic novel. That's what she said. She said she needed six months of solitude and paid the first three in cash. Well, solitude she got. That's the one thing that old place has, and plenty of it. Did you have someone in mind for it?"

"Yes. A couple down from Boston looking to fix up a weekend retreat."

"It would be perfect for renovation. Lots of renovation. Would you like for me to arrange to show it?"

"Well, let me talk to my clients and see when they might come down. Probably this spring sometime. I'm just doing a little spade-work now."

"Oh, fine."

"Say, do you think you could describe the place for me?"

Megan looked toward Duncan, who nodded. He had a pad of paper and a pencil ready.

"Sure," said Barbara, hesitating.

Come on! Megan thought to herself. Come on, you dizzy old horse. Remember!

". . . Well, it's not in great shape, but structurally it's completely sound, so you're not into any major foundation work . . ."

Megan closed her eyes and asked, "What's the interior like? How is it laid out?"

"Let's see. Nice wide front porch. Front door leads to a vestibule. Living room to the left, dining room next to it. Passageway to the kitchen—you could turn that into a pantry—in back. There's a back door off the kitchen, which leads out to a field. Plenty of room for a nice patio. One bathroom downstairs. Little parlor room to the right, a really nice little space you could really make something out of, then a little bedroom or study. The stairs go up from the center vestibule. There's a landing, then up to a second floor with three bedrooms and another bath. None really are a master, so you'd need to take down a wall up there. At the end of the hallway there's a door up to a third-floor attic. The draftiest old dusty place. Nobody ever insulated it or finished it off in any way. Just a lot of dust, but enough space to make it into a rec room or something."

Megan nodded. "Barbara, you've been a great help. Sounds like what my friends are looking for. I'll get back to you and we can make an appointment."

"It's a cold old house. Just needs some TLC. All those old farmhouses need the same. I think they're all haunted, anyway . . ."

She giggled. Megan thanked her again, and hung up the phone. She looked over at Duncan.

He shook a fist in the air.

"We have a chance," he said.

For a moment, Megan felt like a climber who slips on the rocks, then spins out wildly into the air. She seized hold of her emotions, like catching the strands of a rope, and snapped herself to attention.

"We do," she replied.

*   *   *

It was late at night, the darkness mingling with cold and silence. Megan sat on the floor of the living room, with all the weapons and ammunition spread out around her. A single light from the corner of the room caught the hard ridges in her face. She shuffled through her sketches, photographs, and diagrams. Karen and Lauren sat together on the couch. Duncan was standing, looking out the window. Then he turned and reached over and picked up the rifle. For an instant he cradled it in his arms, then he pulled back on the arming bolt.

"Are we crazy?" he asked abruptly. "Have we completely lost our senses?"

"Probably," Megan replied.

Duncan smiled.

"Just so we're all in agreement. If we do this, we're crazy."

"We're crazy if we don't."

"That's right."

Duncan ran his finger down the edge of the rifle barrel. He turned to his wife. "You know," he said quietly, "for the first time in a week, I'm beginning to feel as if I'm doing something. Wrong or right doesn't enter into it anymore."

"Dad? One thing bothers me," Lauren said. "It's just, well, we don't know that she won't release them in the morning."

"That's right."

"So we could be—"

"That's right, too. We could be jeopardizing everything. But the chances are the same, and this way we have one powerful ally."

"What's that?" Karen asked.

"Surprise," Duncan said.

He looked at the three women in the room.

"What we are going to do is the one thing that Olivia will never expect."

"I know one thing," Karen said angrily.

"What?"

"If we continue to do what she says, we're guaranteed a disaster."

"That's right," Lauren chimed in swiftly. "Every time we've done what she said, she's twisted it somehow. She'll do it again. I know it."

Both Duncan and Megan stared at their daughters with some amazement. The shadows seemed to freeze on the faces of the two girls. These are my children, Megan thought. My babies. What am I doing?

Lauren rose up, struggling with emotions. She burst out in a half-sob: "I just want to get him back and get this over! I want everything to be like it was before." She started to say something else, but her sister put her arm out and quieted her.

"It's okay," Duncan said. There was a small silence in the room.

Megan stood up, fingering the .45-caliber pistol. "You know what I keep thinking?" She walked over and knelt down in front of the two girls, resting her hands on their knees and speaking in a soft, steady voice. "If we do this and screw it up, then we will blame ourselves and we'll have to live with that forever. But if we don't do anything, if we trusted Olivia and something went wrong—I couldn't handle that. I couldn't live with it for a minute."

She turned to Duncan, but remained touching the twins.

"I was thinking earlier—I kept picturing all the times on the nightly newscasts where you see pictures of some family caught up in a tragedy. They're always crying and sobbing, the cameras catch them and it's awful. But they're always surrounded by men in suits. Policemen, firemen, detectives, lawyers, doctors, soldiers—hell, I don't know. But it's always somebody official who tried to do something and ended up doing nothing. It never works out. There are never any happy endings unless you make them for yourself . . ."

She took a deep breath and looked back at the twins.

"You remember when Tommy was little?"

They both smiled and nodded.

"And he was so much trouble?"

She could see the memories lighten their hearts.

"All the doctors said one thing first, then another thing the next time, and then another. They were never really certain, so we just trusted ourselves and did what we thought was right. Our family did it together. We saved Tommy then . . ."

Duncan said, "And we're going to save him now."

He looked down at the rifle. "You know what has hurt me the most through all this? Tommy expects us. He knows we'll come for him. I feel like I've been letting him down."

"What about Grandfather?" Lauren asked.

Duncan snorted. "You know what he would say. Shoot first, ask questions later. Let the law work things out afterwards."

Megan pictured her father. If he were here, she thought, that's exactly what he would say. He wouldn't trust anyone to take over this job. Too important to trust to professionals, that's what he would say. She thought of her mother and realized that she would say the same. They would have different reasons: Her father would be all bluster and Marine can-do determination; her mother would be quiet, certain, and probably just as deadly.

"Look," said Duncan suddenly, in a firm voice. "This may be crazy. But it is not wrong. It's the one true surprise we have. And that is its greatest strength. She thinks we're cowed and defeated, but we're not. She thinks we're ready to roll over and play her game. But we're not."

He paused. Then he smiled. "One thing I can't stand is the idea that we haven't done what we could. I want it on my tombstone: He was crazy, but at least he tried."

"Dad!" Lauren said. "That's not funny!"

"But it's true," he said.

There was another silence before Lauren spoke again.

"It is true," she said firmly. "It's our turn."

She rose up and threw her arms around her father.

Karen looked at her mother.

"Let's go over the plan again," she said.

Megan breathed in harshly, as if she was inhaling superheated air that scorched her lungs. She pointed down at a rough diagram of the house and fields.

"The field slopes down behind the house, back away from it to the forest. You two will take the two shotguns and wait down there and cover the back door. Your father and I will go to the front."

"What exactly should we do?" Karen asked.

"I don't really know," Megan replied. "Mainly make sure that no one escapes in that direction, especially with Tommy or Grandfather. Use your judgment. Don't try to shoot it out with them or anything, just keep your heads down and do whatever seems necessary. Keep an eye on that back door. I think everything will happen in front, but . . ." Her voice trailed off.

Duncan picked up the thread: "I don't want either of you exposing yourselves in any way, especially to gunfire. The shotguns are your last resorts. They're just to protect yourselves, got it? Stay down. Mom says there's a stone wall back there. You stay behind it at all times."

He glanced over at Megan, wavering for an instant. He thought of the differences between daughters and sons. If they were teenage boys, he thought, they'd probably be anxious to fight. But they wouldn't be as steady and as trustworthy.

"Maybe—" he started.

"Not a chance!" interrupted Lauren.

"We're all in this together!" Karen almost shouted. "You're not leaving us behind."

"We won't let you out of our sight," insisted Karen.

Megan held up her hand, signaling peace. She looked closely over at Duncan. "It's the damn back door," she said quietly. "I don't know much about this sort of thing, except I know you have to cover that back door. Otherwise we could get hung up in front, and out they'd scoot. Someone's got to be there."

Duncan sighed in agreement. "Listen, you've got to promise one thing. It will be difficult enough to get the Tommys without having to worry about you guys. If you two were exposed to some danger, we'd go crazy. It could jeopardize everything. So stay back, stay out of sight, stay out of the way. Just watch the damn back door and make sure we're covered on that side. Got it?"

"Yes," they said in unison.

"No chances, dammit—don't take any chances! No matter what you see happening."

"We understand."

"Even if your mother or I are in trouble, stay put."

"Come on, Dad . . ."

"Okay," Duncan said. He was filled with dread.

Lauren, though, had brightened considerably. "So, while we're doing nothing, what happens in front?"

Megan smiled. "Your father takes the rifle and covers me while I go through the front door—"

"Megan, are you sure—"

She cut him off.

"Yes. Absolutely. I've thought about it a million times. I probably couldn't hit anything with that rifle, like you can, so it doesn't do any good for me to cover you. I'm quicker than you, though you don't like to admit that. And a smaller target, if it comes to that. And also, I know exactly what the inside of that old house will look like. So I'm going in first."

"Mom, are you sure they're in the attic?"

"Yes. Remember the tape from Tommy that Olivia played for us? He said he didn't like it 'up' there. That's where they are."

"What happens after you get through the front door. And suppose it's locked?"

Megan held up the hunting knife. "For the lock," she said. "And when I'm inside, your father follows. I cover him with the pistol. Everything should be real simple. It will just barely be light, so I bet they'll all still be asleep and we'll be in the house. Hands up and that's it. It will be over."

"A rude awakening," Duncan said.

"It sounds simple."

"It is. If we surprise them."

"They'll be surprised, all right," Lauren said angrily. She rubbed her eyes quickly, as if cleaning some of the week's tears away from her cheeks. Then she picked up a shotgun from the floor and cocked it. "Mom, just show me how this works one more time," she said.

12

THE BACK DOOR

Insistent dawn light sliced through the forest darkness like a razor parting flesh. There had been a hard frost during the night; a thin white coverlet was spread across the fields and rode the edges of leaves and branches. They could see their breath as they moved through the trees, like blowing smoke in an all-gray world. They wore the camouflage outfits that Megan had purchased the day before, so that they blended with the shadows and dark colors that hid from the first moments of day. The twins each struggled with a shotgun; Duncan gripped the semiautomatic rifle, and Megan had stuck the .45-caliber pistol in her belt, alongside the hunting knife. They walked in single file, Megan leading, then the twins, with Duncan bringing up the rear. They traveled quietly, stealthily, pausing to listen to the void around them, then moving on, picking their feet up slowly and setting them down equally carefully. As they passed through the woods, it seemed they were leaving behind everything that they had once known and loved and were stepping into another world; a place of cold and unsettling silence.

Megan pushed some thorny branches out of her way and held

them for Lauren, who was next. She passed them to Karen, who waited for Duncan. Megan maneuvered a few feet farther, then crouched down, squatting, waiting for the family to catch up with her. When they all gathered close, she pointed through the pale light, between a stand of trees, and they could all see the white shape of the farmhouse a hundred yards ahead. Without saying anything, Megan gestured toward the stone wall that marked the edge of the treeline. Then she pointed to the right and left, signifying the directions that the stone wall traveled. The twins nodded.

Duncan whispered, "You take them, get them in position. I'll wait for you a little ways up there, where we can see the front. I'll be right on the wall, okay?"

Megan reached out and grasped his hand.

"Be quiet," she said. "I won't be more than a few minutes."

Duncan turned to the twins. "Please," was all he could say. He could feel his lip quiver and he hoped it was from the morning chill.

"Don't worry, Dad," Karen whispered back.

"You be the one who's careful," Lauren said. She smiled, then reached over and brushed his cheek with a quick kiss.

A thousand fears and thoughts burst through Duncan. He started to reach out, to speak, but stopped. When he looked at the twins' eyes, he saw them as babies, remembered the defenseless, small children who needed to be swept up in his arms and protected.

"Tell Tommy we're waiting for him," Lauren whispered.

"And tell him he's never to cause us all this much trouble again," Karen said, smiling.

Duncan nodded and looked back at Megan. Their eyes met and for just an instant, they both felt a great sucking helplessness. Then he managed a wispy smile that was almost lost in the bare light and thin air. He turned and looked at the house.

"All right," he said quietly but firmly. "Let's get it over with."

Duncan half-crawled through the trees. Megan waited until he had slid from sight and sound, and then she motioned to the twins to follow her. She held a single finger up to her lips, gesturing for silence, only to hear Karen's breathy whisper: "We know we're supposed to be quiet. Let's go!" she urged.

Within a few minutes they had maneuvered around the edge of the field behind the farmhouse and were moving parallel to the back side. The stone wall was in disrepair, chunks had fallen away, and each time they had to cut slightly back from the rim of trees, so as to maintain concealment. They were almost on their hands and knees, bent over, moving from tree bulk to brush, to tree, in stops and starts. Megan kept searching off to her right, across the field, looking up at the house, keeping it in constant view. She cursed inwardly, frustrated, wanting to spot some natural barricade, some hollow that would afford both cover and protection. She suddenly felt an arm on her shoulder and turned abruptly.

It was Karen, gesturing back into the forest. Lauren was looking that way, as well.

"What is it?" Megan asked, nearly frozen with sudden fear.

"Look!" whispered Lauren insistently.

"It's a car," Karen said. "Back there, behind those trees."

Megan's eyes narrowed and she caught a gleam of metal reflecting off a persistent shaft of morning sunlight.

"You're right," she said. "Come on, let's go."

She started forward, only to be stopped by Karen's hand, pressuring her.

"What?" she said.

"Don't you see?" her daughter asked.

Megan looked back again and then did see.

"It's the judge's car," Lauren said.

Megan quietly turned and led the twins through the forest toward the car. It was parked on the edge of what had once been a dirt road. The road was overgrown, grassy; the only real sign that it had once been used was the meager mud swath cut through the trees.

Lauren ran her hand alongside the car, fingering scratches in the paint. "Poor Grandfather," she said. "He was so proud of the silly thing. Why would they put the car here?"

"To hide it, silly," Karen whispered back. "They couldn't leave it out where anyone might see it and recognize it."

"Oh," her sister replied.

Megan looked and saw tracks where the car had been painstakingly turned around. She saw that it was pointed back toward the main road and the exit from the forest. She peered through the window and saw that the keys were in the ignition. There was a bag on the floor of the passenger seat. For a moment she considered opening the car door and inspecting the interior, but then she realized there was no way she could get it open without making a familiar and therefore telltale noise.

"I think," she said quietly, "that you guys better help keep an eye on this."

"Stay here?" Karen asked.

"We can't see anything."

Megan turned back in the direction of the farmhouse.

"All right," she sighed. "Over there at the last big pile of rocks from what's left of the stone wall. But keep your bearings, okay? And keep this car sort of covered, too."

The twins both nodded in agreement. Megan thought how ridiculous her directions were. Keep it covered. She wanted to laugh. As if any of us had any idea what we are doing, she realized. Then she dismissed this revolutionary bit of sense, and led the two girls back to the spot where they could each see the back of the farmhouse, rising up ahead of them. She looked at the two of them, placing them so that they were well down behind the rocks. "Keep down!" she whispered frantically. Then she sighted toward the white clapboard building. The silver, frost-covered field seemed to be like a wave lapping up against its edge, racing away from where they were waiting.

"All right," she said. "Wait here. And no chances. Got it?"

"Come on, Mom. Get going. The sun's coming up and Dad's waiting."

"No chances."

"C'mon, Mom."

She wanted to tell them how much she loved them, but thought they would just be embarrassed. So she said it to herself: I love you two. Please stay safe.

Then she swallowed hard. Suddenly paralyzed with reluctance, she had to order her muscles to move. She closed her eyes tight, for just a second, and turned her back abruptly, scrabbling crablike away through the brush and trees. She did not look back even once because she knew that no matter how brave she thought they were, if she did she would be unable to leave her two daughters alone out there in the woods, facing across such a small distance from so much uncompromising evil.

Duncan hugged the wall, waiting for Megan to appear through the morning mists behind him, keeping an eye on the farmhouse for any signs of movement. He tried to make his mind a blank; he did not want to think about what they were doing or what they planned to do. He tried to segment his life into the seconds that it took to inhale the sharp air, then blow it out again. When he heard animal noises in the woods, he pivoted, only to see his wife crawling toward him.

"Is everything okay?" he asked.

"We found the judge's car. It's hidden on the access road behind where I left the girls."

"Are they—I don't know . . ."

"I guess so. Sure."

Megan looked at Duncan and for a moment felt her will waver. He, too, was caught in the sudden undertow of doubt. Both thought of speaking, then forced themselves to be quiet. Megan slid forward on the damp ground and crawled into her husband's arms, burying her head against his chest. For a moment she listened to his heartbeat; he counted the rising and falling of her bosom.

The moment passed, and they strengthened.

"It's time," Duncan said. "If we wait, someone might be an early riser, and—" He didn't bother to finish his sentence.

Megan rolled over and looked up at the sky. She could see great purple-red streaks of light in the distance, riding the edges of massed clouds. "Red sky in the morning," she said.

"Sailors take warning." Duncan followed Megan's gaze and nodded. "Storm coming, probably. Snow maybe."

Megan turned away and reached out and squeezed his hand.

"Have you been thinking of Tommy?"

"A little."

"So have I. Let's go get him."

Duncan forced a smile through his worry.

"I'm ready. Whenever you want."

Megan peered over the edge of the stone wall. She took a deep breath.

"I'll go first to the car. Then to the edge of the porch. Then to the door. When I'm inside, you count to five, and then run like hell for the car. Then the door. Okay?"

Duncan clicked the safety catch off the rifle. He grasped the firing bolt on the side of the magazine and slid it back until it caught with a sharp click, chambering a round.

"You do the same," he ordered in a firm whisper.

Megan took the pistol in her hand and armed it.

"Ready?"

"Ready."

"I love you, then. Now, go!"

Duncan twisted upward, resting the rifle on the ledge of the wall, as Megan vaulted over the top. For an instant it felt like diving into a deep, black, unfamiliar pool. Everything I've ever been or believed or wanted has come down to this moment, she thought. Then she realized she was running, crouched over, the cool air tugging at her flushed cheeks, her feet barely skimming the surface of the yard. The distance to the house seemed suddenly immense, much farther than she had ever figured, a vast, wide, brightly lit, hazardous world. She gritted her teeth and raced on.

Ramon Gutierrez lay on his bed, watching the light creep slowly up the wall, thinking of murder.

He tried to persuade himself: It is not such a difficult thing. In its own way, it is no different from other crimes.

When he was young, there was always an initiation into the gangs. A robbery, a rape, a killing; the task had been different for each organization. They hadn't been large things in his neighborhood; everyone's familiarity with crime made the acts part of the norm rather than the exception. He had not hated committing crimes; only being caught. The thought jolted him with a flash of hatred for the two captives in the attic. They are dangerous, he told himself. They are very dangerous and they can kill you much easier than you think. Their eyes are like shotguns pointed at your chest. Their memories are like knives that can slash your throat. Their voices are like the electric current in the chair. They can put you away forever. They can kill you dead as any policeman.

Ramon could feel a band of sweat on his forehead.

There was a tugging within him, half pulling toward sleep, half toward wakefulness. He wished that he had managed more than the few hours that he had. I need to be alert, he told himself. He measured the forces within him, and realized his eyes were open, watching the world about him come into dawn's focus.

He remembered prison, and joining the movement. As with the youth gangs, the leadership had always prescribed an act for admission. But the gangs' initiations had a practical streak. The movement had liked symbolism, bombs in particular. He had always thought them a cowardly way of killing people, but he'd understood they were a much safer organizational approach. That was what he had done; helped plant a pipe bomb in the men's room of a government building. It hadn't been his fault that the damn thing failed to explode on schedule.

The memory slid from his mind and he thought of the two captives upstairs. He pictured the two Tommys sitting on the bunks facing him. Then he tried to paint into his vision gunshots, blood, and wounds. He saw them stretched out on the floor, stiffening.

He realized he had never actually killed anyone before, though he had been present when murders had taken place: once during a gang war, when two rivals had been cornered in an alley; the second time after a prison meal, when the flood of convicts had gone to the exercise yards and an informant had been slaughtered in the momentary confusion that overtook the place whenever there were large movements of the inmate population; the third time was Olivia's visit to the executive out in California. He recalled the look on the man's face when he had recognized the inevitability of what was about to happen; a mixture of panic and anger. He had fought. He had no chance and he knew it, but he fought and that made it easier for her. He hoped that the judge and the boy would fight him. Then he could kill them in battle and it would be easier for him, too.

He cursed and swung his feet over the edge of the bed.

The weak light in the room illuminated his package of cigarettes on a rickety old table. He sneezed as he reached out for the pack. Damn this cold, old place, he said to himself. Damn it forever. I never want to see it again.

He tried to make himself think of warm climates. He encouraged himself, thinking, By noon today I'll be flying south with a pocketful of money. He looked over at his small duffel bag, already packed and ready.

He got up and pulled his pants and shoes on. He threw a tattered gray sweatshirt over his head. It had a hood, which he pulled up, like a scarf.

Ramon listened and heard the muffled noise of Bill Lewis's snoring coming from the next room. He clenched and unclenched his hands a few times. Then he went over to the bedstand and found his revolver. He slid it into his waistband. After today, he thought, everything will be different. He imagined it would be very warm in the bed next to Olivia.

He felt a burst of enthusiasm: We will do remarkable things together. For an instant he felt a small sadness for Lewis. He doesn't understand, Ramon thought. Then he shrugged the idea away, replacing it with an undefined jealous anger.

Ramon stepped out into the hallway and looked down toward the locked attic door. I could do it now, while Lewis sleeps. He would be taken by surprise; so would they. It would be done and over and no one could do anything about it. Ramon realized that the gun was already in his hand, but he couldn't remember loosening it from his pants. He looked down and saw it was cocked, but couldn't recall doing that, either. In their sleep would be easier, he told himself. He took a step in that direction and felt his will waver. A cup of coffee first, he said. To keep the hand steady. He replaced the weapon in his waistband.

The stairs creaked slightly as he padded down toward the kitchen.

The house seemed still and frozen; he hated the way the cold seeped through everything. It made the mornings utterly silent and awful. In the south, waking up was to greet friendly noise and warmth that built up into day. He shivered again as he wandered into the kitchen, turned on the hot water tap as far as it would go, and searched for a coffee cup less dirty than the others. After a moment or two, he found one that was satisfactory. He dashed two scoops of instant espresso coffee into the bottom and filled the cup from the steaming tap. He took a sip, made a face and turned around, leaning against the sink, letting the heat from the cup flow into his hands, warming him to his soul.

When he heard the small thud from the front of the house, he was at first confused. What was that? he thought. There shouldn't be any noise. Not here. Not now.

Then, instantly, fear seared him.

His hand shook slightly as he put the coffee down.

He strained his ears, listening for another noise, but he heard none.

It was something, he thought. It was nothing. It was this old house creaking with age. It was the police getting into position. His insides shook with sudden tension, as he tried to persuade himself both that he had heard something and had heard nothing. When he looked down, he saw that his revolver had jumped again into his hand. He thought for a moment of running upstairs and crying out for Olivia. Then he thought: I am stronger than that. What do I need her for, to check out some little noise that will turn out to be my imagination playing tricks? He felt a small bit of disgust for his frayed nerves. Reproof mingled with fear.

He walked carefully, but with deliberate speed, to the front of the house. He peered through a glass panel in the front door, but he could see nothing but the front yard, glistening with the dawn frost.

It was nothing, he said to himself. You slept poorly.

It's close to the end and you're nervous, so you're reacting to nothing.

Ramon shivered once. It is probably nothing, he insisted to himself. Maybe it was the wind. But he could see the trees standing bare and still against the overcast sky.

He did not want to leave the meager warmth of the old house, but he knew he had to make certain. He turned the door handle slowly, and opened the door. It was as if someone had blown a frigid breath around him. He hesitated again, reluctant to step outside.

But he did.

Shaking from the chill, and perhaps from something else, Ramon walked slowly out onto the porch. He held the gun outstretched in his hand, and his head pivoted to the right and left as he swept the yard with his eyes.

Lauren looked up at the back of the farmhouse and asked, "Do you think they're okay?" The quiet had begun to gnaw at the edges of her confidence. She had fought off a dozen nightmare visions in the past minutes. Karen draped an arm around her, hugging her.

"Of course," Karen replied gently. "Why not?"

"We haven't heard anything."

"Well, that means it's going like it's supposed to."

"I wish we'd hear something."

"Are you scared?"

"Sure. Aren't you?"

"Only a little. I'm mad, too."

"Yeah. Do you suppose Tommy and the judge—"

"Oh, they're okay, I just know it. They're probably asleep. You know how Tommy is. If he's a little tired, you can't wake him with a cannon."

"I wish Mom were here."

"So do I."

"They know what they're doing."

"Of course they do."

"Sit closer. I'm cold."

"It's not the cold," Karen said, practical as usual. But still she moved closer. She looked down at her weapon. "When you can see the little red dot, does that mean the safety is on or off?"

"Off."

"Oh. Right." She clicked the safety catch on.

"Why are you doing that?" Lauren asked.

"Well, Dad said—"

"He said to be careful. He didn't say to be stupid."

"What do you mean?" the older sister said, bristling slightly.

"Well, I don't think I could ever remember to find the stupid safety if I had to. I think we should be ready, in case we have to run up there and help."

"They said to stay put."

"Yeah, but what do you think?"

Karen thought for an instant. She wanted to be responsible, she wanted to behave. She wanted to make her parents proud of her. Lauren looked at her sister closely. "I know what you're thinking," she whispered. "I know what they said. But we're here to help! He's our brother, too."

Karen nodded. "I think you're right."

Both girls unlatched the safety catches on their weapons. They bent forward, watching the house.

"Can you feel it?" Lauren whispered suddenly.

"What?"

"I don't know. It's like the wind picked up or a cloud passed over, or something."

Karen nodded. She smiled. "You know, they wouldn't believe this at school."

Lauren almost giggled. "Boy, that's right."

But the slight moment of humor dissipated in the overwhelming still of the morning. The silence swept across them again, and within it an unsettling fear of the unknown. They remained shoulder to shoulder, staring up at the farmhouse. Lauren reached over and grasped her sister's hand. It was as if an electric charge passed through them. They could feel each other's heartbeats, taste each other's breath.

"It's going to be okay," Lauren said quietly.

"I know. I just wish something would happen," Karen replied.

They waited, letting anxiety battle with trust.

* * *

When Megan's foot had slipped on the frost-slick first step up to the porch, her hand, holding the pistol, had thudded down hard on the wood stairs as she caught herself. The noise had stopped her instantly. She thought it was like an explosion. Instead of stepping ahead to the front door, she had ducked back, cowering against the porch riser, hiding by the edge, waiting to see whether she had been heard.

The scraping sound of the front door swinging open scorched her will. She froze, holding the pistol, trying to wedge herself against the porch so that she could not be seen from above.

She had no idea what to do.

When she heard the first creaking step, almost on top of her, she trembled. But she lifted the weapon and insisted: It won't end like this.

She fought the fear that gripped at her arms and legs and all her muscles and joints with a single image: Tommy. Her heartbeat quickened and she felt adrenaline surge through her. I'm coming, dammit, I'm coming for you now.

She tightened, as she heard the footsteps work closer to her hiding spot.

Duncan had seen her slip, heard the small bumping sound, and cursed. He too, had waited, his eyes locked on his wife. She seemed like some small animal, crouched against fear.

The sight of the door opening onto the porch stabbed his heart with terror.

"Oh, my God," he whispered. "They heard her."

For an instant, it was as if all his strength had been sucked from him. He felt light, almost weightless.

Then he saw Gutierrez step onto the porch.

"Oh, my God," he said again. *"Megan—watch out."* His voice was a bare whisper.

He saw the gun in Ramon's hand.

He saw Ramon take one, then another, step toward the place where his wife was huddled.

He tried to command his racing heart to still. He thought: There is no choice.

He wanted to swallow, but his mouth was completely dry. A brief memory flashed into his eyes: He could see the street in Lodi, see himself hesitating, hanging on the van, as if touching the edge of some dark ocean, afraid of being sucked down into the depths. The years screamed at him not to wait, not to hesitate again and lose everything by doubt.

"Keep down, Megan," he whispered.

He took a deep breath and lowered his cheek to the rifle stock. His world suddenly miniaturized, past the black sight, across the yard, over his wife's head and directly into Ramon Gutierrez's chest. He saw Ramon take another step and pause, no more than a foot or two from the edge of the porch, where Megan hid.

He blew out slowly.

"I'm sorry," he whispered. The pressure in his finger against the trigger seemed immense, almost painful. He gently pulled back and fired the gun. The crash of the report seem to shatter the porcelain air.

Olivia Barrow was snatched from a dream of prison. She had been back in her cell, in maximum security, only this time it wouldn't lock properly. She had been able to open the bars at will. In the dream she could feel the sticky cold of the steel, hear the rasping noise as the gate swung back. She had seen herself step forth, alone, onto the catwalk outside the tier, free to go wherever she wanted. She had swelled with an unbridled happiness, a lightness, almost as if her feet were no longer linked to the earth, and she could fly. In the dream, she was joyously fast-walking away from the cell, when she heard a thunderous peal, and for a microsecond she thought it was a storm bursting over her head.

Then she tumbled from sleep into sudden, horrible wakefulness.

She sat up abruptly in bed, ignoring the morning chill, straining to hear.

"What the hell was that?" she demanded, her voice high-pitched.

Bill Lewis had risen next to her. In the weak morning light his skin seemed pale, almost translucent. His eyes were wide, his voice a slippery whine of near-panic:

"I don't know. What was it? I couldn't tell, I was asleep."

"It sounded like a shot."

"Where's Ramon?"

"I don't know. In his room?"

"Ramon? Ramon! Where the hell are you?" Olivia cried out.

There was no answer. She thought: He's gone upstairs and he's killing them. She swung her legs out of the bed and stood naked by the side. There should be another shot. There should be screams. There should be an answer. What is it?

"What's he doing?" Bill demanded suddenly, his words jumbled together by fear. "Is he—what the hell—where's he gone? What's he doing? I don't get it—it's not part of the plan."

Bill Lewis looked wildly at Olivia.

"That's not upstairs," Bill shouted. "That's coming from outside. Ramon!"

Olivia's mind raced with confusion. She screamed orders to herself: *Think! Act!* She snatched a machine pistol from a bedside table. Suddenly she felt a wondrous, peaceful calm, almost a child's moment of satisfied delight, as if she were back in her dream. She felt her nakedness flush, glistening red with sudden warmth.

"What's going on?" Bill screamed.

"Come on," Olivia said carefully. "It's ending."

She strode across the bathroom to the window and peered out. She was aware that Lewis was struggling to get into his pants behind her, cursing as he fought against the stiffened jeans, and she thought how silly that was, how completely absurd, and she laughed out loud.

The noise of the first shot also ripped Judge Pearson from a dream. He had been on a beach, surrounded by his grandchildren, playing in the sand. The hot sun had warmed him, and he'd blinked back the glare. He could see Megan and Duncan riding the blue-green waves. He had turned and spoken to his wife, who had been sitting next to him. "But you're dead," he had told her. "And I'm alone."

She had smiled, shaking her head, and replied, "No one ever really dies. No one ever really is alone." But then, when he turned away from her, his family was gone and the beach was the red-tinged sand of Tarawa, and he was a scared young man again. He heard a single shot race over his head and he buried himself in the sand, pressing his face down sharply as the bullet whistled in the air, only to lift back up, and in the dream say, "But that was real."

And plummet into wakefulness.

He spun quickly to Tommy, who was sitting up ramrod straight on his cot.

"Grandfather!"

"Tommy, it's happening. My God, they're coming for us!"

"Grandfather!" Tommy burst from his bed, leaping into the judge's arms.

Judge Pearson hugged him tightly, then thrust him back.

"Now, Tommy, now! We must help save ourselves."

Tommy swallowed and nodded. The judge swung from the bunk and seized the metal rod.

"Now," he said. "Give me a hand."

They heard a second shot.

"Quickly, Tommy. Just like we talked about!"

He was filled with power, with direction; he remembered a hundred terrifying, paralyzing moments in combat where, despite all the death and horror, he'd acted. It was as if his muscles were no longer aged, his bones no longer brittle and old. He felt flush with the arrogant strength of youth.

The judge lifted one of the bunks and dragged it across the room. With a great shove and crash, he sent it tumbling down the stairs, slamming up against the attic door. He jumped back and grasped Tommy's bunk. "Now yours!" He pushed that one down the stairs, further blocking the entranceway.

Tommy was already dressed, already at the wall, smashing into the weakened area with the metal rod from the bed frame. Judge Pearson jumped to his side. He took the piece of frame and thrust it beneath one of the loosened boards. He blew out once, hard, then levered back as hard as he could. There was a cracking sound, and the creaking of splitting wood. The first board pulled back, like a broken bone. The judge shouted once; a splinter had creased his thumb and shot pain into his arm. But he ignored it and slammed the metal piece into the exposed plaster. It exploded in a dusty cloud. He smashed the opening again, and then a third time. Then, winded, Judge Pearson stepped back, ready to swing the metal again, only to hear Tommy shout:

"Grandfather, we're through! I can see the sky!"

He gritted his teeth, all age, doubt, and infirmity forgotten, and attacked the wall, ripping and tearing at the crumbling plaster and rotted wood with a great cry of victory.

Duncan's first shot had crushed into Ramon's chest like a heavy-weight's punch, knocking him backward, slamming him against the front door of the house, pinning him there. He jerked once, like a spastic marionette. Then he had slithered slowly to a sitting position, almost as if relaxing. He stared out at the yard, still seeing nothing, wondering what it was that had happened to him. He wondered too, why the cold had disappeared. It was his last thought.

Duncan's second shot exploded in the dead man's face.

Megan rose up, after the second report from her husband's gun, and stared wildly at Ramon Gutierrez's body, awash with blood and brain matter. She took a step backward and wanted to scream at the nightmare.

Duncan stood up behind her, back at the wall.

For an instant, everything was quiet again, the silence filling the frozen morning.

He could feel his throat contract, dry, as he saw his wife hesitate and he croaked out a great shout: "Go! Go, Megan! Go! Now!"

Duncan scrambled over the stone wall, nearly dropping the rifle. He grabbed it and stood up, stumbling into a run toward her, still crying, "Go! Go! Now!"

His wife turned crazily toward him. She saw him gesturing frantically toward the front door. Their eyes locked for an instant and he saw her nod. She turned back toward the body on the porch and gave a cry of half-rage, half-fear, and complete determination.

Weapon in hand, she vaulted up the porch stairs and threw herself past Ramon's body, into the house.

"Them!" Olivia cried, a sound mingling a scream with a laugh.

"Who?" Bill Lewis shouted, grabbing his machine pistol.

"Who do you think?" Olivia replied. She pulled the bolt back on her weapon, arming it. She used the barrel to crash through the windowpanes. She could see Duncan running toward the house.

"Cover the stairwell!" she yelled at Lewis.

He hesitated.

"Do it now, you idiot, before they get closer!"

He spun around behind her and jumped through the bedroom door, padding toward the core of the farmhouse.

Karen and Lauren heard the shots and gasped.

In the silence that followed, they each felt a dizzying plunge into immediate fear, like the first moment that a car swerves on a rain-slick street, out of control.

"Oh, my God," Lauren whispered. "What's happening?"

"I don't know," Karen replied. "I don't know."

"Are they all right?"

"I don't know."

"What shall we do?"

"I don't know."

"We have to do something!"

"What?"

"I don't know!"

Both girls, fighting tears and panic and the urge to race from their place of concealment, remained still, stiff with emotion.

Megan tripped as she flung herself into the vestibule, crashing to the floor. For a second she was stunned, then she rolled over, coming up to her knees with the pistol in her outstretched hand, swinging it back and forth, ready to fire at noise, at movement, at ghosts or fears. She could hear her breathing, loud, raspy.

She climbed to her feet and headed for the stairs, which rose up in front of her.

She heard the footsteps above her, slapping against the wood floor, and she threw herself to the side, back against the wall, staring up the stairs. She lifted the gun to be ready, and saw Bill Lewis's face peer over the banister. For an instant they both paused, then she saw the gun in his hands. Both of them shouted out something incomprehensible in that second; Megan fired once, then ducked back into a parlor door, while Lewis opened fire. But his momentary hesitation lost him his advantage. The bullets sprayed wildly into the plaster and woodwork, sending dust and splinters flying.

Megan screamed as a shaft of something tore into her forearm. She reeled back, staring at the blood that welled up through her sleeve. A jagged piece of wood was sticking out through the fabric, caught in her skin. She cried out and snatched it from her arm. Blood trickled down between her fingers. Then she rolled forward, raising the .45, and let loose with a wild series of shots, feeling the great handgun buck and pull at her as she did. The world above her seemed to explode in noise and terror.

Bill Lewis jumped backward as bullets slapped up into the ceiling above him, shielding his face from the sudden onslaught.

He fired again, just as frantically, haphazardly stitching the air with death.

In the bedroom, Olivia watched almost patiently, as Duncan raced toward the house. He came straight on, no zigs or zags, no hesitancy in his stride, barreling forward on a line for the front door. She thought he moved in slow motion; she was surprised, for an instant, that he was there at all. I didn't think you had it in you, math-man, she thought. I never thought you'd try. And now, it has killed you. She could feel a massive bellow of anger rise within her, electrifying her arms, legs, and heart. She could feel her hand twitching, demanding to fire. And so she did, screaming imprecations that rose above the ripping sound of the automatic weapon.

"Die!" she roared. But the word was drawn out and more a guttural, wordless keen. The gun in her hands seemed possessed by the same rage, bursting hot and crazily, tugging and jumping as she tried to aim carefully.

She kept firing at the figure that persisted toward her. He was running with one hand held up over his head, as if that would ward off the shots. Through the instant smoke, she could see bullets kicking up the dirt around Duncan. The hot, acrid smell of cordite filled her nostrils.

"Die, you coward!" she screamed again.

Then she laughed as Duncan fell abruptly, as if tripped by some great unseen hand. He splayed on the ground directly in her line of fire.

"I've got you, you bastard!"

She aimed carefully and tried to fire again, but cursed when she realized the magazine was empty. She swirled about, seizing another clip.

Pain flooded him.

He could taste bitter, dry dirt, where he'd skidded in the ground.

In that first instant, he did not know if he were dead or not. He looked down at himself and saw streaks of blood littering his legs. She'll kill me now, he thought.

But he realized that he had struggled to his feet.

The front door seemed a vast ways away, completely unreachable. He wondered for an instant where the next volley of bullets was. What are you waiting for? he cried to himself. Then he saw that the kidnappers' car was only a few feet distant, off to his left. Reaching down for his weapon and grabbing it by the barrel, he half-hopped, half-tumbled behind the car. Before he could gather his thoughts, a second burst of bullets exploded against the vehicle, screeching and whining like unhappy orphans as they ricocheted off the metal. The window glass burst above him, shattering with an explosion and raining down on his head.

He huddled against the side, and stared down at his mangled legs.

Broken, he wondered? Ruined? What? He thought of Tommy and the twins, of Megan and the judge.

He shrugged. Can't be helped, he thought. Got to keep moving. He pushed up to his feet, gasping with sudden flames of pain that shot through his knees and thighs. He bit back tears and tried to relax. The wave of hurt washed through his brain, making him dizzy. He bit his lip and thought of his family and felt a surge of strength. He buried his head against the side of the car and took a deep breath.

You haven't killed me yet. He would have laughed if he'd had the strength.

Duncan's mind raced with directions, orders, ideas. He recognized he couldn't make the front. But the side of the farmhouse beckoned with cover and he decided to head that way.

He took another deep breath and wondered where the pain had fled. It's there, he thought. Just hiding. Probably an illusion, he realized. He smiled.

Not dead yet. Tommy, I'm still coming for you.

Duncan gathered himself and rose up, lifting the rifle to his shoulder. He pointed it in the vague direction of the upstairs room where he knew it was Olivia shooting at him. Then he started firing, squeezing off the shots as quickly as he could. Through his squinting eyes, he could see the bullets tearing into the window frame and crashing through the window. He kept firing as he moved away from the car, stumbling, struggling, now angling toward the side of the house, where he would be out of her line of fire, wondering how long his legs would last him and surprised that they would work at all.

Olivia reeled back in sudden surprise as the bullets from Duncan's weapon burst against the window and slammed into the wall and ceiling, showering her with glass, dust, and debris. She landed on the bed, sitting, rocking back and forth, not damaged, but astonished by the ferocity that filled the air. Another volley ripped the air around her, and she felt herself falling. The floor thudded against her, hard. It took her a second to realize that she was knocked down, and she picked herself up and jumped back to the window, only to see Duncan, limping, dragging his legs, but still firing his rifle, sweep around the corner of the farmhouse. She fired off a last barrage toward him, cursing as she leaned out of the window.

Then she turned back to the room.

It's just them, she thought. It's just the two of them.

She could hear the gunfire from the stairwell and she thought of the captives in the attic.

The high-pitched ripping sound of the machine pistol stopped, replaced by a flurry of deep-throated roars from Megan's gun. Olivia looked down and saw her red satchel, filled with money. She closed it quickly and threw the carrying strap over her shoulder. She looked up and saw Bill Lewis in the doorway.

"Give me another clip!" he shouted.

She tossed him a clip of cartridges, which he dropped, then bent over to pick up.

"Kill them," Olivia whispered.

He stared at her.

"Go kill them up in the attic," she said in a normal tone of voice, but firmly, the way one would reprimand a small child who knew no better.

His jaw dropped.

"Kill them!" she shouted, her voice rising.

"But—"

She screamed, her voice soaring into a high-pitched siren demand: "Kill them! Kill them! Kill them both! Do it now, dammit! Do it now! Kill them!"

He looked wide-eyed at her. Then he nodded and disappeared through the door, trailed by Olivia's screamed commands. She followed him to the hallway, turning toward the stairwell, readying herself for Megan's assault. Behind her, she could hear Lewis fumbling with the lock.

Megan, kneeling behind the cover of the doorway between the vestibule and the sitting room, was trying to reload the .45 when she heard Olivia's screams rise above the ringing in her ears. The words froze her and electrified her at once, filling her with desperate, wounded mother-anger. She pushed herself to her feet. Her own mouth opened in a great shout of despair and determination:

"No!" she cried. "Tommy!" Filling with rage and hurt, Megan charged up the stairs, oblivious to any pain and harm that might befall her, thinking only of her child, firing as she ran.

The sudden ferocity of her assault took Olivia by surprise and she fired a useless, wild burst toward the banshee battle cries. The bullets slapped angrily into the wall above Megan's head. The explosions knocked Megan to the floor, but did no other harm than slow her down, which she realized instantly could be the greatest harm of all.

She picked herself up again and crawled forward insistently, hugging the stairs, ready to fire.

Olivia was screaming now: *"Kill them! Kill them!"* over and over. She turned back and saw Lewis struggling against the door.

"Something's in the way!" he yelled.

"Shoot it out!"

"What?"

Before she could answer, she heard the crash of Megan's weapon, fired from a few feet away. The bullet exploded into the wall next to her head, creasing her cheek, ripping the lobe of her ear. Olivia tumbled backward, as if struck by a great blow. She was instantly dizzy, confused: She can't have killed me, she thought in utter shock. It's not possible. Olivia put her hand to her face and felt a sticky streak of blood welling between parted flesh. Scarred, she thought. She scarred me. She shouted again, and fired a burst toward Megan, but her own shots were wildly ineffective, because at the same time she was stumbling back into the bedroom.

Judge Pearson took a final savage blow at the hole in the wall and turned to Tommy, breathless, and asked, "Can you get through there?"

"I can, but, Grandfather—"

The judge quickly looked out, catching a glimpse of the forest and the sky, stretching out endlessly. Then he pulled back inside.

"Just go, Tommy, go! Drop to the roof. Get away! Get away, now!"

In the second that the child hesitated, they both heard Olivia's voice screaming her commands to Bill Lewis. The words seemed to fill the air about them, reverberating in the old attic, icy now with winter air.

"Grandfather!" Tommy yelled.

"Just go! Dammit, now!"

"Grandfather!" Tommy seized Judge Pearson's hand.

Judge Pearson heard Bill Lewis pushing at the door. He heard the door open, and crash against the bunk barricade. "Now, Tommy—please!"

He grabbed his grandson and thrust him, squirming feet first, through the small hole. For an instant it seemed the boy would be caught; then, gloriously, he popped through. The judge could see Tommy's hands, gripping the edge of the hole, as he maneuvered for his leap to the roof.

"Go, Tommy, go!" he yelled. Behind him he heard Lewis swearing and pushing against the door. Tommy's hands disappeared, and the judge heard a thump as the boy landed on the roof below. He leaned forward, just to see that his grandson was safe, and yell again, "Get away!" Then the judge turned and picked up the metal rod. He summoned a battle cry from his chest and charged toward the attic entranceway, swinging the metal piece above his head.

As he threw himself against the barricade, the world seemed to explode around him. Bill Lewis had sprayed the door with the machine pistol, and bullets, chips of metal and feathers from the pillows, and wood splinters from the door all howled and screeched in a death song around him. He spun around, as if caught in a sudden gale, knocked to the floor by the force of the wind. He knew in that moment that he was hit, once, twice, perhaps a hundred times. His body screamed commands to him, raging at the insult of red-hot metal piercing cold flesh. A wave of shock and injury washed through him, luring him into immediate unconsciousness. But he fought it off. I can breathe, he thought. I am wounded badly. But I am not dead yet. He pushed himself halfway to his feet, and threw himself forward, trying to use his body to jam the door further.

But his weight had no bulk. He felt himself helplessly being shoved aside.

"Go, Tommy," he whispered. But unconsciousness still did not find him. Instead, black pain clouding his eyes, he looked up and saw Bill Lewis standing over him, oddly hesitant.

Lewis waited for the judge's eyes to lock onto his.

"I'm sorry," he said. "It wasn't supposed to be like this."

"He's out," the judge replied. "He's safe."

Lewis hesitated again.

"I didn't want it . . ." he said. "I wouldn't have . . ."

Judge Pearson did not believe this. He turned his head aside, waiting for death.

After Olivia's last haphazard volley, Megan had struggled up the stairs and saw her adversary fall back into the bedroom. In almost the same moment, she saw Bill Lewis's back squeeze through a door.

In that instant, she knew that was where they were.

She knew she had to get there. She knew she could let nothing stop her. She ran forward, dashing past the bedroom, only peripherally aware that Olivia was standing naked and bleeding a few feet away. Megan charged, screaming like some berserk Valkyrie urged forward by a battle shout of rage and need.

Megan threw herself inside the attic entranceway, tripping and thudding down. She looked up and saw Lewis standing above her a few feet away, holding the machine pistol, frozen in place, like a schoolchild caught misbehaving. He was standing over the judge's body. She screamed and fired wildly.

The first bullet picked Lewis up and dumped him backward onto the seat of his pants. Scarlet blood instantly spread across his chest. He looked strangely at Megan, as if she'd done something unexpected.

She fired again, and this time he spun around and landed in a twisted, misshapen heap in the corner of the attic, his sightless eyes locked onto the hole in the wall.

"Tommy!" Megan called. "Tommy!"

She saw the judge try to lift himself, gesturing at the hole.

"Out," he rasped. "Safe. We did it."

"Dad!"

"Get him, dammit, get him now!" the old man cried, his voice just a bare whisper above death. "Leave me! Get the boy!" He saw Megan nod, and he closed his eyes, satisfied. He did not know whether death would find him in those minutes, or whether he would live, but he swelled with an ineffable pride and breathed slowly, carefully, willing to wait for whatever outcome should arrive. He could sense his heartbeat, pumping steadily within his chest and thought: It's strong. He thought of all the men he'd known who'd fought and died on all the beaches of his youth. They would be proud, he realized. He thought of his wife: I did it, he said to himself.

He waited easily.

Olivia saw Megan flash past her, and squeezed on the trigger, only to have the weapon click uselessly on another empty clip. She seized the final filled magazine from a table, and grabbed the red satchel with the money. Escape, she thought. It's over. She took one tentative step toward the door, then another, flinging herself forward. Run! Get away! Fight another day. Her bare feet seemed light, as if winged. She plunged out of the room and ran down the corridor, leaving Megan struggling to get past the blocked attic door. Olivia grasped the banister and leaped down the stairs, heading toward the back of the house. She nearly fell at the bottom, catching herself as she slid on a throw rug. She dodged past the furniture, angling through the house for the kitchen. She paused there, taking stock for a single moment, using the time to reload her weapon. She was warm, her entire body tingled with combat. She tasted the blood on her lips and looked down and saw that it had flowed from her cheek freely, smearing her breasts like war paint. She roared out, not in pain or anger, but in a sort of exultant fury. She looked about to fix everything in her memory and thought: Goodbye to all this. I need nothing. I am completely free. She remembered the clothing waiting in the judge's car and thought: Escape now. For an instant she figured she would simply be their plague forever, never really eradicated, simply hiding, waiting to surface in the future, whenever she was ready. "You can't beat me!" she yelled out at the top of her lungs. "You can never beat me." She paused hoping for a response, but when none came, felt an uncontrollable anger. She hesitated, staring down at her loaded weapon, struggling with the urge to race back upstairs and continue fighting. It took her a moment to compose herself. *You win by escaping,* she insisted to the side of her that raged on. She laughed once, loudly, falsely, hoping Megan would hear it, then she burst through the back door, carrying the machine pistol in one hand, the money satchel in the other, her mind filling with a vision of freedom.

Tommy clung to the roofline, trying to keep his balance on the steeply pitched surface. The frost from the night before made it slick, and it was hard for him to move. He heard the last flurries of gunfire, and started to crawl away. The cold breeze tugged at him, and he forced himself not to think of his grandfather, and not to hesitate. He had heard his mother's cries, and he knew she was there, somewhere, waiting for him. He battled against tears and confusion, biting back all doubt, and maneuvered toward the edge of the roof.

Megan fought her way back into the upstairs hallway, only to hear Olivia's shouts of defiance coming from the downstairs. She ignored them. She could think only of Tommy, almost overwhelmed with the need to see him and hold him. She raced into a bedroom and went to the window. It overlooked the roof.

"Tommy!" she screamed.

She suddenly saw him, perched on the edge like a resting bird, as if preparing to jump out into the free air.

"Tommy!" she screamed again. "I'm here!"

He turned at the sound of her voice, and cried out, "Mom!"

Megan could see a great, joyous light in her son's eyes. She tore frantically at the window frame. The sash would not budge. She pivoted and saw a chair in a corner. She seized it and raised it high, then crashed it into the glass and wood. She kept yelling at the top of her lungs, "Here I am, Tommy. Here I am!"

The glass exploded outward. She pushed the remaining jagged edges out and jackknifed through the opening. Her hands were cut in a dozen places and bleeding profusely, but she paid no attention. No hurt, no pain, no agony whatsoever could penetrate the swelling of emotion as she saw her son scrambling up the roof toward her. She reached out, crying, "Here, Tommy, here!" filling with volcanic release.

And then she saw Olivia, behind her son. She was standing on the ground outside the back door, staring up at the small figure crawling across the roof.

Black fear enveloped her.

"No!" she screamed. She stretched out her arms for her son's.

As she had dived through the back door, Olivia had heard the scraping noises made by Tommy's feet as he fought for purchase on the roof.

The sound had made her pause in her flight, look back curiously. She had spotted the child at almost the same moment that Megan had. As she watched, she saw Megan throw the chair through the window and then reach for her child.

Olivia stepped back a few feet farther from the house to give herself a better angle for firing. She pulled back the machine-pistol bolt and took careful aim at the two figures in her line of sight.

Duncan had crawled around the side of the house, each foot traveled filling him with searing pain. He felt like a wounded dog struck by a car, too scared and too stupid to realize its legs were crushed, as it tried to run away from the agony, whining its life away.

He had nearly blacked out twice, each time fighting off the seductive urge to slip away into dreams.

When he saw Tommy on the roof, he tried to call out to him, but his voice was dry and barely audible. He dragged himself farther, finally managing to cry out, "Tommy! I'm here!" His voice sounded strong and steady, and this surprised Duncan. He felt a surge of encouragement within him, and some renewed strength propelled him forward, shakily, but steadily.

And then, he too had spotted Olivia.

He watched, stopped in his tracks in utter terror, as she raised the gun and he recognized what was about to happen. He screamed out: "No! No!" lifting his rifle simultaneously. He fired, panic-stricken, in her direction. He fired again, kept firing, kept screaming, eyes almost closed with pain and outrage.

As she was about to pull the trigger, the first of Duncan's crazed shots scorched the air above her head and the second whined inches beneath her nose. For a moment she thought she had been hit, and she fell back, catching herself before she tumbled down. She inadvertently loosed a burst that ripped up uselessly into the sky. She bellowed in immediate fear and anger, whirling about, facing him. She could see him stretched out, prone on the ground, partially hidden by the side of the house, a poor target. She could see the muzzle of his rifle flash.

Another wild shot ripped the air just above her head.

Olivia fired at Duncan, spraying his position with bullets until the gun clicked emptily. She tossed the weapon aside and furiously grabbed at the red satchel. She tore open the top, exposing the money and the large handgun. Seizing the pistol, she looked back at Duncan's position, and saw that most of her shots had crashed into the side of the house above his head. She cursed in immediate frustration. Then she pivoted back, searching the roof, only to see Tommy's hand grasped by Megan's. For just an instant, as she hesitated, the two seemed to move in slow motion. Then, as she gathered herself to aim and fire, they suddenly began moving with lightning speed, and before she could act she saw the child tugged off the roof, through the window, his feet kicking for an instant in the air like a swimmer plunging into the surface of a pond, before disappearing from her sight.

She felt abruptly empty. She turned back to Duncan.

He must be dead, she thought. She crouched and took one step toward him. But then she saw the rifle muzzle rise again, staring directly at her. She ducked fast, and another shot crashed past her.

Megan pulled Tommy toward her with every last remaining bit of strength she could muster, giving a great groan of effort, and the two of them fell back in a pile onto the floor of the house. Megan rolled over, to cover his body, and protect him from any last shots. She heard him grunt, and after a few seconds, he pushed her off him. They sat up, and she pulled him close to her. She realized that she was sobbing his name, hugging him, her own body racked with great tidal waves of joy and relief. After a moment, she felt his own tears on her face, but he pushed her back slightly. She cupped his face in her hands, unable to say anything, her lips quivering with happiness.

He wiped his eyes, suddenly all little-boy tough. "Come on, Mom, I'm okay."

She nodded gratefully.

Duncan had seen Tommy fall through the window into his mother's arms and felt a wild, great joy burst past all the pain within him. We did it, he thought. Oh my God, we did it.

Then he saw Olivia standing across from him. He could see that she had thrown one weapon aside, and now held another. He loosed another shot in her direction and saw her spin away, starting to run. For an instant he watched her back.

He took a deep breath and tried to aim the rifle one last time. For a millisecond Olivia's naked back danced in front of him, directly in the gunsight, and he tugged on the trigger. But there was no report. He too was out of ammunition.

It makes no difference, he thought.

We did it. We are all alive and we did it. We won.

He rolled back and struggled to a sitting position against the side of the house. He took a deep breath and forced himself to his feet, ignoring the pain that seemed to have come alive within him again. He lifted his arm to wave to his wife, to signal that he was all right, which he knew was debatable. He stared down at his bloody legs.

They can be fixed, he thought. Everything broken can be fixed. He closed his eyes and put his head down to rest. He did not think about the bank, about the money, about the past or the future. He felt a completeness within him. He wanted to sleep. He did not realize in which direction Olivia was heading.

Olivia ran.

Naked, bloody, her hair streaming behind her, long legs devouring the ground, arms pumping, like a sprinter who sees the finish line, she dashed down from the back of the farmhouse and started across the long sloping field toward the forest line. Her bare feet kicked up small explosions of white frost from the earth as she raced against the cold and the onset of day, angling for the dark shadows of the trees which would hide her, allow her to escape. She gripped the pistol in one hand, the red satchel of money in the other. She opened her mouth wide, drinking in great draughts of icy air, filling with a wild strength: I'm free, she cried to herself. As the wind flowed past her, she saw herself in the car, in the airport, in a plane headed south, forever loose and unfettered. She gave in to a surge of defiance and success that coursed within her, and sped on, letting the downward momentum of the hill force her faster, in a great sweeping flight toward safety, her bare feet making slapping sounds against the earth that rose up into the gray morning sky.

Karen and Lauren had seen Tommy's struggling dance on the roof; seen Olivia take aim, and seen their brother pulled to safety. They had surged forward once, only to fall back amidst the cover of the rocks. They saw Olivia spray their father with machine-gun bullets, and they had gasped and shouted with fearful rage. But they had seen, too, that he was unhit, and as they had watched Olivia turn and race toward them, they saw their father raise an arm and wave up to the window where Tommy and their mother were.

Their own shouts and cries had been lost in the forest shadows and the insistent racket of gunfire from the house.

They were confused, afraid, in tears.

"What do we do?" Lauren yelled.

They saw Olivia flying directly toward where they were concealed. They saw the streaks of blood that creased her nakedness; she seemed some half-demon, bent on assaulting them.

"I don't know!" screamed Karen.

But then, in the same moment, they both did know.

They rose together, their weapons held up to their shoulders, held steadily, aiming straight ahead, precisely as they had been instructed by their parents.

Olivia saw the two girls rise out of the earth before her like apparitions.

She felt a momentary confusion, but did not slow her headlong charge toward the twins. She lifted her own weapon, aiming at them. What is happening? she wondered crazily. It can't be. It's not supposed to be. I'm free. I'm safe. She tried to hold herself back, to slow down and steady herself, to be able to take aim and save her life, but her momentum pushed her forward inexorably.

Karen and Lauren said nothing, but felt the same indestructible, electric memory inside, a feeling deposited within them so many years earlier, when they were still in their mother's womb and they were the reason she was escaping to a different life. Wordlessly, they fired together; two great blasts that reverberated in the sudden winter still air and closed forever the door to childhood past, innocence, and the simple dreams of youth.

The twin blows picked Olivia Barrow up and dashed her back onto the cold ground. The satchel of twice-robbed money was torn from her grip, tossed aside by the force of the shots, flying through the air. She could feel her weapon ripped from her hand as if by some powerful force. She could see the sky swirling dizzily above her, hear her breath rattling around in her broken chest. The chill from the earth seemed to seep into her and around her like an unwanted embrace. She shivered deep into her core. She remembered her lover's eyes from a different time, when Emily looked at her up from the dusty death street. But it's all wrong, she thought. All wrong. No, I made it. I'm free.

And then death's currents swept her into black oblivion.

The brace of shots from the twins' weapons had penetrated the icy air and lifted Tommy from his mother's embrace. He jumped across the room and stared past the stray shards of glass through the broken window, out across the field, down to the woods. For an instant he had trouble making out his sisters; their camouflage outfits blended with the browns and grays of the forest line. But in a moment his eyes picked them out; they stood stock-still in the echoes, as if seized by the frozen morning light. Then, as he watched, he saw the two of them come alive, and leap out from the woods. Like a pair of frightened deer, they raced across the field, bounding up toward the house. Tommy could see that neither sister glanced at the body that lay sprawled on the ground as they ran past.

Behind him he heard his mother, scrambling through some of the debris in the room. She was talking to herself: "Dammit, where's the phone? Where's the phone?" There was an edge in her voice, a pitch that he'd never heard. *"Tommy! Where's a telephone!"* she cried out. He glanced away from the window for just an instant, and saw that she had located the telephone in a corner beneath a bedstand. She was dialing numbers rapidly.

He returned to the window and from his vantage point saw Karen and Lauren dash up to the house and embrace his father. He leaned out and waved, but said nothing. They didn't see him, but he didn't care, filling instead with a great, wild sense of something that he couldn't put a word to, but which completely charged his insides, like an electric current lifting him and reminding him of the way the first waking moments on Christmas morning thrust him, fighting off sleep, from his bed. He could see the twins positioning themselves under his father's arms and helping him maneuver toward the house. In that moment he wanted to fly toward them and help them as well.

His mother had finished dialing, and he heard her give an address and say, "Please send help immediately. Ambulances. Gunshot wounds. Please hurry." The tone of her voice rode an edge of panic and frustration.

It was in those words that something dark and horrid penetrated his heart. For a second, he felt all the warmth and joy flood away from him, and a dizzying blackness swept across his sight. He gasped and turned abruptly away from the window and raced past his mother, as she continued to speak into the telephone, repeating her plea for help. She reached out as he swept past, then drew back her arm and let him go. "Please hurry," he heard her say, but then he flew on down the hallway, back toward the attic where he'd been held captive. He squirmed past debris and pushed aside the jumble of bedding that still partially blocked the door. Then he took the steps two at a time, oblivious to everything except the dread that swirled within him.

The judge had pulled himself up to a sitting position against a wall. But his eyes were shut and his breathing was shallow and forced when Tommy found him. The boy gasped at the sight of the old man's wounds. He wanted to throw himself down on his grandfather, but was afraid he would somehow injure the old man further. For a moment, he simply hovered indecisively next to the prone figure. Then the boy gently dropped to his knees beside his grandfather. He was scared to touch him, scared not to. The judge's eyes fluttered when he heard his grandson take up the spot beside him.

"Grandfather?"

"I'm here, Tommy."

Tommy took a deep breath to control his frightened heart.

"Don't die, please. Mom has called for help and they'll be here soon. You'll be all right."

Judge Pearson didn't reply at first, but when he did, his voice seemed distant. "Well," the old man said, "we made it, didn't we?"

"Yes."

"Is everyone—"

"Dad got hurt, but he's walking okay. Mom's okay. Karen and Lauren are here, too, and they're okay."

"And?"

Tommy didn't answer.

"Good," said the old man. "Your mom got that one before he could get me for sure." Tommy followed the judge's gaze and he spotted Bill Lewis's body contorted in a corner. The boy quickly turned away. "It's all right," the judge said. "Couldn't be helped." After a second, he added: "Well, we did it. I told you we would, and we did." This time the old man's voice seemed firmer, and Tommy hurriedly blurted out:

"You're not going to die, Grandfather?"

Judge Pearson didn't answer. Tommy could see the old man's eyes roll closed.

"Please open your eyes, Grandfather," he said. He was aware that tears were flowing from his own eyes and he wiped at them without thinking. He raised his voice a bit, finding a command: "Open your eyes. Please."

The old man blinked and looked at his grandson.

"I just wanted to take a rest," he said.

"Please. Just keep talking to me."

"I'm tough," the judge said, as if speaking to ghosts. "A lot tougher than they thought."

Tommy smiled.

"I won't let you die, Grandfather. Remember the walking riddle? Remember? You said to think of it when I was scared and it would help us, like a lucky charm. I'm doing that now. Four legs, two legs, three legs, Grandfather. I won't let you die."

The old man closed his eyes again, and Tommy leaned forward insistently: "Grandfather! Answer the riddle. Who is it?"

Judge Pearson seemed to awaken. He snorted, half-smiled, and answered. "Man."

Tommy reached out and grabbed hold of the judge's hand. For just an instant the old man felt all the child's youth and future flood through his own veins, as if all his wounds were sucking at the boy's inexhaustible fund of vitality. It coursed through him and he felt a great satisfaction inside.

"I won't let you!" the boy insisted fiercely.

"I know," replied the old man.

"Really. I'm not just saying it. I won't."

"I know."

They were quiet for an instant.

"I'm tired," said the judge. "I'm very, very tired. Three legs." Tommy squeezed his hand, and he tightened his grip in reply.

They waited then, gently linked together, just as they had throughout the past week, for whatever would arrive next.